The BeAst and the Brightest

Harvard students are known as the best and the brightest, but sex, deceit, and betrayal by three Harvard graduate students, one of whom loved a woman, Cleo, a would-be advocate of feminism, led to a moral and social disaster. Cleo was faithless, sexually immoral, and untruthful to everyone, even to those closest to her. Betrayed by two friends and the woman he loved, one of those graduate students was almost destroyed, but a wise, grand old lady in Boston, several wonderful French women in Paris, and a former girlfriend in Princeton saved him. These women were real feminists and are the heroes of this novel.

The BeAst and the Brightest

Published by
Hybrid Global Publishing
333 E 14th Street
#3C
New York, NY 10003

Copyright © 2024 by RJ Berrier

All rights reserved. No part of this book may be reproduced or transmitted in any form or by any means, electronic or mechanical, including photocopying, recording, or by any information storage and retrieval system, without the written permission of the Publisher, except where permitted by law.

Manufactured in the United States of America, or in the United Kingdom when distributed elsewhere.

Berrier, RJ
The BeAst and the Brightest
    ISBN: 978-1-961757-60-8
    eBook: 978-1-961757-61-5
    LCCN: requested

Cover design by: Julia Kuris
Copyediting by: Sue Toth
Interior design by: Suba Murugan
Author photo by: Carlos Chavez Photography

All rights reserved for "The BeAst and the Brightest" ©2024 by R. J. Berrier. This book or any portion thereof may not be reproduced or used in any manner whatsoever without the express written permission of the author. This is a work of fiction. All of the names and characters are the product of the author's imagination or used in a fictitious manner. Any resemblance to actual persons, living and are dead, is purely coincidental.

"If I lose my honor, I lose myself."
—William Shakespeare, *Anthony and Cleopatra*, Act 3, Scene 4

"Gentle Octavia, Let your best love draw to that point which seeks
best to preserve it."
(Gentle Octavia, give your most faithful love to whomever most
worthily deserves it.)
—William Shakespeare, *Anthony and Cleopatra*, Act 3, Scene 4

"Les vrai menteuses ne savent pas dire la vérité."
(Real liars don't know how to tell the truth.)
—Sasha Guitry, French actor and writer

"Forgiveness is a strange thing. It can sometimes be easier to forgive
our enemies than our friends. It can be hardest of all to forgive
people we love."
—Fred Rogers

Veritas (Truth)
—Harvard University Motto

Contents

Chapter 1	Serial Male Killer—Blondie	1
Chapter 2	Mr. Money	11
Chapter 3	Coffee Shop Guy	21
Chapter 4	True Friends	31
Chapter 5	Cleo Abandoned	39
Chapter 6	University Press	45
Chapter 7	Schendler and Boston	53
Chapter 8	Prudence and Alexander	65
Chapter 9	Cleo's Game	73
Chapter 10	The East West Literary Conference	77
Chapter 11	Confusion and Love?	91
Chapter 12	*Les Enfants Terribles*	101
Chapter 13	Idyll and Deceit	107
Chapter 14	Deceit and Radiance	117
Chapter 15	Cleo's Boyfriend	123
Chapter 16	Announcement	129
Chapter 17	Danny in Paris	135
Chapter 18	Cleo's Dilemma	147
Chapter 19	The Holidays	155
Chapter 20	Back Together	167
Chapter 21	Back in Paris	173
Chapter 22	Danny's Gifts	177

Chapter 23	Cleo's Confession and Submission	185
Chapter 24	Cleo Plots to Kill Danny	193
Chapter 25	Tallington's Betrayal	201
Chapter 26	Preparing for Paris	207
Chapter 27	Cleo and Nicole	213
Chapter 28	Cleo Murders Siegfried	225
Chapter 29	Nicole's Present	231
Chapter 30	Cleo Rapes Danny	237
Chapter 31	Wonderful Women	251
Chapter 32	Cleo Moves On	261
Chapter 33	Danny Returns	267
Chapter 34	Danny Moves On	275
Chapter 35	Cleo and Vilemann Finale	281
Chapter 36	Cleo and Remington Finale	297
Chapter 37	Love Guides Life	303
About the author		307

Chapter 1
Serial Male Killer— Blondie

Sleeping with a guy was just the ante she paid to play another hand in The Game. The guys never knew what game was being played or that they were going to be the losers; they were always going to get "killed." Cleo did not care how much they might get hurt. They were just characters in her evolving storyline. Cleo's rule was to never let guys into her apartment; that was her realm, her private self. Having them at her place would give them too much control over her. They might think that because they could get into her body, they could also invade her space and her life as much as they wanted. That was not going to happen.

When guys had served her purpose, she'd wad them up and throw them in the trashcan by her desk, and then she'd write them out of her story as if they had never existed. That was the price they had to pay for being guys. If guys got hurt, that showed them what bastards men have been with women and how strong and independent she had become. The next one to be killed was Blondie.

Cleo looked back at Henderson, who was asleep in bed, as the door closed. "Got him," she said to herself. The note she left was her standard, "We both know we're not right for each other, so don't try to contact me. It's over. C."

Blondie was the nickname she secretly gave him. She always had a nickname for her transient lovers, one that depersonalized

2 The BeAst and the Brightest

them, usually without their knowledge. Blondie was very good-looking; he was one of those pretty boys who have a beautiful Greek-god physique and are totally blonde. She had been with him for about three months, sleeping one or two nights a week at his apartment, usually on the weekends. After all, Cleo was a working girl.

One weekend morning, Blondie got up from his bed and walked totally nude over to the bookshelf in his bedroom and picked up a picture. He looked carefully at it and then turned as if to show her his truly great body. He wasn't just standing there; he seemed to be posing. This was her opportunity. She got up and walked over to him, also totally nude, pressed her body to his, and said, "You are such a great-looking guy; you're my Greek god; please show me the picture."

They headed back to bed since it was cool in his Cambridge apartment, and he showed her the picture of him after winning the intercollegiate swim contest for the 100-yard butterfly. He was standing there at the end of a pool, the medal hanging from his neck, with all his swim team buddies around him beaming with admiration. He was wearing a little Jockey swimsuit, cut low, team-issued like the other guys.

Cleo thought, *Any of these guys would have done just as well as Blondie*, but said nothing.

She didn't need the champion for her purposes. Although he seemed very proud of himself, he proved to be just an ordinary lover—actually, a pretty good one—but not a champion in bed. Any of the other guys on the swim team could have served Cleo's purpose just as well, maybe better.

His physique was that of a champion swimmer: broad shoulders, well-developed pecs, long, strong arm muscles, and a small waist. Cleo asked, "How small is your waist?" She knew this would set off another moment of self-satisfaction and bragging. "Just 31 inches, like most male models." Cleo knew she had just scored a point, but she also knew that she needed to cash it in fairly soon, so she divided the time he had left in half. Two weeks would do it. She just had to finalize the kill, the moment, and the way she would drop him. Given Blondie's seeming infatuation with himself and how much he was attracted to Cleo, she knew

Serial Male Killer—Blondie

that he would lose at The Game, her method for controlling males. She would get him.

She had picked him up at the Harvard Coop, the big bookstore and general merchandise mart, where students got their course readings, perhaps enjoyed a coffee before venturing out in the cold, and where the students' parents and Harvard visitors could pick up Harvard-branded merchandise. A lot of would-be Harvard students grew up wearing child-size Harvard T-shirts. That never helped them with admissions. Harvard did make a killing on all that stuff. The magic of the Harvard name sells.

Henderson was looking through the shelves in the Coop's sports section just flipping through books about the Olympics. His impressive physique made him easy to notice, especially given his 6 foot 4 inch frame, but that is not what attracted Cleo to him. He just seemed like an easy mark. He seemed proud to be good-looking and maybe a little egocentric, even mildly arrogant, like some Harvard guys. In short, he was an easy mark for Cleo, who had gotten rid of her previous male a few weeks earlier. All it took was stepping toward him with a bright smile and a "Hi," and the conversation began easily. Clearly, he was used to women looking at him and even approaching him, and he knew how to manage the encounter–not too casual, relaxed enough to put the ladies at ease, but engaged, and then he'd make his move.

"Would you like to have a coffee?"

"Sure," she said.

Cleo would be in experienced hands, and she liked that. That meant few, if any, surprises and no unnecessary drama. He was just going to be the next male she bedded, nothing more.

While in bed together looking at the picture, he invited her to a swim meet the next afternoon to see the competition, where he would have also have the chance to tell her more about his success in the water. He was as proud of his success as an athlete as he was of his looks and his academic achievements. Cleo knew how to judge her compliments—not too much, but attentive to what he was saying and as relaxed as he was. When the swim meet finished, they headed to a local Greek restaurant in Central Square, halfway between Harvard and MIT, and then he invited

4 The BeAst and the Brightest

her to his apartment. Everything was going just as both of them had hoped.

Henderson saw her as an attractive potential girlfriend, an interesting and attractive woman he'd like to know, but unlike her, he never put an expiration date on his relationships. He'd just let things work out. He was clear about three things: he would only marry a beautiful, wealthy blonde, and he would have beautiful blonde children. While not his blonde ideal, she displayed a natural eloquence as flashy as it turned out to be empty, and she was attractive. At 5 feet 10 inches she stood out not only because of her height but because of her hair. She had bright reddish hair, clear skin, a very nice figure, and lovely shapely breasts. Sometimes her eyes could look sinister as if on fire but that was only a fleeting impression which was erased by the radiance of her smile. Her smile brought her good looks to life. Was she pretty? Not really. "Pretty" was not the best word to describe her." Beautiful"? No one would call her beautiful, but she was very good-looking. She turned heads.

Henderson genuinely liked women and not just for sex. He liked to be with women. He never considered them arm candy or just there to complement him. The woman who had just approached him seemed like someone he'd like to get to know. All he wanted for now was a girlfriend. She wanted a fuck and a little companionship, a male body in bed with her. They both thought they were going to get what they wanted.

As a kid, Cleo kept her distance from her brothers, Mark, the oldest, and Tony, her junior, whom she believed were favored by her grandparents and her parents. Well, she wasn't sure about her mother, who had her own life.

Blondie seemed too attractive for his own good, just like Cleo's brother Tony, who was always looking at himself. With his good looks, Tony hooked up with many pretty ladies. He also had many male friends, all good-looking, just like him. He ran with the popular crowd. Cleo's other brother, Mark, was the business guy. Cleo knew that her father had plans for the two boys that didn't include her, except in a secondary role.

She kept her childhood in Napa and her years at San Francisco State a mystery. She got by with making only a few tangential comments about her past. The same was true of her work. She only told guys about being an editor and a writer. She never elaborated; they didn't need to know more. They always assumed that she'd tell them more over time.

After three months, Blondie and Cleo knew each other really well, which upset Cleo. She never wanted to stay too long with a guy, which meant she had to drop Blondie fairly soon. He seemed good for another two weeks, maybe a month, and then she would drop him. She always ended things abruptly, without any explanation as a way of putting them in their place; they were only a male body, only a fuck, nothing more. If they were hurt, that was just too bad.

The kill was essential to her routine, a way of ending the imagined relationship with such absolute certainty that even the dullest guy would realize it was over. The guy would never know why or anything else about her. Sometimes, the guys would call her for several weeks but never get a response. Eventually, they'd get the idea and move on. After all, it had been a short-term affair.

So, after four months, she intended to set up Blondie for the kill by sleeping with him three nights in a row: Friday, Saturday, and Sunday. She told him she needed three nights with him, not just two. "I love being next to you in bed; I just love the feel of your great body and what we do in bed. I love being with you; you're a great guy," she told him.

He put his arms around her while whispering in her ear, "You are my goddess. Do you know that? Can you feel that when I make love to you? Don't our bodies tell each other about the affection and love we are feeling?" She just looked at him and gave him a big, radiant smile. The bright flash of that smile would make him think that everything was going really well. He would think she really liked him and that a nice emotional relationship was developing between them. She was just setting him up for the kill. To avoid revealing herself, she would often use the blinding light of her smile or verbal ballet—turning, gliding, and darting—to distract with the flash of her clever words.

After the three-night sleepover the next weekend, they decided to meet at a restaurant not far from Blondie's apartment

6   The BeAst and the Brightest

on Friday at 6 p.m. The nights were so cold that staying out late didn't seem like a good idea. Cleo met him at the restaurant's reception desk, and as he leaned over to kiss her, she sneezed. A big sneeze. Then she sniffled. He seemed concerned; was she all right? They sat down at a table, and Cleo started to feel worse. Henderson asked her if she felt like staying; she insisted that everything was OK.

"It's just a little cold."

But as the dinner progressed, she felt worse and worse. Henderson could see that she was really suffering, so he paid quickly and got a cab despite the fact that he lived fairly close to the restaurant. They arrived at his apartment just 10 minutes later. She was sick, just a cold, but a bad one.

Once in the apartment, he turned up the heat and gave her a blanket. "How about some chamomile?" he asked.

"Sure."

The tea helped but did not prevent a surge of fever. She was really coming down with a bad cold. Insisting that she had to stay with him, he helped her undress and gave her a big sweatshirt to wear and then held up the covers as she slipped into bed. Tylenol, some cold medicine, more chamomile, and some kisses on the cheeks were offered to make her feel better. Since she liked classical music, he put on some Mozart softly. He kept kissing her cheeks, her neck, and her hands and talking with her until she went to sleep.

Blondie looked at her sleeping in his bed and thought, *Maybe this is the one. She's not blonde and probably not wealthy, but I really like her. I really like her.*

Then he gave her a soft, lingering, loving kiss on the cheek. His thoughts about his life were changing.

The next morning, she woke up aching with fever. Sneezing. She saw Blondie next to her in the bed, wearing a big T-shirt and some cotton lounge pants. She was happy to see that he had no intention of trying to play with her. They spent Saturday with her in bed—more chamomile, toast, and applesauce he bought at the little store downstairs from his apartment. She felt better but was not able to go home. He insisted that she stay. He lent her a book so she could try to read, but Saturday was devoted to sleeping.

Serial Male Killer—Blondie

Dinner Saturday night was some chicken noodle soup he had bought at that same little store. This was "homemade" soup sold in a big buccal, the kind with the metal clip on top. Authentic and delicious. She ate a lot with a few pieces of toast. She tried to watch TV with him that evening but went to sleep without realizing it, curled up next to him. He gently picked her up from the couch and carried her in those strong arms to bed. He tucked her in and tenderly kissed her cheeks.

Sunday morning, she woke up feeling much better. She told him that she was hungry, so he made her a nice brunch: an omlette with some herbs that tasted really good, sautéed potatoes, asparagus, and sourdough toast. Since she was from SF, she liked sourdough bread. She was surprised by how well he cooked. He told her that he had always liked to cook and had learned a lot from his mother with whom he had cooked starting at about 11 years old. Who would have guessed? Then he started talking in the most flattering terms about his mother—a real beauty devoted to her family, worked for free in politics to elect the "right" people. Obviously, he adored her, but Cleo thought she sounded just like the type of woman she did not want to be, a woman focused on being a housewife and mother, someone devoted to others.

Cleo started to realize that his arrogance was actually just a touch of innocent narcissism, not totally unjustified. Despite his masculinity, his beautiful body, and his accomplishments in sports and academics, Henderson had some elements of humility and femininity. Not that he was gay. Sexually and socially, he was all hetero, but softness resided in that classic masculine body that made him tender and vulnerable and able to give of himself. His surface pride and arrogance hid certain feminine sensibilities. Very hidden but real. Cleo did not want her femininity to be at all like his. She wanted to be dominant, not a nurse for someone weaker. There was to be no submission in her life. Her goal, her brand of feminism, was not to be equal to men but to dominate them.

Cleo had rejected her family and its money. She wanted to live her life in literature, even if that meant not being wealthy like her family and many of their friends in Napa Valley. She saw how her mother had been hollowed out to become one of those women who "lunch," who "shop," and occasionally finds a lover who furthers erodes her sense of self. You can only fool yourself so much into believing that this or that lover really cares about you. Her mother knew that the waiters, guys at the gym, and other men she picked up occasionally were using her as well as her using them. With each one-night stand or short liaison, she became harsher and more cynical, and finding any pleasure became an empty pursuit. She would redouble her lunches with her girlfriends and shop with greater passion.

Cleo spent the week at her apartment as usual but had accepted a rendezvous for the next Saturday. She declined a Friday night dinner with Blondie, saying she wanted to get totally over her cold. They met Saturday at the first restaurant where they had eaten together and then headed to his apartment. He put on some music and got her to dance, something she enjoyed but with restraint. Then, right into bed, no sweatshirts, T-shirts, or lounge pants. Doing it, several times, then hugging in each other's arms. She gave him a quick kiss, turned over on her side, and fell asleep.

As she slept, Henderson kept looking at her and felt his heart melting; he was starting to feel a special kind of love for this woman. Why he felt a special affection for her eluded him, but his feelings were real and undeniable. Yes, he liked her and was enjoying being with her. Sex with her was good but a little limited. He believed that she'd loosen up over time and be better in bed. He certainly appreciated and enjoyed her lovely young body. He told her that he loved her smile. But he was starting to realize that she had touched him deeply, and he wanted her to feel the same about him. He had thought that he could plan his life; he thought he knew what he wanted in a woman, in a relationship. His heart was leading him in a different direction simply because of what he thought was a chance meeting at the Coop with an attractive woman. Hearts can change lives. Henderson said to himself that the wise thing to do was to follow his heart. He would let love guide his life. He knew that love is more powerful, smarter, and more authentic than anything the rational mind can imagine. He was strong academically, like most people at Harvard, but he also had layers of social and emotional intelligence.

He put his arm around her, placing his hand next to her left breast. Although lovely to touch, it wasn't her breast he wanted to feel; it was her heart. He wanted to feel her heartbeat. Yes, he knew that love doesn't come from the heart muscle; it comes from your mind and your spirit, but he was deeply romantic and wanted to feel her heartbeat. Did she share his feelings, his incipient true love? Blondie had felt sweet affection for really all of his girlfriends. Despite many relationships, he was not a womanizer and was certainly not a guy who mistreated women. He cared for and respected women as much as they were attracted to him. He had deeply cared about some of these women. He had never hurt or mistreated a woman. While no stranger to love, his feelings for Cleo were becoming more profound than he'd ever experienced; he felt almost overwhelmed by what his heart was signaling.

He said to himself, *Maybe this is true, pure love.*

She wasn't anything he had thought he wanted, blonde and wealthy. He was hungry not only for her body and companionship; he was starting to want to share a profound and perhaps lasting love with her. He was welcoming this whole woman into his heart and his life. This was new and revealing to him. Passion, ardor, and fascination were taking possession of his mind and body within a new, deeper, more expansive dimension of love that was opening up in his heart. He really wanted her; he imagined a life together. No, his feelings weren't just lust or infatuation. This was different. As a wave of tenderness wept through all those muscles, he kissed her several times softly on the cheek and fell asleep.

The next morning, while he was still sleeping, she left early. Her adieu was the usual, curt note. She had never felt any love. He had just been another fuck. Blondie never knew what had happened. He had started to think that she could be "the one." He felt bewildered and hurt, really hurt.

Cleo's note suited her perfectly since it was hard to interpret. Did they both actually know that they were not right for each other?

Had Blondie participated in this decision? No, it was all Cleo, but by saying, "We both know" she was rejecting any responsibility for how he might feel about her decision. She wanted to make the decisions, but not accept responsibility for them. That released her from any concerns, any scruples about how her males might feel about what had just happened. Not taking responsibility was critical to avoid second guesses or any doubt about how she treated guys. She never assumed responsibility for anything since she could so easily twist the story she told others and even herself. She had to be totally free to make decisions without regard for the other person. Cleo appreciated the care she had received the previous weekend, but that did not change her plan; Blondie had to be cut loose. She needed to win this hand in The Game. The time had come for the kill. She was proud of her note. Blondie, that is, John Henderson, had meant nothing to her.

Chapter 2

Mr. Money

After leaving Blondie, Cleo headed later that afternoon to Harvard Square, where she called a guy she had met, James Fitzgerald Braddington, Mr. Money to her, to accept a rendezvous for the next Saturday night. He was to be her next score. She was glad to get his message machine. Leaving a message was so much easier than a conversation. He called her back saying how happy he was to hear from her and was looking forward to dinner together.

She had met him not really by chance at an upscale men's clothing store, Alan Bilzerian, on Newbury Street just off the Boston Public Garden. She was on her way to Trinity Church for an afternoon concert when she suddenly decided to go into the store. No, she wasn't shopping for someone; no guy was going to get a present. The "present" was meant for Cleo. She had gone in remembering an experience in San Francisco at a similar upscale men's store. She was shopping for a male. Suddenly, there he was, Mr. Money. She asked him for advice regarding a sweater for her dad, and it developed from there.

As an undergraduate at SF State in downtown San Francisco, she had encountered one of her first good lovers at Wilks Bashford, a men's clothing store for wealthy men like her father. She had dropped in to buy that requisite Father's Day present, a shirt and a tie. As she looked through the tie drawers to match something to the shirt she had selected, she noticed a guy looking at her

12   The BeAst and the Brightest

with interest. He was in his early 20s, decent-looking, nicely dressed, but casual, as would be expected on a Friday afternoon in California. She asked for his advice about a matching tie. The conversation started, and Cleo knew where she wanted it to go.

Her introduction to good sex had been the summer after her second year at the university when she went with her parents to Australia to see her brother, Mark, who was managing their vineyards in New South Wales. As usual, she was not the center of attention, so she could spend her days at the beach resort where they were staying. She had the classic summer romance with the guy who ran the Jet Ski business. Sexually, he was experienced and talented; she enjoyed him a lot. He knew how to make her thrilled. He'd ask if she was up for a "thrill."

She always said, "Yes. Thrill me, please. Please thrill me."

After the Jet Ski guy, she had decided not to continue her sexual journey with undergraduate boys, who tended to just fumble around down there trying to figure out what worked, what women wanted, and where "it" was. She had tried those guys the first two years at the university and had found them to be "zeros in bed." She had no intention of giving remedial education to her bed partners.

Returning to SF from Australia, she was eager to sleep with more experienced guys, and the one she noticed in Wilks Bashford seemed to fit the bill. They started talking; then she got the invitation she'd hoped for: "I'm headed over to Rickhouse for a drink. Would you like one, too? It's just over on Bush Street."

She said, "Love to."

After drinks at Rickhouse, this guy, whom she nicknamed Tie Guy, invited her to dinner in Chinatown. She agreed. He was polite and had nice manners without being mannered or too self-conscious. Then, to his apartment for the after-dinner delight. They had another drink and kissed a bit, but then she told him that she didn't feel that well, but really, really wanted to see him again, and something about, "Don't be disappointed," then she grabbed a cab. What they both wanted and what he had expected would come later when she was ready. A few days later, she called him, asking if they could get together again. A dinner was set up, followed by a visit to his apartment where, as

Mr. Money

they sipped a glass of wine, she asked him if he liked sex. When she was ready, she went right for it. Her hand in his, they headed to the bedroom. He was much more skilled in bed than those undergraduate guys.

Her time with Tie Guy lasted six months, during which Cleo learned more about how to enjoy herself with a guy but also the limits she would impose on all her sexual relationships. Just the basics. She limited guys to the missionary position and maybe side to side. Nothing more. She didn't want them to treat her like a sex toy, something to devour. Enjoy, OK, but not believe they could do anything with her that they wanted. She had not yet developed The Game, but the essentials had started to fall into place. She would be in charge, not that male, not that guy. She would determine the start, the end, and how it ended. One lesson she learned from Tie Guy was that six months is too long; he had started to believe that they had a relationship. Not acceptable. So, three to four months or less seemed about right.

After that first encounter at Alan Bilzerian, Mr. Money had been calling Cleo, who agreed to meet him at a restaurant that was nice but not ostentatious. The conversation proved to be scintillating but mostly about him. Clearly, he had enjoyed a privileged life of luxury travel to attractive locations, but he didn't seem to be bragging; he recounted details of his trips, which Cleo found captivating. Clearly, he was observant and had a sense of adventure, although limited. He did not want anything too out of the ordinary and certainly nothing physically risky. No unfortunate surprises. He'd just be another serial male who'd end up losing at The Game.

After dinner, he asked if she'd like one more drink at his apartment: a very classic, unoriginal invitation to spend the night.

She would have preferred a direct question about sex, but still, she said, "Yes, sure."

His apartment was in an old brownstone just off Newbury Street, a high-class, that is, expensive neighborhood. The apartment was too expensive for a young guy who didn't have family money. She was impressed by the overall look: expensive oriental carpets complemented with antiques and some stylish modern furniture. Some nice original art. No framed posters. A guy

14 The BeAst and the Brightest

with taste and money. As she took off her cape and hung it by the entrance, she noticed a little table with a telephone. Next to the phone was a slightly oblong black book with orange lettering, *The Social Register*. Cleo had no idea such a thing existed. She assumed he was in it, but she absolutely would never ask him. A social register in America? Was that real? Hard to believe for a girl who grew up in California. But there it was. She again told herself never to ask him about it.

Instead, she asked him about his work, which he described as somewhat boring. OK, clearly, it paid well. He worked for a financial firm started by his great-grandfather that handled government bonds for the City of Boston, the Commonwealth of Massachusetts, and a few other government organizations. He asked what she did and seemed satisfied with a quick description of her work as an editor. She didn't get to the part about being an aspiring feminist writer. As the conversation continued, Mr. Money leaned over and put his arms around her. He kissed her. She just smiled. He asked if he could see her again.

"Sure," she offered. Then, with kisses on the cheeks, she headed out.

As she got into bed, she picked up a book on her nightstand and thought, *What would I tell him about this book?*

Probably nothing. As she got sleepy, she heard her message machine go off; it was Mr. Money, of course. She smiled to herself since she was on top of The Game with him.

The next Friday night, dinner was in a nice restaurant in downtown Boston, followed by another trip to his apartment. Once seated on his couch, he bent over for a kiss. He got that kiss, a discrete one. Then she placed his hand over her left breast and kissed him harder and longer.

"Are you up for sex?" she asked with a mischievous little smile.

Bed came soon. When she was ready, she liked going straight for it. No need for the guy to engage in a prolonged seduction, which might lead him to believe that she had relented due to his sophisticated moves, good looks, money, or compelling personality.

The morning offered a basket of croissants and good, but not great, coffee and orange juice. Cleo's coffee-making technique

Mr. Money 15

beat almost anyone else's. He was a satisfactory lover—nothing great, but competent. She asked if he was married.

"No!"

He seemed profoundly shocked by the question and insisted that he didn't even have a girlfriend. Cleo thought to herself that she'd never be a wife or a girlfriend.

At breakfast Saturday morning, he invited her to go with him to Provincetown, at the very tip of Cape Cod. Cleo thought that the drive would be too long, and she had to be at work on Monday morning. She was not interested in staying with him at a hotel in Provincetown that Saturday night and enduring a long drive back in horrible traffic to Boston on Sunday morning. Sunday mornings were her private time. No, they weren't going to drive; he'd been invited by a friend to go and return in the friend's private Cessna. They were going to make a day of it, a Saturday jaunt. She had never been to Provincetown but had heard that it was a fun place. So, she hugged him and said she would be delighted to go along.

They headed out to Logan, Boston's airport, at about 8 a.m. to meet the friend and his girlfriend, Cynthia. Mr. Money's friend turned out to be a guy almost identical to Mr. Money. All day, Cynthia just smiled. This drove Cleo crazy. She had seen her mother do the same at one social event after another, as if women were just there to decorate the place, smiling happily about everything. The two guys took the front seats, leaving Cleo and Cynthia to take the seats behind them. Mr. Money's friend, John something or other, had gone over the Cessna's checklist carefully, which reassured Cleo. She remembered that John Kennedy Jr. had crashed his small plane somewhere over the Cape, or was it Martha's Vineyard?

The flight was exhilarating. Cleo could see the entire coast, and she watched as the coastline faded to the right of the plane as it cut across the Bay. She then saw nothing but water until Provincetown Airport came into view. John managed a smooth landing, and they were out of the plane in no time. Cleo had really enjoyed herself, even with Cynthia next to her. She thought how fitting it was to go to Provincetown, the site of the *Mayflower*'s landing in 1620, with a guy who was probably in the *Social Register*. She assumed that John was in the *Register*

16 The BeAst and the Brightest

as well, but probably not Cynthia; she lacked the bearing and social ease that comes with generations of money.

Once the plane was secured, they headed over to Commercial Street, which was full of art galleries. As usual in a tourist town, most of the "art" was kitschy, but several of the galleries had really fine art, very expensive, but appropriate for the high-class or at least wealthy clientele who came to Provincetown. Mr. Money explained that some of the clients had probably come in their boats from Nantucket, and, in fact, the harbor was crowded with many multimillion-dollar boats. Provincetown attracted day trippers, but also lots of wealthy visitors. Cleo saw herself in an East Coast version of the wealthy Napa-to-Carmel crowd on the West Coast. She knew it well since her family was part of it, but she would never mention her family or the resemblance she saw between the Provincetown crowd and the people who live in or visit Carmel or Napa.

Cleo saw herself as a budding art critic and noted some things she might have liked to discuss but decided not to with Mr. Money, John, and Cynthia. This was their show, and she assumed that they really didn't care what she thought. She was essentially right. After an hour or so strolling through the galleries, John suggested they head to a restaurant on the Bay side, where he had made reservations. Once at the table, John suggested lobster for everyone and a very good white Burgundy, but he insisted no wine for him. Pilots can't drink. Cleo was relieved. John was a nice character, but she could see her father in him. John would probably marry someone like Cynthia, cheat on her, relegate her to a "ladies who lunch" lifestyle, and spend decades flying around looking for something that would always escape him. The amount of time she was going to devote to Mr. Money was going to be the standard three or four months.

Despite having grown up in a wealthy family, or perhaps because money had never been an issue, she was unimpressed by wealth. She was not materialistic at all. Oh, the lobster was delicious, probably fresh from Maine, and the Burgundy, crisp, smooth, and complex, but her motivations in life were different; she wanted to be a fresh, new voice to help steer American literature and art through her influence as an important editor and

Mr. Money 17

feminist writer. While not turned off by Mr. Money and John's displays of wealth, she really didn't care.

A crème brûlée flavored with lemon and an espresso finished a delicious lunch. They walked back to Commercial Street to visit a few more shops and galleries and then headed back to the airport. Cleo had enjoyed herself, as had everyone. Back at the airport, John once again went over everything on the plane, meticulously going through the checklist. Cleo did not doubt that they would land safely back at Logan Airport.

Once out of the plane, Cleo hugged both guys, smiled at Cynthia, who smiled back, and told Mr. Money that she'd like to see him again, but not until the next weekend.

"Saturday," he ventured.

"Sure. Call me."

She gave Mr. Money a quick kiss on the cheek and then went off in a cab to her apartment. Things were going well. Mr. Money thought he'd just had one of the best Saturdays of his life.

The cab dropped her off at her apartment, but she decided to walk a few blocks down the street to Tuk Tuk Thai, a restaurant with takeout. All the Asians do takeout, right? She went for Asian panang chicken and white rice. Back at her apartment, she put the food on her little table and opened up her copy of Huysmans's *Against Nature*. This is a work of deep pessimism, often characterized as decadent, in which he explores escaping from the mundane horrors of life through aestheticism and religious conversion. What could be more striking after a day of pleasure, luxury, empty, even if intelligent conversation and tourism? Other than superficial pleasures, Cleo could not think of anything of any substance that had occurred that day. Cleo was clear that Mr. Money would just be another serial male to enjoy in bed, nothing more.

Given her interpretation of feminism, women absolutely could not be submissive, not come under the sway of males, of guys. Relationships inevitably led to one person being dominant, and Cleo was determined never to be submissive. She had to become the dominant person in the relationship. On the other hand, she could not imagine a long-term relationship with a guy she would have to dominate. She did not want to spend her life dragging the same male around or making decisions for two people. No, she was not going to get married, not going to have children, not going to get trapped in American life as a couple, but also, she was not going to live without sex. Women like and need sex just like men, and she was going to get her share. The solution was The Game and serial males.

Boston was full of interesting guys, and since there were so many universities, there would be an endless supply of willing males. Hunting would be good, and she would do with them whatever she wanted. She had no concerns about her reputation since she would be defined by her writings, her feminism, and her impact on culture as an editor. In Boston, there would be no "village gossip" as happens in a little place like Napa. She would be known as a major cultural tastemaker and a feminist guide for women.

Mr. Money left her a voice message Monday afternoon suggesting a concert at Symphony Hall and then dinner at a well-known seafood restaurant. "Would 6:45 p.m. in front of Symphony Hall be all right? That's Saturday night."

She called him back on Wednesday, leaving a message on his answering machine at home saying that Saturday was "a go." He was relieved since he wondered why she hadn't called him earlier.

The concert and the dinner were fine. Back at his apartment, the expected happened. The next morning, there were more croissants, coffee, and orange juice. He lived an organized, surprise-free life. Cleo started thinking about a shorter time together. He thought things were going well. Cleo knew she had to assume control. This pattern—dinner, perhaps some entertainment, his apartment, bed, sex, and croissants—continued for the next four weeks. Cleo assumed that this would be his pattern for the next 50 or so years. He had made every decision for them. Cleo knew that she needed to go for "The Kill," the end of her time with him.

Unless she was with somebody, literally some male body, she typically took it easy on Sunday mornings alone in her apartment. Since she slept with some male or another most Saturday nights, she had a habit of announcing early Sunday morning that she had things to do and went straight back to her apartment.

Her standard line was, "I'm a working girl, you know, and you probably have things to do as well."

Sundays were devoted to restoring herself, relaxing and enjoying solitude, a comfort for her. Solitude was a feeling she treasured. Since there was nobody to deal with, she could devote herself to her writing and reading. She'd usually walk over to Copley Plaza unless it was too cold, to her favorite French pastry shop and get a *pain aux raisin,* a raisin bun, and an elephant ear, a *palmier* in French, not the standard croissants. She'd take them back to her place and make coffee her way. She used one of those large French funnels with a paper filter, just like her father had taught her.

She usually didn't follow her father's advice or lifestyle, but he had given her good training in coffee preparation and wine appreciation. As far as she was concerned, his good advice stopped there.

Once she had her coffee, the palmier, and the pain aux raisin, Cleo was eager to pick up her copy of Huysmans again. This book is an account of a person who dedicated his life to the "finer things." She wanted to see herself as equally passionate about literature and art. She also embraced the idea of being independent and not relying on others to define what she should like, how she should act, or how she should enjoy herself. She certainly did not want any male to define her.

Chapter 3

Coffee Shop Guy

Early one Monday morning, she headed to the Coop at Harvard Square to buy a book. Since she didn't have to be at work that day until 10:30 a.m., she had time to drop into The Coffee Spot, a little place just off Harvard Square, for something hot to drink. The place was packed. Walking up behind some guy who was alone at a small table, she asked, "Can I sit here?" She was about to launch an adventure that would last more than a year and end with a murder and a rape.

Once she had her coffee, the guy asked her what she was reading—just like that. He had noticed her Coop bag and thought it looked like she had a book in there. This was the first time a guy had started a conversation focused on something that interested her. He let her talk about the books she was reading, what she had just bought, her passion for literature, and her job at Schendler Publishing, one of Boston's prominent, serious publishing houses. She talked on and on … almost losing herself in her passion for literature until she realized that she had to take off to be at work in downtown Boston in just 20 minutes. As she hurried out, she gave him her number and said, "Call me."

"Nice to meet you, Cleo," he said.

Once out in the street, she realized that she had no idea who he was or what he did. She didn't even know his name. Had he said it?

Her father had invited her to be in the wine business as well as her brothers, but she knew that she'd end up with a boring job, her brothers as her bosses, a dominating husband, and maybe even a couple of brats. That is not what she wanted. Her mother was often assumed to be a trophy wife since she was good-looking and did all the right social things, but actually, she was her father's first wife. She looked the other way as he maneuvered from one mistress to another. She also knew that there were indiscretions in Australia and Chile, but why rock the boat? His bedtime companions had ceased being of any interest to her.

Cleo's mother was more wedded to her fairly easy and luxurious lifestyle than to her husband. Everybody knew the score, so there were few hard feelings, even if some chagrin and some distress had seeped into her life from time to time. Cleo was vaguely aware that her mother might have attempted suicide at some point as she adjusted to her flexible marriage, but eventually, she succumbed to the lifestyle provided and defined by her husband. Honest discussions rarely occurred in her family. Members of her family did not air their dirty laundry either inside or outside their little family circle or even admit what type of or whose "laundry" they preferred. Everyone knew that their independence and preferences in life depended on being as autonomous as possible. Everyone in the family lived their own lives.

Cleo had two sets of living grandparents. Her paternal grandfather had started the vineyards in Napa Valley as a young man, and the business had grown and prospered along with the rest of the California wine industry. He had been, in fact, one of the recognized leaders of that industry. When her father suddenly took over the business, her paternal grandparents moved to Sydney for no apparent reason. Given the distance, Cleo and her family rarely saw them. When her father visited her brother and their operations in Australia, he almost always went alone.

Cleo remembered just a few occasions when her paternal grandparents visited her family. These get-togethers were usually limited to a fancy lunch at Jack's, the famous SF restaurant. Everybody seemed to be on their guard during these lunches, which felt more like a council of war than a family reunion. Her paternal grandparents always left the area or did other things for dinner. They never ventured just the short distance to Napa.

Coffee Shop Guy

Her paternal grandfather was friendly, especially with the boys, but did not interact at all with Cleo, which was just another sign that the boys counted for more than she did. She seemed to be a non-person to him. His behavior demonstrated his macho attitude toward women. Cleo felt that she didn't even count as a human being to him.

Cleo's maternal grandparents lived in Carmel, a charming, upscale tourist town on the coast south of the Bay Area. They represented the third generation of a banking family from Kansas City. The second generation had increased the family's wealth considerably, but the third proved less capable, as so often happens. They contented themselves with tennis, bridge, charities, and some travel. They did visit Napa ever so often and invited Cleo's family to big occasions in Carmel: birthdays, Thanksgiving, Christmas, etc. Cleo liked them, but the relationship was never close with her or her brothers, although when they were together, her maternal grandparents always tried to pay special attention to Cleo, as if to reassure her. The four grandparents never seemed to be together at the same time. Maybe they just didn't get along; that happens in families.

Several days passed, and she had almost forgotten that guy in the coffee shop, but he had intrigued her. Wednesday night, she found a message on her answering machine from him inviting her to a concert Friday night at a famous church in the Italian North End and then, perhaps, dinner.

She had heard about the concert and thought, *Why not?*

His message included his number, which she called the next day, trying not to appear too eager. He then left her a message on her machine to meet him at the church at 7 p.m. "OK, it should be an interesting concert," was the total of this message. So, they would meet again without any more interaction than had occurred during their accidental meeting at The Coffee Spot.

This invitation from Coffee Shop Guy raised the issue of Mr. Money. Cleo had fallen into a pattern of spending Saturday and sometimes Friday nights with Mr. Money. She wasn't quite ready to cut him loose, and she knew almost nothing about this other guy. So, she left Mr. Money a nice message on his answering machine saying her boss' boss had invited her to a conference in NYC over the weekend, something about the National Book Awards, and since many authors would be there, she needed to go. Lies can work. He bought it. Her message included the fact that she'd get some time with her boss' boss. Her boss, a wonderful woman, had severe MS, which dramatically restricted her movements. A trip to NYC was out of the question for her, so Cleo was invited to take her place. These details added credibility to her lie.

When Cleo met this "mystery man" at the Old North Church, she asked him his name, saying she was a little embarrassed. "Danny," he said.

"OK, Danny." He was going to be her first Danny.

The concert was fine, but Cleo was most interested in what might happen afterward. Leaving the concert, he asked if she had enjoyed it.

"Sure, very much," she said.

They walked several blocks to a restaurant Danny knew and found a table right in the middle of the place. It was a typical red-sauce Italian American restaurant filled with students and pseudointellectuals as well as people who were just in the mood for pasta. It was lively and colorful. Cleo thought that Mr. Money would never be found in a place like this, but OK, that was him.

They had just gotten their menus when Danny asked her, "So, what did you actually think about the program and the performance?" Her antenna went up. What was this guy's game? Could he actually care what she thought? Did he know how interested she was in art, literature, and music? Did he understand that she thought of herself as a taste-maker, guiding literature and the arts? If so, how did he know this about her when she knew essentially nothing about him? OK, she had talked about her job at Schendler when they met at The Coffee Spot. Surprisingly, he seemed to have remembered what she told him. She told herself to be cautious and began with a general statement. Then, he talked about a similar concert he had attended in NYC and commented on how the two compared.

She wondered, *What the hell does this guy do? Who is he? Why doesn't he start his patter like all the other males? Doesn't he know how to talk up a girl?*

As dinner was ending, she asked him where he lived. "Halfway between Central Square and Harvard Yard in Cambridge. I'm at

Harvard," he said. Since she had the weekend free of Mr. Money, she wanted him to invite her to his apartment in Cambridge. But it was such a terribly cold night, and he had met her by taking the "T" from Harvard Square, leaving his car at his apartment. Parking was always almost impossible in the North End, especially on a snowy winter day. The thought of a taxi ride to Cambridge and then going from there to her apartment the next morning seemed crazy. So, she broke a rule and invited him to come to her apartment. They grabbed a taxi and were there in just ten minutes.

This was the first time in years that she had let a guy into her world, and she knew almost nothing about him. Once in her apartment, he helped her remove her heavy wool cape, a garment that women were starting to wear to stand out among all the ski jackets and heavy down coats usually worn in Boston on a winter day.

She had a routine to seduce guys since her method was to bed them as soon as possible, which helped her and her potential bed partner avoid learning much about each other. Meet, unzip clothes, and "fuck." Yes, she liked that vulgar word more than "having sex" or "sleeping with somebody." She never said it out loud, but that is what she thought she was doing, fucking. That is also the word used in a phrase made famous by her favorite feminist author, Erica Jong. She advocated that women enjoy themselves and learn about their sexuality by "anonymous, zipperless, fucking." Cleo had read her book many times; she considered it her feminist Bible. Cleo had bought it at the SF State University bookstore as an undergraduate and was impressed that it was still for sale many years after it was published. Cleo aspired to write a book on feminism that would be another great feminist classic, equal to *Fear of Flying*.

Jong explained that the encounters she advocated are "zipperless" because "when you came together, zippers fell away like rose petals, underwear blew off in one breath like dandelion fluff." Cleo took this to mean that avoiding the dance of seduction, much discussion about each other, or making out were not only unnecessary but were also to be avoided. She felt authorized to initiate sex directly, such as, "Are you up for sex?" or

26   The BeAst and the Brightest

"Where is your bedroom?" Cleo developed her routine to avoid personal interaction, which led directly to fucking.

Cleo was inspired by both of Jong's descriptions of sexual encounters. Sometimes Jong used the word "zipperless" to mean quickly out of your clothes, and sometimes "zipless" to imply no relationship, just fucking, a sexual encounter for its own sake without emotional commitment. Jong wrote, "For the true ultimate zipless A-1 fuck, it was necessary that you never got to know the man very well."

Cleo's interpretation was that her males would have an expiration date of about four months. Cleo tried to be faithful to both terms; they suited her purposes perfectly. She only remembered in her Jongian Bible what fit her purposes. That is all she really wanted, a male giving her some pleasure and then a male body in her bed until the next day. Also, she liked to have a guy to do things with as long as the relationship didn't get serious, at least for her. Sex needed to be handled so that it did not imply or include an incipient emotional relationship.

Her routine was a big hug, a charming kiss, a flashy smile, another hug, then rubbing her hands over the guy's pecs and making some positive comments. The guys would then inevitably try to touch her breasts, and she would not resist at all. She believed that almost all guys lose their ability to think once they have caressed a girl's breasts, and she was almost always right. Then, the preliminaries would get cut, often almost totally skipped. Off with his shirt and her sweater and bra, and then she'd drop her skirt. A little more touching, a few kisses, and then she'd deliver her "killer" line, "When I'm with a guy, I don't like to take off my panties … pause, pause … I'd like you to take them off me." If males lost their ability to think once they had touched her breasts, she knew that they couldn't think about anything except "it" as they removed her panties. Never had this line failed to get the reaction she wanted. This routine assured her of a male in bed with her remaining in control. She got everything she wanted. The guys could believe that they had seduced her, but no, she'd got what she wanted on her terms.

As soon as Danny had helped her with her cape, she intended to begin her routine. But he had walked over to her bookcase

Coffee Shop Guy   27

and started looking at her books carefully. Then he started asking questions about what she was reading, what she liked most, her favorite authors, etc. She fell into a literary conversation, the subject she was most passionate about.

As she talked, she kept thinking about her routine, but she couldn't seem to find a way to transition from what she cared about so passionately to getting this guy into bed. Bedding him seemed somehow less interesting, or at least less urgent. Two hours passed, and she was totally sucked into talking about her views on literature, this or that author, and art. She offered him a glass of wine and they both sipped the wine slowly as she talked. She told him about her work at Schendler Publishing, how she had come to Boston from San Francisco for this job, this opportunity, and so on. She skipped the part about what she had done to get the job. Another hour and a half passed by.

It was nearly 1:30 a.m. when he got up and said how much he had loved, yes, his word, loved their evening, but that he needed to get back to Cambridge. She was caught short. Was he leaving without doing anything with her? Was he not interested in her? Could he be gay? Was he too shy to do anything to take the first step? He was about her age, mid-20s, so she doubted he had no, absolutely no experience at all.

Why hadn't she asked anything about him? Looking around the apartment for his coat, he turned and put his arms around her and said, "You are a really terrific woman." She lost it. All she could do was put her arms around him and give him one, then multiple passionate kisses. He responded with his own, tender kisses. Then, leaning down to look directly into her eyes, he asked, "Are you with anyone? Do you have a boyfriend?" Cleo had never thought of a guy as a boyfriend, nor did she want one, but here was this guy trying to see if he could fill that role. She just shook her head no. Then he looked at her and asked softly, "Do you think we should stay together tonight? Do you want to stay together?"

The questions seemed genuine, lovely, and innocent.

"Yes," she gushed.

He cut short her routine by taking hold of her sweater at the waist and lifting it over her head. Instead of heading right for her breasts, he took off his shirt and started kissing and hugging her

28   The BeAst and the Brightest

gently but passionately. He wasn't gay. She suddenly realized
that she wanted him. She really wanted this guy to be with her.
She actually liked him. He was the first guy she had met in many
years, maybe ever, that she really liked. She wanted him, not just
his male body, not just for a fuck. She wanted to be with him,
whoever he was. He had awakened something deeply hidden in
her, something she feared, the desire for some sort of relationship, even with a guy. That meant that she made love with him
just as much as he made love with her. For the first time, maybe
ever, she was not just fucking; she was loving him and letting
him love her.

Waking up Saturday morning, she looked over in bed and
saw this guy, this guy she really liked. She had no idea why, but
she really liked him, and she was glad to be with him. Since he
was still asleep, she put her arm around him and nestled her
head on his shoulder. She felt happy and content. She hoped
that he was happy, too.

When he woke up, she realized that she had nothing special
to offer for breakfast since she never expected to have someone
in her apartment. She kissed him and offered herself, "Do you
like to do it in the mornings?" After making love, they were both
starving, and she offered what she had to eat: coffee and toast.
He seemed delighted. Cleo started her coffee-making routine,
and he complimented her on the type of funnel she was using
and her overall approach to coffee. As soon as the toast popped
out, they ate their first breakfast together. Being together seemed
to be somehow natural to both of them.

There they were, eating together at her little dining table after
a night of talking about her literary interests and lovemaking,
and she knew nothing about him except his first name, Danny.
She thought that this was a lovely name after all of her John's
and Jim's, alias James, and lots of others. So, she asked, "Tell me
about yourself."

He was a third-year Ph.D. student in economics at Harvard
with an emphasis on the role of government finance depart-
ments. He mentioned growing up out west, including attending
Stanford in Palo Alto for his undergraduate work. He was studying European economies and talked about how much he loved
Italy. With Stanford he had had a chance to spend a total of a

year and a half studying in Italy. So, what was his last name? She asked. "Dolcetto," he said, "Daniel Dolcetto." She almost laughed out loud since it fit him perfectly. He was sweet.

"*Dolce* means sweet, right?"

He was what his name implied: sweet but clearly intelligent.

She teased him a little about his name, which launched him into an impersonation of an Italian guy standing behind his gelato counter saying, "So, pretty lady, what'll it be … *cioccolato* (chocolate), *fragola* (strawberry), *limone* (lemon)?" He did both the Italian and the English words with a hilarious Italian accent. She laughed out loud. She caught herself since this was the first time a guy had made her laugh out loud in a long time. She seemed embarrassed about laughing, but then he offered, "*Une femme qui ri est moitié dans ton lit*," adding that this is a French expression—"A woman who laughs is half in your bed."

She said, "I'm already there, all of me."

They both laughed. So, the next move was her taking him by the hand and leading him back to bed, where they got under the covers and started kissing.

Cleo's kissing technique was well-honed. She'd smile, a radiant smile that lifted the tips of her lips upward into a welcome, and then, just as the guy's lips approached hers, she would pinch her lips together so that the kiss was brief and hard. She felt that letting a guy's lips touch hers was enough. No smooching, no tongue, absolutely no tongue, then separation. Guys didn't seem too happy about the way she kissed, but getting to have sex with her was compensation, ample compensation.

That morning with Danny, she let herself go. He caressed her for a long time, slowly, as if to appreciate every part of her body. He said, "You are so lovely, so sweet," over and over. She had never felt sweet but liked to hear that he thought she was. He would kiss her slowly and softly with a sensuality that seemed innocent, nothing for effect, just deep appreciation for the woman who was in his arms. She felt like she was melting; she didn't resist; it felt good, right somehow. She kissed him softly on the lips, over and over. This was not her; he had touched something that set her on a different path.

Then he ran the tip of his tongue over her lips. She tensed but couldn't resist letting him slowly, gently put his tongue in her mouth and roll it around. He was opening the little door in her that led to her feelings and was nurturing them so that they were becoming the most sensuous and satisfying she had ever experienced. She did the same to him, slowly coming into his mouth and rolling her tongue around, giving him as much pleasure as possible. He asked, "Isn't it wonderful to be together, just us here together?" Her antenna went up. Who is this "us?" What was happening to her? She could not let this guy derail her life's plan just for a French kiss. No way, but then she slipped back into a tender mood. Being together was all so sweet, so innocent, so loving.

They stayed in bed, hugging, kissing, and talking for the next two hours. All of this was new to Cleo. She felt like a virgin discovering sensuality and feeling loved. Was this type of feeling, this sensuality and warmth with someone she really liked, better than just fucking? She was profoundly frightened, like a virgin having her first experience with sensuality, with love, but she wasn't that. She was a mid-20s feminist with a career and a destiny, and no one was going to take that away from her. As noon approached, she told him that she had a lot to do. As they got dressed, he again leaned over, smiling, and said, "You are really a lovely woman. I like you so much. I like it when we're together." She liked hearing that but was upset that he had said it, especially the "we." There was no "we."

Chapter 4

True Friends

Cleo made herself a sandwich for lunch and spent that Sunday afternoon reading Huysmans. At about 7 p.m., she walked to Pizza Napoli for a four seasons pizza, which she took back to her apartment. As she ate, she decided to write a letter to an old friend, Nicole, with whom she had gone to elementary and high school in Napa. Nicole had lived with her mother and stepfather in Paris for the last five years. Nicole had come to visit Cleo in SF every year, but Cleo had never made it to Paris, although she was sure that one day she would. Nicole was the only friend from those school days with whom she had stayed in touch. They had been, in fact, best friends, and Cleo valued Nicole's continuing loyalty to their friendship. She always knew that she could count on Nicole to listen to her without judgment. They had shared some intimate experiences, all innocent, just part of growing up, but these intimate moments had deepened their feelings for each other and brought them much closer together.

Nicole had grown up in an extremely wealthy family in San Francisco who were major industrialists in the United States and Europe and who were also big investors in Napa wine. Although they had an elegant townhouse in Pacific Heights, they lived most of the year in Napa Valley. Wine was her father's passion. Nicole was into sports, including soccer and lacrosse at school, plus horseback riding and skiing. Sports did not interest Cleo, who preferred books, but these differences were never a problem. They were close friends.

When they were 12, they started having sleepovers on the weekends with each other. They alternated sleeping at each other's houses; their houses were just a half mile apart. Nicole was an only child, so Cleo was almost a sister to her. Cleo's two brothers ignored them, so the link between the two girls was very tight. Nicole had a large group of dolls, each of whom had a name, a distinctive personality, and a role within the "family." Nicole loved her doll family and played a lot with them. Her doll family was part of her emotional world. Cleo was not into dolls; in fact, she only had two as a very young child, but she never connected with them emotionally. Instead, she'd say, "Read me a story." By 12, she had read many stories by herself.

During summer vacations, Cleo and Nicole were often separated since both families took time off to travel, usually in June, immediately after school let out. The dads needed to be back right after the Fourth of July because of their vineyards. Activities picked up a lot in July, and August was devoted to preparing for the harvest and, crucially, wine-making. Of course, all this required their fathers' financial expertise and attention to the operational details of the vineyards.

When the girls had just turned 17, Cleo's parents went to Australia to see her brother, Mark, who ran their operations down there, and Cleo's paternal grandparents. For some reason, Cleo wasn't invited to go. She had a choice of spending two weeks with her maternal grandparents in Carmel or going on vacation with Nicole's family. She was ecstatic when Nicole's mother insisted that Cleo come with them. In fact, only the two girls and Nicole's mother were going since Nicole's father had other things to do. They went to Hawaii. The girls were so excited since it would be their first trip to a tropical island. Nicole told her mother they had some things to buy for the trip but did not specify bikinis. Nicole was sure her mother would be cool about them wearing bikinis. Nicole and Cleo had fun trying on different ones and giggling about which was too "tiny."

Nicole's mother had found a super first-class hotel on the northern shore of Kaua'i. They took Hawaiian Airlines to Honolulu and then a hopper flight, on Hawaiian, of course, to the island. Once on the flight from San Francisco to Honolulu, Hawaiian Airlines made them feel as if they were already on the islands. The hotel, the beach, and their rooms were all magnificent. Nicole's mother had her own room; the girls shared one with a king-size bed and a great view of the ocean, just as they had hoped. They were going to be inseparable. The girls thought that they would do nothing but run to the beach, but the first morning, Nicole's mother insisted they all have breakfast together on the patio overlooking the beach, the ocean, and the palms. All so lovely. Her mother did not want to be alone; being alone was not an option, at least for meals. The girls looked carefully over the menu, and both ordered waffles, something they almost never had at home. The waffles came with authentic maple syrup but also a couple of big slices of fresh pineapple. No big deal, they thought, until they tasted this pineapple; it was sweet and so delicious, the best they had ever tasted.

They couldn't resist asking the waiter about this pineapple. Was all Hawaiian pineapple so sweet, so lacking in acid, and such a beautiful color? "No," he said. "These are special pineapples selected by Mr. Rockefeller when he was building the Rock Resort on the Big Island. They are very special, grown only for some of the hotels in the islands. Enjoy them." The girls threw themselves on every bit of each slice.

"This is the best pineapple in the world," they said. The waffles were wonderful, too.

Nicole said naively, "This is how millionaires live."

"No," her mother replied, "this is how billionaires like the Rockefellers live." They all laughed. Actually, everyone at the table was used to luxury, but the tropical environment, the view, the quality of the food, and being there together had really enchanted them.

After breakfast, the girls ran back to their room, changed into their swimsuits, and hurried to the beach. They would be wearing those bikinis for the first time. The bikinis were not really tiny, but they were pretty small, much less than the girls had ever worn. They felt so grown-up, so free, and ready for fun on the beach and in the water. Nicole told Cleo, "I feel like we're becoming grown-up women." They spent the entire morning at the beach, playing in the water, which felt warm, very warm to

Northern Californians. They also found a hammock at the beach between two palm trees, just like in the postcards.

The girls climbed into the hammock and snuggled together. Nicole put her arms around Cleo, and they smiled at each other. They were just teenage girls having fun, enjoying the sun on their skin and the feeling of a real friend lying against them. Life was good. They put on cover-ups and then ran to have lunch on that same patio with Nicole's mother; everybody ordered a tropical salad and iced tea. As lunch finished, Nicole's mother asked them if they wanted to go back to the beach or take a helicopter ride to see a famous part of the island, Waimea Canyon, often called the Grand Canyon of the Pacific.

The idea of a helicopter ride in such an exotic place was super exciting, so they looked at each other, and both said, "Yes," with an emphatic shake of the head. The girls ran to their room, took a quick shower to get the sand off them, and dressed rapidly. The hotel offered a car and driver, so they arrived at the heli tourism office in just about 15 minutes. Kaua'i is a small island. Once on board, they put on their headphones so they could talk with each other, and off they went. What fun going almost straight up. The view of Kaua'i and the ocean was terrific, but nothing compared to the magnificence of the canyon. The helicopter took them right up in front of a waterfall and then circled back around to show them more of the canyon before heading back to the heliport. Everyone had been thrilled to see the canyon from a helicopter. The girls thought they had just seen Eden.

The car taking them back to the hotel stopped at a little roadside stand that offered eight different types of tropical ice creams. Then, they headed back to the hotel. Dinner was on that same terrace.

Each day followed a pattern: breakfast with waffles, pancakes, or French toast and pineapple, beach, hammock, lunch with Nicole's mother, and then more beach time. One day, Nicole's mother told them that they were going to another part of the island to a restaurant with a magnificent view, and they should get cleaned up, put on something really dressy but appropriate for a tropical climate, and be ready for a nice dinner.

The girls had planned to stay as late as possible at the beach but needed to take a shower since they both had sand all over them. They also wanted to take a nap before meeting Nicole's mother. Nicole headed to the shower first. Since it was a big stand-up shower large enough for four people, Nicole asked Cleo to join her.

Cleo hesitated but thought, *What the hell, we're both girls.*

They washed themselves and then each other all over. Cleo and Nicole both thought that the touch of their friend's hands on their bodies and especially on each other's breasts was delicious. Nicole dried herself off and then helped Cleo dry her back. The girls put on big T-shirts and laid down together on the bed. They were both exhausted from the beach, the trip, everything. Nicole looked at Cleo and thought that she was the best friend possible. They would always be friends, always together. Nicole said, "Isn't it wonderful to be here together, just us? We will always be best friends. We'll always be together."

The days continued to follow a pattern, starting with a wonderful breakfast: waffles or pancakes, the great pineapple, and then the beach. Lunch was followed by more beach time. One afternoon, they went to a little shopping area just to look around and get some presents for a few people. Nicole asked her mother what she was going to get for her father, but her mother said, "He has everything he wants." So, nothing for Dad.

Another day, Nicole's mother arranged a flight on Hawaiian to the Big Island to see the volcanos, particularly Mauna Loa. This largest of Hawaii's volcanos was erupting, so they got to see the lava flows. This was the girls first time at a volcano. They had a great time and were excited to hear the roar of the earth's interior. At the gift shop, they bought lava bracelets to wear back home. The black stone was highly polished. They were told to be careful, however, since it can break. The flight back to Kaua'i was short, but the girls once again felt tired, so they took another nap. This time, Cleo leaned over in the bed, kissed Nicole on the cheek, and thanked her for the wonderful time together. This had been Cleo's best vacation ever.

That night, Nicole and Cleo had a nice dinner of fish and rice with Nicole's mother and then they watched a show on the beach—flaming torches, drums, etc. Touristy but fun. After the show, the girls headed to the hammock, but a highly interlaced couple was already there, so the girls headed farther down the beach, giggling and wondering just what was going on in that hammock. They believed they both knew but were unsure about the details. Just how do you do it in a hammock? Neither of the girls had "done it" yet, which added a lot to their curiosity.

Since the hammock was taken, they laid down on mats on the beach and looked at the wonderful stars. They thought they had seen beautiful skies in Napa, but this was something else. They talked, and then Nicole leaned over and kissed Cleo on the cheeks, telling her how wonderful it was to be together, "Just us," she said. "We're so great together." Then another giggle. Then the girls kissed each other on the mouth, not a long, sensuous kiss, but a real kiss on the lips. They knew they loved each other and would always be best friends. They also wondered what it would feel like to kiss a boy on a beach and when that would happen. They were both almost ready for boys.

Once back in the room, they put on their light, short cotton nightgowns and laid down on the bed. The big bed felt so good, so relaxing. Since the night was warm and a nice breeze was coming off the ocean, they left the big patio doors to the terrace wide open to feel the warm breeze and hear the roar of the waves breaking on the beach. Both girls looked at each other and felt the profound intimacy this vacation had created. They began to hug, giving each other kisses on the cheeks, and then Nicole sat up and pulled her nightgown over her head, saying, "I want to feel the breeze all over my skin, all over my body." Cleo thought how right it was to enjoy the breeze, so she pulled her nightgown off as well. They laid there enjoying the breeze for a few minutes. Then they started caressing each other carefully at first, letting the warm night breeze caress their bodies, adding to their pleasure. They both had found their special pleasure place down there several years earlier but now wanted to feel each other. They wanted to know what it feels like to touch another person down there, to give pleasure to another person.

Starting slowly, gently, sweetly both girls explored each other discretely, very gently and discretely. The sensation felt new, wonderful, and innocent. They were just learning about their bodies, about other people's bodies, and what physical intimacy means. They knew what it felt like to touch their own breasts and their special pleasure spot, but now they could see what it felt

True Friends 37

like to explore another person, to give pleasure to another person, someone they loved. Neither of them felt embarrassed or shy; they were such close friends that this experience could be shared without any second thoughts. After a few minutes, Nicole said, "I think we're growing up, and it feels great."

"Yes!" Cleo shouted.

After a few more kisses, the girls fell asleep hugging each other, both very happy to be there together.

Chapter 5

Cleo Abandoned

Once back in Napa, Nicole found out why her dad had not come to Hawaii with them. None of her dad's things were in the Pacific Height's house; something dramatic had occurred. Nicole's parents had decided to divorce just before the trip, which had given her father time to deal with some of the legal and financial issues and have his personal affairs removed from the townhouse in Pacific Heights. Nicole and her mother were getting the townhouse while Dad would stay at their place in Napa, close to his beloved vineyards. Nicole was very upset but not that surprised since her parents had been arguing a lot, and her dad had spent more and more time "traveling." Actually, he had decided to keep one of his mistresses in Napa.

This meant that Nicole would have to change schools; she was going to be in San Francisco, about an hour and a half away from Napa Valley. The girls cried because they were going to be separated—Cleo in Napa and Nicole in San Francisco. The move to Pacific Heights happened fairly quickly. Just as soon as the movers came for some of their possessions, including Nicole's dolls, she was gone. The girls had spent almost every day together since returning to California from Hawaii, and both felt overwhelmed by the news of Nicole's move to SF.

For Cleo, it was devastating since she had a very emotionally distant and complex relationship with her family, especially her brothers and her mother. The paternal grandparents were in

40   The BeAst and the Brightest

Sydney; the maternal ones were much closer, but still, Carmel is a half-day drive from Napa, and Cleo saw them only rarely. Although this would soon change, Cleo wasn't ready for boys; Nicole was her soul mate, and she was leaving Cleo just as they reached a new level of intimacy.

Cleo felt angry at Nicole, even if she understood the circumstances. She asked her parents if Nicole could live with them and continue to go with her to Napa High School for the next year. The trip to Hawaii had occurred at the end of their junior year, so they just had one more year in high school, their senior year. Cleo's parents were somewhat open to this suggestion, but Nicole's mother was unwilling to consider the idea since she would be alone in San Francisco, and if Nicole stayed with Cleo in Napa, Nicole would be near her mother's ex and his mistress. Nicole's mother would not let that happen. After much crying and hugging, the girls made a pact that they would visit each other on the weekends. One weekend would be in Napa and the other in San Francisco. Of course, this meant they needed someone to drive them and pick them up, an hour and a half each way. This proved hard to manage.

The visits started much more spaced out than the girls wanted; the first month, Nicole visited Cleo in Napa just once. Nicole's second visit to Napa was almost five weeks later. Cleo was never able to make it to SF. Cleo told Nicole that she would visit her over Christmas, but then Nicole's mother announced they were going to spend the holiday with a special friend in Paris. Cleo was not invited to go along. Cleo felt more and more abandoned and angrier at Nicole because of what was happening. Cleo was being abandoned. She understood all of the "realities" but hated them.

When Cleo found out about the trip to Paris, she told Nicole that this was the end; they would never be friends again. Nicole insisted it was just a trip, and they would reunite once they came back after New Year's Eve. Nicole left for Paris, wondering if this were true. She had begun to make friends in her new, fancy, private school in SF, and she liked the urban girls who were more sophisticated than her classmates in Napa and more experienced with guys. Many of them had "done it."

Cleo Abandoned   41

Nicole quickly found a guy she really liked who was fun and good-looking, so she "did it" with him. She was incredibly eager to see Cleo the next weekend to tell her about this first experience. Nicole was all gushy and happy about what had happened. It was wonderful. She really adored the guy. She was somewhat surprised when Cleo said that she, too, had "done it," but she seemed much less happy about the experience. Cleo said that she knew a guy at her school who had done it with several of the girls, and she had chosen him because he'd know what to do. Cleo told Nicole, "It was OK, but I'll be better with someone I really like. With him, it was just sex, nothing more."

Nicole fit in easily at her new school. She became more interested in clothes, art, and boys than she had been in Napa. She had always liked to go skiing, so once back in SF, she and some of her new friends planned a ski trip toTelluride. Nicole invited Cleo, but she wasn't interested in skiing. She felt more abandoned, and her anger toward Nicole grew by the day.

Nicole's feelings of intense friendship and sense of profound intimacy with Cleo had never changed. Even with the new friends in SF and a boyfriend, Nicole still felt more deep friendship and closeness with Cleo than with anyone else, but Cleo had tremendously mixed feelings. Yes, she remembered their intense friendship and the fun and experiences they had shared, but Cleo felt that Nicole had somehow wronged her by leaving Napa.

Then things got much worse. At the end of the school year, Nicole's mother announced that they were actually moving to Paris, where Nicole's mother had a "special friend." They were going to get married. This friend turned out to be a fabulously wealthy Italian who had several magnificent houses in Europe, including a private residence in Paris in the 16th Arrondissement, a small castle in the Carpathian Mountains, and a large penthouse apartment with a terrace on the roof near the Piazza Navona in Rome. Nicole's mother tried to tell Nicole that this would be a wonderful adventure, a new life for them. Nicole was stunned by all this news and these dramatic changes: first, the divorce and then the move to SF. Now, a move to Paris and a

42   The BeAst and the Brightest

stepfather. She didn't know how she was going to adapt to living in Paris; she didn't speak French or anything. She certainly did not know how she would announce this to Cleo.

Cleo was devastated when Nicole told her about the move to Paris. She pleaded with Nicole to ask her mother if there wasn't some way for her to stay in the U.S. to go to a university together, but Nicole told her that she wanted to "give Paris a try." The idea of living in Paris excited Nicole, whose SF friends were crazy with jealousy; they saw living in Paris as a great, exciting adventure, so chic.

Instead of being an hour and a half apart—Napa to downtown SF—they were now going to be separated by zillions of miles. Were they ever going to see each other again? They both cried a lot, hugged each other, and Nicole swore they'd be friends forever. They would try to visit each other. Nicole promised to return to SF, and she implored Cleo to come to Paris. Cleo made Nicole promise to come back to visit her. "Yes, of course, you are my best friend. There will never be anyone in my life like you." Nicole asked Cleo to swear to come to Paris, but she hesitated, saying, "I don't know if I can or if my parents will let me, but I'll try."

During the four years Cleo spent at SF State, Nicole did come back at least once a year, and the girls had wonderful reunions. Gone were the days of intimate touching; they had both experienced guys but seeing each other brought back wonderful memories. Cleo never decided not to visit Nicole in Paris, but she never got around to actually planning the trip. She'd make excuses involving her family, never true, a guy, rarely true, or the requirements of school, only partially true. What was determinant was Cleo's anger at being left in Napa and then at the university in SF.

Nicole's first two years in Paris were spent at an international school where she started learning French and Italian as well as tidbits of other languages. The students were from all over; the only thing that united them was their parents' money and a desire to get out of school and just have fun. That is just what Nicole did, and she did it with relish. Nicole's parents moved from townhouse to castle to penthouse apartment. Nicole was

Cleo Abandoned

initially overwhelmed by the money and the opulence of Paris and Rome but quickly got used to having wads of 500 franc notes in her wallet along with 10,000 and even 100,000 lire bills. The supply of these notes seemed unlimited. This was not the life she had chosen, but she was enjoying it.

Chapter 6
University Press

Cleo was a good student who was very passionate about literature, art, and writing. She imagined writing the ultimate feminist novel of her generation based on her life, which would be a template for a new generation of feminists. Her ambition was to become a senior editor at a substantial publishing company where she could help shape American culture. Her major impact would be through her own story, which would help young women define feminism, leading a life independent of men, if not totally separate from them.

Sexually, like most women, she needed guys. She didn't imagine having a guy with whom she would have any sort of permanent relationship. She'd find ways to be satisfied sexually but be essentially independent of men. She had no interest in women sexually, so it'd have to be guys. The intimacy with Nicole had just been girls growing up. She was sure that they were not the only young girls to have experimented with other girls to understand intimacy. Her sexual life was going to be with guys, but she was not ever going to submit to a guy; he would have to submit to her. That is what she thought her life's work would be—writing about feminism as dominance and freedom from emotional ties. She wanted to live her entire life consistent with those ideas. She also imagined herself as an editor of serious literature at a major publishing house who would direct American

46   The BeAst and the Brightest

culture toward her feminist ideas. She was single-minded in pursuing these two goals, which she saw as mutually reinforcing.

During her time at SF State, she worked on the university newspaper as an editor and part-time writer. Her work on the school newspaper paid off when she graduated by giving her entrée to the University Press as an intern to an assistant editor. This starting position did not come with a glorious title, but her foot was in the door, and she threw herself into the work with gusto. She was so happy. Her dream was going to come true.

As a very attractive young woman, she had no problem getting her share of guys. Some were OK, but apart from random, short-term sexual escapades, she didn't really connect with any of them. She learned that she needed to be in charge since some of them were just bastards who wanted to get her into bed once or twice and then drop her, often without even a goodbye. Several were married. She hated them for using her like that. Guys could be such bastards! She didn't find most of them to be good lovers, anyway. She had her share of males who just explored down there as if looking for something they had lost. A few asked her for what she thought was weird stuff sexually, and she refused. She was absolutely not going to let guys use her to satisfy their infantile male sexual fantasies. No way!

Two years at the University Press led to a promotion to assistant editor. She loved her new position since she now had more frequent contact with both current and prospective authors. San Francisco had become a fairly vibrant literary scene where the most important authors made visits when they didn't live there. Not that SF was Boston or NYC or London or Paris, but a lot was going on. Sometimes, major literary events would be held at UC Berkeley or down the peninsula at Stanford. She loved going to these places and meeting authors. She met a lot of them. Several tried to get her into bed, and more than a few succeeded.

Often, she initiated the process that led to bed. Since she was direct about sex, these encounters typically started during the day when they first met and finished the next morning. To ensure she could connect with these authors, she would find the right moment and then use her most direct lines, such as, "I know you're away from home and probably feeling lonely. How about

University Press 47

we stay together tonight? Do you like sex?" or "Are you up for sex?" or "Isn't there a minibar in your room?"

She thought it couldn't hurt her career to know some of these authors, to have a special relationship with them. Although somewhat allergic to one-night stands, she felt slightly humiliated as a feminist to let more powerful and older guys use her, but it did seem to help her career. She told herself that they were just using her for sex, but she was using them for something more important: advancing her potential role as an influential editor and a feminist. When she was with these guys, she didn't participate much in sex; she just let them do their little things with her. This also minimized her potential emotional reaction to being totally naked in bed with them and "doing it." Sex was traded for positive comments about her work by these authors to her boss, Frank Cooperman. Sure, these very short-term sexual encounters were beneath the feminist she wanted to embody, but it was only sex, and she never mixed up her emotions or feelings with sex.

She did have a clear idea about right and wrong. Right meant being able to have sex with whomever she wanted without any consideration for other people. Thinking about other people would limit her, and that would be wrong. She also felt that sleeping with guys, regardless of their relationship with another woman, was justified since it facilitated her rise as an influential feminist. Anything that stood in her way was wrong. She felt that her approach to morality was both pragmatic and justified since she was destined to be an influential feminist. She couldn't let anything stand in her way, certainly not other women or outmoded traditional ideas about appropriate behavior, manners, decency, or morality. Men had created those to control women, and Cleo would have none of it.

One author in particular, John Fleming, was attracted to Cleo who knew that he was one of their best sellers. He was a nice-looking guy in his early 40s. He was very trim since he worked out a lot and had an abundance of totally white hair. His good looks were augmented by a nice smile and a good sense of humor. He wore very nice clothes casually but with style. Cleo was very interested in sex with him since he could be helpful to her. The first time he met Cleo, he remarked that she was very

48   The BeAst and the Brightest

attractive and said that Cooperman, her boss, had good taste. Cleo got the hint so that when he invited her for a drink at his hotel, she understood what they were going to do.

Since she liked to be direct, she showed up without a bra, wearing a light white cotton blouse, and a big smile. They met in the bar, but quickly, she used one of her lines about the possibility of a minibar in his room, where she proposed they could talk without the distraction of other people in the bar.

Once in the room, they both were very direct with each other. She opened her blouse a bit slowly, undoing the top button while looking straight into his eyes, and he took the hint to continue unbuttoning her blouse. He quickly took off his shirt, and then they both quickly undressed each other and jumped into bed. This was pure zipperless fucking. He was fairly vigorous and skilled, but Cleo wasn't there to appreciate his sexual ability; she wanted him to tell Frank how smart she was. He came on her twice and then, relaxing, said, "So, what can I tell Frank about you?" He had understood the exchange perfectly, sex for support for her career.

"How about you like how I edit your books? How about I have a special skill as an editor?"

It was a done deal. He showed up in SF several times over the next year, and a command performance ensued. Fleming delivered the recommendation after each of these sessions with the skill of a good writer who knew how not to be repetitive or too obvious but still get his message through.

Cleo lived fairly separated from her family during the years at SF State and at the University Press. Her mother had decided to buy a very nice apartment near Coit Tower and was spending much more time in SF than in the Valley. Cleo's father almost never went to the apartment; that was her realm. By respecting her privacy at the apartment, her father could have his own life and lovers at the house in Napa. Once her mother had bought the apartment, she shopped and lunched with more and more fervor. She traveled a lot, usually taking this or that guy with her. Cleo didn't try to keep up with it, either the men or the destinations. She had her own life. Cleo saw her mother rarely even though she was living near Coit Tower, not too far from Cleo's

University Press

apartment. Occasionally, Cleo would see her father and brothers in Napa, but the brothers were spending almost all of their time at their respective vineyards in Australia and Chile. Cleo had no interest in the family business and had never had close ties with her brothers, so she preferred going to Napa just to see her dad. Being there in those hills, seeing those vineyards, and being back in her house revived and refreshed her memories of those childhood and high school years. She always thought about Nicole, and when she was there, she occasionally wrote her.

Her letters to Nicole were the only vehicle she had to express herself somewhat honestly. In fact, their correspondence was an essential outlet both girls had to tell someone what was going on in their lives. Cleo would tell Nicole about the books she was editing and the horrible manuscripts she hated and had rejected. She'd also refer to a sexual relationship with a guy or two, but only in passing. She'd only write a phrase or two about these relationships, phrases that hid as much as they revealed. In fact, the guys she had sex with other than the authors meant almost nothing to her except a little physical pleasure. During this time, Cleo never had anyone she would consider a boyfriend, nor did she want one.

Cleo felt that she could write anything to Nicole without ever being criticized or told to live differently. There was no restraint with Nicole. Well, almost none. Cleo didn't tell Nicole about her sexual relations with authors; she wanted Nicole to see her as a feminist, independent of guys, and she thought that trading sex for help with her career with a lot of different guys was beneath a real feminist, but she needed to do it anyway. She felt no hesitation or shame about what she was doing but knew that Nicole might not understand, you know … trading sex for career advancement, doing it with a lot of different older guys. During this time, Nicole had a significant relationship with an Italian guy named Bepe, who was living part-time in Paris. Nicole wrote that they were totally in love.

Nicole was obviously living a lifestyle very different from Cleo's. When she was first in Europe, Nicole threw herself into the high life, vacationing in Greece, where the guys were "beautiful, plentiful, and free for a night, a few days, or a week." She had always loved to ski, so she usually spent a month each winter

50 The BeAst and the Brightest

in Switzerland or at Val d'Isère in France with friends. They'd ski all day and party at a discotheque until early the next morning. While Cleo was all about having an impact with her feminist ambitions, Nicole was all about having fun and luxury. Despite very different lifestyles, somehow, the closeness they had once felt was rebuilt letter by letter as both girls opened up to each other about their lives. The distance between the two girls gradually lessened; they felt very close again. Cleo had almost forgotten her anger at being abandoned, and what she saw as the betrayal of their friendship, so she wrote regularly to Nicole.

Nicole hid her social awareness because she knew that Cleo didn't like any reference to Nicole's expensive SF private high school. Nicole had stayed in touch with several of the friends she made the year she was there, her senior year. As times changed, Nicole realized that the homogeneous, white, and wealthy private school needed to be part of the larger society in San Francisco. So, during a reunion trip, Nicole, with some friends, organized a scholarship fund for Black, Hispanic, or Asian girls with promise. Within three years, they were able to fund 10 scholarships. Nicole understood how privileged she was and wanted to help some girls who did not have any of the advantages in life she enjoyed. As a feminist, Nicole felt a responsibility to help other women.

Nicole understood that Cleo hated that school since it had separated them, so Nicole never mentioned her work or her new family of girls to Cleo. But during her trips to SF, Nicole always saw Cleo and continued to tell her that despite all the changes in their lives, "You are my best friend; I'll always love you. You can always count on me. That is what a friend is for, right?"

Cleo's boss, Frank Cooperman, was no dupe when it came to hearing lavish praise about Cleo from so many of his authors. Sure, she was good at her job, but the type of praise, the frequency, and the timing were due, he suspected, to more than her work. Fall was a time when authors came to SF for a literary conference and to promote their books on the West Coast. One of Frank's longtime, best-selling authors, John Fleming, had also become a good friend over the years they had worked together. Frank knew that Fleming was an attractive bachelor who liked good-looking women and who slept with a number of them. Given Fleming's positive comments about Cleo, Frank felt comfortable making a remark to Fleming about Cleo's good looks and asked, "John, so have you had a chance to get to know her more deeply after work at night?"

John just nodded and said, "I find her very welcoming; she is easy to get to know. That red hair is just one indication of her … well, you know."

The men smiled at each other. Frank had been calculating his chances with her as well. If she were willing to have sex with authors just to influence him, why not seize the opportunity to let her influence him directly? He thought he'd be crazy to pass up this opportunity to have a sexual relationship with an attractive young woman, especially one very open to casual sex.

Frank started looking for an opportunity to be out of San Francisco with Cleo. A conference or other business reason to travel together somewhere would suit his purpose. As a married man with two kids, he was going to be careful. He had to come up with a good plan. The opportunity dropped in his lap one day when an old friend, Alexander Remington, the chief editor of Schendler Publishing in Boston, asked if he was interested in sponsoring an East Coast/West Coast series of literary discussions at a conference in Boston.

Remington thought they could get the Boston PBS channel to cover the literary discussions; the publicity would be well worth it. Schendler and Frank could invite authors whom they believed represented the two costal cultures to the conference. Frank and Alexander could organize discussions among three or four authors who would read a book written by an East Coast or a West Coast author and then discuss it as a group. Frank immediately jumped at the idea. Cleo would become the coordinator; she would have to travel with him, and he would have his chance.

Frank presented the idea to the university president, who saw the opportunity but wanted another university to be involved, not just a business like Schendler. Frank and Alexander worked on this request and were able to get a joint sponsorship with the University of Massachusetts in Boston. Harrison Jones, a professor of English literature, was selected to be the key contact to work with Frank and Alexander. The project would move ahead, as would Frank's plan. The next step was a planning meeting in Boston; Cleo would be invited to go along as the coordinator. Early on in the project, there seemed to be no pressing need for a coordinator, but Frank was determined to bring Cleo along with him.

Of course, Cleo was thrilled by the opportunity and excited about the first list of potential authors Frank and Alexander developed, which included several authors she knew intimately. Cleo was determined to prove her worth to both men. Frank asked if she knew Boston, and she answered, "No, I have never been there but am dying to go."

NYC and Washington, DC, were the only cities on the East Coast she had seen, and those visits were on trips with her family when she was first in Napa High School. That is when her family still took vacations together. That stopped when Cleo was a junior in high school, the year she and Nicole went to Hawaii.

Cleo enjoyed seeing the monumental public buildings in DC, but she was most interested in the Smithsonian. In general, she didn't care about politics, and Washington left her indifferent. New York City! Seeing that town convinced her of one thing: She would spend her life on the East Coast and maybe in NYC. She was excited to see Union Square and Times Square, Wall Street, and the Statue of Liberty. She loved going to the theaters and visiting the museums. Yes, all that was great. But what she really wanted to see were the great publishing houses—Penguin, Random House, HarperCollins, MacMillan Publishers, Simon and Schuster, and Hachette, among others. Every night in the hotel she would dream of working in one of those storied publishing houses, editing books, accepting some for publication while rejecting others. She wanted to help feminist authors and write her own book advocating and defining feminism for her generation. She wanted to be a fresh, new voice for feminism. Yes, NYC, or certainly the East Coast, was where she was going to be.

Chapter 7
Schendler and Boston

Imagine how excited she was to accompany Frank, a respected publisher at a university press, to help organize a literary event in Boston and with Schendler Publishing, one of America's oldest and most serious publishers. They got a flight from SF to Chicago's O'Hare airport, where the layover was prolonged due to bad weather, but eventually, they arrived in Boston. Given the time difference between the coasts, the prolonged layover in Chicago, and the length of both legs of the trip, they arrived late. Flying into Logan Airport, Cleo saw almost nothing due to the lateness of the hour and dense fog. The taxi trip from Logan to the Copley Plaza Hotel was fast given the lack of traffic at that time of night. They both got their keys and headed to their adjacent rooms. The trip was tiring, and they had a lot to do the next day, so Frank led the way to their rooms, saying, "See you in the morning." As he got into bed, he imagined Cleo next to him, not just in the room next to his, but next to him in bed. He'd have to find an opportunity and the guts to make a move.

Even when you think you know what a hotel or a city might be like, the experience of being there is often very different. To really know a city, to know if you could live there, you have to get a firsthand feel of its texture, its rhythms, its architecture, and its people. Cleo's first impressions of Boston were all positive.

At breakfast in the hotel with Frank Cooperman and Alexander Remington, and throughout the first day, she started feeling

54   The BeAst and the Brightest

that Boston was going to be her new home. Everything about Boston pleased her: the scale of the buildings—less intimidating than Manhattan; the streets—less frenetic, but still alive; the ambiance—less about money, but very serious. Everyone she looked at seemed more interesting, more educated, and more intelligent than their equivalents in California. Even the weather seemed more serious. The snow and the cold seemed to invite a day of reading rather than fun in the California sun. The clothes people wore seemed more serious without being pretentious. She loved it.

Now, she just needed to find a way to get there. Frank, Cleo, and Alexander were joined the first day by Oliver Friedman, an editorial assistant to Remington. They discussed how to organize the events, the involvement of the local PBS station, which authors to invite, and a million details. Oliver, a guy in his early 30s, was there to take notes and weigh in on certain decisions about logistics. He wore big, round glasses and a vest, but he wasn't bad-looking. Cleo wasn't sure about him, but he seemed OK. He tended to ignore her, which pissed her off, but she recognized that she was the most junior person in the room.

The first night, everybody was invited to dinner at Durgin Park, a Boston landmark restaurant. Not that the food was so good, it wasn't really very good. The appeal of the restaurant was that it had been there forever, and the waiters and waitresses had been there for ages, too. They were known for their curtness—"What'd you want?" Durgin Park was a Boston institution. The menu was dominated by traditional New England food: baked beans, Yorkshire pudding, crab cakes, and steamers.

Cleo didn't know what steamers were but went for them to learn more about Boston and to seem more "local." Frank and Alexander selected the prime rib, the restaurant's specialty. Oliver ordered crab cakes. Cleo liked the fact that he didn't just do the same thing as his boss. His choice also led to a conversation about crab cakes, a short conversation. Since Oliver was much more interested in books than food, Cleo started to like him. As a guy, he seemed to be a loser, but at least he was very interested in and knowledgeable about contemporary American literature.

Cleo sat between Frank and Oliver. Both seemed to want to talk with her, but she was focused on the guy who mattered most to her, Alexander, the editor of Schendler. After dinner, Cleo and Frank took a cab back to the Copley Plaza, and he invited her for a drink in the bar. She was worried that Frank would see Oliver as a substitute coordinator for her. She knew that Frank was her ticket back to Boston, so she got ready to make her move. Without any hesitation, she flashed that smile and said, "It's noisy here; wouldn't your room be better? You have a mini-bar, don't you?"

Frank was relieved and thrilled at this suggestion since he had never cheated and didn't know how to take the first step with Cleo, who was, after all, not just much younger but also his employee. Going up in the elevator, Frank tried to figure out how to make a move while they were talking and drinking a glass of wine. He thought he was going to have to make a move and was nervous about how to do it, but Cleo knew how to be as direct as possible. They were going to have sex.

As soon as he closed the door, Cleo put her hands on his chest and rubbed them up and down, saying, "I'm so thankful you gave me this opportunity."

He reciprocated by putting his hands on her breasts. "Why don't you take off your shirt," she said. As he unbuttoned his shirt, she pulled her sweater over her head, revealing her breasts. She wasn't wearing a bra, sure of the effect this would have on him. Then zippers started sliding down so fast she didn't even have to use her line about panties. Once in bed, the deed was done, with no enthusiasm on her part and a huge sigh of relief and pleasure on his. He laid back on top of the bed, totally nude, and just smiled at Cleo, a huge smile of contentment. This was the first time in 15 years that he had enjoyed sex with someone other than his wife.

He said to himself, *That was good, that was really good—I really needed that.*

Cleo looked at him and thought that she was glad he wasn't bad-looking for a guy his age. That would make her "work" easier. Cleo kissed him on the cheek and said, "That was so nice, but we're both so tired; I need to sleep in my own room."

56 The BeAst and the Brightest

With that, she was dressed and out the door in a couple of minutes. Frank was disappointed that she was leaving, but given what had just happened, he was satisfied. He had scored, sort of, with an attractive young woman. Actually, she had gained points with him; she was sure to have a ticket back to Boston.

The next day, the meeting went well. Cleo sat on one side of the table with Frank, who kept smiling at her, and Oliver. She wondered why Oliver was on their side of the table, but maybe there was no specific reason; he had to sit somewhere. Usually, Cleo could tell when she was going to be approached by a guy, but not his time. She was fascinated by Boston, the discussions during the day, Alexander, and even Oliver, who seemed to be just as passionate about books as she was. After a lunch break, Oliver took Cleo on a tour of Schendler, during which he respectfully introduced her to some key people. She met several division directors, including Johnny Littman, who was introduced as the head of general literature, Schendler's most important division. She then met several more of the division directors, including a couple of women.

One lady in particular impressed Cleo. This was Prudence McClinton Higginbotham. She was introduced using all three names: Prudence McClinton Higginbotham. The lady did not get up from her seat but held out her hand and said with a distinctive upper-class British accent, "You are lovely. Are you interested in books?"

"Oh, yes," Cleo exclaimed.

She then launched into a passionate recitation about her love for books, how thrilling it was to be in Boston, how happy she was to meet her ... until Oliver leaned over and said softly, "That's wonderful, just great, but we really need to let Ms. Higginbotham continue with her work." Cleo felt somewhat embarrassed, but Prudence McClinton Higginbotham saw something she liked— herself, only younger, much better looking, and healthy.

Higginbotham was British through and through: public school, then Oxford, followed by a marriage to a professor of classics at Oriel College, Oxford. For reasons she never understood, the marriage only lasted three years. Then, she met a visiting professor from Boston to whom she became engaged. That meant a move to the other side of the pond, as she called it to

Schendler and Boston

her friends. She hated leaving her beloved Britain, but for love, she would make that sacrifice. While they were engaged, she discovered that she had MS, which eventually left her unable to walk steadily and fearful of falling. Oliver did not tell Cleo more of the story but did say that she had not gotten up to greet Cleo since standing was difficult for her. Then Oliver said the magic words, "Ms. Higginbotham might be looking for an assistant."

Cleo looked at Oliver, smiled, put her arm over his shoulders, and said softly, "You are so, so nice to tell me that."

Oliver loved the feeling of her arm on his shoulders and her comment about being so nice.

That afternoon, the conference discussions ended early at 2:30 p.m. since Alexander had other appointments. Cleo was asked to call Harrison Jones, the literature professor, to give him an update on the conference. She had been told to keep him in the loop, but he wasn't going to be directly involved. This was going to be Frank and Alexander's show. Oliver offered to give Cleo a little tour of Boston in his car. Cleo gladly accepted. Her plan seemed to be coming together. Cleo loved seeing the sites: the Public Gardens, the state capitol with its golden dome, and Faneuil Hall. Then Oliver took the "Salt and Pepper" Bridge over the Charles River into Cambridge, past MIT to Harvard University. Oliver made a point of saying that he was a Harvard graduate, which didn't impress Cleo much since he seemed to be somewhat of a loser, but perhaps he was a smart loser.

They then turned back over the Charles River again into Boston past the Museum of Fine Arts, the Boston Symphony, the Isabella Stewart Gardner Museum, then down Huntington Avenue to Copley Square and her hotel. Cleo invited him in for a drink. Once in the hotel, she used the line that had worked with Frank the previous evening. "It's noisy here, wouldn't my room be better? I have a minibar, you know?" As they went up the elevator, Oliver became nervous but was reassured when Cleo flashed one of those pregnant smiles so full of promise. Oliver's heart started beating wildly; he had no idea what might happen; she used the same technique as the night before—hands on his chest, his shirt off, her sweater off, zippers down, quickly doing the deed, then the line about needing to do some work and then get to sleep.

58   The BeAst and the Brightest

"I'll see you tomorrow," she said as she hurried him out of the room. Poor Oliver had not slept with many women, actually only a very few, and never one nearly as attractive as Cleo. The time was only 6:30 p.m. Cleo had handled Oliver in just three hours, complete with a tour of Boston, a quick "seduction," and a minimal tumble in bed. Oliver was in heaven. His nickname was Useful Idiot. He would be the first of two useful idiots.

Once Oliver was out the door, Cleo called Frank. He had been upset to learn that Cleo and Oliver had taken off without his knowledge to tour Boston. Somehow, he feared the worse, so he was delighted when he got the call from Cleo. "Do we have plans for dinner, just us?" she asked. Frank was relieved to see that nothing had happened except a little tour of Boston, not that Oliver seemed to anyone to be a ladies' man. Frank was new to cheating, so he was extremely nervous, but his interest in Cleo had not been satisfied. He hoped for more.

"Sure, we're eating together," he said. Frank didn't know Boston well, so on the fly, he suggested a well-known restaurant on the Bay, Anthony's Pier 4. Off they went.

The restaurant was very large and somewhat noisy, and the food was only good enough to satisfy tourists who wanted to eat at a landmark seafood restaurant with a view of Boston Bay. Neither of them mentioned the previous evening and what they had done. Frank was nervous and uncertain about how to mention it to Cleo or broach the subject of their relationship. They decided to skip dessert and grabbed a cab back to the hotel. Since Frank was uncertain how to approach Cleo, he said, "If you are still hungry, we can have dessert in the bar."

Cleo looked straight at him and asked, "Wouldn't a special dessert be better in your room?" Frank understood in a flash what dessert she had in mind, a very sweet dessert.

Of course, she had no sexual or emotional interest in Frank; she was just assuring herself another trip to Boston and guaranteeing her role as the conference coordinator. Again, a quick but vigorous toss in bed was followed by a show as she slowly stood up next to the bed, being sure to let Frank see her totally naked, and then she slipped on her tiny thong panties. She was putting the hook in deeper. "How about a drink? If you put on your boxers, we could get something from your minibar."

He slipped on his boxer shorts, got out a little bottle of wine, poured two glasses, and sat down on a couch next to Cleo, who was still just in her thong panties. She knew she had been very passive during sex, so she wanted to spice things up. As they sipped the wine, Cleo gave him an occasional kiss. As they finished their wine, she brushed her breasts over his face. "That was great again, boss," she said with an ambiguous smile. This line was, however, delivered with a nice kiss on both of his cheeks. She then finished dressing and headed to the door. By using the word "boss," she was defining his role: a boss with a special advantage. Frank understood that he was getting measured rations, but he really liked what he was getting.

Back in her room, Cleo realized that she had given herself sexually to two guys the same day and just a few hours apart, which was a first for her. That was no big deal, but she understood that she needed to be smart about how she handled them. Nothing she had done concerned her at all—certainly not any moral issues or the need to be truthful with these guys, but she would need to be careful about what she told them. The less they knew about what she was doing or with whom outside of the business meetings, the better. She was happy and a little proud of how she had handled herself and managed these two guys who were important to her success.

The next morning, the discussions proceeded quickly since, after a lunch of sandwiches in the conference room, Frank and Cleo needed to head to Logan for the return flight. Cleo exchanged smiles with Oliver and Frank. Both seemed very happy. Then, an unexpected moment came when Alexander said to Frank, "What a good idea to bring Cleo; she added so much. I hope she'll return." Cleo knew she was getting closer to living in Boston.

Once back in SF, Cleo wrote a note to Alexander saying how much she had enjoyed meeting all of the people at Schendler, especially him and Prudence McClinton Higginbotham. Oliver got a short note saying how much she enjoyed meeting him, "the tour and everything else, especially everything else." Then she

60   The BeAst and the Brightest

added, "I take you at your word that you can help me find a position at Schendler, maybe with the impressive Ms. Higginbotham. Alexander thinks the world of you, and you seem to know everything that is happening at Schendler. Until we meet again, yours, Cleo." Oliver was thrilled by the words, "especially everything else" and "yours, Cleo." He felt a marvelous complicity with her. Every night, as he was going to bed, he read her note over and over, savoring every word.

The next trip was just a few weeks later. Cleo had avoided any discussion with Frank about what had happened between them in Boston. Frank was OK not discussing any of that in the office in SF, and did not want anything to happen anywhere near SF. He had to be careful. Cleo and Frank took another flight through Chicago's O'Hare Airport to Boston and the Copley Hotel. Frank and Cleo glanced furtively at each other in the elevator as they headed to their rooms. Cleo said, "We were great together, but I feel bad since you are married …" Frank understood that he had served her purpose. Cleo had feared that she couldn't deliver the morality line about him being married because she really didn't care; she didn't emotionally understand the issue, but she had to be able to use it, and the line had its effect.

Frank remembered their drink on his couch and how she sat there almost naked and the feeling of her breasts brushing against his face, and now this! Mentioning his marriage seemed like a low blow by someone who had given herself sexually to a lot of men, including many of his authors who were married. Frank was upset by Cleo's mixed signals. He asked himself whether she was ever honest and straightforward with anyone.

Well, he told himself, *it was nice while it lasted.*

Cleo had slept with Frank because she wanted a ticket back to Boston. Now, she wanted Oliver to help her get a job at Schendler. Frank realized that he had deluded himself. He had dreamed momentarily about having a real relationship with Cleo because she liked him and was attracted to him. His cynical sexual opportunism had transformed into a narcissistic delusion that she might like him.

The next morning, the same group—Alexander, Frank, Oliver, and Cleo—continued to discuss the conference. Cleo hoped to avoid dinner with Frank and thought that he might not even

Schendler and Boston

invite her because of what she had said about his wife. Cleo was, in fact, totally focused on Oliver, so she planned to invite him to dinner with her that night. But Cleo's plans got derailed that afternoon when Alexander said that Oliver had mentioned that she might be interested in a position at Schendler and asked her if she would come to his office at about 6:30 p.m. to discuss possibilities. She told everybody that she wanted to do room service for dinner and would go to bed early but whispered to Alexander, "I'll come by to see you later, at 6:30. Your office is on the sixth floor, right?"

Frank and Cleo took a cab back to the hotel, where Cleo grabbed a snack from a cart in the bar. She ate it quickly in her room. She had no idea what might happen. A short cab ride took her back to the Schendler building, and she went up to the sixth floor to find Alexander's office. She saw that nobody was on the entire floor; everyone had left much earlier. She noticed two big mahogany doors that led to the publisher's office and wondered if she should just go in or knock. She decided just to open the doors. He was in shirt sleeves, having draped his suit coat over the back of a big, deep couch in his office. This was the first time she had seen him in shirt sleeves.

Cleo was invited to sit on the couch, and Alexander offered her a drink. A wine bottle and two glasses were on the coffee table in front of the couch. She was only able to nod and say, "Yes, that would be great."

"Would you like some wine or something stronger?"

She looked at the wine bottle, then, pointing at it, said, "That would be fine. You know my family is in the wine business." He asked her more about the vineyards and her education and then said, "I think we could use a very attractive, intelligent girl here."

"Do you really find me attractive?" she asked, flashing her smile. "I think you are, too, very attractive," she ventured.

She leaned over toward him, licking her lips as voluptuously as possible as if preparing to kiss him. He noticed that she had opened her blouse since the business discussion that afternoon and had removed her bra. He responded with an open-mouth kiss. This opened the door to more kisses, clothes off, and a quickie in the missionary position on that big, deep couch. The way he handled her suggested that she probably was not the first and would not be the last on that couch. The couch seemed to have been selected for just this sort of thing since it was long and deep enough to lay back on comfortably. Alexander seemed satisfied with a quick one. That worked for her as well. "To conclude the encounter, he said, "We'll try really hard to get you here."

She said, "I like your hard thing." This type of somewhat vulgar, unrefined comment was unlike her, and as soon as she had said it, she wondered how he would react, but it worked. He looked like a sophisticated but restrained, if not uptight, New England gentleman, but he was no virgin or prude. She was almost certain about getting a job and moving to Boston.

As she got dressed, he kept the slightly off-color comments going by saying, "About that job and everything else, I'll work hard, very hard at it," and smiled at her. She smiled back and gave him a lovely kiss on the lips.

Back at the hotel, she had a voicemail from Oliver, which she ignored. But the next morning, she intended to consolidate her position by being sure Oliver was on her side. That was going to be easy. She made a point of sitting next to Oliver at that big conference table and touching him on the shoulder a couple of times and then once or twice on the leg. No one noticed except Alexander, who was the most astute person in the room. He didn't care since he hoped Oliver would carry some of the water for him.

That night, Oliver stayed with Cleo the entire night in her hotel room, which was the best night of his life. Poor Frank was lying in his bed all alone. He imagined Cleo alone in her bed in another room in the hotel and wished that he were with her, enjoying her lovely young body. Cleo had, in fact, asked for a room on a different floor so Oliver or any other guy would not be seen coming or leaving her room.

Cleo and Frank saw their Schendler counterparts the next morning just for two hours. Instead of the standard sandwiches at lunch in the conference room, Alexander invited them for a lunch of fried clams, a Boston classic, in his private dining room. Everybody toasted each other and drank a glass of good white wine to the success of the project, and Frank and Cleo headed back to Logan for the long trip home. Cleo thought that everyone, except poor Frank, had gotten what they wanted, her more than anyone. A little sex with two Schendler guys was all it took to advance her career as an editor and feminist writer. That is all that mattered to her.

Chapter 8

Prudence and Alexander

Once back in SF, Schendler didn't wait long to make a move. First, Alexander called Frank to say how happy he was with the project. He then said that one of their senior editors, a Ms. Higginbotham, was looking for an assistant and had been impressed by Cleo. Alexander said that they were considering making her an offer and wanted to tell Frank about this personally to avoid any unpleasantness. Frank understood without knowing what had actually happened that had led them to be interested enough in Cleo to make her an offer.

Despite feeling that his sexual relationship with Cleo was probably finished, he thought that maybe, just maybe, on subsequent trips to Boston, he would be able to sleep with this attractive young woman. He also felt vulnerable to blackmail since she could make it known that they had slept together, and the news might get to Frank's wife. Her move to Boston would make this much less likely. So, he said graciously to Alexander, "Of course not. I would not think of standing in the way of Cleo's career. I think you'll be happy with her."

Alexander replied, "I'm sure we'll enjoy having her here. I'm sure she'll give us satisfaction." Frank didn't understand the full meaning of those words. Frank could not imagine that Alexander and Cleo had done anything together, certainly not what he and Cleo had done, and Oliver was clearly out of Cleo's league,

66 The BeAst and the Brightest

so Frank just thought that they had seen her intelligence and needed someone.

Saying goodbye to her family was, in fact, thrilling for Cleo. Boston was about as far away from her family as possible, and she relished the idea of seeing them even less frequently. Her father said he'd be sure to see her when he came to the East Coast, and her mother made the same comment, muttering something about getting the opportunity to do some shopping in NYC. Cleo wasn't quite sure what the connection was between shopping in Manhattan and seeing her in Boston, but she knew which was more important to her mother. Before leaving, she spent a weekend with her grandparents in Carmel, which made everyone in the family feel better; at least it looked better.

The night before she left, her father organized a nice dinner for her at Bix, a swanky supper club in SF with a 1930s ambiance. Bix describes itself as a place where it would be difficult for a woman to overdress. Cleo bought herself a really nice dress for the occasion at Bix as well as for fancy functions in Boston. The dress was very form-fitting, discretely, but definitely sexy, with a décolleté sure to be noticed but still appropriate for a professional, good-looking young woman with something to show. She knew she'd be wearing it at parties or fancy soirées in Boston. Her destiny was going to play out in Boston. She felt very sophisticated heading to Boston. At Bix, a large black woman sang the blues while leaning on a piano. Cleo thought she sang very well. Cleo felt another surge of emotion about growing up. She was becoming the formidable woman she had always aspired to be.

Frank also organized a goodbye party for her at lunch. Frank, Cleo, and four of her co-workers went to Fog City, a nice restaurant near Levi Strauss Plaza Park. Frank offered wine, saying that, exceptionally, he'd like a glass at lunch. It seemed fitting for Cleo because of her family's business and since she'd be far from the California wines. He proposed that they share a platter of fresh shellfish, which Cleo loved.

She smiled, raised her glass, and said, "Thank you so much. I wouldn't have this opportunity except for the University Press, and especially you, Frank. Thank you, thank you. You will always

Prudence and Alexander

be special to me in so many ways, and I can't wait to see you again in Boston. I'm really eager to see you and excited about being with you again in Boston, you know, being together."

Frank weighed every word and was very pleased by her response. He thought, *Well, maybe.*

Cleo quickly found a nicely furnished apartment in the Back Bay section of Boston. She did not move her furniture from the SF apartment, only some of her books, clothes, stereo, and a few of her cooking things. She was devoted to her big French coffee funnel, but other than that, her cooking would be simple. Thank goodness for takeout.

Prudence McClinton Higginbotham turned out to be the grand dame of literature that Cleo had imagined her to be. In addition to her important role as an editor, she had written several novels, all of which had been published in Britain, not by Schendler. She did not want the appearance of being favored because of her job. To her, being straight and narrow and avoiding even the slightest hint of impropriety was essential to her entire person. She was British and about as straitlaced as they came, but she was also kind and empathetic. She welcomed Cleo into the office warmly and said how delighted she was that such an attractive, intelligent young woman would be joining her.

Their working arrangement fell into place easily and quickly. Prudence made the first selection of manuscripts to read and gave a selection to Cleo for a first look. Prudence made a habit of first reading books by authors already published by Schendler or to whom Schendler had given an advance. Cleo liked exploring authors she didn't know, but her division got so many unsolicited manuscripts that she had to have some criteria to select those that would get even a first cursory reading. Given the volume of manuscripts, she realized why Prudence had requested an assistant.

Often, Cleo would start a manuscript only to see that the writing was not up to Schendler's standards. These authors quickly got the standard rejection. Cleo tried to give special attention to manuscripts from authors she knew to be feminists or who might be. She also looked for "feminist" titles. Prudence was open to publishing feminist titles but told Cleo that their division could not be limited to that theme, however important. Cleo said she understood but thought that when she was in Prudence's job, she'd use it as a feminist bully pulpit.

Despite her two failed relationships with men, one unexplained divorce, and one guy leaving her because of her MS, Prudence seemed to idolize men. Cleo understood that her love and sex life were on hold, if not suspended for good, so she tried to be understanding. She had a totally different take on men than Prudence; they were all bastards, but above all, she wanted to gain Prudence's respect and admiration.

Prudence saw that Cleo had a talent for an apt phrase or a clever turn of words. As a writer, she liked that. She also saw that Cleo thought of herself as a feminist, and she wondered whether Cleo would be able to write a significant pro-feminist book or whether her brand of feminism was just a guide for her own life. Cleo never mentioned her mentor, Erica Jong, or her advocacy of "anonymous, zipperless, fucking," or that relationships should be "zipless," that is, without any affective feelings for each other. Given Prudence's positive attitude toward men, Cleo understood that Prudence would be shocked by this approach to feminism. Cleo just positioned herself as a feminist. In any case, the working relationship developed smoothly. Occasionally, Alexander would ask Prudence about Cleo's work, saying that he knew he had taken a somewhat unusual step of bringing her to Boston, a town not lacking in talent.

Upon arriving at Schendler, Cleo understood that she had to deal with Oliver, poor Oliver. On her second day at Schendler, she went to his office to tell him, "You are such an attractive and great guy (she believed nothing like this but knew he would like to hear it) that I am glad that something happened between us, but since we're now working together in the same company, I think it is better if we don't continue."

Oliver just sat there for a minute, swallowed hard, and said, "I understand." What he thought was that, once back in SF, she had decided that he was not the guy for her, something she never would have considered. Of course, he would never have thought that she had done anything with Frank or Alexander; he thought he was the only one she had shared herself with in bed.

Prudence and Alexander

Poor Oliver. He could not imagine that she used sex as an asset to achieve a professional goal and could sleep with guys without involving her emotions. He didn't understand that she could be totally faithless. He had taken her word as truthful that she found him attractive. Women rarely let Oliver think they had any interest in him, especially a woman as attractive as Cleo. He knew he shouldn't feel this way, but he was really hurt. Somehow, she had made him dream, but it was just that, a dream. Every day at Schendler was a constant source of pain for him, renewed every time he saw her. He resisted the suggestion that she had just used him. When this idea came to him, he fought to reject it since he wanted to always think of Cleo in the most positive way possible. For her, he was just a guy she had used to advance her plan, her ambition. This type of cynicism, harshness, and complete indifference to other people's feelings was simply beyond Oliver's imagination.

On the other hand, Cleo knew she needed to be careful how she reacted to Alexander and strategic about the liaison between them. She didn't know if he had "done her" just to show that he was the boss and could get whatever he wanted or if she was being introduced as part of a stable of women he occasionally enjoyed on that big, deep couch. When she got the job offer, she sent him a note from San Francisco, "Thank you, Alexander, for working so hard, so delightfully hard, to find a way to get me to Boston." After she sent it, she wondered if continuing the off-color comments about "hard" was too crass, too obvious, but Alexander liked it and kept it in his top desk drawer.

Cleo didn't know when he would invite her for more sessions on that couch or in a hotel room, but she felt sure that he would make a move. She understood that Alexander was going to be critical to her plan, to her career and she'd have to play her cards with him as well as possible. She understood that he had the upper hand and absolutely did not want to do anything that would jeopardize her job or her new life in Boston.

She didn't have to wait too long for an answer to her questions about Alexander. Cleo had been there for just two weeks when, one afternoon, he dropped by her office to invite her to come up to his office about 6:30 p.m. to discuss how things were going. Despite being her boss and in command of her career, she told

70   The BeAst and the Brightest

herself she should just consider him to be another guy when it came to sex. This thought reassured her. At 6:30 p.m. sharp, she went up to the top floor, got off the elevator, and saw that everyone had already left. The usual "closing time" at Schendler was 5 p.m., so by 6:30 p.m., the top floor was deserted. His secretary always left precisely at 5 p.m. This time, she knocked on his big mahogany office door and heard, "Come in, Cleo."

He again offered her a glass of wine, which she drank quickly and then asked for another. She needed something. He was now her boss and held her career, her destiny in his hands. They quickly finished their drinks, and as they were putting their wine glasses on the coffee table in front of the couch, he leaned over and kissed her, but only on the neck. She didn't know why the kiss was on her neck. He was essential to her success, so she decided to take the initiative. Quickly kicking off her shoes, she started unbuttoning her blouse. Then, standing up in front of him, she unzipped her skirt, which, with a little wiggle of her hips, fell to the floor. Her actions spoke more clearly than any words. His reaction was almost immediate; he unzipped his slacks, and she helped him pull everything off. As she pulled down his shorts, she noticed that, despite his lanky, somewhat wiry thin body, he had a big penis. She thought it looked funny for such a thin, tightly wound guy to have such as big one, but so what? It was just funny to see.

She was still wearing her bra and panties. The bra came off quickly, and as he leaned back on the couch, she came over him and brushed her breasts against his face, rubbing her nipples over his lips. He seemed enthralled. His reaction gave her the opportunity to use her line, "When I'm with you, I don't like to take off my panties … please do it for me." His eyes lit up like those of a small boy looking at a Christmas tree. He took the sides of her panties in his hands, and down they came. As she stepped out of them, he put them on the cocktail table next to her bra. Then he leaned back on the couch, inviting her to come on him.

He had been on top the last time, and she was somewhat surprised about this movement, but she knew what to do. Despite the initial awkwardness, there was no fumbling around. He let her take charge. Taking his penis in her hands, she rubbed it with

Prudence and Alexander

some expertise, and as he got much harder, she led it into her as she laid down on him. A few minutes of shaking around elicited the happy tremor and sigh she hoped for, and he seemed to want so badly. He leaned all the way back on the couch and said, "Oh Wow! Oh Wow!" as if he had been saving up sperm and sexual emotion since their last encounter. She wondered if she was his only sexual outlet.

Before turning around to get dressed, she stood in front of him totally naked. She noticed how disheveled he was. He looked much less imposing laying there, having just enjoyed a full orgasm thanks to Cleo. After all, he was just another guy, an important one to her, but just another male who needed a screw. He looked up and smiled at her, saying how wonderful it was to share these moments with her. But then he added, "We need to be discrete and pace these little moments together out a bit—like once a month or every five weeks." He looked at her to see her reaction to this plan. She wondered how many other women he enjoyed occasionally on that couch. Four-to-five-week intervals seemed too much for a guy who wanted sex. Surely, other women were fulfilling his desires. She'd have to be sure to please him more than any of these other women. She would give him whatever he wanted, however he wanted it, as often as he wanted it. She now knew the terms of their deal, his support for her career for an orgasm every month or so.

All her instincts were to protect her plan, her career. She told him, "I would love that; you are so right. I like being with an attractive gentleman from time to time who is such a good lover." Their entente was complete. He offered her another glass of wine, and she accepted. They sat there on the couch, totally nude, touching each other a bit. As they finished their wine, they both started getting dressed. She gave him a brief kiss on the mouth, and quickly, she was out the door. She was happy with her performance and their deal and determined to beat out other women, if there were any, for his attention.

Chapter 9
Cleo's Game

Cleo was determined to be successful at Schendler, so during the first two months, all she did was work. Even at night and on the weekends, she'd read manuscripts or edit pages of books in progress in her apartment. She wrote short but smart analyses of books she thought Higginbotham might want to consider. One afternoon, Higginbotham invited Cleo to dinner at her apartment, which was on the ground floor of a building right across a side street from Schendler. Because of her MS, the company had made getting to and from work very easy. "You like Chinese, yes?" she asked.

Cleo nodded and said, "Of course."

The invitation was for that Friday night. Higginbotham asked if that was convenient or if it interfered with other social arrangements or obligations. Cleo said, "Of course, I'd love to see you." In fact, she was delighted to reinforce their relationship.

The evening at Higginbotham's apartment was just lovely. Prudence had ordered Chinese to be delivered, and it was good. She offered Cleo a glass of dry white wine, which she liked, and the conversation started easily and flowed quickly from subject to subject—all about books, authors, sales, ideas, etc. Cleo was in heaven. They were becoming real colleagues, a sentiment which was strengthened when Higginbotham said how happy she was with Cleo's work and how pleasant it was to share time with such a lovely young woman.

74 The BeAst and the Brightest

The next day, Cleo ventured to ask Higginbotham a question about Alexander. She was afraid to go straight to that subject, so instead asked if Oliver was married or had a significant other. Higginbotham said she didn't know for sure but thought not. Cleo said, "That's too bad because he is a nice guy. He'll find somebody, I'm sure." Higginbotham nodded her agreement. Then Cleo asked about Alexander. "No, he's not married; he's divorced but has a long-term relationship with a lovely woman, Diane Bouquet. They live together in a big townhouse not far from here."

Cleo couldn't restrain a little twitch. She was surprised. "What is she like?" she asked, trying to be as nonchalant as possible.

"A lovely woman … do you know her work? She writes interesting novels known for being very sensitive from a woman's point of view. She's an important and influential feminist."

Cleo didn't know what to say or whether the better part of wisdom was just to be quiet, but she added, "Diane Bouquet. Is she French?"

"Her father was French, her mother American," but then Higginbotham said somewhat proudly, "she was educated in England. She met Alexander after his divorce, and they have been together for some time."

Cleo asked if Schendler had published her books, but no, that, too, would not be appropriate. Higginbotham had assisted Diane with the same publishing company that Prudence had used for her books. Cleo took a deep breath; she needed to think. Then Prudence added, "Diane and I are dear friends."

How was Cleo going to handle the reality of this Diane? Cleo knew that she had to think clearly; too much was at stake. She had to make a success of this job, this opportunity to realize her dreams. Then it came to her: Alexander had never mentioned this person, Diane. Cleo had not noticed a picture of a woman in his office, but she'd be sure to look around more carefully next time. All Cleo had to do was ignore her as well. Cleo would be more comfortable being intimate with Alexander without seeing a picture of Diane in his office.

Cleo thought that she should at least know the titles of Bouquet's books and something about them. After work, she headed for the first time to the Harvard Coop. Cleo had not taken

Cleo's Game 75

the time to go to Harvard except for her brief tour with Oliver. She was enthralled by all the people, the books, and the sense of being in a major intellectual center. She was right where she wanted to be. Finding Diane Bouquet's books was no problem at all. The help desk directed Cleo to them. She found a place to sit where she could write, then pulled out her little notebook and wrote down all of the titles, the dates of publication, and the description of the books on the back cover. She thought she might want to find some reviews to add depth to her knowledge.

As she was finishing, a guy sat down next to her and asked why all those books by the same author were strewn all over the table. She hesitated, then asked him if he knew this author. No, he wasn't into novels. He preferred science—experiments, facts, reality—he insisted. He then proceeded to tell her that he was a graduate student studying astrophysics and started going into some detail about what he was doing in that area.

Cleo thought he might be interesting for her, but not because of astrophysics. He introduced himself as George, just George. Cleo said her first name. He was OK-looking, with dusty blond hair, bright blue eyes, nice lips, but a somewhat ruddy complexion. He was tall and slightly muscular. In short, he had a fairly attractive male body. Except for Alexander, she hadn't had a regular bedmate since leaving SF to work at Schendler and was ready for one. So, she leaned over and asked, "Are you up for something, like a coffee?" His face showed his amazement that she had gone right for it before he could even try. He hadn't had to chat her up very much at all.

Not that he was so compelling or incredibly attractive, but she knew he would be an easy mark. She just wanted someone, some guy to sleep with, and he seemed to be available. He thought that Cleo also seemed to be available, except that women as attractive as her usually already had someone or would be hard to get. Not Cleo. So, he invited her to dinner right around the corner at a little place he described as "Mostly frequented by students, with OK food but convenient."

While eating, she asked him where he lived. He had an apartment a very short distance down Mass Ave, not far at all, at 19 Pleasant Court. "Will you invite me for an after-dinner drink at your apartment? I'm new in Boston and don't know many

76   The BeAst and the Brightest

people." He couldn't believe his luck. As a modern woman, a feminist, she was not afraid to indicate that she was open to sex. She liked sex. She was ready for it. A little moment with Alexander had not satisfied her needs.

They walked the few blocks from the restaurant just off Harvard Square down to Pleasant Street and turned left to his apartment.

She thought, *This evening might be more than pleasant; it might be stimulating, really stimulating.*

She was really ready for sex. His second-floor apartment had two bedrooms, but she quickly learned that he lived alone. A quick look around the apartment revealed that he furnished it with secondhand or cast-off student furniture. The central feature of the main room was a huge TV and bookcases crammed with folders, books, files, videotapes, etc. Cleo was curious about the two bedrooms, but a quick look at the second bedroom revealed that tables had been placed around the walls, and piles of papers covered every inch of these tables. George explained that this was material, stacked by chapters, for his dissertation. Lots of research was piled on those tables; George was a worker.

The after-dinner drink proved to be problematic. Beer, some vodka, a Diet Coke, and a bottle of American "blush" wine were all that was available. Cleo went for the Diet Coke. George poured a large can of beer into an enormous German beer stein and then launched into a detailed story about going to Germany for Octoberfest. Cleo was losing interest rapidly. After a few minutes of telling her about Germany while he gulped down that beer, he excused himself to go to the bathroom, and Cleo took a look at all those things on the shelves. He was into porno. Porno videotapes. That was probably why he had that big TV. As soon as he came back into the room, she said she really had to go and bolted for the door. Not every guy was worth it. She didn't want to give him anything, certainly not sex. He didn't even get a kiss or a thank you for the Diet Coke. This was the first guy she had turned down in some time. On the positive side, she had learned that the Coop offered males as well as books and Harvard-branded merchandise. The Coop would be a good place to hunt.

Chapter 10
The East West Literary Conference

Cleo had not given up her coordinator responsibilities for the East West Literary Conference when she took the job at Schendler. In fact, she had become the main contact with the local PBS station that came through on their pledge to film some of the discussions among well-known authors for later broadcasting. Cleo loved being in contact with TV; she could easily imagine herself being interviewed about her upcoming book on feminism, which someday she was sure she would write. She had to stay in contact with Frank in SF and with Oliver, her Useful Idiot, at Schendler to be sure what she was doing was compatible with their plans and arrangements. She also kept Harrison Jones, the professor at U. Mass, informed about how the conference was developing. She was assiduous about talking with him since she wanted to build as many bridges in Boston's intellectual world as possible. She thought that she might need contacts outside publishing in the future. Her role as a coordinator became essential. Authors were constantly agreeing to come, then backing out, and then saying they could only come for one day or the other. Lots of complications.

After a month of solid work, both at her job and as conference coordinator, Cleo found that Oliver, although somewhat of a loser, was not a bad guy, and after her episode with George, the astrophysicist, she didn't want to take too many chances or devote too much time looking for another male, but she was

78 The BeAst and the Brightest

still eager for a regular bed partner. She had too much to do to look for someone new, so she cozied up with Oliver who was incredibly surprised by her renewed interest but also thrilled by it. He started believing that her previous involvement was due to his appeal. This would not be the last time Cleo hooked up with a loser just to achieve a goal. To Cleo, he was just a guy with a dick, someone she could sleep with occasionally and whom she could totally control, and there was nothing really wrong with him. Oliver thought his life was as wonderful as possible. He started dreaming that Cleo would fall in love with him.

The conference finally took shape. Two days before the conference, Frank arrived in Boston and went straight to the hotel, arriving at about 4 p.m. Cleo met Frank right after his arrival. She tried to be warm, greeting him. "Hi, Frank. I am so glad to see you again, and here at this conference you were so critical to organizing."

"Hi Cleo, nice to see you again, too." He actually wasn't that glad to see her; he still felt the sting of rejection, but he had some hope for a renewal of the pleasure she had given him based on what she had said at her farewell lunch. In particular, he remembered her saying, "I'm really eager to see you and excited about being with you again in Boston, you know, being together."

Oliver came over, and Cleo was scared he might seem too intimate, too comfortable with her, but he knew where the guardrails were. He wasn't that clueless. Plus, Oliver had just been shaken up by hearing rumors that Cleo and Remington were getting together after hours in his office.

The first night Frank was in Boston was devoted to final preparations for the conference. Alexander, Frank, Oliver, and Cleo worked as a team at the hotel to address all those last-minute changes that always occur. Cleo looked at all three guys and realized that she had had sex with all of them. She'd have to be super careful and smart. Alexander headed home about 8 p.m. By 9 p.m. that evening, Frank, Oliver, and Cleo thought that they had handled everything and could wrap up for the night. Since none of them had eaten since lunch, Frank invited both Cleo and Oliver to a late dinner at the Hotel's Oak Long Bar, taking one of the little tables usually set for two, but when Cleo sat on the banquette under the windows, Frank scooted in next

The East West Literary Conference 79

to her, so Oliver had to take the chair in front of them. Oliver looked squarely at Cleo, wondering if the rumors he had just heard about her and Remington were true. He hoped with all his heart that they were just malicious talk.

They all went for traditional comfort food: hot French onion soup and a little steak with french fries. Cleo declined the fries, opting for a salad instead. Frank offered a bottle of red wine from one of Cleo's family's vineyards in Napa. She leaned over even closer to Frank and said, "You really are a great guy." He registered and measured every word. As they finished coffee, decaf for both Frank and Oliver, Cleo put her hand on Frank's leg under the little table and said how glad she was to see him again. He asked himself what was going on. Her hand stayed on his leg, moving up the leg just a bit. Frank hoped he knew what that might mean. Was he dreaming?

As soon as Oliver headed home, saying, "See everyone soon; can't wait for the conference to start," Cleo said to Frank, "I really liked our previous times together. I didn't say some of the right things. I really liked being together, you know, together." Frank nodded, not knowing actually what she meant, but then she clarified, "I'm staying at my apartment tonight, so, your room?" with a complicit little smile.

This is usually what a guy would say, but she was used to being open about her sexuality; she never wanted to be the little submissive woman waiting for a guy to take charge. Frank said, "Yes, my room."

Once out of their clothes and lying on the bed, Cleo was a little more sweet and "loving" than usual with a guy. She was trying to erase her comment about his wife. She told him she wanted to sleep next to him all night, both nude. They did it twice, in the missionary position as usual. Frank was thrilled; Cleo was sleepy.

Frank had ordered a room-service breakfast for two. At 7 a.m., Frank heard a knock on the door.

"Room service."

He jumped up, put on one of the robes provided by the hotel, and answered the door. When the little table with the breakfast trays was rolled in, Frank said, "Thank you very much," and then closed the door. As he looked around, Cleo got out of bed and walked toward him to give him a little kiss on the cheeks. Then she sat down and offered to pour Frank a coffee. She had not bothered to get a robe; she was still nude. Frank dropped his robe, kissed her, and said, "Wow."

As they sat there nude, eating their breakfast, Frank couldn't help but look at her; his eyes were glued to her face, her breasts, and her long legs, which she crossed outside the table so Frank could see them. He was on fire. He believed that he would always be welcome in Boston, just as he had imagined or dreamed. He thought that he and Cleo had a real relationship. Poor Frank. To Cleo, he was nothing more than an asset she could use to advance her professional interests, absolutely nothing more. As she got dressed, Cleo said she had to go to the office but would see him at the pre-conference cocktail hour at the hotel that evening. Frank's head was spinning.

The conference started as planned. Everyone was very busy. Alexander and Frank did the pre-conference cocktail hour with skill, chatting with all of the authors, making appropriate introductions, and keeping people apart who didn't really like each other or might clash. The usual crowd control at a professional cocktail hour. Cleo was moving through the crowd, taking care of things, only to be hailed by Alexander, who was standing next to a very nice-looking, well-dressed woman Cleo did not recognize. He offered, "Honey, this is the new person we hired from Frank's shop; you know, I mentioned her. Cleo, this is my companion, Diane Bouquet."

Cleo smiled slightly and said, "So nice to meet you. I know your work. I especially liked your latest book, *Daylight for Women*." Then, with another smile, she said to Alexander that it seemed everything was going well. He agreed. Then Cleo turned and looked back at Diane with a very controlled smile but didn't say anything. Cleo now knew who she needed to avoid. Diane knew who she needed to watch. Before leaving the cocktail hour for dinner, Alexander came over to Cleo, saying, "Really great job, Cleo, you know how to handle yourself."

Cleo sought out Frank before he left the cocktail hour and said how glad she was that the conference was finally off to a good start. That was all. Frank had been thinking all day about her since the previous night and what it meant to have a relationship

The East West Literary Conference

with Cleo. He couldn't get over having enjoyed a breakfast completely nude with her after a night of sex in bed together. He was totally on fire and profoundly confused. Cleo's statement about being glad the conference was starting was so matter-of-fact, so lacking in warmth, that he felt compelled to ask, "Do you really like me? Do you have feelings for me?"

She looked at him straight in the eyes, not aggressively, but not tenderly either, and offered, "What do you think? Whom did I sleep with?" He didn't know what he thought, but her ambiguous comment was not what he had hoped for. He just stood there looking at her while trying to tame his emotions. Then she said that she had things to do so that she would see him in the morning. Frank felt his emotions being whipsawed.

Cleo and Oliver worked closely during the conference but didn't say anything about their relationship; they just worked. Oliver seemed preoccupied and jittery. Cleo was totally focused on the team from PBS and the authors. She tried to impress the TV crew as much as possible, hoping that they would remember her. Most of the authors showed up, and the discussions were as animated and interesting as everyone had hoped. Alexander was a whirlwind of activity, going from one discussion to another. Sometimes, he and Frank alternated leading the discussions. Cleo was always there to help. Everyone seemed extremely engaged and happy about how things were going. The first afternoon finished up at 5 p.m., and everyone got ready for another cocktail reception at 6 p.m. Dinner was at the hotel at 7:30 p.m.

At the cocktail reception, Frank could not help but think about the previous night with Cleo and their amazing breakfast. He approached her and asked straight out, "What about tonight?"

She smiled as much as she was able and then said, "Let's see; so much is going on." Frank just moved on. That night, Frank slept alone fitfully.

The next morning before things got off to a start, Oliver asked Frank if he could talk with him in private. Oliver seemed incredibly nervous but was able to say, "Frank, you have known Cleo for much longer than any of us. There are rumors, just rumors, mind you, that she might be having an affair with Alexander.

Again, it is just talk, but do you think it might be possible? I mean, since you know her so well?"

Frank was stunned. He started shaking all over. "Oh, my God," he thought. "How could she?" He had hoped that his relationship with Cleo meant more than the one-night stands she had accepted with so many authors; he wanted her actually to like him. He thought that maybe they were developing a real relationship. Oliver's question dispelled his fantasy. He just stood there for a minute or so, looking at Oliver and not knowing what to say, but he managed, "I'm sure these are just rumors. I would not believe them." Oliver agreed and asked Frank to forget, totally forget that he had ventured to ask him such a sensitive question and affirmed that he didn't believe these rumors at all; they were probably just slander.

Oliver said that he thought that Cleo was "terrific, a real lady, and very intelligent."

Frank knew that these were very likely to be more than rumors. His understanding of Cleo was becoming clearer. He now fully realized what she was capable of and how she could treat people, how she used them, even those closest to her, even him. He felt a moment of panic about what might happen. He was terribly exposed, having given into Cleo's sex appeal and lack of any morals. He realized that she had cynically manipulated him and that he had done something terrible. He recognized his own cynicism and regretted his actions. He had been nothing more than a sexual opportunist. He felt humiliated and ashamed of himself. Evidently, Cleo didn't have any scruples. Frank thought that she was not only sexually active; she was depraved, totally lacking a moral compass. He thought that he needed to teach her a lesson she would not forget.

The second day of the conference went off without too many problems. Cleo was happy to go to the cocktail reception before the final banquet that evening. She put on the really nice dress she had bought in San Francisco, and several authors who knew her intimately commented that she looked "spectacular" or something to that effect. Oliver looked at her as if he were going to have a heart attack. He bit his lip to control his conflicting emotions. Alexander approached her, whispering in her ear that she looked "stunning, really appetizing,"

The East West Literary Conference

83

Frank thought, *What a waste; she has enough going for her without, you know, doing all that.*

Cleo thought Frank might say something about getting together, but he just moved on. Cleo was moving from group to group when she noticed Diane Bouquet, Alexander's companion. She came over to Cleo and said that she had heard that Cleo had done a good job and that she seemed to have gotten to know Alexander well. Cleo didn't know what she meant. Cleo trembled a bit, then regained her composure to say, "What a wonderful pleasure to help him organize this conference; it's been a success, don't you think?" Diane just smiled at her. Cleo was starting to realize that she'd be happy when this conference ended. She always liked being able to control everything, especially her bed partners.

Just before the final cocktail reception ended, Littman and a couple of his authors were talking in the bar. After a couple of drinks, these guys loosened up enough to share some confidences. The liquor-inspired revelations made clear that several of these authors had enjoyed Cleo's attractiveness and bedtime skills. She was starting to get a reputation. One author referred to her as "The Easy Editor," which elicited a big laugh from the group of guys. The little world of publishing at Schendler was somewhat like a village. Littman immediately crossed her off the potentials list; she was never going to get a position in his division.

At dinner, Frank walked by her table and put a little note in front of her that read, "My room, 425 at 10:30 p.m." He had never been that direct, that brazen. She knew that she needed to agree to keep him on her side, so she put the note in her purse and, a few minutes later, walked over to his table and said, "What a nice note. OK."

After the banquet, she talked with a lot of people to keep busy, but at 10:30 p.m., she knocked on the door of room 425. Frank was only wearing his slacks. He has taken off his shoes, shirt, etc. She noticed that his suitcase was by the door. He had a bottle of champagne and two glasses on a coffee table. Cleo smiled and said, "Looks like we have things to celebrate." He popped the cork and poured two flutes of champagne, He toasted her contribution to the conference and its success. She returned the favor by toasting him.

84   The BeAst and the Brightest

Then he started undressing her. She had never seen him so sure of himself or so eager to take charge. His determination to enjoy himself was evident, and Cleo decided that this once, she'd give him whatever he wanted. She'd thrill and totally satisfy him. He seemed to be incredibly hungry for her, so much so that she wondered what was going on between him and his wife, who hadn't come to the conference. He took her several times, each more aggressively and thoroughly than ever before, turning her over and over, coming into her in new positions. As it got late and they started looking very tired, Frank said, "You need to stay with me all night."

Early the next morning, he took her again, pounding his sex into her with all his force. All he said when he finished was that he had to get ready to head to the airport. She wondered what was going on, but in any case, he was headed to SF. He checked the time as if he had an appointment. He got out of bed, saying she should stay under the covers despite the fact that the room was warm. He only took a couple of minutes in the bathroom. She heard his electric shaver but only for a minute or two, then he came out fully dressed. He checked his watch again to see what time it was. As he walked across the room, someone knocked on the door.

"Room service."

Frank's order was arriving exactly on time, as he had insisted. Everything had been carefully choreographed. Frank opened the door, and a waiter pushed a little table with a breakfast tray into the room. Frank reached into his coat pocket and put a little note on the breakfast table. A full American breakfast was on the tray: coffee, eggs, toast, sausage, hash browns, marmalade, orange juice, the works, but just for one person. Cleo wondered why Frank had ordered this big breakfast just for one person. Was it only for her? Was he not going to eat with her? The waiter noticed the attractive young woman sitting up in the bed, holding the covers up to her chin. He strongly suspected that she was nude, given how tightly she clung to the sheets. He had seen similar scenes before, so he just looked at Frank and said, "Enjoy your… breakfast."

Frank looked back at Cleo, saying, "I'm leaving, too. I left a note for you." Quickly, he turned away from her and started to

The East West Literary Conference
85

follow the waiter out into the hallway. He hadn't kissed her or said anything about their night together. As the door was about to close, he leaned in and said, "Cleo, remember this: Cynical sex is a two-way street." Then the door closed. She jumped out of bed and walked naked over to the breakfast table to read the note. "Feel free to use my name for a recommendation in your next career move." He signed it, Frank Cooperman.

Cleo felt a surge of anger. The bastard had just used her cynically and brutally for sex. He had just fucked her three times, really hard! That SOB! Cleo was blind with rage. "I'll never speak to that bastard again! That old SOB!" She cursed him and let her rage explode for the next 10 minutes or so, just standing there naked in front of the breakfast tray he had ordered for her. "He ordered this tray just to put me down! He fucked me just to humiliate me. Men can be so petty and mean. He just fucked me. I'll never let that happen again! Doesn't he appreciate what I have given him? How can he be so cruel, so brutal? Men treat women like shit!"

As she calmed down a bit, she helped herself to the coffee and ate the eggs and then a couple of pieces of toast with marmalade. Sex can make you hungry. She even ate some of the hash browns and drank the orange juice. She poured herself a second cup of coffee and sat there, still totally naked, thinking about where she was in her career. "I'll never need him. No way will I ever ask him for anything!" She started thinking that the success of the conference had put her in a position in her career where she didn't need fatuous recommendations from random authors or anybody at Schendler except Alexander, so she'd stop the one-night stands when male authors came to Boston, except Fleming, of course. And no way was Oliver ever getting anything more from her. Alexander was going to be the only one she did things with for her career. She didn't need anybody else. That was behind her. Fleming would just be for fun. She didn't regret anything she had done or think that she had done anything wrong, but she needed to shift gears.

She went into the bathroom, where she found a little package supplied by the hotel with toothpaste and a toothbrush. After brushing her teeth, since she was already undressed, she stepped into the shower to finish cleaning up. As she was drying off, she heard a knock on the door and "Room service."

She was pissed about being disturbed, but she grabbed the bathrobe provided by the hotel and went to the door. She was feeling outraged and ready to do anything to get back at Frank, so she opened the door, letting the room service guy see her standing there nearly nude. The bathrobe was open in the front; she had left the belt in the bathroom. Then, with a little shake, she let the bathrobe drop off her shoulders. This was a way of getting revenge for what Frank had done to her. The nude performance was for the room service guy, not Frank. The room service guy looked at her, up and down, for maybe 10 to 15 seconds while she smiled at him. Then he went straight to the little table and, as he left the room, said, "Thank you. I hope you enjoyed your breakfast; I certainly did."

Cleo liked his style. He thought she was a professional. Something similar had happened to this room service guy several times since the hotel was used occasionally by high-end prostitutes who understood the importance of being nice to the staff and knew how to tip a guy without using money. This had typically happened when the room service guy worked the night shift. This type of occurrence would happen early in the morning, around 2 a.m., when the professionals wrapped up their work, but occasionally, they seemed to have spent the night. In any case, Cleo had appropriately tipped the room service guy, and he left happy.

Frank felt very alone on the plane going home to SF. He knew that he had hurt Cleo and felt really bad about it. He regretted what he had just done. But he hoped that Cleo had learned something. Cynically using people is a two-way street, particularly when it involves sex. That certainly did not excuse what he had just done. He knew that treating Cleo like that was shameful, but he had been hurt. Actually, he had hurt himself, and he knew it. Cleo had held out the promise of renewed youth when an attractive young woman could become interested in him and could want to be with him and enjoy intimacy with him. He had learned that Cleo was unrestrained in cynically using sex to advance her career, but that was no excuse for what he had done. He had given into temptation and knew that what he had

The East West Literary Conference 87

done was wrong, morally wrong, and socially stupid. How could he have ever thought she really wanted a relationship with him? He had wanted to take an opportunity to have sex with an attractive young woman, but then he started believing that she could care about him and that they were developing a relationship. He knew he had acted like an old fool. He had hurt himself and short-changed Cleo. He should have shown her a more positive way to live; he should have exemplified a higher moral standard, but he hadn't. He considered sending her a note but knew that he should not put anything in writing; he could not trust Cleo enough to give her something that could prove his betrayal of his wife. He would never again make that mistake. He would never again interact with Cleo. She was now dead to him.

The next week, Alexander opened the door to her office. Cleo expected another appointment, but instead, he said, "You did a very admiral job presenting yourself to everyone at the conference, including Diane. Our relationship is lovely, and we both want it to continue, but a relationship would not be appropriate with other employees."

Cleo just looked at him and nodded. She tried to smile, but only the very tips of her lips opened up a bit. She didn't know what he knew about her and Oliver if anything, but she knew she had to protect her relationship with Alexander. Had Frank said something? Had Oliver or anyone else mentioned a relationship with her? She was mortified to think that Alexander might know that she was sleeping with Oliver. Did Prudence suspect or know something about her and Oliver? Cleo's stomach started tying itself into knots. She knew she had to cut it off with Oliver; she'd have to do something and fast to "kill" Oliver.

The rest of the afternoon and evening she tried to figure out a plan; she had to get rid of Oliver totally and to do so in a definitive way. She mulled over different strategies and different ways of doing the deed. Then it hit her. More than anything, he wanted to protect his job. He was not confident that he could easily get another position at his current level in Boston, and he couldn't imagine leaving a city where he had lived for over a decade. His savings were meager, so losing his job would put him in difficulty very quickly. Poor Oliver. He had shared all his insecurities with Cleo, so she knew how to get him.

Monday morning, she went directly to his office. She went right to the point without saying hi or anything else. "Alexander may suspect something, and we are treading on thin ice. We have to stop now. We could both lose our jobs. Don't try to contact me about anything personal. From now on, it is just business."

Oliver looked shocked, then looked down at his desk and muttered, "I understand," as Cleo turned and closed the door. In fact, he suspected he knew why this was happening. He thought that Remington had precipitated this sudden and totally unexpected rupture. He had been shaken up by the rumors about her and Remington and had started to suspect that they were true. Now, he was almost sure they were true. He was hurt and angry, very angry at Remington as well as Cleo.

Cleo had been so brutal, so direct, that he understood that the game was up. He just had to come to terms with it. She had said nothing about having liked him or their time together. He was accustomed to rejection and disappointment, but no woman had ever slammed the door so hard with no expression of feelings or regret. Cleo hadn't said anything about him or her feelings for him, which hurt him. He wondered if she had any feelings at all for anyone.

Cleo saw all relationships with men as win/lose. Somebody would be dominant and get more from the other person than they gave. That was just how the world created by men worked. Society's rules were stacked in their favor because men had created them, and men usually won; they had written the rules of the game. Some guys were more decent toward women than others, but many were just bastards who hurt, abused, beat up, and even killed women. Even her father, who never physically or verbally attacked her mother, had hurt her by putting her in a little box where she could only play the role he had prescribed for her. She had not defined her life; her husband had. That was also true of Cleo's maternal grandparents, who were nicer and seemed happier than Cleo's parents, but their relationship with each other and with other members of the family fell into the typical pattern. Her grandmother was second in everything to her husband. Her paternal grandmother seemed more dominant, especially when she was with Cleo, but not with the rest of the

The East West Literary Conference 89

family. Cleo thought this was probably due to her grandfather's preference for her brothers.

If Cleo hurt men, she did not care. She never felt sorry, remorse, or shame. Had men had those feelings when they hurt women throughout the centuries? Absolutely not! In fact, hurting males was just payback for the centuries of terrible injuries men had inflicted on women. Her role in life was not to make men feel good. If they enjoyed sex with her, that was OK because she was getting what she wanted and what she needed—basic sexual pleasure and a body next to her. She was careful to limit men's pleasure. They only got what she was willing to give, and that was just the basics. She approached everything she did with men from the perspective of win/lose, and that win/lose philosophy was all she used as a moral compass. She was fine having sex without affection. She was determined to win.

Cleo's sex life was developing in Boston along three tracks. The first was the guys at Schendler whom she slept with to further her career. For the moment, this was limited to Alexander, but she was trying to figure out how to approach Littman. The second track was with authors with whom she was open to one-night stands. Yes, she again started to have these one-night stands with authors. She found that male visiting authors were easy targets, and she hit on several of them. When she saw that a male author was interested, Cleo almost always complied. But she was sure she got the feedback to Schendler she wanted. The third track was with serial males she'd pick up here or there.

After "killing" Oliver, Cleo needed to find a guy whose bed she could occasionally share. She just wanted guys she could sleep with and with whom she could enjoy Boston. She liked having a guy to do things with. Cleo started picking up serial guys at the Coop, in men's stores, and at the public library. That led to a succession of males and a clear idea of The Game and the rules she would follow. As she won hand after hand at The Game, her pride in herself and her confidence increased in her role as an independent, strong feminist who would never let men dominate her. She had learned to handle men so that guys like Blondie, Mr. Money, or any of the others she used were totally under her control. She could enjoy them for sex and some companionship without ever being submissive or letting a real relationship develop. She had both her personal and professional life in order. Now, she just had to get Alexander to help her move to a higher position at Schendler. Maybe she could get Littman interested enough to help her.

More Chinese dinners started taking place at Prudence's apartment, and Cleo started telling Prudence tidbits about her life—never very much, just enough to tighten the bonds between them. Cleo started to understand Prudence's British reserve; she did not ask probing personal questions. Prudence allowed Cleo to share what she wanted to when she wanted to. Prudence did not express any judgments about anything Cleo shared with her, and this reserve disarmed Cleo, who started feeling closer and closer to Prudence. She was welcoming but never judgmental. Cleo felt she could be herself with Prudence within limits. Prudence had found in Cleo a younger and much better-looking version of herself. Cleo's presence allowed Prudence to live more freely and go farther in her imagination. She had a template for what her life could have been, and that was Cleo.

Chapter 11

Confusion and Love?

Meeting Danny, the Coffee Shop Guy, had thrown Cleo's life into some confusion. After that first sweet night together, when he left her saying how great it was for "us" to be together, she was eager to see him again. She wondered whether that night was just a fluke; would she have the same reaction to him when they were together again? All she knew was that she really liked him, and he had made her feel different than other guys. She liked that feeling. He didn't wait long to call her. He got her message machine. "Hey Cleo, there is a talk at Harvard by a professor of comparative literature from the Sorbonne in Paris about current trends in European literature. Sounds like the kind of thing we would enjoy hearing. How about meeting tomorrow at 5:30 p.m. in the Annenberg Hall, near the Art Museum? Meet me there, and we'll go together, OK?"

His message sounded like they had been friends for years. His tone of voice was that of a longtime friend, not a guy she had recently hooked up with for one night. She liked his familiarity, his directness, and even his presumption that they were somehow "together." He had used that "we" again. Of course, she was not looking for a relationship and certainly not a boyfriend. But she wanted to see him again, and she liked the feeling of having a guy friend who felt comfortable with her and with whom she could be herself. This was a feeling of both friendship and attraction she had never felt before with a guy.

92   The BeAst and the Brightest

When she got to Annenberg Hall, he was standing at the front door looking around for her. As she approached him, he threw his arms around her, gave her a big kiss on both cheeks and said how happy, how very happy he was that she could come. She was happy, too. Then he took her hands in his, leaned over toward her, and said, "Can we kiss?" The question seemed so sweet, so innocent, that Cleo's heart actually seemed to jump in her chest. She thought that was the sweetest question she had ever been asked. Her response was to give him that kiss he wanted, a very sweet, tender kiss. Then he led her into the auditorium, asking where she would like to sit. Clearly, sometimes he was taking the initiative; but then letting her decide some things. That was new to Cleo.

Before the talk started, Danny said that he knew she was passionate about literature, English-language literature, that is, but that she would probably like to get some insights into what was happening in Europe. She might even hear about some authors she might be interested in publishing in English. She thought he might be right and was impressed that he seemed to be interested in helping her with her job. The talk, in English, of course, was interesting, even though the professor spoke with a very thick French accent. Cleo realized that she had been living in a totally English-oriented world and that non-English European literature was vibrant and something she needed to know about, at least a little. As the talk ended, Cleo told Danny that she had found it really interesting and said, "Thank you for letting me know about this; it was sweet of you."

"I got a kiss, didn't I?" he said with a big smile. She leaned over and gave him another. Then they just looked at each other for a long, lingering, tender moment.

Cleo couldn't imagine leaving him right after the talk; she wanted to stay with him. After all, it was a Friday night. She really wanted him, but not just for sex. She wanted to be with him. He felt the same about her. Since he had his car nearby, he invited her to go to a "crazy fish restaurant in Somerville, just behind MIT with a weird name, Legal Seafood." Cleo thought this was the weirdest name for a restaurant she had ever heard. Danny described it as "very simple, quirky, but the fish is pretty good." So off they went.

Confusion and Love? 93

The restaurant was in Somerville, a solid working-class town right behind Cambridge. Cleo had never heard of it and thought how strange that a working-class community was adjacent to MIT and Harvard. The restaurant was, in fact, very basic. As they sat down, Danny imitated the Sorbonne professor's accent so well that he made Cleo laugh again. Laughing out loud felt new and wonderful to her. She started feeling like she was with a real friend, not just a male to bed. The catch of the night was on a big blackboard and the sides were rice or fries and mixed veggies. Cleo went for grilled halibut, and Danny said that sounded good for him as well.

"Rice for both of us," he told the waiter without asking Cleo. Then he looked up and said, "Oh, I'm sorry I should have asked you, but you are so trim and pretty, I thought you'd prefer rice to fries. I should not presume to answer for both of us?" There was that "us" again. She told him he was right; she would prefer rice and that it was OK to order for her. She liked the compliment about being "trim and pretty" and was not upset at all at his taking charge. She sort of liked it.

At dinner, he asked her a zillion questions about her reaction to the talk, and she responded by asking him what he thought. She was impressed by how he thought about literature and how European literature differed from much of English-language lit, well, American literature. She was genuinely surprised that he listened to her, not for effect, but because he seemed to care what she thought. Was this guy really just studying economics? Was he for real?

As dinner finished, he offered to take her home since the weather was awful and getting to Back Bay from Somerville would not be easy. She said, "OK, if you'll stay with me." Danny was somewhat surprised by this direct invitation, but he could not imagine dropping her off with just a little kiss. He was becoming crazy about her and wanted more than anything to be with her.

He told her, "I'm crazy about you."

Cleo gave him a very big smile and said, "Let's go."

Once in her apartment, Cleo planned to go right into her routine, but Danny asked for a hot tea since it was so cold. Actually, Cleo wanted one, too, so she made chamomile for them and put out some little anise-flavored cookies she kept in her apartment.

They chatted for a few minutes, drank their tea, and started caressing each other and giving each other little kisses and talking about this and that.

Cleo thought, *This guy wants to make out with me; he wants us to talk. He wants us to get to know each other.*

This was new to Cleo, who was used to getting guys right into bed for intercourse. She started relaxing and cuddling with him, exchanging little comments, kisses, and hugs. Then, he started unbuttoning his shirt. Cleo just looked at him. He asked her if he could help her with her sweater. "Sure," she said. Then the clothes came off in seconds, and they were in bed again.

Cleo was so happy; this guy was a lover and potentially a friend, something she had never experienced. Her deal with guys was fucking or "sleeping with a guy," as she called it, avoiding the more vulgar word. This was different. He was really loving her, and she wanted to love him back. They spent the entire weekend together. On Sunday, Danny said he had some work to do, and Cleo wanted to read, so they went to Danny's apartment, and Cleo cuddled up in a big reading chair while Danny worked at his desk. Every so often, he'd come over and give her a little kiss and a hug and then return to his desk. They were just happy to be together, and Cleo felt that she had more than a guy to sleep with; she had a lover and a friend, the first friend she could be with easily since Nicole left Napa. Cleo liked being with someone who would let her be herself, let her read, write, or do whatever she wanted. She felt free to just be herself with him. He was not only her first real lover; he was becoming her best friend, her only one except Nicole. Being with him was as relaxing as the solitude she enjoyed on a Sunday morning, except that every so often, he'd give her a hug and a kiss. This was better than solitude. This was solitude with warmth and love.

Cleo thought that her life was falling into place. Her job was going well; she had worked out an arrangement with Alexander that she believed would help her advance at Schendler. She and Prudence were working well together and liked each other, and now, she had Danny. The only negative was that Cleo really didn't like the idea of having a boyfriend. Theoretically, she needed to have an endpoint with a guy, a moment when she would cut him off suddenly, without warning, and that would be

Confusion and Love? 95

that. The Game with the guy would be over with her winning. She would not get trapped in a male/female relationship. But for the moment, she wanted to be with Danny just as they were. She wanted a lover friend. Her first. They seemed to be happy together.

They had made plans to meet the next Friday night at a Greek restaurant at 7 p.m. and then go to a movie at Harvard, but unexpectedly, Alexander dropped by her office saying, "How about tonight at 6:30 p.m., as usual?" His intonation made it sound like a question, but she really didn't think it was. She took it as a command rendezvous. This was the first Friday evening rendezvous she was going to have with him. Every other encounter in his office had been during the week. She wondered what was up. She was going to have to cancel with Danny, an inconvenience that upset her, but she didn't feel she had a choice. So, she called Danny's apartment and got the answering machine. "Sorry about tonight, but my boss' boss has something we just have to do, so I'll not be able to meet you. Very sorry. I'll call you tomorrow." This would not be the last time she deceived Danny or had sex with someone when she might have been with him.

When she came into his office, she saw that Alexander had his tie off and two buttons of his shirt undone. He said that a business dinner had been canceled with an author who had decided to take off early, so he was free "for a couple of hours." He was more aggressive and physical with her than usual. He seemed rushed to get right to it, to sex, but once in her, he took his time, enjoying her lovely body, and he told her so. This was not the usual quickie; she felt he was really "doing her." He took his time and seemed to relish her more than in the past. While he was in her, he also put his tongue in her mouth, which she didn't like, but ... well, she felt that she had to comply. After his climax, he told her that he really needed that, and she said that she had gotten that impression.

As they physically separated, they sat on that couch Cleo was getting to know so well and talked, both totally naked. He once again offered her a glass of wine, which she accepted. They talked on and on, drank their wine, kissed each other on the cheeks and occasionally on the lips, and touched each other here and there. At one point, he leaned over and kissed her on both nipples. She responded by rubbing his penis with both hands just long enough to get him erect again. Then he reached out to her, and as she leaned back, he came into her again. This time, his business was accomplished faster, but it did elicit another happy moan from him. Cleo looked at the clock on his desk: 8:25 p.m. She looked around the room to see if there was a photo of Diane. There wasn't.

She had spent almost two hours with him. This was the first time she had done it twice with him during the same rendezvous. Maybe she was gaining his favor over those other women, if there were any, whom he enjoyed on that couch or elsewhere. She just hoped that Danny had gotten her message, but she didn't want to call him. Her voice message promised to call him on Saturday, and she decided not to change the plan. Plus, after having sex twice and having spent so much time with Alexander totally nude, she wanted a little time to be alone. She walked over to the Copley Hotel and ate at the bar where she, Frank, and Oliver had eaten dinner. As she ate, she thought about Danny and hoped he had gotten her message. Thinking about what she had just done with Alexander, she told herself several times, "It's no big deal, just sex."

Danny had waited at the Greek restaurant for almost 45 minutes, sitting at a table for two. Finally, he realized that she wasn't coming and ordered something since he was getting really hungry. He called her apartment from the restaurant but got her message machine. He hoped against hope that, somehow, Cleo would show up. A chicken kebob, rice, and a Greek salad would do it. He thought that this would be fast to prepare, and once he was served, he ate quickly. He called her apartment again from the restaurant but again got her answering machine. His message asked if everything was all right and to please call him. He was concerned about Cleo and planned to call her as soon as he arrived at his apartment. Back at his apartment, he listened to his messages and was relieved that she had told him about needing to work late. He was relieved to know she was OK. Since she had said she'd call him on Saturday, he decided to work at his desk and wait until the next day to talk with her. He couldn't help but think how much in love he was with her, and he hoped she felt the same.

Confusion and Love? 97

At 11 a.m. on Saturday, Cleo called just to say hello. Danny was so glad to hear from her; he was relieved that she was OK, but asked what her boss thought was so urgent on a Friday night. Friday night publishing emergencies seemed weird to him. She said, "You know guys, bosses, you're always at their beck and call, and he is a fanatic about certain editing things, so we spent hours going over a manuscript." Danny thought this seemed strange but accepted her "explanation" and then asked, "So, do you want to come over tonight for the dinner party?"

"Sure," was all she could bring herself to say.

That Saturday night, Danny had planned a dinner party at his apartment with his best friend from Stanford, Chuck Stimming, who was nearby at Tufts studying international politics. He wanted a career in the Foreign Service or a similar diplomatic job. He was bringing his girlfriend, Susie, who was also at Tufts. The other guest was John Tallington, a fellow graduate student in economics and Danny's best friend in the graduate program. Since John did not have a girlfriend, Danny had invited Carol Baker, a Harvard friend who was studying African art. Danny thought that John and Carol might hook up.

John was a very tall, stringbean of a guy. In fact, his nickname in the department was Smallie, since he towered over almost everybody. He was also incredibly thin. He wore metal rimbed glasses with big, round lenses, which he would polish each time someone spoke to him as if to find time to figure out how to handle a conversation. A graduate of Tulane, he was clearly from the South, but his Southern accent had lost a bit of its honey during his years in Boston. Social skills were not his forte, but he seemed to be a normal, nice guy, nothing more. He was reasonably smart, so he and Danny could always find reasons to talk together.

The dinner party went well. Danny had prepared authentic Italian lasagna he had learned to make from the Bolognese cook at the Stanford campus in Florence. This was not a noodle pie with cheese and red sauce, but a proper, multilayer, delicious lasagna with real ragù and béchamel sauces just like they use in Bologna. He also added real Parmesan from Italy since that added sharpness as a counterpoint to the rich sauces. Salad and gelato for dessert made a really nice meal. Cleo was her usual sparkling self, and the conversation took off rapidly and never lagged. Danny thought that everybody had a good time. John and Carol talked with each other a little bit, but he left the party first, followed by Carol 15 minutes later. Cleo thought that they were probably never going to hook up; John had been too passive. The hour got late before Chuck and Susie left.

As Danny and Cleo were cleaning up, Cleo mentioned that she really liked Chuck and Susie. Danny asked her about John and Carol. Cleo said she liked Carol, who talked a lot about African art in a way that was interesting and entertained everyone. Carol had made jokes and comments about some of the sexual images in that art and wondered why we couldn't be more open about our sexuality. Danny asked Cleo whether or not she thought that Carol was mentioning all these sexual images as a way of signaling John that she was open to something. Cleo said she liked the direct way Carol talked about sex, with no hang-ups, but had noticed that John didn't seem interested in Carol and didn't respond to her very well. He seemed closed off and didn't have much to say that was interesting.

Cleo never mentioned having friends in Boston or talked about a previous boyfriend in the area. When Danny asked who her friends were, she just talked about Nicole, who was in Paris. Cleo could be very social in a group, but given her lifestyle, she didn't want or need a lot of people around her. She wanted to be able to do whatever she desired without having to explain herself or justify her behavior to "friends." Besides, her goals in life were focused on her career—editing and writing to foster her brand of feminism. What did friends have to do with that? Plus, given her sex life, she didn't want everybody to know everything about her. She didn't need reproaches or comments about morality or truthfulness or being faithful. She hated the idea of explaining to friends why this or that male had been dropped, and she certainly didn't want "killed" males interacting with people she knew, her friends. She was happy to be able to handle people and to play The Game without having to justify herself to anybody. She liked to hunt and kill alone.

During those first two weeks with Danny, Cleo had been getting calls from Mr. Money asking what was going on. He had at first just asked her to call him. Then, as the days went by, he seemed more and more insistent. Cleo hadn't "killed" him off yet but had decided that his expiration date had arrived. She thought about just sending him a note but wanted to find a more emphatic, definitive, and fun way to kill him. She wanted to play with him before his execution, like a cat with a mouse. So, she called him saying that she had been very, very busy. She asked him if she could come over to his apartment that Wednesday evening and of course, he called her right back, asking her to please come at 6:30 p.m. He'd have dinner ready at his apartment. She showed up with the usual big smile. As soon as she knocked on the door, he was there, saying how happy he was to see her. They exchanged kisses and hugs, and then he invited her into his big salon, where he had a bottle of champagne. Cleo was ready for a drink. They both had a flute of the champagne before heading to the dining room for a prepared meal of crab salad, toast, green beans, a fruit cup, and vanilla ice cream for dessert. She passed on the ice cream.

Their conversation was somewhat awkward, so to enliven the staid atmosphere, Cleo got up and went around the table to sit on his lap. Giving him a big kiss, she asked, "Have you missed me? I have missed you. Shall we make up for time lost? I bet you are ready for sex. I am."

They headed right for the bedroom and intense lovemaking. Mr. Money was ecstatic. Cleo thought that she had really primed him for a major fall. They made love like crazy. As Mr. Money laid back on the bed with a huge smile, Cleo asked for another flute of champagne, saying, "You know champagne gets you ready to go again, did you know that?" He almost ran back into the salon, where he grabbed those flutes, filled them almost to the brim, and headed back to the bedroom. They clinked their flutes and started to drink, sitting up in bed. Before even finishing this second flute, they started doing it again. As they finished another round of sex, Cleo flashed her smile, took another sip of champagne from her flute, and asked, "Wasn't I right; it did get you ready to go again?" She was enjoying toying with him.

Mr. Money let out a particularly happy moan the second time. Then he fell asleep. Cleo left him her standard note around 1 a.m. but added that she wanted "to enjoy another fun moment together one last time." When he saw the note the next morning, he didn't know what to think. He was both happy for that last "fun moment" and deeply perplexed, profoundly offended, and very angry. He told his friend John about this strange evening, and John said that Mr. Money would be better off without her since "she is not the type of person people like us should associate with." That settled the issue for Mr. Money.

Leaving his apartment, Cleo was able to jump in a cab and arrive at her place in Back Bay in just about 10 minutes. As she got ready for bed, she saw a message on her machine from Danny. He was just calling to say hello and talk, "if she was free." Since she didn't answer, he wondered what she was doing. Thursday morning, about 11 a.m., Cleo called Danny, hoping to get his message machine. She left a message promising to call him later that evening. She never wanted to be too eager to return a call from a guy, any guy, even Danny.

Chapter 12

Les Enfants Terribles

Danny had wanted to talk with Cleo on Wednesday, but by 10 p.m. on Thursday, she still hadn't called him. Danny started getting anxious and concerned about her. He was so eager to talk with Cleo that he called her, asking what she wanted to do that weekend. She acted as if everything was OK; she didn't apologize for not calling him. Danny was confused and somewhat upset but glad to talk with her.

Cleo had been thinking about her favorite film, *Les Enfants Terribles*, by Jean Cocteau, an extremely influential French playwright, novelist, poet, and filmmaker of the first half of the 20th century. Cleo liked him for two reasons. First, his writings and films were highly influential creative works. Cleo dreamed that her book on feminism would equal his creativity and artistry. Second, Cocteau's influence on culture was very significant. Cleo thought she could have an equal influence as an editor and writer. She aspired to have an equal, pro-feminist cultural impact.

She loved *Les Enfants Terribles* so much because of its theme, drama, and extremely dark image of an intense relationship between a sister and her brother who played a sinister game with each other. This great classic was shown every Friday night at midnight at an iconic movie theater, The Brattle, just off Harvard Square. Cleo wanted to see it with Danny; she wanted Danny to appreciate and understand her fascination with this film and its dark magnetism.

102 The BeAst and the Brightest

They decided to meet at 7 p.m. and eat at Danny's apartment. They decided that since the film started at midnight, they could lay down and take a little nap, which was proceeded by making out on the bed and then having sex. Both were happy when they headed off to Harvard Square on the way to The Brattle.

The film is about two siblings, Elizabeth and Paul, who engage in an intense relationship in which each tries to outdo the other. The siblings would strive to irritate or infuriate each other. They lived together in a chaotic bedroom. Elizabeth would try to bait Paul, who would respond by being taciturn, which drove Elizabeth mad. Their relationship evolves into "The Game," a psychodrama that they decide can only be played in their shared bedroom, which becomes "The Room." Winning at The Game involves being the person with the last word or dramatic move, which gives the winner a sense of superiority as the loser is consumed by anger and frustration.

As they grow older, love affairs, betrayals, and intercepted letters fuel the rivalry between the siblings. At one point, Elizabeth manages to get Gerard, who is in love with her, to marry another woman, Agathe, whom Paul loves. This breaks Paul's heart, and for the first time, Elizabeth regrets what she has done. She has robbed Paul and Agathe of their love and happiness. Paul takes poison in despair. When Elizabeth learns that Paul is dying, she believes he decided to kill himself to win this final move in The Game. She realized what she has to do. She shoots herself a few moments before Paul's death, trying to be first to die, trying to win this final move in The Game.

Cleo watched this film, which she had seen many times before, with rapt attention. Danny's reaction was mixed; he appreciated the artistry but was disturbed by the central theme, which seemed excessively dark and destructive. When Cleo asked him what he thought, he begged off, asking for some time to reflect since the film evoked so many things in him. Cleo could not help but ask, "You liked it, didn't you?" She wanted him to absorb the essence of the film. To her, this film captured all of life—its drama, its intensity, its darkness, its fatalism, its self-deception, and its destructiveness.

The film ended late, and they had eaten early, so while the dinner had been good, they needed something more before

Les Enfants Terribles

heading back to Danny's apartment. Cleo said they should go to The Coffee Spot, where they had met. When Cleo and Danny arrived, the place was just about two-thirds full, so they didn't have any problem finding a table. Cleo said how lucky she had been to go to The Coffee Spot when there was only one seat left, the seat across from Danny. He was thinking the same. They ordered coffee, grilled cheese sandwiches with a slice of ham, and a small cup of tomato soup.

Cleo was torn between two visions of her life. Both included her destiny as a significant writer and cultural influencer, like Jean Cocteau. In one version, she'd continue to play The Game, switching lovers at will but never getting caught up in a traditional relationship with a guy. She would never be a wife, get married, or have kids.

The other vision was completely new to Cleo. This vision involved a relationship with a guy like Danny, maybe even with Danny, based on love and mutual respect. But she doubted that this type of relationship was possible. Wouldn't one person or the other be the winner or the loser, just like in *Les Enfants Terribles*?

As she tangled with these questions, she recognized how much she liked Danny, and he seemed to love her; at least he was clearly infatuated with her, and his interest in her didn't seem motivated just to have a woman for sex. He was passionate about making love with her, but he seemed to value the entire person that was Cleo as well. Could something like this last? Could she continue to be in that type of relationship without being smothered, without having to shoot herself like Elizabeth or be poisoned like Paul? She suspected that the whispered comments about a suicide attempt by her mother—did that really happen?—had been with barbiturates. Cleo wanted to be intense, dynamic, and impactful, not slumber off into oblivion because of a relationship with a guy.

Leaving The Coffee Spot, these questions seemed to lose their meaning as they reached Danny's apartment. Before opening the door, he turned to her, saying, "Thank you, Cleo, for sharing this experience with me, this powerful film. I see that it is really meaningful to you, and now it is to me as well. I am learning so much from you." She put her arms around him and said how terribly happy she was to hear that. No guy had ever told her how much she was bringing to him except sex and a little, perhaps insignificant, companionship. Cleo thought that Danny was helping her learn about life and herself as well. But what was the lesson?

Danny had a way of making love gently that totally relaxed her but also created a little tingle in her clitoris that exploded into a full orgasm. Even the little muscles in her inner thighs would tingle and shake, her breasts would seem to expand, and her nipples would almost explode with pleasure. She had rarely let herself feel this type of intense sexual emotion, except with that Jet Ski guy in Australia and one or two other guys; Fleming was one of those. She had learned to control her emotions and limit her reaction to the sex act by letting herself enjoy minimally the feel of a guy in her and against her body. For years, her approach to fucking limited her emotional reactions. Yes, she got some pleasure, but that was all, rarely an explosive orgasm, but also no emotional vulnerability or emotional ties. She was OK with that. With Danny, all restraint had fallen away. After making love, Danny would always tell her that he loved her; he loved her totally.

Cleo's questions about guys and her relationship with them continued to bug her, but the next three weeks were lovely. Planning for the next weekend, Danny suggested getting a B&B in Marblehead, a seaside community just north of Boston. Cleo thought this was an attractive idea, but what would they do there? She remembered the day spent window shopping and eating at a nice restaurant in Provincetown with Mr. Money and his friends and initially was turned off by the prospect of having a similar experience with Danny, but then he mentioned taking a sailboat with a captain for a little voyage out into the Atlantic, and that sounded wonderful. She had heard a lot about Marblehead since arriving in Massachusetts and was curious. Having a fun thing to do sealed the deal. Cleo was not averse to just having fun, especially with someone who meant something to her. Despite herself, Cleo was becoming attached to Danny.

The weekend turned out to be great, especially since the weather was perfect for a sail on the ocean. Danny was charming,

Les Enfants Terribles   105

and the sailboat was wonderful. Cleo liked going forward to the bow and letting the spray cover her. She was wearing a long yellow slicker with a hood provided by the skipper to keep her somewhat dry, but she loved the experience of the spray. Danny seemed thrilled by the boat, the wind, the spray, and above all, Cleo. She knew that he had splurged to pay for the B&B and the sailboat, so she offered to pay for dinner Saturday night.

They both got dressed up, and Danny said he had a little present. Cleo took two boxes from him. What could they be? She opened the first to find a bottle of French champagne. The second had two crystal flutes from Baccarat in France. "Cleo and Danny" was etched on both flutes. Danny said they could use these to celebrate all their wonderful times together in the future. Cleo thought this was a delightful present but wondered what he meant by "together in the future." They both enjoyed a flute of champagne before heading out for dinner.

What do you have to eat on the coast of Massachusetts? Lobster, of course. The one she had eaten in Provincetown that Saturday with Mr. Money, John, and Cynthia had been really delicious, but this one seemed especially wonderful because she was with Danny. He kept looking at her with the most enthralled expression. Danny thanked her for the dinner, and Cleo let slip, "I'm having a wonderful time just being together, just us."

Once back at their hotel, Danny said that a flute of champagne seemed to be the best nightcap, but Cleo said, "I certainly hope you're not going to sleep without ... you know, celebrating." Danny served the champagne and clinked glasses with her, saying, "Here's to many, many more wonderful anniversaries and many, many more celebrations."

She made love with him with more intensity, more adventure and abandon than she had allowed herself in years. She experienced more than sex; she felt freer than ever to enjoy the sensuality of love. She felt so free because she trusted him so much and believed he really loved her. And he trusted her. She could totally let herself enjoy both physical pleasure and love with him. Yes, she thought, love can be as sensual and fulfilling as sex. She surprised herself with this thought. She had always associated sleeping with somebody with nothing more than physical, sexual release, with a little pleasure, if not a full orgasm. She started to understand that sensuality with someone you love, sharing something with someone you care about, is wonderful, and that makes sex even better, actually profoundly satisfying.

Cleo and Danny had both experienced one of the best weekends of their lives. Danny thought they were both truly in love. Cleo felt both happy and uneasy. What was happening to her?

Chapter 13
Idyll and Deceit

Several months went by with the two of them continuing their idyll. Cleo had put *Les Enfants Terribles* out of her mind, as well as the troublesome questions she had asked herself about guys, Danny, and relationships. She just focused on her work and Danny. Cleo and Danny were supposed to get together one Friday night, but that afternoon, Cleo got a call from one of Schendler's major authors with whom Cleo had been having sex when he came to Boston, Fred Fried. Yes, she had continued to have some sexual rendezvous with a few important authors despite her relationship with Danny. She was careful to schedule these during the weekdays so Danny would not get suspicious, and she always left around midnight rather than sleeping all night with them. She could always tell Danny that they had just talked late. Fried's books were being handled by Johnny Littman's general literature division. Cleo had a great relationship with Prudence, but her group was tiny—just Prudence, Cleo, and a secretary—and she hoped to move to Littman's bigger division.

Cleo knew that she'd have to change divisions to move up at Schendler, and Littman's division seemed to be the place to be. Fred Fried was their best-selling author, so Cleo did everything possible to show her interest in him. He was very responsive. She knew he wasn't a prude since his novels contained some very explicit group sex scenes. Cleo wondered if these reflected his life or were just fiction. Given the very standard

108   The BeAst and the Brightest

sexual experiences with him in hotels in Boston, she assumed it was just his imagination. He seemed OK with her "only the missionary position" approach to sex.

That Friday afternoon, Fried called Cleo, telling her he wanted her to spend the weekend with him at his house in Marblehead. He would send a Town Car for her, so all she had to do was to be ready for the pick-up at her apartment. He said that two other couples she'd want to meet were going to be there as well. Marblehead is just 45 minutes on a regular day north of Boston, but with Friday afternoon traffic, he suggested a pick-up at 4:30 p.m. Cleo knew that Prudence would grant her an hour or so on a Friday afternoon. Of course, Cleo could not mention Fried. The invitation did pose a major conflict with Danny, who expected to spend the weekend with her.

Cleo would have to give Danny an excuse for the weekend; she was sure he already had plans, but she needed to be with Fried and was intrigued about who these other people could be. Surely, Fried would have invited some friends who were also writers. She would have an exciting literary weekend with Fried and his literary friends.

Cleo's excuse was that a division head, Johnny Littman, was supposed to go to a literary conference at Amherst that weekend, but he had fallen sick, and Schendler had asked Cleo to fill in for him; it was an opportunity for her to show Schendler that she could handle herself and move up in the organization. She said that Littman had recommended her, which meant that he was interested in her joining his large, dynamic division. She had to go. Imagine her relief when she got Danny's answering machine, not him. She ended by promising to call him on Sunday after-noon when she got back to Boston.

She mentioned that Boston was only about two hours from Amherst, so she should be back fairly early on Sunday afternoon. Cleo ended by enthusiastically saying, "This may be a major opportunity for me." She said it with such conviction that she almost believed it herself. In any case, being with Fried would be good for her career if he put in a good word for her about her professional, not her sexual skills, and she was intrigued about who these literary friends could be. To her, the ability to invent a credible and interesting fable illustrated and substantiated her

Idyll and Deceit

talent as a writer. Novels are no more than written lies, just words after all. They are just fiction, like life, something we make up.

The Town Car arrived at her apartment right on schedule, and the traffic heading north was as intense as expected. Traffic always bottled up going through the tunnel from downtown Boston to the airport and points north, and that Friday was no exception. Cleo was relaxed, however, in the back of the Town Car. She had been at a hotel in Boston three, maybe four times with Fried. He was just a standard guy in bed, OK to good, but nothing out of the ordinary; he was just a guy with a penis. Sex with him was sort of once, maybe twice, and done, no big deal, not like the hot scenes in his books. His imagination exceeded his actual sexual techniques and appetite. Authors can write about things they have never experienced, and wild sex was probably one of them. Cleo wasn't even thinking about Fried, just who she might meet at his house. Having left a message for Danny, she had put him completely out of her mind. All she could think about was what this weekend with literary people might offer.

Fried lived in a large old New England-type house comprised of three stories with a major staircase that led up to the bedrooms from the entrance. He greeted her in a polo shirt, tan slacks, and a cardigan sweater—the uniform for New England in the summer. Even in summer, the evenings could be chilly along the coast, which explained the cardigan. The greeting included a couple of kisses on the cheeks and a quick one on the lips. She kissed him back somewhat awkwardly. She had to get back into the mode of, "It's just sex." He took her to his bedroom on the second floor, which was dominated by a very large, four-poster bed covered by a white comforter. She expected him to take her under that comforter without any preliminaries or hesitation. She remarked that the "comforter" looked warm and snuggly. Fried corrected her saying that the "comforter" was a real German *federdecke*. Then he asked her to get ready to go out for dinner since they had reservations just 40 minutes later. Her sessions with him in a hotel had been clothes off and right to sex, but she was going to spend the weekend with him; she was glad that he was giving her a little time to reorient herself to "It's just sex."

Right on time, she presented herself in the salon, where he had poured two glasses of sherry. Cleo was used to a more

110 The BeAst and the Brightest

informal way of life and didn't really go for sherry, but she took a glass and flashed a big smile at him, saying, "Here's to a wild weekend in Marblehead." She had no idea why she said wild; that is not what she anticipated, but she was letting herself go, so "wild" just slipped out. Many of the sex scenes in his books were, in fact, wild, so maybe that influenced Cleo to say that word. Fried seemed excited, offering to clink his glass with hers.

"Yes, here's to a wild weekend."

Dinner was the expected fish or lobster. Instead of the literary discussion she had hoped for, all he wanted to talk about was places abroad where he had traveled, things he had seen, etc. Anecdotes about these trips included comments about "such beautiful women," "women everywhere," or "great women." Cleo started wondering if he was just trying to get her into the mood for sex, something he didn't have to do since she didn't need to be seduced, or if he had experiences with group sex abroad that he used in writing some of his sex scenes in his novels. Cleo didn't want to ask and didn't want to know.

In the car going back to his house, they passed the restaurant where she and Danny had eaten. Life is full of coincidences. Other than that, she didn't think about Danny that whole night. She was sure he had found things to do that weekend; he would probably just work in his apartment. Once back at Fried's house, he offered her another drink, which she accepted. She asked for white wine. "OK," he said. While Cleo sipped her wine, he helped himself to a scotch on the rocks and then another.

Cleo thought, *Great, he'll probably fall right to sleep once we are done with sex.*

Actually, he was hungrier for her than she had experienced when they were together in the hotel in Boston. He wanted to do it several times and he kept feeling all over her. It seemed like he had more than two hands since he explored every part of her body. She just let him do whatever he wanted since it wasn't kinky sex. She just said to herself, "Let him have his little fun, it's just sex." Cleo was relieved and able to relax once he turned over and went to sleep.

The next morning, he didn't seem interested in sex. Cleo thought that the previous night had probably satisfied him, given his age. He was probably running low on sperm. They

Idyll and Deceit

had breakfast, and then he started talking about the book he was writing. She was so glad to be talking finally about literature and his book project. She quickly became very active in the discussion, mentioning scenes and writing styles from his earlier books. They seemed to get energy from each other as the discussion proceeded. The conversation then turned to other authors who Fried thought might interest Cleo and Schendler or whose writing he liked. Cleo knew she had made the right decision to spend the weekend with him instead of Danny. She couldn't wait to meet his literary friends.

After a light lunch at a little vegetarian restaurant right in the center of the town, they took a walk in Marblehead, dropping into a bookstore he frequented. The owner and Fried knew each other, which led Fried to introduce her as one of his preferred editors. This comment thrilled Cleo. She thought that she was on her way to a more significant job in a bigger division at Schendler. They spent an hour just looking through books, discussing them, and sometimes critiquing them. Fried seemed interested in Cleo's comments and never contradicted or corrected her. Of course, this made her feel really great. Here she was with a best-selling author on the East Coast, talking about literature. She could not have been happier. Fried said that he had planned to have the dinner in his house catered, so there was no preparation needed, but his friends were expected to arrive somewhat later, so they might want to get something light to eat before going back to his house. A little place down the street from the bookstore seemed like a good choice. Cleo opted for a salad while he devoured some fried clams.

Back at his house, he suggested that they take a "little nap." Cleo knew what to expect and went right up to the bedroom and laid down on the bed, getting ready to take off her clothes. She opened the top three buttons of her blouse to show her breasts. Fried joined her, just taking off his shoes. They kissed, hands exploring under their clothes, but before things got really serious, he said, "Let's just rest so we can enjoy ourselves fully tonight. It'll be wild." Cleo just thought he was picking up on her word.

Then Fried said that these friends were two couples they could "do things with." For once, Cleo was slow on the uptake.

112 The BeAst and the Brightest

As a writer, she valued her ability to observe little things and make inferences about them. But she could miss the forest for the trees. "What's that?" she asked naively.

Fried said, "You know, like in my books, they are swingers and into group sex; we'll have a great time. It'll be wild."

Cleo sat up straight in the bed. This was totally unexpected, although his books were filled with scenes of group sex. She had thought it was just fiction, his imagination, his skill as a writer. "I really don't think I can," Cleo muttered, almost at a loss for words. "This is not what I expected. I can't. That's not me."

"Sure, it is," he insisted. "You like sex, you a free girl; you'll have a great time. They'll like you; you're a good-looking woman. It is more fun with multiple people. I love it; you have to try it. I'm sure you'll really enjoy yourself and discover new ways to have fun. The guys will really get it on with you. And the other two women are young and good-looking and really hot, really into fun sex. That red hair and your unbridled appetit for sex are proof that you like to get wild."

Cleo could feel her anger rising inside her. "No, that's not me."

"Oh, come on, do it for me," he insisted, "I know you're not a prude. You enjoy sex; you'll see how great it is; you've read my books, right?"

"No," she blurted, "I have to go." Fried looked mad.

"Look, I brought you up here to have some fun; I want more than just an occasional, boring humping in a hotel, real fun, real wild group sex. Come on, I'll put in a good word for you with Littman. Wouldn't you value that?"

Cleo was willing to trade sex for help with her career, but she wanted to be the one to initiate and control what happened. In theory, she had nothing against group sex, but she wanted to control the situation and decide on the participants. She also was more willing to doing it with multiple guys than with guys and women together. In fact, having sex with two guys at the same time was her most frequent sexual fantasy. She was open to doing it with two guys but hadn't had the occasion. She'd never seen other women getting fucked, and she wasn't up for that. The idea of doing it while other women were in the room seemed weird, too weird, even disgusting. Here, he, this guy, had set her up for something she had not bargained for, and she was angry. "I'm leaving; either I'll call a company for a ride, or you should." Her eyes were aflame. She quickly buttoned up her blouse. Her back stiffened.

"What am I going to tell my friends? They are coming here just for this. I told them that you'd be up for it, that you'd be great."

"Your problem, I'm leaving," she shouted.

He looked terribly aggravated, no, really mad. "OK, but if you leave, that is it between us."

"Fine," she said. He went into the other room where he phoned the car service.

"Just get your things and get out," he screamed.

"OK, that's what I'm doing."

"Just get out, you little cunt." Yes, he used the most vulgar word possible. Cleo had never imagined that anyone would use that word to mean her. Her anger boiled up higher and higher.

"I'm going, and you are a bastard. You know that, right? A real bastard!" She hurried up the stairs, put her few things in her bag, and ran back down the stairs. She wanted to be gone as quickly as possible.

Fried shouted, "Wait on the front porch for the car. I don't want to see you anymore."

"Fine with me, you old bastard."

Once in the car, Cleo's anger kept exploding. "Guys are such bastards, just bastards." She kept saying the same thing about men to herself over and over.

Why should I ever think a guy, a male, can be a decent human being and can treat women right? They have no respect for women; we're just things to be used and abused.

She started thinking about her book on feminism. She'd have to tell men exactly what she thought about them. *All bastards, all damn bastards.*

As soon as she arrived back In Boston, Cleo looked around her apartment for a bottle of wine, which she opened quickly, then sat down in her big reading chair. *You just need to deal with it*, she said to herself.

Men are bastards.

114 The BeAst and the Brightest

Her anger was burning hot, and the glasses of wine did not extinguish the flames. With each glass of wine, her anger grew more intense. Cleo didn't use alcohol to control her emotions, but this was an exception; she was so uncontrollably mad.

How could he think I'd do it with just anybody, people he invited without telling me? How could he think that I'd go for group sex?

Of course, she knew his books, and several contained scenes of group sex. She had slept with him without any process of seduction on his part. From the first smile, he knew the deal— sex for a positive recommendation. But to Cleo, he was totally responsible; she had no responsibility at all for what had just happened in Marblehead. He was just a bastard.

Cleo drank almost two-thirds of the bottle of wine without noticing how much she was gulping down. After an hour or so, the alcohol began to have its effect on her, and she calmed down a bit. At about 8:30 p.m. she headed as usual to Tuk Tuk Thai for something to eat, which she brought back to her apartment. She was wondering what that bastard Frank was telling his friends. Had they made it a five-some? Did the three men regret only having two women to play with? Had Fried recruited another woman he knew to have an equal number of guys and women?

Cleo tried to read something, but the wine had taken its toll and she fell asleep late, very late. Sunday morning, she woke up at 9:45 a.m. hungry and somewhat calmed down. She headed over to get something to eat, but her pastry store was out of her favorite, pain aux raisin. She settled for an elephant ear and a croissant. She enjoyed just reading the newspaper and relaxing. The mess with Fried had really upset her, and she felt she needed some time alone. Cleo didn't give a thought to Danny, whom she had promised to call Sunday afternoon until he called. She didn't pick up. Her answering machine took the message. "Hey, lady, did you have a good time? How was Amherst? Were there people you liked to meet? Give me a call; I'm thinking about you, sweet lady."

She thought, *He's probably a bastard just like all the other men. I don't need to call him. He doesn't deserve it. Let him wonder what's going on.*

Idyll and Deceit

In fact, Danny was wondering why she didn't call, but assumed that she had gotten back much later than she expected. He was sure they'd talk the next day. Cleo's animosity toward men was burning inside her. First, Frank had "fucked" her the last night of the conference.

How could Frank have done that to me?

And now Fried had assumed that she would willingly participate in group sex just because she had let him screw her in a hotel, what, three or four times without much of a process of seduction. Well, she thought, he was now out of her life. How could Fried believe she'd have wild sex with people she didn't even know?

Cleo valued guys just for their utility, nothing else, certainly not as people since they were all bastards.

Chapter 14
Deceit and Radiance

Cleo didn't pick up the receiver of her phone until Tuesday afternoon when she heard Danny's voice on the answering machine. Her anger against him for being a guy had subsided, and she had started thinking about the next weekend with him. She had not given a moment's thought to how she would end things with him or even if she would. This was totally new to her. The only person with whom she had maintained an open-ended relationship was Nicole.

Danny suggested getting together Friday night for dinner at his apartment and then going to a movie at Harvard. Cleo said, "No, I'll think about what I want to do this weekend and call you tomorrow, OK?"

Danny thought this response was a little strange, but he decided to wait to hear from her. She left a message Friday morning on his answering machine saying that she was busy Friday night but that they could get together Saturday "for lunch." Danny started wondering seriously what was going on. Why hadn't she called him when she got back in town from Amherst? What was she possibly doing Friday night without him? Would she spend more of Saturday with him or was it just lunch? He started thinking that something was going on that she did not want him to know about. Was she with somebody else? He decided to leave her a message that he was looking forward to seeing her on Saturday and said that some of his friends were organizing a party and he'd like for them—Cleo and Danny—to go together.

118   The BeAst and the Brightest

In fact, Cleo did not have other plans for Friday night. She got Italian takeout and headed to her apartment to eat and read. She thought that not being with him Friday night would put her back in control. If he started worrying about their relationship, that was OK since she needed to get the upper hand. But about 9 p.m. that evening, she started thinking about him and began to wonder if she would lose him. She did not want to lose Danny. Was she making mistakes that would lead him to dump her? He had a lot going for him and could easily find another girlfriend. Cleo started thinking that she was being stupid.

I just met a guy I really like, and I'm pushing him away.

She finished the bottle of wine she had opened Sunday night and got into bed. Cleo never cried, but she did feel a wave of emotion, of longing for Danny, sweep through her body. She wished that he were next to her. She'd need to repair whatever damage the previous weekend and this unexpected Friday night apart had created.

On Saturday, she showed up at his apartment with a huge smile, open arms, and a real kiss—a soft, loving kiss—the kind she rarely gave anybody but had grown accustomed to giving to this guy, Danny. He responded with kisses, took her hands in his, and said how happy he was to see her. "Is everything all right?" he asked.

"Sure."

Then he asked the crucial question. "Are you seeing anyone else?" Cleo tried to look hurt or shocked, but she couldn't. She just said, "Why would you think that? You're the only guy I'm with. I'm really into you. Don't you know that?" Danny said he was sorry he had asked her that and that he, too, was into her, only her.

"After the weekend without you, I was just disappointed not to see you Friday night, that's all." They just smiled as best they could at each other. Then Danny asked, "Are you up for lunch, and how about that party tonight? Are we going, you know, together?"

Cleo sensed the hesitation in his voice that the events of the last weekend and then an unexplained Friday night apart had created and wanted to repair the damage she had caused. "Of course, I'm dying to be with you." They ate at a little Portuguese

Deceit and Radiance

restaurant just behind Central Square. Cleo seemed happy to be with Danny and occasionally leaned over and gave him a little kiss on the cheek or put her hand on his leg or her arm around his shoulders. She wanted to reassure him.

To seal the deal, she said that she had not felt very well on Thursday and Friday, so she had just slept. She had not mentioned feeling bad to him since she did not want him to worry. Then she returned to the lie about Amherst. Cleo started talking enthusiastically about the conference and all the authors and academics she had met. Being there as the representative of Schendler had been a real thrill for her, and although she had missed being with Danny, she thought that the weekend had helped her career a lot. Cleo's verbal skills allowed her to invent completely false stories, so vibrant with details and so engaging that she almost believed them herself. Her real life could be turned into fiction, and vice versa.

As they were finishing lunch, Danny said the party would begin at about 8 p.m. and asked Cleo what she wanted to do. "How about wild sex in your bed?"

Danny looked surprised but was so ready for it that all he could say was, "Let's go." The door to Danny's apartment was still closing when she pulled off her sweater, revealing her breasts, no bra. Danny took off his shirt, and they hugged and kissed, long, luxurious kisses. Then everything came off, and Cleo pulled him toward the bed, saying, "You can't imagine how much I need this. I thought about you and doing this with you all last weekend and last night, but I just didn't feel well at all. I am so hungry for your body and everything else, of course."

Danny responded by saying, "I love being with you, too." They made love slowly with affection. Danny caressed her all over, including turning her over on her stomach and rubbing her back and the back of her legs.

Cleo lifted her hips and turned her head toward him and, looking back at him, said, "Come into me like this." Danny understood that she was ready for a new experience with him. Perhaps this is what she had meant when she said, "wild sex." Danny thought, *Not exactly wild*. He was experienced, but he was happy that Cleo was ready to explore new sensations with him. Maybe this was "wild" to her since she had restricted their lovemaking to the basics, primarily the missionary position. Cleo was happy about the effect this move had on him; it was the first time she had allowed a guy to have sex with her like that. She enjoyed this new sensation, especially since he put his arms around her and held her breasts as he whispered, "You are so beautiful. I really love you."

They both "came" at the same time, and then they laid down on their sides, looking at each other. Danny caressed her and said, "Isn't it wonderful to be this much in love?" Cleo typically would have said her usual, "Sure." But she couldn't. She tried to give him her standard, deceptive smile, but the tips of her lips would not move into the ritualistic position she used so often to communicate so little, so little that was true at least. She was starting to lose control of herself, her real self. Instead of a smile designed to betray as well as to enchant, a radiance had been lit inside her that was propagating ever deeper inside her body. She leaned over and gave him a long, soft kiss with all the tenderness she was able to muster. Danny could feel that radiance in her body; the feeling of love was penetrating the barriers she used to protect herself from emotions, and was liberating the longing for love hidden profoundly within her. That lovely radiance started to burn so brightly that it began shining in her eyes. She was just looking at him. Her eyes were radiating love. Their eyes met in a long embrace. This was the one moment in her life when she might have felt pure love; she thought that perhaps she was responding to real love, not just desire, and she wanted to give love herself for just that one extremely lovely but very brief, fleeting moment.

They stayed in bed a little bit before starting to get dressed. Cleo helped him button up his shirt, saying, "I'll help you, but I prefer to unbutton it." She was just teasing him a bit, but she did it with a real smile. Danny had forgotten all of his worries about what might be going on with Cleo.

Danny and Cleo headed to Harvard Square to the Coop, but as they approached the Square, Cleo said she'd like a coffee at The Coffee Spot. "Do you think we can use the same table? That table means so much to us." Danny was charmed again. He loved to hear her talk about "us." Their table was taken, but the one next to it was free, and that was good enough. As they

Deceit and Radiance   121

sat down, Cleo said that it was so wonderful that they both liked coffee. They could not help but laugh. Any doubts about Cleo disappeared. Danny swore to himself that he would never again doubt her. He would always trust her completely. How could he have ever doubted such a wonderful woman?

Danny couldn't possibly doubt the woman he loved and the guys who were his friends. He was eager to introduce her to his friends in the department, except that he would never have introduced a close professional colleague in the department, Vilemann, to Cleo or invited him to any social event. He was obviously a vulgar, tough bastard, but he was also a "colleague," studying the same general field in the department, so Danny maintained a professional relationship with him. Danny wasn't that naïve. Was he somewhat naïve, as well as kind and innocent? Yes, but that meant he needed to surround himself with good people he could trust.The party was held New Year's Eve 1999. The whole world was nervous about what would happen to all the computers once the year changed from 1999 to 2000. Would everything go haywire? Danny and his friends had decided to welcome in the new millenium together at a party. At 8 p.m., they headed to the party with some of Danny's econ friends, which was just getting started when they arrived. About 20 people were there, all drinking and dancing and talking on the couch or sitting around on the carpet. Cleo had expected to see John Tallington, but he had decided to study instead of coming to the party. One couple had started kissing and making out. Soon, they headed to one of the bedrooms. Danny introduced Cleo to everyone, being sure to tell her their names, and described her as "the best-looking, sweetest girl I have ever met, and the best editor in Boston." This last comment directed the conversation to Cleo and what she might want to talk about.

Danny got Cleo to dance a bit. She didn't consider herself a dancer, but she enjoyed swirling around with Danny, and he was having a great time. Swirl, kiss, swirl, kiss, swirl, kiss, kiss. Although she could be very social in a group, Cleo wasn't much of a party girl, but she was really enjoying herself. After two hours, she was exhausted. She sat down with a couple of Danny's friends, who asked her what she did as an editor.

Cleo was happy to sit and talk about her work, about feminism, and about novels some of them knew. Around 1:30 a.m., she and Danny started feeling really tired and decided to head to his apartment. They undressed and went to bed without making love. They had already had a very satisfying day and were tired. She put her head on his shoulder and hugged him.

She asked him what he thought might happen in the morning, thinking about the computer problem. Danny said that he would kiss her, then they could make love. Cleo liked the answer.

As she fell asleep, she thought that this might be one of the few times she had gotten into bed with a guy without fucking. She liked that. She felt happy and satisfied. She told herself she was maturing and might even love Danny. She thought that she was becoming a more mature, grown-up woman. She wasn't sure, but she thought that she might be in love, at least a little. The thought both pleased and surprised her. It also frightened her. She wondered how long "we" would be together. Yes, they were becoming a "we" even to her, but somehow it didn't feel right. Could Danny or another guy fit into her life's plan?

The next morning, they kissed, made love and then prepared a nice brunch. Cleo made the coffee while Danny make delicious omlettes, sautéed potatoes, and sourdough toast, her favorite.

Chapter 15

Cleo's Boyfriend

Cleo had never talked about specific guys with Prudence. She limited herself to saying that she had gone here or there with a guy she knew without mentioning his name. She wanted Prudence to know a little about her life to strengthen the personal relationship between them, and Prudence enjoyed hearing about Cleo's activities without asking probing questions. The fact that Prudence didn't ask questions or make comments about her behavior made Cleo even more open with her. These stories fueled the imagination of this lovely woman, Prudence, who was restricted to living in her apartment, her office, and rarely anywhere else.

But on Monday, Cleo mentioned having a friend, Danny, whom she liked very much and told Prudence that she would like to have an opportunity to introduce him to her. "The next time we have Chinese food at your place, would you like for me to invite him?"

"Of course, my dear. I'd enjoy that very much." Prudence invited them to come over that next Friday night. Chinese takeout in hand, Danny and Cleo showed up at Prudence's apartment right on time. Danny believed that showing up together was further proof that they had become a "we." Cleo was sharing more of her life with him. He would be the only one of Cleo's bed partners whom Prudence would meet.

124   The BeAst and the Brightest

Prudence sat in a large easy chair; two crutches were leaning on the side of the chair. "Excuse me for not getting up. I'm so delighted to meet you." Cleo busied herself in the kitchen, opening up the Chinese food and putting each dish they had ordered in a separate bowl. Prudence did not eat out of a carton, and the dishes were to be shared. Cleo opened up three TV tables and put the food on the coffee table in front of Prudence so that she could serve herself. "It looks delicious," she said.

As they ate, Prudence said that Cleo had told her that he was studying economics at Harvard, and Prudence said she found that fascinating. With this introduction, Danny described very briefly what he was studying but said that he shared Cleo's love of literature. He admitted that his knowledge of English-language literature was embarrassingly limited, but he had gotten into Italian literature when studying in Florence.

He complimented Cleo as a great guide to English-language literature. She had introduced him to authors he had heard about but never read, like Huysmans. He mentioned seeing *Les Enfants Terrible* together at The Brattle. That shifted the conversation in a direction that everybody could enjoy, and Prudence noticed how he had managed this transition. He was not all about himself; he was focused on Cleo. They talked for a couple of hours, and then Cleo said that they had better go since Danny had to go back to his apartment in Cambridge. Prudence understood very well by their behavior that evening that they were sleeping together but appreciated Cleo's tact. Cleo wanted Prudence to think that she was a proper woman, a lady. To avoid any misunderstanding, as soon as they were outside, Cleo told him, "You better come home with me, fellow. You're staying with me."

That dinner at Prudence's apartment started a regular every second Friday takeout dinner with Prudence. Prudence enjoyed seeing this young couple together, whom she believed to be in love. During their discussions, Danny realized the extent to which Prudence was a profoundly cultivated person. Danny was amazed, for example, how much she knew about Florence and the great land-owning and banking families and the Renaissance artists who made its fame even thought she had only been there one time. She had become an avid traveler in books. Prudence started seeing Cleo and Danny almost as family, as her children.

Cleo's Boyfriend

Danny thought she was charming, and he liked her immensely. Prudence and Danny were becoming friends.

One Friday night, Cleo mentioned that she liked to give people nicknames. Of course, she was not going to mention how she used them. She asked Prudence what nickname she would give to Danny as she gave him a big smile.

"Siegfried," Prudence said. "Yes, I think Siegfried would suit you."

Danny seemed surprised, "I'm Italian. Do you really think I'm a Siegfried?"

"Well, you are very romantic, tender, sensitive, and, of course, intelligent, so somehow Siegfried just came to me."

Danny and Cleo just looked at each other and said in unison, "Siegfried, it is." Her description of him touched Danny. Leaving her apartment, he asked, only half fishing for a compliment, "Cleo, do you think I'm romantic, tender, and sensitive?"

"What do you think, Siegfried?" she said.

One Friday evening, when they were not going to Prudence's apartment, Danny and Cleo met at his apartment for a night together. Danny said that the next weekend, they couldn't do anything together. His advisor had just given him a project that consisted of writing a grant proposal that gave graduate students like him enough funding for a year to do their dissertation research. The Harvard Grant Office's deadline for these proposals was the next Monday. Danny had always planned to do his dissertation about the role of the Ministry of Finance in Italy. This grant was just for France, but his advisor wanted him to compete to gain practice writing grants and to get feedback. Writing it would take all weekend. Danny told Cleo how much he would miss her but hoped to finish the proposal by Sunday afternoon. Maybe late Sunday afternoon, they could see each other. They almost never slept together on Sunday night since they both had to work, her in Boston and Danny at Harvard in Cambridge. Cleo said she understood but said, "You're spending Sunday night with me... all night with me, even if you come late." Danny thought that this was a very sweet invitation that would motivate him to get that grant written. He accepted Cleo's invitation.

The next weekend, he started working Friday afternoon and plowed forward almost without eating all day Saturday. He was glued to his typewriter. He had learned a lot about the inter-action of the French government with French industry, work-ing with his dissertation advisor during two summers in Paris. Danny had never studied French, never had even one class, so his French was very rudimentary, but he spent most of his time with numbers, and the French people he worked with were all elite cadres, as the French call senior leaders of an organization. They all spoke excellent English. Danny liked the experience of learning about the practical side of finance beyond academic theory. He also enjoyed being in Paris and admired his advisor's knowledge and connections. So, he put all he had learned into this grant, which would be easy to convert to Italy. He did not feel that this effort or the time spent was a waste of a weekend with Cleo since he was going to spend the rest of Sunday with her. At about 3 p.m. Sunday, he finished typing the grant pro-posal, headed to Harvard to make copies, dropped off one at his advisor's office, and slid one into the mail slot in the door at the Harvard Grant Office. He realized that this advisor was right: It had been a good exercise. Then he rushed to Cleo's apartment.

"You see... I couldn't miss enjoying some time with you, lovely lady." Cleo greeted him with kisses and hugs and offered to take him to that Portuguese restaurant where they had eaten one time. Danny and Cleo both liked having "their regular places." It seemed to increase their closeness, their "we-ness." Danny always said, "We like this" or "We like that." Every time he said something like this, Cleo felt pleased but wondered if this type of equal, loving relationship was, in fact, what she wanted. Was an equal relationship without domination or submission even possible? Would becoming a "we" divert her from her advocacy of feminism and her destiny as a great editor and writer?

She had never imagined herself "with" anybody. Could she and a guy have a relationship without one or the other dominat-ing? What did he think about feminism? Cleo regularly tested him by articulating something fairly strident about feminism or by making very negative comments about males. Danny would say she was absolutely right and then add how much men had dominated, mistreated, limited, even attacked, or killed women and that it had to stop. He said that a society in which women were absolutely equal to men would be a much better world. He

Cleo's Boyfriend

told Cleo that he saw her as a great spokesperson for feminism. He was eager for her to write her book. How could Cleo not like this guy? He didn't try to dominate her. He supported her and gave her space to be herself. She never felt on guard around him. She could do and say whatever she wanted. Only occasionally when she would talk about how horrible guys were, he'd ask, "Am I like that?"

"Oh God, no," she'd say, and she didn't think he was.

The next Friday, they went to see Prudence and then spent the weekend together just working, reading, having a good meal out Saturday night, and going to a film Cleo wanted to see. It was just a relaxed weekend for a couple at home. The next weekend, they drove up to Marblehead to stay at that B&B they knew. Danny suggested the restaurant where she and Fred Fried had eaten, but Cleo was scared that she might run into him, so she insisted on going to another place somewhat out of town.

They were looking at their menus when Fred Fried came up behind Cleo, walked around the table, and looked straight at her, saying, "Hello there, Cleo; I didn't expect to see you here." Her heart almost leaped out of her chest. She looked up and saw Fried staring at her. He had knives in his eyes. He had not forgotten or forgiven anything associated with that weekend. Cleo's verbal ability was about to be tested. She simply said that it was strange to see him since she thought he preferred Provincetown for its social atmosphere. She had no idea what he would say. He looked right at Danny and said, "Good luck with this one." With that, he turned to the two much younger women standing right behind him, and they left the restaurant. Cleo's heart was beating like crazy. Danny noticed that the two very young women were wearing very form-fitting dresses, cut very high on their thighs and extremely décolleté, so he doubted they were his daughters.

Danny asked, "What was that all about? Who is he, and who are those two women?" Cleo had to invent something on the spot.

"Oh, nothing. He is one of Littman's authors, and I helped edit something he wrote. He was not happy about some of the changes. He is a touchy author, that's all."

"What did he mean by good luck with this one?" Danny asked.

"He tried to pressure us to print what he originally wrote, but we refused. That's all. He said I was stubborn and an idiot. He can get insulting, but that's his problem."

Danny just offered that he understood that some authors can be touchy. Danny asked Cleo if she had noticed how young those two women were and how they were dressed. She just said, "NO!" Danny decided to drop it.

The rest of the weekend went by smoothly. Danny knew that he was totally infatuated with Cleo and had started to think that she was going to be his life partner. Cleo realized that she not only liked Danny but might be in love with him. This idea both frightened and enchanted her. As they headed back to Boston, Danny said, "I can't imagine not being with you."

Cleo just smiled and said, "You're so sweet, Mr. Dolchetto, I mean Siegfried."

Chapter 16

Announcement

The next week, Danny called Cleo on Thursday, saying he wanted to talk with her about something important, and asked if they could get together at his apartment at 6 p.m. on Friday. They now had the habit of spending at least Friday and Saturday nights together, and she didn't understand why he needed to make a date for Friday night. What intrigued her was his mention of "something important." What could it be? Was he going to propose to her? If so, what would she say? Her emotions became almost uncontrollable. What if she turned him down cold, saying she had no plans to get married, ever? What if she said yes? Could she really imagine herself as a wife?

Arriving at his apartment at 6 p.m., he kissed her and said that they needed to talk about something. She could feel her back straighten up. Her mouth became dry. Her eyes widened. What was he going to say? He started by telling her that it was good news but that it posed some challenges for them, challenges he firmly believed they could surmount. What could it be? Was he sick? "No," he answered, "nothing like that. Surprise, surprise, I won that grant to France. I was the first person they decided to give it to this year. My advisor called me this afternoon, and I am totally excited. This will give me a year in Paris to do my dissertation research so I can finish my degree."

Cleo just looked at him. How was this possible? He was going to leave her for a year and for Paris, just like Nicole. He

130 The BeAst and the Brightest

was going to abandon her, just like Nicole. He wasn't going to marry her; he was leaving. Cleo had not realized that the grant would enable him to be in Paris for a year to do his research. Consternation turned to anger. How could this be happening? After so many guys and so many years, she finally found someone she liked, and now he was leaving her. It was over. Anger surged through her body. She was almost blind with rage, but she tried to maintain a calm exterior.

"Look, Cleo, we can make this a positive for us. I'll come back regularly to be together, and you can come to Paris to be with me. Sure, there will be a lot of time when we are apart, but many couples who love each other have faced something similar and have emerged strengthened. We can also write to each other."

Cleo was looking right through him; all she knew was that this guy had changed how she thought about men, well, about this one guy, and now he was going to abandon her; he was going to hurt her. She heard him say that they could visit each other, but she and Nicole had said the same thing, but the visits between Nicole and Cleo had not been frequent. Cleo had never devoted the time and money to go to Paris to visit her friend. Cleo didn't blame herself for this lack of visits; the whole thing seemed unrealistic. She wasn't sure why, but she had never gone to Paris to see Nicole. She'd probably never go to Paris to see Danny, either. He'd just leave, and that was that.

Cleo managed to say that she was happy for him, but he knew that this was a hard blow to both of them. Danny kept saying that they could visit each other regularly and that they could make this an adventure. Danny even said that she could spend time writing her book advocating feminism, and he'd work as hard as possible to come back as soon as possible. Danny asked her if she had ever been to Paris. Cleo said, "No, but I have a friend there, an old girlfriend from elementary and high school."

"Perfect, you can visit her when you come to see me."

Danny said he'd come back at Christmas and New Year's, and then in March or early April. "Imagine April in Paris together, what could be more wonderful?" He'd come to see her right as summer began in June. Then, she could come to see him in late July or early August. He suggested a little summer vacation

Announcement 131

together at the beach. He'd probably be back in Cambridge in September. Danny believed with all his heart that this program would keep them excited about each trip to be with each other, and they'd have enough time together to keep their love vibrant. Cleo just listened to him. Danny was profoundly disturbed by Cleo's bewildering response but thought that she'd accept the challenge of this year since he believed they truly loved each other. Danny believed that love can be a force that makes wonderful things possible.

When he met Cleo at The Coffee Spot, and as their relationship developed, he started to believe that he had met the love of his life. She was everything a woman could be: very attractive, intelligent, loving, affectionate, passionate about her career, and independent. She was a very lovely, modern woman. Would they marry? Danny thought they would, but he needed to get his dissertation research under his belt, write the thing, and then get a job. He imagined living with her when he returned from Paris and then hoped that they would make a solid commitment to each other. He certainly didn't have the financial means to support two people. While prestigious, the Harvard grant was meager, very meager.

Danny kept insisting that they would stay together, but Cleo thought, *You bastard, just when I met a guy I like, he does this to me. All guys are bastards, even Danny.*

Danny tried to tell Cleo that if she could get her feminist novel written and he could do his dissertation research, they would both have major accomplishments behind them and could just focus on being together when he got back. With his dissertation in hand, he could get a job and start making real money, enough to support them. Cleo just looked at him. She didn't know whether to cry or slap him.

Danny and Cleo kept seeing each other as if things were not changing, as if he were not leaving. During all this time, Danny kept showing Cleo how they could "stay together" by four visits, two by him and two by her. She'd just say, "OK, but I don't know if I can come over there. I have limited vacation days." Danny assured her that he would come back at Christmas. Cleo never said she thought this separation would be too hard or that she'd

132   The BeAst and the Brightest

prefer to break up. She seemed honestly open to the idea that somehow things would work out, even though she was both terribly unhappy and angry about the situation. Cleo did tell Danny about her friend Nicole, who had lived in Paris for some time, and told Danny that this friend would be happy to help him settle into Paris. Danny was happy to hear about this friend whom Cleo could visit when she came to Paris.

Cleo's ambiguous attitude toward Danny's plans to exchange visits really shook him up, but when he asked her if she was willing to commit to staying together, to writing and visiting each other, she said, "Sure."

Danny had learned that sometimes she substituted an unclear response rather than a more straightforward answer, but to date, these ambiguous responses had not caused any arguments or problems between them; everything had just worked out. He had not learned that Cleo guided her life by deceit. He remained hopeful. He was in love with Cleo and thought she loved him, too.

Danny thought that he and Cleo could work things out if they both just tried, if they worked at it. Visits would help a lot, and Danny started thinking about the first one at Christmas. Cleo got in touch with Nicole, who seemed happy to help Danny get into Parisian life. Cleo's attitude toward Danny didn't seem to change during those last six weeks.

Twice, they ate at Prudence's apartment, and Prudence said that Cleo and Danny seemed to have worked out a good plan to "stay together despite the distance." She even said that they made "a wonderful couple." Cleo bristled at that comment since she had never imagined herself in a "couple," but she was able to thank Prudence for that nice comment. Danny was very happy to get this support and endorsement. Prudence said, "Paris is wonderful, particularly with someone you love."

Cleo just said, "That's what I've heard."

The night before he left, they had a special meal and spent the night intertwined in her apartment since Danny had given his up. His best friend and fellow graduate student, John Tallington, helped him store his possessions and agreed to check in on his car, which Danny put in a garage. John had done this for Danny twice before when he spent summers working with his

Announcement

dissertation advisor in Paris. John seemed happy to help. John had appreciated Cleo's and Danny's attempt to hook him up with that woman at the dinner at Danny's apartment, even though it hadn't worked out. As Danny left, John said, "Good luck with everything."

Danny thanked him for his help and said, "I'll be back at Christmas, and we'll get together. I'll be staying with Cleo. *Ciao.*"

Chapter 17

Danny in Paris

anny was not totally reassured that Cleo thought they could or should stay together that year, but as soon as Danny got to Paris, letters began to be exchanged. Six days on average were needed at that time to get an airmail letter across the Atlantic so Cleo would get one every week. Danny waited patiently to get a letter from Cleo and respond to it. International phone calls were impossibly expensive. Cleo's first letter was very sweet, reassuring, and very personal. Danny fully appreciated her skill as a writer since he could hear her voice in every sentence. Reading and rereading these letters and "hearing" her voice through these little airmail letters made him feel that she was almost next to him in his little Parisian apartment. Danny could not wait to get back to be with her at Christmas. He read her latest letter every night before going to sleep. He missed her terribly but believed that at the end of the year in Paris, they would be together.

Danny's apartment was on the Left Bank, just a block from the Saint-Germain-des-Prés church and two famous cafés, Les Deux Magots and Café de Flore. Both cafés had been known in the 1950s as literary hangouts, and Danny was excited by the idea of going to one or the other with Cleo. Just behind the Place St. Germain, there was a lively food market, Marché Buci, with everything he might need. By chance, the two apartments he had stayed in during those summers in Paris were in the same neighborhood as his new place, just blocks from each other, so

Danny felt like he was "coming home" and didn't have to spend time finding his way around.

On the first day in Paris, Danny headed to Gilbert Jeune, the big bookstore where French students for more than a century have bought textbooks, novels, and all sorts of literature. He was going for books to learn French. He quickly fell into a routine of doing his research in the mornings, having a quick lunch at a café or in his apartment, and then studying French until late at night. He was making progress but realized that he needed conversation with French people to learn to speak the language correctly. Lessons would have been too expensive, so he had the idea of making a little sign—English to French, Français à l'anglais—which he mounted on a menu holder and went to his favorite Café Mabillon, just a block or so from his apartment. Tourists dominated Les Deux Magots and Café de Flore, hoping that just being there would make them literary giants or at least seem cool. Neighborhood people went to Café Mabillon. He asked the manager if he could talk to people—no money involved—to learn French.

"*Bien sûr,*" was the response. So, he put up his little sign, ordered a café and waited for someone to ask him what this was about. He explained that he'd give English lessons for a certain time—5, 10, 15 minutes, or longer if the person interested in improving their English would help him with French for the same amount of time. The lessons started quickly since a lot of educated French speak some English but would like to know more or improve their pronunciation. Many people wanted to learn how to swear in English or say something related to sex. Danny learned some choice words and expressions in French, plus many words about anatomy. Everybody likes sex. Well, almost everybody.

Some days, he would go to Café Mabillon; others, he'd head toward the national theater where a lot of students and artists congregated at Café Odéon. One day at Café Odéon, a perky, extremely pretty woman in her mid-20s came by and asked for lessons. She was smartly dressed, and Danny noticed that her makeup was very subtle; her makeup and perfume added to her good looks but did not dominate them. He also saw immediately that she was very nice and friendly.

Danny in Paris   137

He thought, *What luck to meet such an attractive Parisienne.*

She needed help with pronunciation, particularly the "th" sound, which can come out like "zz." Danny showed Sandrine how to use her tongue and lips to say "th." Danny couldn't help but think that she had delicious lips regardless of her pronunciation.

Sandrine worked for a marketing firm that had lots of English and some American clients, so knowledge of English was critical to her job. And she wanted to be understood more than seem charmingly French. She was French and charming enough.

On the first day, she spent 30 minutes on her pronunciation and then helped Danny with French. Neither saw the time pass. "*Zut alors*, I need to go," she exclaimed. "This was great, I'll come back." She got up to go, then turned back and gave Danny three *bises*, typical of young people. These were just three air kisses, but they made Danny feel very Parisian, especially since Sandrine was so pretty and so charming.

Because of Sandrine, the next day Danny went to Odéon, but Sandrine didn't show up. Instead, a strikingly beautiful blonde woman about the same age as Sandrine walked up to his little table and said, "Danny, I'm Christelle, Sandrine's friend. She is busy, but I'd like a lesson, OK?"

So, the lessons started with Christelle. Again, the lessons ended with three bises. Some days, neither girl showed up, but Danny had other visitors to his little café table, his little café classroom. The café managers seemed OK with the arrangement since many people just did five or 10 minutes of English and then the same amount of French, and they always bought something: a café, a glass of wine, an aperitif, or even something to eat.

In addition to the two girls, Christelle brought a friend, Loïc, whom she introduced as a *petit ami*, a boyfriend, not just a *copain*, a friend. Loïc had worked in the same marketing company as Sandrine and Christelle, but he had moved to an ad agency. His specialty was graphics and photo shoots, so working in an ad agency made more sense for him. He was very good-looking, very French, and extremely sociable. He was tall and thin but had the musculature typical of soccer players. He also had a great sense of humor and loved telling jokes that Danny understood in French, sometimes. The jokes were, in

138   The BeAst and the Brightest

fact, a good way to learn vocabulary and gave clues to French culture. Humor is both universal and local and can be deeply embedded in language.

After a few weeks, while taking a lesson, Loïc said, "The girls really like you, and the four of us should have dinner sometime."

Since Danny didn't have any social friends and was feeling lonely, especially so far away from Cleo, he was eager to start a social life beyond the café lessons. Nicole and Danny had met each other several times at cafés or for dinner, but only very occasionally. She was nice but didn't really help him integrate into life in Paris. Her circle of extremely rich friends didn't include poor students. During those dinners, he went on and on about his love for Cleo, and Nicole just listened and smiled. Danny's social life revolved around those little lessons at the cafés and writing letters to Cleo. He kept his morale up by reading her latest letter every night in bed before going to sleep. The letters reassured him that their couple was strong enough to endure a year of separation, with visits, of course.

A couple of days later, Sandrine showed up at Café Odéon and gave Danny three bises before she sat down. She looked at Danny and said, "Let's have dinner with Christelle and Loïc next Friday, *d'accord*?"

"Sure, I'd love to!" Danny said. He was thrilled to have some social life, and he really liked all three. Sandrine and Christelle were charming, intelligent, and friendly, and Loïc seemed like a nice guy, so Danny thought he was starting to settle into life in Paris with friends. Sandrine mentioned a Moroccan restaurant on the rue Saint André-des-Arts, not far from his apartment.

"20:30, ça va? OK?"

Danny was standing outside the restaurant people-watching when Sandrine came up behind him and put her hands over his eyes. She asked, "What is it?" Danny looked around and smiled at her, then said, "You mean, who is it?" They both laughed at her mistake.

Christelle and Loïc came a few minutes later. Everyone gave each other lots of *bises*. Danny loved this tradition, which seemed so much better than a handshake, especially with these lovely women. Danny had to get used to receiving and giving air *bises* to guys; it's a cultural thing. Sometimes, they were closer

Danny in Paris   139

than just "air." When he lived in Italy, Danny had gotten used to talking with Italian guys who stand much closer together than Americans, but kisses, even air kisses near the cheeks, were another thing. Eventually, Danny got used to those male air kisses, but it took him a little time; it's cultural.

All four ordered couscous, and Christelle suggested a bottle of Rosé wine. The conversation started quickly in French and English and bounced easily between the two languages. As the couscous and Rosé diminished, the conversation grew even more animated. Christelle asked for the check, which they all split, and then she announced that they should all go to her apartment to dance.

Christelle's apartment was one Metro stop away in a very imposing stone building. The entrance gates were of beautiful wrought iron. Past the gates, a large courtyard opened up to reveal a set of five steps leading to a magnificent stone building. Once in the foyer, which was covered with beautiful marble, Danny was confronted with a classic 19th-century wrought iron elevator, which is considered a point of prestige and class, something frequently found in expensive classical buildings. The contrast with his little student apartment could not have been starker.

Christelle's apartment was on the fourth floor. As she opened the door to her apartment, Danny could see a large salon beautifully furnished. Hallways went off in both directions. Either Christelle had a much bigger job than he had thought or family money. Sandrine told him it was the latter. Despite her extremely good looks and money, she just seemed like a million other nice, polished Parisian working girls. She had no hang-ups or pretensions. She had never made any references to having money or a prominent, wealthy family. She put on some music and headed to the kitchen. Sandrine and Danny sat down on a couch, and Sandrine leaned over and said, "Danny, we're so happy to know you, to be with you."

"You guys are terrific, too," he said.

Christelle came out of the kitchen with a bottle of champagne and asked Loïc to get some flutes. "Danny asked, "What is the occasion?"

Sandrine said, "It's our first night together." Danny didn't fully appreciate what this might mean. Everybody clinked their flute

140   The BeAst and the Brightest

and took a sip. "There is nothing like champagne," Danny told
them. Christelle put on some music, and she and Loïc started
dancing. Danny put his arm around Sandrine's waist, and they
joined in. The girls changed partners during and between dances,
and everybody started joking, drinking champagne, and just letting themselves go. They were all having fun.

After about an hour, Christelle and Loïc headed down one
of the corridors. Sandrine looked at Danny and whispered, "The
other bedroom is this way." As she took his hand and started
down the other corridor, Danny put his arm around her, not as a
hug but to stop her.

"Sandrine, you are a wonderful woman, but you know that
I have a girlfriend, a serious girlfriend, Cleo, and I, well, I just
can't." He had talked several times about Cleo to Sandrine and
had mentioned that she was going to come to Paris to see him,
but Sandrine had not realized how serious he was about her.
Sandrine had assumed that this Cleo was just a friend who might
come to Paris. Sandrine was also very attracted to Danny. She
looked at Danny as her eyes blinked and widened as if asking,
Is it that serious?

"I think we're going to be together for a long time, maybe our
whole lives … I just can't."

Sandrine put her arms around Danny, holding him for what
seemed like a long time with her cheek pressed against his chest.
Then she gave him big kisses on his cheeks, paused for some
time, and then said, "Where does a girl find a guy like you?"
Danny was stunned by this question. She repeated, "Where are
there others like you?"

Danny returned the compliment by saying, "Sandrine, you
are so wonderful that a zillion guys would do anything to be
with you." They went back into the salon to find that Christelle
and Loïc had not come back. Sandrine and Danny finished their
flutes, not saying much to each other but giving each other little glances. Sandrine explained that Christelle and Loïc lived
together and had been lovers for many years. Danny asked
Sandrine if she wanted to stay or if he could walk with her to her
apartment.

"Let's walk," she said.

Danny in Paris 141

Sandrine's apartment was just three blocks from Danny's, and the walk from Christelle's apartment took only about 20 minutes. During that walk, Danny and Sandrine looked at each other several times. Sandrine realized that Danny really wanted her as much as she wanted him, but he was not willing to cheat to betray his love for Cleo.

As they walked, Sandrine started giving Danny smiles—little ones at first, then big happy smiles since she understood the situation and wanted Danny to know that she understood her relationship with him; she would be a *copine*, a friend, but not a *petite amie*, a girlfriend. As they approached her apartment, Danny put his arms around her and gave her three *bises*. These were not air kisses but soft, lingering kisses on her lovely cheeks. He told her, "You are absolutely lovely and a really wonderful woman."

She responded with her own tender kisses and then said, "How about a lesson at Odéon on Tuesday afternoon?"

The next week, everything fell into place. Danny focused on his research, and the two girls and Loïc each came by for an English lesson and to help Danny with his French, which was getting better. Christelle started coming more frequently, and about the third lesson after the evening out with them, she put her arm around Danny's shoulders and whispered, "Sandrine told me all about the other night. Loïc and I have a wonderful love story. Your Cleo is lucky to have such a wonderful love." Danny said that he realized that he and Cleo had a wonderful love story.

The next day, Sandrine came to the café and told Danny she needed to talk with him. She said she wanted to apologize, to clear the air about her invitation to spend the night with her. She told Danny that she hadn't appreciated his commitment to Cleo; she thought that perhaps this woman, Cleo, was just someone he had just gone out with or was just a friend. She said that she had never slept with anyone who had a serious relationship or was married and wouldn't because it would be morally wrong, and she respected women too much to do that. She said, "I'm not that kind of person; I'm a feminist, you know. Women have to support each other, and I don't cheat; I'm not a cheater. I want to be able to respect myself, to live happily with myself, and

142   The BeAst and the Brightest

deserve the respect of others. I'm not a cheater." She seemed really upset. Danny leaned over and gave her a little kiss on the cheek and said that he knew she was terrific, no harm was done. He put his arm around her shoulders and gave her a little hug. Sandrine looked terribly relieved but also looked longingly at Danny. Danny realized at that moment that she really loved him, so he said, "If I didn't have Cleo, I would have accepted your invitation enthusiastically."

Sandrine offered to buy two flutes of champagne to celebrate. Danny asked, "What are we celebrating?"

"The continuation of a wonderful friendship … and more language lessons."

Once they had their champagne, they clinked glasses, smiled at each other, and drank that delicious liquid. Then the lesson started.

The next time he saw her, Danny asked Sandrine whether she had a *petit ami* or a *copain*? She didn't seem to be bothered by the direct question. "I had a *petit ami* for two years, Gerard, who was from a small town, Gap, in southern France. He was studying here but intended to return to work with his father in the family's hardware store. So, we knew he'd be leaving. I couldn't imagine living in a little town like Gap, and he was devoted to his family and the business, so we knew that, at a certain point, he'd leave. He left just before you showed up in Paris. There is another guy I know, Alfred, who is very nice, but … I'm not going out with him right now."

Danny gulped down some champagne. He realized that he could take the place of this guy, Gerard, but he couldn't because of Cleo. Danny took Sandrine's hands, kissed them, and said, "You are a wonderful woman, very, very pretty, too; you'll have another love in your life very soon." Sandrine tried to smile but instead leaned over and kissed Danny on the cheeks. Their understanding was complete.

In fact, that entire year, Sandrine did not get together with any of the guys who wanted her, including that guy named Alfred, who called her every few weeks. After Gerard's departure, Alfred had hoped to become Sandrine's boyfriend. She was thinking about Danny and having him as a friend was enough for her. She wanted to be his warm, loyal friend. Having a really good guy

Danny in Paris

friend and feeling love for him was enough for her. She could skip sex for a time. The four friends went out to eat or dance fairly regularly, but nothing ever happened between Danny and Sandrine except friendship—real, close friendship.

Danny could not help but ask Christelle how long she and Loïc had been together. "Let's see, 12 years now," she said in French. To an English speaker, the number 12 in French sounds a lot like the number two. Danny wondered if he had misunderstood. Danny thought she was kidding.

"Come on, how old are you?"

"I'm 25; I've been with Loïc since we were 13." Danny looked quizzical.

"How is that possible?"

"He moved into the house just down the street from where I lived, and we became best friends. We'd walk to school and home together, and sometimes, he would come over and play dolls with me. I loved my dolls, and we played with them until we were almost 15. I'd also play soccer with him and his friends. I was good, you know. So was he."

Danny was intrigued. "So, when did you two, you know ..."

"You mean start being lovers and having sex?" Christelle had a way of talking directly without artifice about subjects that other people avoid or dance around. "One day, I looked at him and knew that I loved him and that he was the guy for me. I asked him if he felt the same. We knew we were in love with each other. Soon after that, when we were 17 and a half, we asked our parents if I could have the Pill since Loïc and I wanted to start making love; we wanted to sleep together and enjoy sex. Our mothers asked us to wait until he was 18. His birthday is two months before mine. So, that was it. I was his 18th birthday present, and he was mine, two months early," she said with a big smile.

Danny couldn't help but remark, "I bet he really liked his present."

"We both did," she said, laughing. "After that, we'd sleep sometimes at my house or his. It was wonderful right from the start. He's the only guy I have ever made love with."

Danny asked, "Really?"

"Sure, we sincerely love each other; why would we need other people?"

"So, both of your parents were OK with your becoming lovers?"

"Of course, they are lovers; they sleep together and have sex. Why shouldn't we?" Christelle had a way of saying the most basic truths, simple, compelling truths, straightforwardly. Danny thought she was absolutely terrific. She exuded authenticity and honesty.

"So, who is the dominant one, you or Loïc?"

"We're equal. We decide everything together." Then she leaned toward Danny with a funny look on her face. "Why should one of us need to be dominant? He's a modern guy, and I'm a modern woman."

Danny asked, "Do you consider yourself a feminist?"

"Of course. Women have to take a bigger role in society and have to live together with men and men with women; neither should be dominant. That's such old thinking. But men need to change just like women are changing. Too many guys are babies or brutes. They need to understand that male characteristics and female characteristics are things we share. Men need to stop fearing their softer side." Then she paid Danny a compliment. "You're like that—you're a guy, but you have a soft side."

Danny thanked her, then added, "I like your feminine side a lot, and your guy side, too, but less."

She smiled and then quoted a well-known feminist, Emma Watson: "Both men and women should feel free to be sensitive. Both men and women should feel free to be strong. It is time that we all perceive our gender on a spectrum, not as two opposing sets of ideals."

Danny had thought that maybe her feminism was a product of the times, but obviously, she had read some feminist literature as well. In any case, she seemed to be a wonderful representative of feminism.

Anybody could see that Christelle was extremely beautiful, and she wore very smart, chic clothes and laughed easily. She was incredibly attractive. Her surface glittered; her personality shined, her silhouette and posture impressed, but what Danny was seeing and what had attracted Loïc was more than that

Danny in Paris

lovely surface. She had depth and intelligence and both sympathy and empathy. Her depth reflected and enhanced her beauty; she was a totally beautiful person, not just a pretty one. As he got to know them, he realized that Christelle had told him the truth about Loïc having been her only lover. Loïc told Danny that it was true of him as well. Danny said that Christelle was very beautiful and very nice, so she had little competition. Loïc said, "Yes, she is beautiful, but I love her for everything she is." Danny started to be convinced that they would be happy and together forever.

Chapter 18

Cleo's Dilemma

When Danny left, Cleo was unsure what she was going to do. Could she start The Game again with guys whom she would just pick up here and there? After the deep, new, wonderful, but somewhat troubling feelings that Danny had evoked in her, that didn't seem possible or even something she wanted to do. Could she live without sex until Christmas? Maybe? Danny had promised to come back during the Christmas to New Year's period, but that was three and a half months away.

Cleo kept thinking about herself as a dominant feminist who would never live to please a man. But she really liked Danny, the way he treated her, and the way she felt when she was with him. She had decided not to break up with him before he left for Paris. Yes, she had been very upset, even angry, that he was leaving her, but she never wanted to break up with him. She felt that she might love him, or at least she liked him too much to decide to break up. This is what had reassured Danny.

Did those feelings make her less of a feminist? Had he sabotaged her version of feminism as dominance with kindness and love? She was unable to answer these questions, preferring just to focus for the time being on her work. She thought about starting her novel to define her feminism but decided to wait until she had resolved her issues with Danny. She needed to understand

148   The BeAst and the Brightest

whether she could have a relationship with a guy who was totally comfortable with her feminism and with her work.

As she kept asking herself these questions, a guy started calling her and leaving messages, saying that he knew that Danny was in Paris "for a year" and wondered if she was all right. Maybe she would like to get together for a coffee or something. He left several messages, including one that asked if she had heard from Danny and leaving his name, Jim Vilemannn. He also mentioned studying with Danny in the same department. Finally, Cleo called him back.

Their first meeting was at a coffee shop in Central Square. Jim was not good-looking at all. In fact, he had a big nose, somewhat hollow cheeks, and a very bad, unattractive swarthy complexion. His father was German. His mother was a Brazilian creole which accounted for his short stature and his swarthy complexion. At 5 feet 6, Cleo towered over him, but so what. Cleo thought that since he was a friend of Danny, she could learn something more about him from this guy. Instead, he talked a lot about himself. He had gone to Duke where has was just an average student except for economics, but somehow he had gotten into Harvard for graduate school. He mentioned that some people thought he was "brilliant," but that brilliant is a big word.

As he talked, Cleo felt herself being pulled into some strange dark matter as if he were a black hole that could just swallow somebody whole, not leaving a trace. There was nothing about this guy that she liked, but he did have some strange, dark charisma, a strange dark magnetism that she could not ignore. That darkness was not just his complexion, but something deep in him that attracted her. In fact, she felt trapped by what he was saying as if some bizarre magnetic rivalry was developing between them, pulling them together, not pushing them apart. After one cup of coffee, Cleo got up and said, "Nice to meet you, but I have to go."

As she got up, she thought she'd never see him again, but then he said, "I'm sorry. I just talked about myself. Let's talk about you at lunch. How about tomorrow?"

Cleo could not believe she said, "Yes, OK."

Lunch was the same thing. He spun a voracious, sticky web of words mostly about himself that neither interested her nor

Cleo's Dilemma   149

seemed very relevant to anything in her life, but she just kept listening and listening. Something about this guy fascinated her, but she had no idea what it might be. He seemed totally disinterested in literature or music or the arts. He had traveled outside the United States just twice to London and Paris, as a tourist, nothing more. Only when she asked him why he was studying economics did he start to reveal himself.

Economics is all about competition between strong and weak companies, between good and bad ideas, and between players who just enjoy being in the game and those who are in the game to win and will do anything to win. Winners don't care what happens to the losers; they just try to keep on winning. Cleo started thinking about *Les Enfants Terribles* and the rivalry between Elizabeth and Paul for domination.

Vilemann went on to say that he believed that the world is best described by the German philosopher Hegel. We are engaged in a war of all against all. There are no moral guidelines, restrictions, or restraints. The most aggressive and the least constrained by moral guidelines wins. What's morale and what's fair competition are defined by the winners, not the losers. Life is "solitary, poor, nasty, brutish and short" in Hegel's famous description. This view of the human condition led Hegel to believe that we all must submit to the authority of a sovereign (a guy, of course) who would use his individual power to dominate and control society. To Cleo this seemed to be an ideal posture for someone like Vilemann, who described himself as aggressive, as someone who wants to dominate, to win. He was also egotistical, ruthless, insolent, and controlling. Cleo was fascinated by him.

As Vilemann went on and on about Hegel and competition, Cleo asked herself why she was willing to listen to this. She hated the idea of being submissive to a guy who would be the winner by dominating her. But she saw the world in ways that matched Vilemann's description. Men and women are in an unavoidable war in which there are winners and losers, just like the rivalry between Elizabeth and Paul in *Les Enfants Terribles*. Female winners shouldn't care what happens to the guys who lose. Had Cleo ever had any feelings of guilt because of how she treated guys? Did she care what Blondie thought of her or if he felt bad about her leaving him so abruptly? No, she had not given a single thought to him since she left him that night, and she honestly didn't care what had happened to him. She sincerely didn't care what had happened to any of her males. With men, nothing was more foreign than guilt, shame, remorse, or regret. She was the winner in these encounters, and she made the rules about what was right or wrong.

Cleo wondered why an enthusiastic feminist like her could submit to this guy who was clearly a macho bastard. In what way did he seem interesting or attractive? Wasn't he just the type of tough bastard that she hated? If someone had described him to Cleo, she would never have believed that any intelligent, modern woman could be attracted to him in any way or certainly not feel any love; he loved himself too much, and he was too much the brute. But Cleo was attracted to him; she saw so many elements in him that were like her.

His indifference to traditional morality matched hers. She had never had a second thought about the males she slept with, including guys who had serious girlfriends or were married. Many of the authors she had slept with were in a serious relationship or married. Alexander had that Diane Bouquet. What she had done was just fucking, just using sex to advance her career. She saw nothing wrong with that. Vilemann had been in Cambridge for several years, but he didn't have a steady girlfriend. Just as Vilemann didn't seem to have a girlfriend, Cleo saw herself as forging her life without a permanent partner. She would use men as part of her zipless sexual journey, nothing more. This Jim was so much like her despite his macho ideas. In fact, his macho ideas matched her version of feminism, which demanded that women dominate men.

Once Vilemann started talking about Hegel, nothing seemed to stop him, and Cleo did not want him to stop; she was captivated by what he was saying. Cleo had never heard anybody talk like this, but what he was saying tracked closely with her own ideas about men and women. They, too, were trapped in a war of all against all, and Cleo had learned to play The Game so that she was the winner. The whole world was like Elizabeth and Paul. Now she realized why she was drawn to Cocteau's film and this tough guy.

Cleo's Dilemma 151

Cleo was faced with a stark choice: Should she flee or embrace this guy who was so much like her? He asked if they could have dinner together. That night, they slept together at Cleo's apartment which let him into her life, not just her bed and her body.

In bed that night, she asked him if he had a girlfriend. "No, I just move from person to person. When things change, I just leave. Maybe you think that's tough, but it is what it is. Traditional sexual morality is bullshit. People should just do whatever is good for them." As she looked at him, she thought that if they ever had a kid, it might look like a medieval devil in a Hieronymous Bosch painting, given her bright red hair and his swarthy skin. But of course, neither of them ever considered having a child. Cleo was not shocked by his statement of sexual freedom and lack of concern for other people's feelings because she did the same thing; she never considered other people's feelings. Sharing her body with someone did not imply any relationship; to her, it was just sex, zipless fucking. If some guy got hurt, that was his problem. She did not pick up on Vilemann's use of the word "person."

He came over the next night to sleep with her again. He was rough with her during sex, plunging his sex into her without much regard for her feelings or how it felt. His approach to fucking matched his ideas about being aggressive and tough. Getting her into bed had been easy; all he had to do was to take a little time and spin his verbal webs. Except for that time when he mentioned that Danny had left her for a year, Danny was never mentioned by either Cleo or Jim. Vilemann had achieved his goal of taking a rival's girlfriend from him. He saw this conquest as proof of his superiority.

When he learned that Danny had gone to Paris for a year, he wondered if he could "bed" Danny's girlfriend, and he had succeeded. He had never met Cleo but had heard that Danny had a very good-looking girlfriend. As he lay there in her bed, he felt strong and proud. He was stronger and cleverer than Danny. He considered Danny a rival in the department, so hurting him by taking his girlfriend seemed like a brilliant thing to do. He was surprised at how easy it was to get her into bed.

152 The BeAst and the Brightest

Did he worry about what Danny might do when he found out? Vilemann thought that he would deal with that later. He felt sure he'd come up with something. Now, he just wanted to enjoy her long enough to taste his victory fully. She was his, his prey, just female meat. She was just Danny's loss.

After starting to sleep with Vilemann, every time Cleo got a letter from Danny, she would open it carefully, almost hoping that he would tell her that he had a new "friend" in Paris. If Danny had a friend, Cleo was free to move on, too. But really, she did not want to move on from Danny. She really liked him, and no guy had ever made her feel love and sincere tenderness, at least a tenderness she had been willing to accept. He seemed balanced with both male and female characteristics. He was sensitive, like many women, and was multidimensional, like many women. He liked cooking. He liked literature and music, but in bed and elsewhere he was all guy, a real male. But he was also loving and tender. Her sexual response to him was unlike anything she had experienced, except for that guy in Australia and a couple of others. Plus, she had not been with a guy who could just let her enjoy some time "alone" while he was in her apartment.

Despite sleeping with Vilemann, she still wanted to hold onto Danny. He was not only a lover, but he had also become her best friend. She couldn't imagine breaking up with Danny since that might mean a renunciation of the ability to have the type of lovely, comfortable, enhancing feelings he had created in her. So, she would write him a sweet letter back giving him her news, but not mention Vilemann.

Cleo's relationship with Vilemann bumped along. He wanted to make all the plans and decide everything for them. One day, he was in her apartment and saw a letter from Danny.

"Why are you still getting shit from that guy?" he asked.

Cleo fumbled around for a moment, not knowing what to say. Finally, she said, "Well, he keeps writing me."

"Don't you think it is time to end it with that guy? I mean, he can't be anything to you; he's such as loser."

Cleo's Dilemma

Cleo wanted to defend Danny, to say that Danny was a much better guy than that bastard standing right in front of her, but she couldn't. "Let me deal with this, OK?"

Then Vilemann started criticizing Danny as a loser again, and Cleo had had enough. "I'll do what I want to with Danny, OK?"

Vilemann turned and looked Cleo right in the eyes and said, "Who is better than me? Who is a winner and who is a loser?" Vilemann wanted to be able to declare total victory over Danny and move on from Cleo. To him, she was just prey; bedding her was just a way to hurt Danny. Cleo told him that she wanted a little time off, so he should please leave. Vilemann felt so sure of himself that he turned and left, saying, "I'll see you on Friday evening for dinner and a sleepover."

Chapter 19
The Holidays

In fact, once Cleo had written a letter to Danny giving all her news, she calmed down and called Vilemann, asking when and where they should meet on Friday. Vilemann had won. Their relationship developed in fits and starts with them jockeying with each other trying to determine who was dominant and who would be submissive. This continued all through September and October. Slowly, Vilemann gained the upper hand. He was making all the decisions for them. He decided what they did for entertainment, where they ate, and even what she should eat. He stoped waiting for invitations to spend the night with her; her'd just invite himself whenever he wanted or would just show up. He became more aggressive and vulgar. One evening he called her saying that he was going to come over and that she should take off her panties to be "ready for my dick."

The first week of November, he announced one evening at dinner that, "I have been invited to have Thanksgiving with one of my professors. He invited me for 4:30 p.m., so I'll pick you up about 4 p.m. at your apartment."

Cleo was confused. Was she invited, too? Vilemann just said, "They'll be OK with me bringing someone." Cleo felt like baggage, just something Vilemann was dragging along. In fact, that was all she was to him.

When Cleo was growing up, Thanksgiving at her house was always filled with tension and disputes among the members of her family. One time, all four grandparents were at their house in Napa. She was only four, so she didn't understand what might have happened between her and her paternal grandfather one night as he was putting her to bed or why there was so much arguing and anger. Her parents took turns taking one or another of her grandparents aside and would argue with them. There was a lot of shouting. Cleo did not know what the fights were about; she was only four. So, for whatever reason, Thanksgiving always degenerated into arguments and bickering. Tension always filled the atmosphere at her house at Thanksgiving. After that Thanksgiving, her paternal grandparents moved to Sydney despite her grandfather's role in the California wine industry.

The Thanksgiving dinner with one of Vilemann's professors was at a large house in Concord, just west of Harvard Square. On the way to his professor's house, Vilemann went on and on about where the Continental Army had met the British and the "one if by land, two if by sea" story as if Cleo had never heard about the American Revolution. She just let him talk. They arrived right on time. The door was opened by a young woman, a senior at Harvard College, who said, "You must be Vilemann, Jim Vilemann," Cleo realized that they had never met before.

Then an older man, maybe in his mid 40s, appeared and greeted Vilemann, saying, "There you are, glad to see you." Vilemann smiled, and they all went into the salon to the right of the entrance to the house. A large staircase led from the entrance area to the two floors above. A fire burned in the large fireplace in the salon. Jim and his professor went first, leaving Cleo and the young woman to follow. The professor asked if anyone would like a drink "to kick off the festivities." Jim said, "We'd both like a white wine." Cleo just nodded.

As the professor came back in the room, Cleo stood up and introduced herself by saying, "I'm Cleo, a friend of Jim's." Then, the younger lady introduced herself as a friend of the professor. Cleo thought that she might be one of his students.

Cleo was furious that Vilemann was almost totally ignoring her, so she took him aside and said, "That was embarrassing. Why didn't you introduce me?"

Vilemann said that he was going to "get around to it." That further infuriated Cleo, who decided not to make a scene and

The Holidays

just shut up and get through the dinner. Here was another tension-filled Thanksgiving. Cleo was seated next to the younger woman whose name she never really got.

During the very traditional dinner—turkey, gravy, some sort of dressing, mashed potatoes, string beans, cranberry sauce, etc. Jim and his professor talked about economics, gossiped about things in the Econ Department, and about people they knew. Cleo was totally excluded, so she tried to talk with the young woman. In fact, she was one of his students who seemed totally taken by his knowledge and experience. After a few glasses of wine, she also said that he had promised to help her get into Harvard's graduate program. Cleo understood the deal—sex for help with her career. Nothing new there. Cleo knew that women, even feminists, have to do what is necessary to be in a more powerful position in the future.

The meal finished with two types of pie—pumpkin and minced meat—in the salon with coffee. Cleo declined the desserts but took a coffee. More chit-chat between Jim and the professor filled another hour. Cleo became angry at being ignored and was ready to end this charade. Finally, she stood up and said, "Well, this has been great. Thank you so much."

The professor took the hint and stood up as well, but Vilemann just stared at her as if to say that he wasn't ready to leave. Once on her feet, she headed to the hall closet, and the professor followed to give her the heavy wool cape she wore. Vilemann followed, as did the young woman. Pleasantries were exchanged all around. The only thing the professor said directly to Cleo all evening was, "So lovely to have you join us."

On the way back to Boston, Cleo fought to contain her anger; she expressed it by not saying a word. She tried being as taciturn as Paul in *Les Enfants Terribles* to see if this would annoy Vilemann. Vilemann understood that she was upset about something but didn't know what. He had thoroughly enjoyed himself. Finally, he said, "What are you upset about? Was that other woman boring?"

Arriving at her apartment, Cleo could only say, "I'm going to be really busy this week, so no sleepovers. I'll call you."

Vilemann just said, "OK."

158   The BeAst and the Brightest

Cleo didn't like this response. Was she losing him? Did she want to lose him? Yes, because he was an ugly bastard, but no, because he got to her in a way that attracted her to him. His macho intensity mirrored her fervent feminism. His understanding of life as war was parallel to how she played The Game. His disdain for traditional morality, for not feeling bad or regret about anything he did, was just like her ability to ignore traditional sexual morality. He never apologized or said he was sorry for anything. Cleo had never met anyone as tough as that, except that she saw herself in him. How could she give up someone who so closely resembled her? Vilemann was the mirror image of Cleo.

She had two guys in her life—one a fascinating, tough guy who seemed to be able to capture her despite her feminism. Then there was Danny who had enabled her to feel love and to be comfortable with a guy who complemented her without threatening her in any way. But did she really love Danny, or had she just realized that she could feel love for someone, for a guy? Was her attraction to this barbarian, Vilemann, love, or something else? And, of course, there were her episodic sessions with Alexander, but that was just business, at least to Cleo. She tried to read a bit to put these questions out of her mind but couldn't. She wondered what Danny had done for Thanksgiving.

Cleo worked assiduously that week trying to put Vilemann and Danny out of her mind. Vilemann did not call her on Monday or Tuesday. While aggressive, he knew how to pace his interactions with her. Alexander did drop by that Tuesday to invite her to see him the following day, "6:30 p.m. as usual?"

"Sure," she said.

That Wednesday evening, Alexander came on to her with more passion and took longer to finish his business than usual. Cleo wondered what kind of Thanksgiving he had endured. Maybe he and Diane had fought. Who knew? Cleo just wanted to get home. After seeing Alexander, she found a message from Vilemann on her machine inviting her to a concert on Saturday afternoon, followed by dinner. Cleo decided to wait until the next day to say OK.

On Wednesday, she opened her mailbox to find some publicity flyers, a bill from the utility company, and an airmail letter

The Holidays   159

from France. Danny's letter began by saying what a wonderful Thanksgiving he had enjoyed since he had spent it with her in his dreams and imagination. His letter went on and on about how thankful he was to share a love story with her. He went on about how he imagined her in Paris with him during this Thanksgiving and where and what they had eaten, how they loved drinking champagne with their dinner, and how thankful they were to be together. He concluded by saying that he could not wait to see her at Christmas. He didn't want to be separated during another major holiday. He then went on to say that he had invited some French friends, Sandrine, Christelle, and Loïc, to dinner at a restaurant where a traditional American Thanksgiving meal was served. The chef had lived and worked in Chicago for three years and loved the tradition of Thanksgiving. He offered the traditional menu at his restaurant with an amazing French touch, so the food was wonderful. Danny's friends thought that Thanksgiving was, "So American, so positive and optimistic," and they had enjoyed being together. Danny had told his friends how thankful, how profoundly thankful he was to be "with Cleo." They said that they hoped Cleo felt the same. Danny said he was sure she did. "She's such a wonderful woman."

He told them how eager he was to see her at Christmas and New Year's. But when he went back to his apartment, he felt a terrible sadness. He wondered what Cleo had done for Thanksgiving. Being away from her was crushing him.

At dinner on Saturday evening, Vilemann announced that he had made arrangements to spend Christmas " just the two of us" at a little inn near Lake Champlain in Vermont. He described it as charming and cozy, adding that the inn took Christmas seriously. So, there would be lots to do, as well as time together to relax and enjoy the place.

Since Thanksgiving had been difficult, she didn't want to cause any more trouble between her and Vilemann, so she said, "That sounds great." Only a little later did she think seriously about what that meant for Danny. How was she going to manage his expectation that they would spend Christmas and New Year's Eve together? She thought it would be easier to lie to Danny, who was in Paris, than to Vilemann, who was right there in Boston with her.

160   The BeAst and the Brightest

The letter she wrote to Danny explained that her parents were going to spend Christmas and New Year's Eve with friends in Manhattan. They had not seen Cleo for almost two years and were insisting that she come to New York and spend the holidays with them. "My relationship with my parents is complicated, as you know, Danny, so I really need to patch things up with them. I just can't say no. This is a big disappointment for both of us. I miss you as much as you miss me, but I'm free from the middle of January. Prudence and I have tons of work to start next year, so I need a few weeks to get all that done; please plan to come anytime past the first two weeks in January. I can't wait any longer than that to see you."

This letter hit Danny hard, like a tough punch in the chest. He had been looking forward for months to seeing her at Christmas. When he first learned about the award to do his research in France, he had talked about Christmas as a critical time to reconnect with her. She would be off work, allowing them to spend a lot of quality time together. Danny was incredibly disappointed about Christmas but believed what Cleo had written. He had sworn never to doubt her. After a few hours, he pulled himself together and began to plan the trip back to Boston to be with Cleo. By that weekend, he had worked out the flights and could write her the details of his visit.

Danny had nothing to do for Christmas. He was going to be all alone, and the distance in time and space with Cleo was really weighing on him. He didn't want to mention his bitter disappointment to the girls; they knew how much he wanted to see Cleo during the Christmas to New Year's holiday.

When Christelle met him the next day at the Café Odéon for her English lesson, she asked him when he was going to Boston. He stammered a bit and then said that something had come up and that he was going later in January. "So, you are not going to be with your Cleo for Christmas or New Year's?"

"No, she has to be with her parents in Manhattan." Christelle looked concerned. "Are you sure it is her parents?" The thought that Cleo had lied to him and might be with someone else was something he did not want to believe. He loved her and trusted her completely.

The Holidays   161

"Absolutely. I'm sure she'll be with her parents." Christelle decided just to let it go. Danny then told Christelle about his plans for January and how Cleo had told him how much she was disappointed, but the essential was that they would be together. Christelle decided just to begin the lesson.

Christelle told Sandrine about her conversation with Danny. Sandrine wondered if Danny was fooling himself, but since he was going to see Cleo, it seemed that everything was all right. Sandrine and Christelle thought it best to see what happened in January. But Christelle still worried about Danny. She asked her parents, who lived in Poitier, a lovely city just west of Paris if she could bring a friend, a really good friend from America, to spend Christmas with them. They welcomed the idea. Her father was the deputy to the *Assemblée Nationale*, the French parliament, from the region and was also the mayor of Poitier. In France, a person can hold more than one political office at the same time. He also was the hereditary owner of the Château de Poitier, the principal castle in the region. So, there were plenty of bedrooms and a house staff. Danny would be welcome.

Christelle knew how much Sandrine liked Danny; actually, she knew that Sandrine was in love with him, so she had cleared this idea with her before inviting Danny. Sandrine was super happy. She didn't want to leave Danny alone at Christmas. Sandrine's parents lived in La Rochelle and had their own ideas about who Sandrine should be with. These ideas focused on Alfred de Chamberly, a guy Sandrine had dated occasionally and liked a lot, so bringing an American to Christmas instead of Alfred would not have been a good idea. Sandrine's parents knew and were very enthusiastic about that fellow Alfred. Sandrine was very close to her parents and three siblings, a brother and two sisters, so she wanted to be with them at Christmas.

Christelle's mother picked them up in Paris in her Citroën DS Luxe Edition and drove like mad to Poitier. Arriving at the château, Danny was shocked. Christelle had not told him anything about her family, the château, her distinguished father, or her grandfather, who had been a close companion of De Gaulle during the war. De Gaulle had appointed her grandfather to the French *Cours Constitutionelle*, the rough equivalent of the

162   The BeAst and the Brightest

American Supreme Court. Her grandfather had been awarded the highest civil honor, the title of *grand officier* of the Legion of Honor by De Gaulle himself. Her father was also in the Legion of Honor as a *commandeur,* a high level. True aristocrats know they don't have to show off.

The first person Danny and Christelle saw when they opened the huge doors of the château was her grandfather, who insisted on speaking English with Danny. He had a distinctive, upper-class, Etonian English accent. Her father was meeting with some men who had been chopping wood on his property; he offered them a sherry as they talked business. Then he handed each of them a little envelope with their Christmas bonus. They all shook hands and wished each other a happy holiday, and her father turned to greet Danny.

Christelle's father was extremely gracious. Welcoming Danny, he offered him a sherry. This was not the one he had offered to the workmen; that one was too ordinary. He offered a much finer sherry to his guests. Danny said it was delicious. They all sat down by a big fire in a large stone fireplace and talked a bit. Her father said how happy he was that Christelle and Danny were teaching each other their native language. "Culture is carried by language, you know."

The grandfather was sitting with them and started telling stories from WWI, which explained his command of English. He had been in charge of a group of English nurses who were the daughters of members of Parliament. He had married one of them. Despite being in his 90s, he was incredibly sharp, and his stories were amusing. Danny was fascinated by Christelle's family.

Loïc took their bags upstairs while Christelle showed Danny around the château. They started on the first floor, visiting the large kitchen with an enormous fireplace where meat was roasting on a large iron spit. Then, they visited a large, elegant dining room where they would eat all their meals. They took a walk around the grounds, including two greenhouses, one for growing vegetables in the winter and one for Christelle's mother's passion, orchids. At the orchid greenhouse, Danny saw Christelle's mother again, who greeted him with *bises* and a big smile. "I'm really glad you could be here for Christmas."

The Holidays   163

Her mother was almost as beautiful as Christelle and as friendly as well. Loïc said something funny to her, which caused her to break out laughing. Then, turning to Danny, she said, "Loïc always makes me laugh, and we love him." Danny could see where Christelle got her incredibly good looks and her straightforward, unmannered personality.

Then they circled back into the château to see more of the first floor, including the library, her father's office, and some of the spectacular orchids her mother had placed around the house. The second floor contained three large bedrooms, one of which had an enormous antique bed. "That's for Mom and Dad," she explained. Christelle's childhood bedroom was just down the corridor. Her childhood bedroom was all feminine, with a huge space for all her dolls, bookcases filled with volumes and souvenirs from her trips with her parents, pictures of guys who were famous singers, etc.

Next to her dolls, five soccer balls were placed along with a series of pictures of Loïc at different ages, some just of him and others of him and Christelle. Loïc had joined them, and Danny asked Loïc if he remembered playing dolls with Christelle.

"Sure, they're like our kids." Then he started pointing out each one, telling Danny their names, how well they did in school, which one was athletic, how they got along with the others, etc. Then Loïc started telling Danny what a great soccer player Christelle was. He went to a closet where she stored trophies she had won as a soccer player. Pointing out Christelle's trophies, Loïc got an incredible look in his eyes, filled with emotion. "Christelle was not only a good mother to her dolls, but she was also a tough soccer player; she was a striker, the one who shoots the goals. All those trophies are hers."

Danny could hear the deep love and admiration Loïc felt for Christelle. Danny offered, "She obviously scored with you; you're a great guy and perfect for Christelle." She came over and kissed Danny on the cheek, saying, "You are sweet, you know." Then Christelle said, "Let's go on."

Danny then followed Christelle up one flight of stairs to the third floor to show Danny the bedroom where she and Loïc slept when they were at her house. The furnishings were more like Christelle's apartment, with a mix of expensive modern

164   The BeAst and the Brightest

and antique furniture. Danny's guest room was next to their bedroom.

One of the bookcases in Christelle and Loïc's bedroom contained a rather large photo of 10 people, five guys and five women, lined up standing on a beach, all completely tanned, all nude. All of them had their arms around each other and huge smiles. There was Sandrine, Christelle, and Loïc, along with seven other *copains*. Danny asked Christelle if Gerard was in the picture, and Christelle pointed him out. He was standing next to Sandrine with his arm around her waist. Danny said he looked like a nice guy. Christelle explained that all these friends usually spend a week or two at the beach together every year and said, "We have so much fun. Sandrine's parents own a big beach house that they let us use. A large official naturalist beach is within walking distance of the house, so we go there for a few hours every day."

Danny asked if her parents were OK with her having a picture of them all nude.

"Sure, why not?" She seemed surprised by the question. "What's the big deal about being nude? We all know that girls have girl bodies and boys have boy bodies. What else is there to know?"

The simple logic of this statement seemed to be all that needed to be said. Then she smiled and added, "We're all adults. We know what boys and girls are like. Boys are just boys and we girls, well, we girls are prettier—don't you think? Just look how pretty Sandrine is?" She was playing with Danny at this point. "Plus, we've all been really good friends forever, and we've gone to that beach for years." Then Christelle added, "What's better than being nude and feeling the sun on your body and sunbathing and swimming naturally with all your friends, people you love and trust completely? What could be more lovely and sensual?"

Danny could not find a reason to add much, so he said, "Sounds great to me." Christelle never bragged, hid anything, or apologized for anything in her life. She was just who she was; she was comfortable being Christelle, and she made everyone comfortable being with her. Her life was an open book.

Another time, the issue of naturalism and nudity came up, and Danny asked Christelle why she was comfortable being so

The Holidays 165

open about sex. "What does nudity have to do with sex?" she asked, looking surprised. "Nudity has to do with sensuality, with feeling with your whole body, with all five senses. Sex is just one thing you can do with your body. Nudity, naturalism, and sex are totally different. You know I go nude sometimes with my friends, but I only have sex with Loïc."

Danny had just gotten a lesson from someone not raised in a Puritan culture. Christelle had just articulated a European concept of sensuality, all five senses; to her and many Europeans, sensuality and sex are totally different. She had also made clear that since she loved Loïc, he was her only lover. Christelle's feelings and emotions toward people shaped her sexual behavior and guided her sexual morality. Christelle's life was transparent; nothing was hidden, just like in the pictures of all of these friends in the nude.

Danny started to understand how Christelle could just seem to be a working girl and nothing more but have the apartment and the spending money she enjoyed. His appreciation for her grew by the day. Danny asked Christelle why she worked since she obviously didn't have to. "I'm a modern woman. I want to contribute and be valued for what I do, not for what I have or who I am." She seemed to be an authentic feminist, living her own life with love, contributing to society through her work, and doing so without apologies or pretense. And everything she had said about Loïc and their relationship seemed to be real. Christelle's family treated Loïc like a member of the family, not just a *petit ami* boyfriend.

Back in Paris, Christelle, Sandrine, Loïc, and several other friends had organized a New Year's Eve party at a discotheque near Christelle's apartment. Danny was invited to go along. Everyone danced like crazy. In addition to Sandrine, Christelle, and Loïc, other *copains* made up a group of 10. Danny recognized them as the group at the naturalist beach. A French girl named Aurélie, two German girls, Brigitte and Stéphanie, and three guys, Andrian, Rolf, and Helmut, made up the group. Danny was greeted with lots of *bises*. Aurélie said, "So this is the delicious Danny!" He felt more and more welcomed into this happy group as one of the friends. Everybody danced with everybody. They seemed totally relaxed with each other, and the

166 The BeAst and the Brightest

girls changed partners from dance to dance, so nobody was left out, including Danny. Danny wished with all his heart that Cleo had been there to celebrate New Year's Eve with him and his true friends.

Danny remembered one of Ben Franklin's famous sayings: "A true friend is the best possession." Danny could see that all these friends possessed something incredibly valuable: They were all true friends, there together to support, love, and have fun with one another.

After this Christmas break, Aurélie started coming to Danny's café classroom and became one of Danny's more frequent and serious students. She would study the subjects—grammar, pronunciation, or vocabulary—that she and Danny had discussed. She was also very diligent about helping Danny with his French. He told Sandrine that he really liked Aurélie, and Sandrine said that in addition to Christelle, Aurélie was her very best friend. "I know that Aurélie will always be there for me, no matter what happens. We trust and rely on each other. I'll always be her friend; I'll always be there for her. That's friendship, right? Plus, she's really nice and very pretty. Don't you think she's pretty?"

"Sure, she is very pretty but not as pretty as you, not nearly as pretty as you." Sandrine got the compliment she had hoped for. Danny was so sweet.

As soon as he was back in his apartment from the New Year's Eve party, he wrote a long letter to Cleo telling her all about Christmas and New Year's, adding that he hoped that everything had gone well with her parents. In fact, Cleo had just had a short telephone call with her parents who were in Napa, and she had been bored with the inn. Vermont had been cold, freezing cold, so activities outside the inn were almost all canceled or seriously abbreviated. Plus, Vilemann had been a pain, as usual, so she was happy when it was over. After that awful Thanksgiving, why hadn't she just told Vilemann that they were through and let Danny come to Boston to be with her for Christmas and New Year's as planned? She didn't know the answer to that question but hoped that seeing Danny in January would help clarify her thoughts about these two totally opposite guys.

Chapter 20

Back Together

Danny had to wait two weeks before jumping on the plane to Boston. He couldn't wait to get on that plane and see his Cleo. As soon as the plane landed at Logan, Danny got his luggage and jumped in a taxi to Cleo's apartment. After just one knock on her door, Cleo flung the door open, threw her arms around him, and kissed him passionately and tenderly. She was, in fact, very glad he was there.

They almost ripped off each other's clothes and jumped in the bed to make love like crazy. As they finished, Cleo said, "Danny, I needed that so much. I've been storing up all my affection, all my love for you, all my sexual longing, all these months. It has been too long."

Danny said, "Let's do it again." Cleo just smiled at him, and they went right at it. Danny knew that those months alone had been hard on Cleo. Her body told him about her loneliness, her hunger for him, her unfulfilled sexual desire, and her passionate, tender affection for him; at least, that's what she wanted him to believe.

She told him, "We can't be apart this long again, OK?" Danny kissed her and said that she was so right. The previous night, Vilemann had spent the whole night naked in bed next to her, but as she was giving herself to him, she was thinking about Danny. She had also done it with Vilemann the next morning without any concern about Danny's arrival since Cleo knew that his plane landed later that afternoon.

Cleo was glad to see Danny since she needed to be with him to understand her own plan going forward. Vilemann had been told that she needed that week alone to work, and he should not bother her. Exceptionally, she had let him sleep with her almost every night that week to prepare him for a week without sex with her. He seemed OK with a little time by himself. She had to hide the two pictures of Vilemann she kept on her desk and get out the picture of Danny and the picture of her and Danny together in Marblehead. She also had to put Vilemann's toothbrush in a drawer and check around to see if he had left anything else that might cause a problem.

Oh God, she said to herself. *Where is Danny's toothbrush?*

She couldn't find it, so she had to buy another one for him. She also disabled her answering machine so that if Vilemann called, Danny would not hear his voice, leaving a message in Cleo's apartment. The day of Danny's arrival would be another occasion when Cleo had sex with two different males on the same day. But she thought, *It's just sex.*

Cleo told Danny that she did not have any vacation days piled up; she claimed that she had only a week of vacation a year since she was so junior and had used the vacation days here and there. Her story about vacation days wasn't true, but Danny believed her. So, she'd have to work while he was there. Danny was very disappointed since he wanted to spend as much time with her as possible; Christmas would have been ideal since she would have spent the holidays with Danny without having to work. In fact, Schendler closed between Christmas Eve and January 2, but Cleo hid this from Danny.

Since Cleo was working during the day, Danny went to Harvard to see his advisor, who was pleased with his progress, and Danny had lunch with his best friend in the graduate program, John Tallington, who said that his car was safely in the garage and that he had checked on it recently. Everything was OK. If there was a problem, John had Danny's address and phone number in Paris in case he needed to contact him. Danny had tried to fix up John with Carol Baker, the African art student, at a dinner party before leaving for Paris, but they hadn't connected. John was still alone but said that being a graduate student was more than filling up his time. Danny talked about seeing Cleo

Back Together   169

and how happy they were together. Danny wished that John could someday find such a great woman to be with him. John said it was good to see him again, and Danny agreed that being with his friend was great. Danny said that he couldn't stay away from Cleo for more than three months, so either he'd come back in April, or she might come to Paris to be with him. John had heard for several months from other econ graduate students that Jim Vilemann had a new girlfriend, Cleo, but John had decided not to get involved. He decided not to ask Danny about his relationship with Cleo or to contact Cleo to understand if she was still with Danny, but cheating with Vilemann.

Monday evening, Cleo and Danny had been invited to dinner at Prudence's apartment. They got Moroccan takeout. Prudence greeted them warmly, giving Cleo a hug and a very big hug to Danny. She remarked how happy they seemed and then let the conversation drift to Danny's life and research in Paris and the work Cleo was doing at Schendler. As dinner was wrapping up, Prudence said that Cleo seemed so much happier since she had met Danny, and Danny said that he was crazy about her. Prudence said, "I can see that."

Cleo and Danny talked a bit more, helped Prudence dispose of the plates, etc., and then they were off. "Take care of her," she said to Danny. Then she turned to Cleo and said, "Take good care of this one. You won't find anyone who loves you more." Cleo just smiled. She had learned how to hide the ugliness of her treachery behind a screen of outward radiance flashing from her smile. Prudence smiled back at her.

Since Cleo had to work, they only had one weekend together. The other days, Cleo had to work until 5 p.m. On Tuesday, Alexander came by to make an appointment once again for the next afternoon. That next day, Cleo called Danny to say that she had to work a little later than usual.

She just told herself, *These things happen.*

After her little sexual moment with Alexander on that couch she was beginning to know so well, she arrived at about 8:15 p.m. at her apartment. Cleo was happy Alexander had settled for a quick one and then seemed OK with her leaving. Back at her apartment, Cleo suggested Tuk Tuk Thai and eating there since it was so convenient. Danny was OK with whatever she suggested;

he just wanted to be with her. That night, Cleo would have been happy to pass on lovemaking because she had the vivid image of Alexander nude on the couch; she could almost still feel him laying down on her and his penis in her. She had no moral compunctions about having sex with two guys the same day; she just noted that this was happening again and just a few hours apart. But Danny was so eager that she pretended to want him and let him come into her. Then, with a kiss, she turned over and quickly fell into a peaceful, deep sleep.

The week with Cleo went by in a flash, but Danny savored every minute. Cleo seemed as happy as Danny. They spent a lot of time making love and just hugging and kissing. Once again, Danny had done something to her during those days together. Cleo felt that Danny was shining a light into her heart. Each night, as she turned off the bedside lamp to sleep, she felt Danny's light brighten in her, warming and opening up her heart so something could grow in there. Was it love? Cleo knew that Danny could not imagine that she had shared her body with someone else just before coming back to her apartment that Wednesday night, or that she had another regular bed partner, or that she had let Vilemann have sex with her the morning he arrived. She was proud of her ability to control her emotions and manipulate guys. She had complete confidence, even pride, in her ability to deceive, but she did feel that light in her body.

Vilemann liked to fuck; he was not tender or loving at all. Whereas Danny was passionate, Vilemann was aggressive. Danny was sweet and loving and gave Cleo space to be herself; Vilemann was tough and domineering but as engaging as a whirlwind. Cleo was torn between the two of them, but during that week, she rediscovered the feelings that Danny had awakened in her, and she liked them. She liked the woman that Danny thought she was.

As Danny packed his bag to head back to Paris, he felt sure that their relationship was intact. He thought that Cleo had demonstrated her character by staying true to their relationship. He had believed since first heading to Paris that if something changed for Cleo, she would at least be open and honest with him. Beyond loving Cleo, he believed in her. He respected her and was sure she felt the same. He thought she was a wonderful

Back Together   171

person. His only hesitation was her relationship with her family, which she never seemed to want to share with him. She hadn't said anything about Christmas or New Year's Eve with her parents. When Danny asked her about Christmas in Manhattan with her parents, she just said it helped straighten things out a little bit. All she would say about New Year's Eve was, "We had a nice dinner." That was all she wanted to say. Was there something in her past with her parents that prevented her from being totally open with him? Perhaps, but with time, Danny felt sure that Cleo would open up, wanting him to understand the dynamics in her family so that there would not be any secrets between them. He wanted to know and understand the whole person, the woman he loved. He didn't know that her heart was a dark den of deception, not a beacon of warm, loving light.

Danny was holding Cleo tightly against his body and was kissing her neck, her lips, and her face. Then he said that he needed to get in the taxi to make his 5:15 p.m. overnight flight to Paris. He gave her one more hug and kiss and said, "Cleo, I really love you; I love you so much," then headed toward the elevator. He had gotten Cleo to promise to come to Paris in April, and if that was not possible, he promised to come back to see her. Prudence had given her the day off to be with Danny. Cleo hesitated between going to the office and working in her apartment. She elected to stay put since it was already almost 3:30 p.m. Anyway, all she had to do was read a manuscript. Toward 9 p.m. that evening, she was feeling a little lonely, so she called Vilemann and asked if he'd like to come for a sleepover.

"I'll be right there."

Cleo exchanged the pictures and toothbrushes and activated her message machine. Danny could never have imagined that his departure would be the occasion for another two-guy day.

Chapter 21

Back in Paris

Sandrine was the first to show up after Danny returned from Boston, and she wanted to know all about the trip and his relationship with Cleo. He told her how wonderful it had been to see Cleo, how nothing had changed between them, how they had enjoyed a dinner with Prudence. Danny also mentioned that he had told Cleo about her and his other friends, how much French he had learned from them, and how they had helped him keep up his morale. He had told Cleo that they'd all get together when she was in Paris. Sandrine leaned over and kissed him on the cheek several times. "You're our sweet American … English teacher." They both laughed. Sandrine reassured Christelle and Aurélie that their Danny was fine, everything was fine.

Danny kept his spirits up whenever he saw Sandrine or Christelle at the cafés. Aurélie came as well, and Danny and Aurélie became better friends. Aurélie, whose name implies something golden, was not only very good-looking and a serious student of English; she combined intelligence with a lovely glittering charm. Danny could see why she and Sandrine and Christelle were such good friends. One afternoon, Aurélie was at the café classroom, and the subject of her weekend came up. She mentioned having spent a three-day weekend with Andrian at a beach in Southern France, a nudist beach. Danny asked her how she felt about being at a nudist beach. She launched into a

174   The BeAst and the Brightest

passionate assertion that men need to "grow up" and accept that women are their equals and have to be respected.

"Whether I have my clothes on or not, I am a person, not just something to leer at or worse. We're not living in caves any longer; at least women aren't. It's time for men to come out of their caves. Modern women want real men, not brutes. Are men so primitive that seeing a woman, clothed or not, is a signal to hassle or, worse, rape her? Why do men hassle women in the street? Aren't they grown-up enough to act on something other than their most basic caveman impulses?"

Danny said she was right and that women like her are leading the fight. Aurélie just looked at him and said, "OK, but it's time men took some responsibility to grow up as well."

Danny was in awe of her and all her feminist friends. He asked her about her boyfriend, Andrian. "He is great; he's a real modern guy, a real man. You know that we really love each other." Danny asked her if she thought he was a modern guy as well. She smiled at him and kissed his cheek, saying, "Is that the kiss you wanted and deserve, 'Caveman.'" In the future, Aurélie would kid him by calling him "Caveman." Many French women were convinced and passionate feminists. Danny thought they were great, just like Cleo.

Danny kept notes of interesting things from his research trips to major French cities, which he included in his letters to Cleo. She told him how happy she was to travel with him through his letters throughout France, and she told him about the books she was working on and some of the terrible manuscripts she had had to evaluate. She told him how much she had enjoyed his visit and how much Prudence liked him. Danny thought that life could only get better once he was back in Boston. He could finish his doctorate, get a job, and live full time with Cleo. Every time he thought of Cleo, he couldn't help but think about the wonderful relationship Christelle and Loïc enjoyed and how happy and free they seemed to be with their parents. He dreamed about being with Cleo in Paris and introducing his new friends to her.

One of the issues that did haunt him was how he and Cleo could both have good careers and be together. Danny's career goal was to get a tenure-track job at a name university. He aspired to be a tenured professor. Danny's friend from Stanford,

Chuck Stimming, was studying at a university near Boston to become a Foreign Service officer. In fact, this friend did get into the government and had a great career ending up in a high position in the Treasury Department. Danny did not want this type of career, which requires either being single or having a spouse who is willing to move since upward movement is dependent upon accepting new posts in countries chosen by the State Department.

Danny would need to get a university position in Boston or New York City where Cleo could have a significant career as an editor on the East Coast. Danny accepted the reality that he might not get a tenure-track job as a professor in one of the major universities in one of these two cities. Tenure-track positions at name universities become available only rarely. Danny was prepared to find other types of work, maybe in a think tank or study center, so that he and Cleo could be together. There were lots of opportunities in Boston and NYC. As an economist he had more flexibility than Cleo, and he was ready to consider different career paths to be with her. Danny thought she was certainly worth it. He would have to change his life's plan, but he could still have a good career, and he and Cleo would always be together. Cleo meant more to Danny than anything else.

Chapter 22

Danny's Gifts

With all the travel and meeting new people in France, the next three months flew by. Danny had been asking Cleo if she could come to Paris to visit him in April, but she said that her work was so pressing that she didn't see how she could manage it. Plus, she had the problem of no accumulated vacation days. She pointed out that their division at Schendler was just Prudence and her and that Prudence was becoming somewhat weaker, so Cleo had to pick up some of her workload as well as her own. None of this was true, but believable since Danny had seen how crippled Prudence was with MS.

Danny started planning another trip to Boston. He asked Cleo for dates that would fit her schedule. Cleo had been sleeping with Vilemann more frequently on weekdays as well as on Friday and Saturday nights, so she didn't think she could just tell him to stay away for a week as she had done in January.

Vilemann was also starting to look for jobs and had found a possibility in the Bay Area as an econometrician at a brokerage company. He seemed very excited by the idea of being in San Francisco. When he mentioned this to Cleo, she said that she could not imagine moving back there. Vilemann said that he understood. He did not express any regret or consternation about the fact that his move to SF would separate them.

178   The BeAst and the Brightest

Cleo's reaction was to become more confused and angry. She wasn't sure if she liked him or loved him, but here was another guy who was about to leave her. When she asked him how he felt about this problem, he answered, "That's life. Life can be tough, but you have to do what you have to do." He was pure Hegel.

Cleo started to realize that he might just be playing his version of The Game with her. Was he with her just for sex, some companionship, and nothing more? She had never thought that a guy could be playing The Game with her and that he might win. She started to realize that one of them—Vilemann or she—would win at The Game. But did it have to be that way? She had experienced ephemeral moments when she thought that she might love Vilemann. She had experienced the same type of fleeting moments with Danny. She wasn't sure how people feel when they are in love. Love seemed like such a big word, so hard to understand, so difficult to feel, so challenging to trust, so ephemeral.

Before he left for France, she thought that she might love Danny; she had thought that he might ask her to marry him before leaving for France. She was hurt that he hadn't mentioned marriage. But was that what she wanted to be, a married woman? Was that the feminist she wanted to be? Had she discouraged Danny by criticizing women who get married? Could she imagine herself married to Danny? If Vilemann got a job in the Bay Area, would he want her to go with him? Would she agree? Cleo had a clear idea of what she called her "feminist self." Could her "feminist self" ever be happily married to a guy, a male?

Cleo had been putting Danny off for two months about coming to Paris and had found reasons why this or that week in April would not work for them to be together in Boston. Danny became increasingly anxious and unhappy about not going in April. Vilemann had been holding out the idea of a trip to SF to check out possible jobs, but he had not settled on a date. Cleo had been hoping to find a week in May when Vilemann would be in San Francisco. Danny got even more anxious when Cleo didn't agree to a date in May. Sandrine and Christelle once again became concerned that Danny was somehow deluding himself about this Cleo. Finally, Vilemann said that he'd be gone the first

Danny's Gifts 179

week of June. Cleo immediately let Danny know that she saw a break in her work that week and that she'd love for him to come to be with her. She tried to write an extra sweet letter, and Danny loved reading and rereading it. January to June without seeing Cleo seemed like an eternity to Danny, but her sweet letters kept coming, and these thoughtful, loving letters reassured him.

Danny once again got a ticket to Boston and showed up at her apartment just an hour after the plane landed. Cleo threw her arms around his neck and gave him really soft kisses. She told him how glad she was to see him again. Danny expressed the same feelings. Cleo poured two glasses of wine, and just as he was sitting down, she saw those pictures of Vilemann propped up on her desk. She quickly grabbed them and shoved them into a desk drawer. She quickly looked for Danny's pictures but could not remember where she had hidden them from Vilemann. She had completely forgotten where she had hidden the picture of her and Danny together in Marblehead.

The affection each seemed to feel for the other led fairly quickly to clothes falling off and lovemaking in her bed. As they separated, Danny kissed her neck, lips, and face and said how much he had missed her and how much she meant to him. "I can't wait to be back permanently and be with you all the time."

Cleo was an expert at finding a phrase that seemed to capture the moment but which camouflaged or twisted the truth. This time, all she could manage was to repeat his innocent phrase, "all the time," and smile at him. Cleo wasn't sure what he meant by all the time, but Danny thought it was crystal clear; they were in love and would live together as soon as possible.

Danny suggested heading to a restaurant where they had eaten once before on Boylston Street. Cleo agreed. Once at their table, Danny started talking about the short time remaining before he returned and how sure he had been that they could get through this year with their feeling for each other intact. Danny mentioned having made some friends in Paris, and how much he wanted Cleo to meet them. He told Cleo he really wanted her to come to Paris to meet these people who had been very nice to him. He talked about how much he had missed her.

Cleo started to see where this was going. Danny was really in love with her and was starting to think about a life together.

180 The BeAst and the Brightest

This had always been her greatest fear: becoming trapped in a marriage. What was she going to do?

Well, she thought, *he is going to be here for seven days. Let's see where this is going. My thoughts will become clearer as the week goes by.*

As they finished dinner, Cleo mentioned getting tired, so they walked back to her apartment. Danny held her hand all the way. Holding hands with a guy was something Cleo had done only rarely. But she had gotten into the habit of holding Danny's hand; holding his hand felt both innocent and intimate. Back in her apartment, Cleo excused herself to brush her teeth, and Danny unpacked his bag. Cleo hid Vilemann's toothbrush and got out Danny's. She had forgotten to deal with this detail.

Danny had brought a lovely lace camisole with matching bikini panties from Paris and a bottle of excellent perfume. He had seen Cleo wear a camisole and pantie set, but the one he had for her was much more elegant and much sexier. As she came out of the bathroom, Danny held out two boxes wrapped as gifts. Cleo opened the first and said how nice he was to give her such an elegant and expensive perfume. The second present, the camisole and bikini panties, surprised her, but she liked them, she liked them a lot. She promised to wear them, but another day. She said that she was too tired to change and suggested they go to bed. She slid the two presents into a drawer in the bathroom and headed to bed.

Once next to each other, Cleo put her head on his shoulder, and he started caressing her gently. Cleo wasn't that tired; she had always enjoyed his caresses and loving words, so she just looked at him and said, "Please don't stop." More caresses led to lovemaking, and despite being tired, Cleo wanted him again. Danny said it felt like they had never been apart. Somehow, Cleo felt the same; he had once again touched something deep within her that he knew how to reach. Cleo felt happy and contented to be once again in his arms, and she told him so.

As he had done in January, he saw his advisor on Tuesday afternoon, and once again, he expressed satisfaction with Danny's progress. He and John Tallington went to the Econ Café, where they talked for an hour or so. Of course, Danny talked a bit about Paris, but a lot more about Cleo. Danny mentioned that when

Danny's Gifts   181

he came back, he was hoping they could get a place together. Danny put up a little notice on the graduate student bulletin board saying that he'd be back in September and was looking for an apartment for two people. Any ideas would be appreciated. John knew that Cleo and Vilemann were still going around together but could not get up the nerve to tell Danny. Anyway, it was none of his business. He did not think that friendship meant having each other's back, especially when a girl was involved, plus he lacked the courage to bring up this explosive news.

Danny and Cleo spent the next few days together having fun, eating out, going to a play at Harvard, and making love. Cleo knew that she enjoyed lovemaking more with Danny than with almost any other guy she had been with, but this both pleased and scared her. She was not going to let her life be defined by sex. She wanted a sex life, but she certainly wasn't going to marry a guy just because she enjoyed him a lot in bed. She told herself that all she really needed was a standard, somewhat sociable guy with a penis, and every guy had one.

Prudence had invited them to her apartment on Wednesday evening. Everybody seemed genuinely happy to see one another. Danny referred to a period when Prudence wasn't feeling good, but she seemed unsure what he meant or what he might be talking about. She just said that she was doing fine. Danny asked her if she had ever been in Paris, and she started talking about a wonderful trip with her first husband. She remembered some places they had visited and even a couple of the restaurants where they had eaten. She seemed transported back to a happier time when she was with a man and healthy. Danny said that he'd like her to encourage Cleo to come to Paris to be with him at least once before he returned. He promised that they'd have a wonderful time in that romantic, lively, and exciting city. Danny said that, "Paris is full of life; you'll love it, and I have great friends you'll love to meet. I talk about you a lot with them and they are dying to meet you." Cleo just listened. In fact, she had never been to Paris, even to see her best friend from school, Nicole.

The next several days seemed to flash by, and the moment arrived when Danny needed, once again, to head to the airport. The evening before he left, he bought a bottle of champagne and asked Cleo to get out those flutes with Cleo and Danny engraved

182   The BeAst and the Brightest

on them. Cleo found them in the back of a kitchen cabinet where she had hidden them from Vilemann, and they each took a flute.

As Danny poured the champagne, he said that he hoped they'd use these to celebrate wonderful events in their lives for many years. "We'll have a wonderful time together in Paris, you know. I really hope you can come." Cleo just said she'd consider it. Then they touched their flutes together, and Danny said, "Here's to our love."

Cleo just said, "That sounds wonderful." They then went out for a special meal and once back at the apartment, they sat down on her couch to enjoy a second flute of champagne. Danny mentioned his gifts, the camisole and panty set, and the perfume, but once again, Cleo deflected his request to put them on. She said that she'd like to keep them for when he comes back permanently.

"Is that an incentive to come back when we're together all the time?" she asked with a big smile. The mention of being together permanently so pleased Danny that he was OK with not seeing her in his sexy gift. Cleo initiated this session of lovemaking. She wanted him to believe in their love.

They had both really enjoyed being together again. Cleo was surprised that her feelings for him were still so strong. She was attracted to him but hated the dilemma that he posed for her. In a way, her confusion seemed to reveal that he could set the agenda for them, that he could dominate their relationship even without trying. He could dominate her simply by loving her. Was she going to let love guide her life? Would love take her off the path she knew she wanted to follow?

She wanted to avoid making any comments or promises to him. She needed a few days to reflect on the week they had just spent together. For several months she had been torn between Vilemann and Danny and maybe between both of them and just restarting The Game. She was good at The Game and knew that finding a guy to play with would be easy, just another shopping trip to the Coop, the public library, or a men's store like Alan Bilzerian. Wasn't that what she needed to do? So, her choices were to restart The Game, Vilemann, or Danny. To understand what she wanted to do, she needed to see Vilemann once he

Danny's Gifts 183

returned from SF but also to find a guy she could enjoy in another hand of The Game. That would help her clarify her ideas.

Cleo's plan of action became clear when Vilemann called her to say that things were going great in San Francisco. He was going to spend another six days out there before coming back to Boston, which gave her enough time to find another guy.

After work, she headed to the Coop, not for a book, but to score. The first day she didn't find anyone even minimally worth approaching, and she remembered George, the porno astrophysicist, but the next day at the Coop, she connected with a senior at Harvard named Joe, a guy five years younger than Cleo, who seemed blown away by how approachable she was. Actually, she had approached him with a big smile. He was tall, muscular, and rather good-looking. He also had a nice voice, so Cleo thought that he'd serve her purpose very well.

Since he lived in a dorm with another guy, she invited him to dinner near her apartment, then as the dinner ended, back to her place. Once in her apartment, she offered him a glass of red wine and poured one for herself as well. Then she excused herself and headed to the bathroom. Danny's sexy camisole pantie set was still in the box in a bathroom drawer. She knew that coming out of the bedroom in this lingerie would set the guy on fire, and she was right. She also put a little of Danny's perfume around her neck and on her breasts.

The guy almost exploded when he saw her. She had to calm him down a bit so they could finish their wine; he drank his glass in a few gulps. The camisole and bikini panties seemed to fly off as in a hurricane. He literally flew at her, pulled her into bed, and shoved himself into her. He was just OK in bed. He sniffed her breasts a lot and said she smelled really good. She decided to make a date for the next day. She needed a little time with this male before Vilemann returned. She wanted this to be a real test of her feelings; she wanted to clarify her strategy.

Senior Joe, as she called him, came over three days in a row. He seemed to think that she was some sort of angel who had fallen his way. He couldn't believe his luck. How was he so fortunate to have attracted such a good-looking and sexy woman? One evening she came out of the bathroom just wearing the camisole, nothing else. On the third day, it was just the bikini panties.

Senior Joe was in heaven. He was on fire. The day before Vilemann returned, she told him that, in fact, she was engaged and her guy was returning the next day from a trip to the West Coast, so they could not see each other ever again. With that, she pushed him out the door. Cleo had not really enjoyed this little tryst. Maybe the guy was too young, or she was tired of The Game, but it hadn't been that great just to have another anonymous guy in bed with her, another *pénis de passage*.

Chapter 23

Cleo's Confession and Submission

Cleo thought the world of Prudence and always wanted to have Prudence on her side. She knew that Prudence believed that Cleo and Danny were in love and were a "wonderful couple," but Cleo wanted to keep her options open, so she decided to take a risk and tell Prudence that, in fact, she had been seeing another guy. Plus, she knew that Prudence didn't ask probing questions or make judgments about her behavior. Cleo didn't want to come out and tell Prudence directly that she was sleeping with someone else or reveal that he was a student friend of Danny's. She just said that she was unsure what might happen between her and Danny and that she had been going around with another guy.

Prudence just listened without reacting outwardly and, much to Cleo's consternation, looked steadily at her for a long time. Finally, Prudence said, "You owe Danny the truth. You must tell him what's going on."

The truth, Cleo thought. *Who knows the truth?*

The truth is often elusive and open to interpretation. Cleo sat there a few minutes expecting Prudence to say something else, but she just looked at Cleo and repeated, "You must tell Danny the truth."

With the revelation that Cleo had another lover, Prudence's belief in Cleo was shattered. She knew that something horrible was going to happen, and the only way to minimize the damage to Danny was for Cleo to tell him the truth. Of course, Prudence did not know anything about Alexander or any of the other guys Cleo had been sleeping with or The Game. Prudence had never doubted that Cleo was a young woman guided by basic morality and honesty. Of course, she wasn't, and now Prudence started to see the real Cleo. Cleo decided not to talk anymore about the new guy she was seeing.

After the three days with Senior Joe, Cleo knew that restarting The Game didn't make sense for her; she needed to be with Vilemann again to sort out her feelings about him and to understand what path her life should take. Vilemann had taken a red-eye flight back to Boston. When he arrived, he told Cleo that he was exhausted and would call her. In fact, he didn't call her for two days. This was part of his strategy always to keep people guessing so that he would have better control over them. Like Cleo, he always intended to win in any relationship and to win when he was ready and on his terms. In fact, he had found a temporary bed partner in San Francisco, a good-looking young boy. He was a carnivore of any available attractive meat. This "guy meat," as he called it, was why he had stayed longer in SF. Arriving back in Boston, Vilemann needed a day or so to reorient to what he thought of as "female meat," plus he liked to keep Cleo guessing as to his intentions.

On one issue he had made his intentions clear; he kept asking her to do new things in bed. She had been sucking him off for some time, but he had never wanted to give her oral sex. She wondered why, but she was relieved. She had never let a guy go down there on her. Sex with him had never been good, but she thought that by doing new things, maybe they'd both have a better sexual experience. When she would give him blow jobs, often he'd climax and then not have sex with her, so she got nothing except frustration. He never seemed to care whether or not she had any satisfaction or pleasure. As well as being all about himself during sex, he had never been tender or loving. After fucking, he never seemed to want just to kiss and hold her or talk with her. He'd turn over on his back, saying he needed to catch his breath and relax. When she tried to kiss him, he would ask her to "Suck my cock and kiss my balls." Or he'd run into the bathroom, saying he wanted to clean her "pussy juice" off his dick.

Cleo's Confession and Submission

When he said this, Cleo thought, *Am I so dirty; is it so disgusting?*

After his return from SF, the first time they got into bed, Vilemann said that they should vary their sex life even more. He said that he didn't want her to get bored with their sex life. "If you get bored, you might dump me," he said.

Cleo felt a moment of panic. *What if he is getting bored and is considering dumping me?*

Had he been with another woman in SF who did things in bed with him that she had not done? Cleo never wanted to lose out to another woman. So, she asked him, "Have you been with another woman?"

"Of course not; you're the only woman I have been with."

Cleo wanted more, so she asked him straight out, "Do you love me?"

"Sure, you are the only woman I am sleeping with. Doesn't that mean anything to you?"

"Sure," she said.

Cleo was only minimally satisfied with his response, but then he said, "The next time I go to SF, I want you to go with me, OK?"

"Absolutely," she gushed.

Her apartment only had one bathroom. She had put his toothbrush away for Danny's visit. She remembered she needed to put his toothbrush back in the holder, so she said, "Let's get ready to go to sleep, but first, I only need a minute, and then it is yours."

She came out of the bathroom with her big deceptive smile and said, "It's all yours."

He came out of the bathroom nude, as usual, and headed to bed, and she once again noted that he was not good-looking at all. Was he ugly? Frankly, yes; his was not a good body. But that is not what had attracted him to her. She brushed her teeth and then slipped on Danny's camisole and bikini panties, plus two squirts of perfume.

So, he wants to vary our sex life. OK, I'll give him this.

Coming out of the bathroom, she said, "I thought you might like this." Vilemann thought she had bought it just for him. Cleo got what she wanted; the camisole and bikini set cut off any further conversation and led right to another round of fucking.

Danny's gift of a camisole and bikini panties had helped Vilemann switch to female meat, Cleo's meat.

Vilemann saw his opportunity, so he asked her if she had ever done anal sex. Cleo was horrified, especially when he said how much he enjoyed it. She wondered how many women had let him do that with them. Had he done that with a woman in SF? Had he lied about not being with another woman? At first, she couldn't imagine letting him do that to her, and she wondered why he would even think about that. In fact, her sex red lines had been moving. She had been agreeing to whatever he wanted sexually, even things that left her feeling somewhat soiled and disgusted. She hadn't refused him anything. His dark charisma had sucked her into a very black place. But anal sex was still a bright red line. So, she said, "Anal sex is a no-no, a big NO-NO!"

As she wondered what was up with him and his sex demands, he started going down onto her lower belly with his mouth, and she thought he might try oral sex with her. She was not ready to agree to that.

"Please don't," she said, trying to be nice about it.

"Don't worry, I don't like it down there," he answered.

The next time they were together in bed, he again went down toward her sex, and she tensed up.

Was he going to do it to her anyway?

Instead, he reached under the pillow where he had stashed a penis-shaped sex toy, which he slipped into her vagina. She felt invaded, shocked, and offended, but she let him slip it into her and push it in and out.

"This will get you wet," he explained.

She felt horrible but did feel the tingle of the vibrator. After playing with it in her, he came into her and did her as aggressively as possible. She was upset and confused, but he offered, "This will get you ready for what I really want: anal sex. You'll love it. I do."

Cleo was almost beside herself but kept telling herself, *It's just sex. I do want to go to SF with him. I really do.*

But anal sex was a giant NO-NO! All she could say was, "Please, let's not talk about that; I can't imagine doing that."

Cleo's Confession and Submission

One weekend night, she slept at his house. Getting ready for bed, she opened the vanity in his bathroom and saw another type of vaginal, penis-shaped vibrator. She was shocked.

Oh my God, is he using that with another woman?

She also saw another object that looked like a sex toy. She had to ask him about these things.

"Look, I don't have another woman. I just prefer the vaginal sex toy we use, that's all. The other thing is for anal sex, but you have refused to do that. Right? Right!"

He was becoming very annoyed, even aggressive, so Cleo just decided to drop it. At least he hadn't continued to ask to let him do it in her butt. She wondered why this was such an issue for him, but at least he had stopped talking about it. Had he used that anal sex toy with other women in the past? She didn't want to ask and didn't want to know.

Cleo didn't want to continue to ask Vilemann whether he was hearing from the people out in SF or how that might influence their relationship. She was encouraged that he wanted her to go on the next trip to SF with him. She thought that a trip to SF would finally help her decide: Vilemann or Danny. Finally, Vilemann gave her an idea about her next step with Danny. For some reason, Vilemann talked again about Hegel and how he, Vilemann, was always a winner.

When Danny got back to Paris, he called Sandrine to arrange to get together. They had a short talk on the phone, during which he told her that he'd had a great trip and that everything was OK with Cleo. Sandrine called Christelle and Aurélie to reassure them. As well as Sandrine and Christelle, Aurélie liked Danny, and didn't want anything bad to happen to him.

The next day, Sandrine told Danny that since Paris was starting to have summer weather, she and some of their friends were going to a pool on the Seine that Saturday, and they wanted him to go with them. They arranged to meet for lunch at a café near the pool at noon on Saturday. Sandrine said, "It's the kind of place you'll need a swimsuit."

Danny was a little amused by the comment about needing a swimsuit and a little perplexed about the idea of a pool on the

190   The BeAst and the Brightest

Seine, but he showed up at the café with a swimsuit. He had just bought it since he hadn't imagined swimming in Paris.

In fact, a floating pool had been in the Seine since 1785 to allow Parisians some relief from the dirt in the city and the summer heat. The pool underwent several major transformations—at one time, royals and Hollywood stars frequented it—but by the 1960s, the clientele was ordinary Parisians. During the 1960s, the women's movement was in full swing in France, and women started wearing monokinis or taking their tops off to do topless sunbathing. French women called it doing "mono."

Danny met everyone at the café Sandrine had mentioned, and they all ordered a light lunch. Danny ordered a croque monsieur, a toasted ham and cheese sandwich made with gruyère, Parmesan, and a little béchamel sauce. This café staple plus a salad made for a nice lunch. Sandrine, Christelle, Loïc, Andrian, Aurélie's boyfriend, and two other of their friends, Thérèse and Jean-Claude, were all together at the café.

After lunch, they all headed to the Deligny. The guys went to the men's changing room, and the girls headed to the opposite side. Big mats were laid out on the deck in two areas that were used for sunbathing—the area around the pool and a mezzanine one floor up. Danny followed Loïc up the stairs to the mezzanine, where they found mats with enough room for the entire group.

As they spread out, here came the girls wearing tiny bikinis and big smiles. Sandrine's was royal blue, Christelle wore a white one, and Thérèse had on a bright red bikini. The girls posed together, saying they were like the French flag: *bleu, blanc, rouge*, (blue, white, and red.) Aurélie was wearing a white two-piece swimsuit with a very abbreviated top that did a poor job of covering her ample and very attractive *poitrine*. Given what she had said about nudism and the need for men to come out of their caves, Danny made every effort not to stare at Aurélie, but she was very attractive.

Danny kept saying to himself, *Be modern, be modern, no caveman stuff*.

They each had a little bag they used for suntan lotion and other things. Danny didn't notice what the other guys were wearing.

Cleo's Confession and Submission

As the girls laid down, they took off their tops. Despite trying to be as "modern" as possible, Danny flinched a bit, but Loïc, Andrian, and Jean-Claude seemed not to notice. It's cultural. They all started talking and enjoying just being in the warm sun after a rainy, cool, or even cold Parisian winter. Danny realized that being European meant learning more than the language; it also implied accepting the culture that the language transmitted.

After a half hour or so, Sandrine said, "Let's all go swimming." Then Sandrine turned to Danny and said, "Guys can swim topless, but we have to put something on to hide ourselves. Isn't that stupid, really stupid? Women have to hide part of themselves at a pool, at most beaches, or anywhere else. Women need to be visible; we need to take our place in society and make some of the rules." Then she continued, "Don't men know we girls, we women all have breasts? Is that such as big surprise? There are too many rules made by men. Men make dumb rules like what women can and can't wear to control them. Do men have to cover up their big ugly bellies when they drink too much beer? Do men have to wear a hat when they are bald? I think women's breasts are a lot better looking than a bald head." She looked straight at Danny as if to get his agreement.

"Absolutely," he responded.

Sandrine continued, saying, "If women made the rules, they would be fairer, more equal."

Aurélie piped up, saying, "Yes, guys with big beer bellies or bald heads should have to cover them up, yes, yes, yes, *oui, oui, oui.*"

Danny said that he thought that women like them were changing things, to which Sandrine said, "Not fast enough." As Sandrine finished her discourse, the girls reached into their bags, took out their tops, and started putting them on. After all, they did want to go swimming. Loïc helped Christelle with hers, but Danny didn't dare help Sandrine or Aurélie. Then they all went swimming. Once back on the mats on that mezzanine, the tops came off again. Sandrine and Aurélie had once again confirmed their feminism with Danny. They were going to be women, feminist women, who help women make progress.

Chapter 24

Cleo Plots to Kill Danny

Cleo's next letter to Danny mentioned that one of the manuscripts she was reviewing had a passage about Hegel, and she wondered what Danny thought of him. Danny's response helped Cleo decide what to do, although Danny could never have guessed what his letter to Cleo would mean to her and him.

She wrote what she had heard Vilemann say repeatedly. Hegel thought that no agreements can exist in society, so there are no rules and no accepted moral guidelines for conduct. What matters is who is most aggressive and most covetous of other people's things. Immoral behavior cannot exist since there are no rules. Society is just the result of a constant war of all against all. There is no objective or societal agreement about right and wrong. What is right is defined by the winners.

Danny wrote back his usual chatty letter to Cleo and then responded to her question about Hegel. Danny said that Hegel captured some aspects of life, but he, Danny, could not imagine living in a totally Hegelian world. He did not see how this led to positive relationships between people, between men and women, or between nations. Imagine seeing a potential rival or enemy in every person you encounter. Imagine thinking about how every person you know could be exploited for some personal benefit. Can you imagine what kind of world it would be if everyone tried to dominate everyone else, to use people? Danny

194 The BeAst and the Brightest

could not imagine how people could live in a world without love, friendship, trust, and fidelity.

"Cleo, I am a lot more Kant than Hegel. Kant believed that we are all free to live our lives as we want with whomever we want as long as we do not hurt other people (my Kantian minimum standard of morality, of civilized behavior in a society). The Kantian moral imperative is to do what is right, to be honest, and to avoid hurting other people. Cleo, it has been a long time since I read Kant, but what I remember is that everybody should act as if they are a law-making member of society. Their choices and values become guidelines for other people, and together, these guidelines define a society. If I treat someone with respect or love, and they do the same, and so on, then treating people right becomes the moral norm for society. Unfortunately, the opposite is also true.

"A key principle for Kant is that a person should never be used as a means to an end. A person should never be exploited for any purpose. Honesty in relationships is paramount. In short, Kant believed that human action is only morally good if it is not for some imagined personal benefit that hurts others.

'Kant also believed that we cannot judge our own behavior because cheating and other sins can be delectable; we can savor the pleasures of deceit, and we can try to betray shame. We must hold ourselves accountable and act responsibly, but we cannot be our own judge without regard to the desires, needs and judgments of other people. We can try to ignore those broadly held concepts of right and wrong, which free us, protect us, and allow us to live in society. We can't want everyone to treat people right but abuse that standard by doing whatever we want. We can't cheat and lie but hope that everyone else is honest. A shared morality allows individual freedom limited only by the injunction against hurting others. When deceit, dishonesty, or violence hurt others, we have stepped outside of society and have committed a wrong; we have done something terribly, morally wrong. The only possible morality is that which is shared based on an ongoing social dialogue that illuminates our shared moral values."

Again, it has been a long time since I read Kant, and I am not a student of philosophy, but I think this is the essence of his

Cleo Plots to Kill Danny

much more sophisticated thought. I certainly believe that being dishonest with someone, hurting them for some personal benefit, real or imagined, is morally wrong. You are such a good person; I'm sure you are much more Kant than Hegel. Did your manuscript mention other philosophers or just Hegel?"

Cleo read and reread this letter. *He is such a baby*, she finally said to herself. *So naïve.*

She did believe that women have to consider every man to be a potential enemy and that the only attitude for a woman, for a feminist, was to play The Game so that she won and he, whoever he was, lost. Equality was a myth used by men to dominate women. She had been right all along to use men for her purposes but not let them know the type of battle that was being fought or that they had an expiration date on them, a date beyond which they would mean nothing to her—when they would be dead to her. Vilemann was right to see society for what it is: a harsh battle for domination and nothing else. Danny's presence in her life had held out a flower, leading her to a garden of love, but she saw it as a poisoned weed that would take over and smoother her feminism in an outdated illusion about love, morality, and honesty.

This meant, of course, that she needed to have an expiration date for Danny. Cleo did not know what that date was, but she knew it needed to be soon, probably before he came back to Boston. She was uncertain about whether Vilemann should have an expiration date. Could two Hegelians live together? Why was she so fascinated by him? Why had she put up with this relationship for so long? The answer, of course, was that she was so much like him. They were both predators who were dishonest and totally immoral sexually. She was more attracted to tough guys and bad boys than guys like Danny.

But there was also a clear difference between them. Vilemann was evil. He did evil things to people to demonstrate his superiority by hurting them. Vilemann was an evil, despicable guy who was a predator to show that he is a winner, the dominant person in any confrontation. He enjoyed hurting people because that showed his strength. He knew that being cruel and brutal was just part of the game, how he would win. He took pride in his barbarity.

Cleo was a predator because she needed a sexual life, but she did not ever want to be dominated by a man. She wanted total freedom to use a guy as long as she wanted to and the freedom to discard him when she was ready. As a feminist, she had to be totally free sexually and liberated from traditional social arrangements, especially marriage. Cleo was predatory to affirm her version of feminism and to develop material for the book of her life. She could not care what happened to her characters. She had to be above morality, above honesty. She had to be totally shameless. This behavior required an ability and willingness to deceive without any second thoughts. If a man got hurt, that was just too bad. If men felt that she was evil or immoral because of the dishonest way she treated them, that was because she was the winner.

With each hand of The Game, she thought she was getting better at it; she thought she was asserting her feminism and confirming her independence. She was just getting more cruel, brutal, and cynical, becoming more like Vilemann.

The most immediate problem was Danny. She needed to kill Danny. She knew that she had it in herself to get rid of Danny, but that was only part of what she had to do. She needed to kill him in a way that would eradicate that part of her that he had been able to touch, the radiance he had lit and brightened in her. His light had become a terrifying threat to her destiny that had to be extinguished.

She now considered the potential for love in her to be a source of vulnerability, a weakness that needed to be exorcised. Danny's light in her had to be snuffed out. She knew that finding out about her and Vilemann would hurt Danny enormously but delivering that blow might not be enough to eliminate her vulnerability to love someone, a weakness she was coming to despise. What would she do if he came back to her offering to forgive her, saying he understood why she had an affair? He would say that he understood that their separation had been too hard for her. He would insist on his love for her and his belief that she loved him, too. She did not want to find herself in that situation. She was not sure she could resist an expression of love from Danny. She needed something else, something that would devastate him totally, that would convince him absolutely that they were through, or even better, that "we" had never existed.

In the vernacular of The Game, she needed to kill him, absolutely destroy him, and exorcise that part of herself that had responded to his love. Or, as she said to herself, *He just found a weakness in me that he exploited to manipulate my feelings.*

Vilemann would be one of the knives she would use to kill Danny; she needed another.

Cheating on Danny with one of his friends, knowing that both the woman he loved and a friend had betrayed him, would be a tough blow, but perhaps not fatal. Their betrayal would feel like a knife right in the heart, but that one knife might not kill him. He might not understand that she had never been his, that she had never loved him, and that neither she nor Vilemann had any respect or concern for him. He had to understand that he was nothing to her, had never been anything to her. Cleo also needed to persuade herself that she had never loved him, maybe never even really liked him very much. She needed to believe he had been nothing to her, just another serial male in her bed, another *pénis de passage*. Cleo knew that she needed another knife, but what could it be? She reread his letter and, with each rereading, became more disgusted by his innocence. "He does not mean anything to me," she said. "We had sex a few times, but that was it. And he left me."

She knew that her relationship with Vilemann would be a critical part of her scheme, but she had to come up with something else. The hour got late, and Cleo had to work the next day, a Monday. She'd just sleep on it. She was avoiding Prudence, who seemed much less open to her since she had revealed that she was with another guy. Cleo knew that Prudence liked Danny a lot, and there was so much about Vilemann that she certainly would not like. Introducing Vilemann to Prudence was out of the question. In fact, Cleo was trying to minimize her interaction with Prudence since she always asked if Cleo had talked with or written Danny telling him the truth.

Cleo kept asking herself what she could do that would devastate Danny and remove the soft spot, no, the weak spot in her that he had touched. What? What? As she sat at her desk thinking about the Danny problem, Alexander poked his head in her office saying, "How about tomorrow evening?"

Cleo absolutely didn't need that diversion from her dilemma but said, "Sure, as always." Later that day, Prudence asked Cleo why Alexander dropped by. Cleo said that he wondered how things were going for her.

Prudence knew better. She had worked for Schendler long enough to know about Alexander's extramarital activities. An affair with a pretty young intern had been the cause of his divorce. Prudence didn't know if he had learned his lesson, but she was starting to doubt it. She had heard about affairs with a number of young women, including a young female employee, but she didn't know exactly what had gone on or what might still be happening. Now, she was seriously concerned about Alexander and Cleo. She just hoped that she was wrong about them, but the fact that Cleo was cheating on Danny worried her. Was she also playing around with Alexander? Was Cleo the type of woman who could maintain a sexual relationship with two men, no, three men at the same time? The thought revolted Prudence, who absolutely did not want to believe Cleo was capable of such a thing.

In fact, the frequency of Cleo's visits to Alexander's office had picked up. What started as a visit to his couch an average of every five weeks or so had shortened to three weeks. Recently, he had invited her two weeks in a row. She was starting to think that she should cash in by asking him for a transfer and a promotion. He couldn't get sex for free; sex was something he had to pay for. She was a professional and needed to climb the corporate ladder at Schendler. He had to pay for sex. Professionals have to be paid. He had to give her something, do something to help advance her career.

Cleo wondered why his requests for visits were becoming more frequent. Maybe his relationship with this Diane had deteriorated. Cleo had wanted to give him more than other women. Maybe she was winning by giving him more satisfying sexual releases than these other women. Maybe she was better-looking and sexier? In any case, she was proud of her success with him. Cleo liked the idea of beating other women and dominating Alexander. But she also felt that too much was going on in her life to deal with doing it with Alexander every two weeks; what if he wanted it every week or more often? Her job and her career meant too much to risk offending Alexander. Dealing with Alexander, Vilemann, and Danny had become too much, so she had to simplify her life. Getting rid of Danny made more and more sense.

Chapter 25
Tallington's Betrayal

Finally, Cleo had an idea involving that guy who was at Danny's dinner party, John Tallington, Danny's best friend. He seemed like the kind of guy who was passive but opportunistic. He seemed to be just another loser, even if like Oliver, an academically smart loser. He'd be easy to manipulate, or so she hoped. That afternoon, after work, she went to Harvard to the Econ Department. She explained that she was a friend of Danny's who was in Paris and wanted to get in contact with one of his friends. The secretary asked what class this friend was in, and Cleo told her that he was a Ph.D. student. The secretary reached into her desk drawer and produced a list of the graduate students in that department. There he was: phone number, address and all, John Tallington, the guy who was at Danny's dinner party. "Thank you very much; you have been so helpful." With that, Cleo headed to her apartment in the Back Bay.

The next afternoon, Cleo called John Tallington. "Hi, John. You probably don't remember me, but we met at a dinner party at Danny's house. Yes, it has been months, a long time. I was just wondering if we could get together for a coffee or something. By the way, have you heard from Danny recently? No? Not since he was here? Well, it would be nice to have a coffee with you. When? OK. Tomorrow afternoon. How about The Coffee Spot near Harvard Square, 5:30 p.m.? OK, it's a date."

202   The BeAst and the Brightest

John was intrigued. Why would Cleo call him? Something must be up. He had known about Vilemann and Cleo for most of the year, but now she was calling him. So, right at 5:30 p.m., he showed up at The Coffee Spot just as Cleo arrived.

"Hi, so nice to see you. It has been too long. Yes, let's sit," she said with a big smile. Once they were at a table and had ordered two coffees, Cleo asked him again if he had heard from Danny since his last visit. "Well, we're in the process of breaking up. Yes, being apart for a year has been too much. I think he may actually have a girl in Paris. That's probably why we could never figure out a time when I could go over there to see him. I really wanted to see him in Paris, but he was never able to come up with dates that worked for him. I think he has another girl. I don't really know, but it seems that way. I just wondered if he said anything to you about a girl over there. Did he ever mention a Brigitte to you? I know Danny tried to fix you up with that girl he invited to that dinner party. Did that ever happen? ... Do you have anyone special? No? Well, I think Danny has found a girl in Paris, maybe that Brigitte. I can't really blame him. A year has been a long time, and I bet that a lot of girls over there would like to have a tall, good-looking American boy. We're not totally broken up, but it is happening, and I'm feeling sort of sad and a little lonely, but what can you do? When he was here, he pretended that everything was OK, but I know it isn't and, well, I know you are his best friend, and he might have told you something about his girlfriend over there. No? Well, I've learned that he is good at pretending, at dissimulating, you know, hiding the truth."

Was Cleo telling him the truth? Of course, based on what he had heard, he was certain that Cleo had been sleeping with Vilemann, so maybe they both had cheated. Maybe Cleo had cheated with Vilemann and Danny with this Brigitte. Then it hit him: If she had slept with Danny and Vilemann, why wouldn't she sleep with him? If she was breaking up witih Danny, maybe she was breaking up with Vilemann as well.

Tallington had not had a girlfriend or sex for the last two years and was dying to have a girl in bed with him. Of course, he had not dreamed of having a girl as attractive as Cleo. He had never been that lucky, but maybe. If she were telling the truth,

Tallington's Betrayal

he might "get lucky with her." If she were lying about breaking up with Danny, he could always use her deceit as a screen to protect himself, to excuse himself. He could always tell Danny, "She deceived me."

John knew that she had contacted him for a reason. Was she looking for solace following a breakup with Danny or with Vilemann, or did she want another affair? Maybe she had broken up with both Vilemann and Danny. John didn't dare ask Cleo more questions about her relationship with Vilemann or Danny. He certainly didn't want to mention to Cleo that he had known for months that she had been sleeping with Vilemann. In fact, Cleo didn't know that Tallington knew about Vilemann and her.

In any case, John thought that he could be the beneficiary if she had broken up with either Vilemann or Danny. But what about Vilemann? Everybody knew that he was a fairly mean, low-minded, but academically smart guy. Were they still together? John thought it better not to ask, just to see where things went. Cleo kept playing the part.

"I'm just feeling a little lonely and want to have somebody to talk with … and I remembered you as a really nice guy." Cleo was watching John carefully to see any hint of what he might do, but it seemed that he was just following along with her like a little puppy dog.

She thought, *Men can be so stupid, so weak.*

Taking the initiative again, she said, "Maybe we can get together for dinner sometime? Yes? Great. Tomorrow."

They easily agreed on where and when. Cleo reached over the table putting her hand on the table palm up. John took it and gave it a little squeeze, saying that tomorrow would be great. As they stood up to leave, Cleo put her arm around him, gave him a little kiss on the cheek, and said, "I thought you'd understand," which was another of her stock statements that said whatever the person she was with wanted it to mean.

Cleo invited Tallington to a restaurant in the North End where she and Danny used to go. She knew that Tallington would not know that she and Danny had considered it one of their regular places, a place where "We like to go," as Danny used to say. Eating there with Danny's best friend was another step toward liberating herself from Danny—a way of advancing her betrayal of that guy that made her feel powerful. What a clever, brilliant idea.

During dinner in Boston, Cleo didn't say anything about Danny, just how nice it was to be with John. "You know, John, at that dinner, I could not imagine why you didn't have a girlfriend; you're such a nice, smart, attractive guy."

The flattery was almost too obvious, but John loved it. He resisted asking himself why she was interested in another of Danny's friends instead of one of the hundreds of thousands of guys in Cambridge who could have provided emotional solace or a penis at least. In any case he didn't want to know the answer to that question. He saw a chance to have sex with her, and that is all that mattered to him.

He started thinking, *My God, I do have a chance with her. She is almost throwing herself at me.*

He thought that since she had slept with both Danny and Vilemann and maybe others, getting her into bed with him might be easy. The deal was done when she invited him for a drink at her apartment. She followed her script. A glass of wine, kisses on the cheek, turning to open her blouse a bit to show more of her breasts, then leaning over for that first kiss. "Can you stay with me tonight? I can't bear to see you leave me. I don't want to be all alone."

Then she disappeared to the bathroom for a quick change into Danny's gift of a camisole and bikini pantie set, plus the perfume. In five minutes, the camisole came off, and she led him toward the bed. Then she used the line about not wanting to take off her panties … she wanted him to help her take them off. He helped her lower those panties. Cleo was proud of herself for having found another clever way to betray Danny. Tallington now belonged to her. Danny was starting to be killed.

As John came into her, he suspected that he was entering not only into her body but into a tangle of lies; he just didn't know exactly what lies or about whom. He knew he was doing something terribly wrong, terribly morally wrong, but he simply didn't have the strength to resist. He had always known that he was not brave, but his moral cowardice was now on full display. He only knew that the moment he came into her, his life would change, as well as Danny's. He knew that he was betraying his

Tallington's Betrayal

best friend, but he was too weak and cowardly to do the right thing, so he just enjoyed the moment as much as he could and tried not to think too much about what was happening, but he was a little scared.

Tallington had forgotten the words of Aristotle, "Courage involves pain, and is justly praised; for it is harder to face what is painful than to abstain from what is pleasant." Or maybe he knew that but didn't have the backbone to abstain from sexual pleasure with Cleo. He liked screwing Cleo. He was proud that he had bedded her. Maybe he was a more attractive guy than Danny. Danny had lost her, maybe. Tallington thought that he could be the winner, maybe even win her love. Males love to compete for women.

Cleo looked at him totally nude as he was falling asleep and gave him the nickname Useful Idiot #2. Tallington was of no interest to her. Tallington reminded her of a waiter at a banquet who, when cleaning up, sees some really good wine left in a bottle. He pours himself a glass and takes a dessert left untouched in the center of the table. As he enjoys the wine and dessert, he imagines that he is the type of person who was invited to the banquet. He looks around with the inflated, empty arrogance of a small-minded loser as if to say, "Look at me." But when the manager comes in and sees him sitting down and drinking, the manager orders him to get back to work. Drinking someone else's wine confirmed to him that he was clever and not a total loser. The wine told him that he, too, was worth something, even while disproving his worth and demonstrating his lack of integrity. Even though he knew that he was not worth that much, he was still pleased to drink that wine. He was a loser, a social idiot just like Oliver, but a useful idiot because his betrayal of his friend would enable Cleo to rid herself of what it was that kept her writing to and thinking about Danny.

Tallington's penis had become Cleo's second knife. She wanted Danny to be dead to her; otherwise, his sweetness and sincerity would continue to threaten her. Tallington was going to help Cleo kill his best friend. He had become an accomplice to murder and rape.

He understood that maybe he had not attracted Cleo, that maybe she had no real interest in him. Maybe he was there to serve her purpose, whatever that was. He lacked the balls to ask what game she was playing; he just went along with her plan. He never imagined having the strength of character to write to Danny or call him to ask if he and Cleo were still together or if his friend was suffering because of the breakup. Tallington didn't ask because he really wasn't Danny's friend, and he didn't know the meaning of friendship. He didn't dare to ask Danny anything, fearing the response.

Their first night of sex with Tallington was just three weeks after Danny had headed back to Paris. It was now the end of June. Cleo knew that Danny was probably coming back early in September, and she wanted to execute her plan at least a month before he was to return. That would give everybody an opportunity to adjust to the new reality and for emotions to calm down. That meant she had to go to Paris to do the deed no later than the first week of August. Given that schedule, she had to put up with sex with Tallington for maybe four weeks or so, but she knew how to separate sex and her emotions and feelings; she had been doing that with Alexander for many months and had done it with innumerable other guys. Tallington was not even there for some short-term sexual pleasure; he was there for one purpose—to help kill Danny.

She knew that dumping him would be easy. He was the kind of shallow person who wants to be seen as honest and decent but is too weak to do the right thing when faced with a challenge, the choice between doing the right thing and committing a mortal sin. Cleo knew that he would be easy to discard and forget.

Trying to diminish his culpability, he told himself that maybe he was just making a mistake. But was betraying your best friend just a mistake? He was becoming an accomplice to murder and rape, which are crimes, moral sins, not mistakes. Christians think that coveting a neighbor's woman is a cardinal sin, but maybe Tallington didn't remember that, or maybe he is not Christian. Maybe he was totally immoral or just too weak and arrogant to do the right thing.

Chapter 26

Preparing for Paris

Cleo would need to be in Paris the last week of July or early August. She told Vilemann that she was going to Paris to see her friend Nicole and finally deal with Danny. Vilemann had seen Danny's letters in one of Cleo's desk drawers, so he knew that they were still writing to each other, which is why he was still with Cleo. He wanted to own her. He wanted Danny to feel the extent of his loss; he wanted Danny to discover that he was screwing "Danny's girlfriend."

When Vilemann challenged Cleo about Danny, she excused herself by saying that he was still writing her and begging to get back together when he returned to Boston. She did not tell him that she had continued her sweet correspondence. In fact, she had just sent him a treacherous letter meant to delude him and set him up for his assassination.

Vilemann knew very well that she had started sleeping with Tallington since he had been stupid enough to tell other grad students in economics about him and Cleo. Tallington couldn't help but brag about his conquest. Of course, this cemented Cleo's reputation as a whore among the male econ grad students. If Tallington could have an affair with her, they were sure anyone could bed her. Vilemann thought it better to keep this knowledge to himself for his kill with Cleo. Cleo thought that she had been clever to assign each guy to regular days of the week. Vilemann got the weekends. Tallington was Tuesday and

208   The BeAst and the Brightest

sometimes Thursday night. Sometimes, she had dinner with one of them, except when Alexander held her up for an hour or two. Given his assigned schedule, Tallington was almost certain that Cleo was still sleeping with Vilemann, but he was too happy to have a chance to screw Cleo and spend some nights with her to raise the issue of Vilemann. Tallington knew he was part of something totally immoral, sordid, and deceitful, but also deceived himself by dreaming that Cleo would fall in love with him. Could he really believe that she would fall in love with him, even as she continued to sleep with Vilemann?

Vilemann told Cleo that he was concerned that Danny would come back extremely angry and blame him for everything. He asked Cleo point-blank whether she had slept with anyone else, someone who could be called out to take some of the blame. He was hoping that she'd lie about Tallington, and she did. Cleo said that a brief affair had occurred with Tallington just after Danny left.

"That was just before we met," she said.

Vilemann almost laughed in her face since he knew she was lying but thought that this would be perfect. Danny would be terribly offended that his best friend, Tallington, had betrayed him by sleeping with Cleo, especially since Danny would believe her assertion that Tallington was the first of her bedmates. Vilemann was overjoyed to hear her lie about Tallington. Cleo thought that she only had to hide when her affair with Tallington occurred and to imply that it was over. Cleo feared that Vilemann would be incredibly angry to learn that she was sleeping with someone else, not just him. Cleo thought that he might dump her if he knew that she was sleeping with Tallington as well as him. She felt comfortable deceiving him since she knew that lies can work and believed that she had the ability to manage more than one lover. Of course, Vilemann didn't care since he was just playing with Cleo to hurt Danny.

Cleo told Vilemann that she wanted a few days in Paris with Nicole; then she'd go to Danny's apartment and tell him about her and Vilemann. She'd tell Danny that she'd be back in Paris the next week. After a week to reflect on what he had just heard, he might get his hopes up, so telling him about Tallington would be especially devastating. She was sure that two blows spaced

Preparing for Paris 209

out by a week would kill any trace of Danny in her and would convince him that it was absolutely over with her or that they had never had a relationship of any value to Cleo.

Vilemann got excited by this plan and told Cleo that she had to be brutal and definitive with Danny. She could not explain herself or get into why these things had happened. She just had to hit him and leave. Vilemann wanted Danny to feel like Cleo had done a "drive-by shooting." Cleo agreed. Part of how Cleo played The Game was to hit hard and never explain or justify herself. She didn't care about avoiding hurt feelings. Danny would be the next to be killed. A lot of blood had to be spilled; Cleo wanted to see Danny's blood flow. His flowing blood would cleanse her of the weakness he had exploited in her.

Vilemann insisted on going to France with Cleo. She thought that he wanted to support her and see that she didn't falter. She thought that his desire to go with her was another proof of his commitment to her, but really, he had other interests. He agreed that Cleo should spend some time alone with Nicole before killing off Danny. While she was in Paris, he'd go to Cannes, a place he was excited to visit. He mentioned having been in Paris but never on the Riviera and thought that spending some time down there in the summer seemed preferable to Paris.

He offered to arrange for a hotel he had heard about in Cannes and suggested that after the first encounter with Danny, she could take a train to meet him. Cleo thought that having some time with Vilemann after killing off Danny and being in a relaxed environment on the Riviera would help clarify her thinking about Vilemann, so she went along with this plan, which allowed her to achieve her primary objectives: get rid of Danny, see Nicole, and maybe get a better sense of what she wanted to do with Vilemann. Another advantage of this plan was that Nicole and Vilemann would not meet each other. Cleo didn't believe Nicole would like Vilemann. His suggestion to come to Cannes to be with him seemed to be proof of his interest in living with her.

After a few days with Vilemann in Cannes, she could go back to Paris, deliver the second blow to Danny and meet Vilemann at the airport for the trip home. Vilemann was going to take a plane straight from the south the morning of their afternoon flight to

Boston. So, he'd just meet her at the airport. That gave him an extra night in Cannes, rather than coming to Paris to be with Cleo. That suited her since she didn't want to have to deal with him immediately after her second encounter with Danny. He'd insist on a blow-by-blow account of what happened and want to know how much Danny had suffered. Cleo was not up for that.

Nicole was thrilled to get Cleo's letter and immediately called her to say how excited she was to finally be with her friend in Paris. Cleo told Nicole that the third day in Paris she was going to see Danny to break up with him. Nicole insisted that Cleo should stay with her since things were that bad with Danny.

Nicole had gotten together with Danny at a sidewalk café, just to catch up right after he returned from seeing Cleo the first week of June. Danny had told Nicole that they had a wonderful time together in Boston and talked about how happy he would be to wrap up in Paris and be back with Cleo. He talked about how much in love they were and how he hoped they would live together when he returned to Boston. So, when Cleo told Nicole that she was going to break up with Danny, Nicole knew that it was going to be traumatic. She knew that Danny was profoundly in love. She'd need to do something to support Cleo, who, she thought was breaking up with Danny despite the love they had shared, and that meant so much to Danny.

Nicole assumed that Cleo was madly in love with someone else. How else could she understand why Cleo would be breaking up with Danny? Nicole believed that the breakup would be tough on both Danny and Cleo, very tough, since Nicole believed that Cleo had loved Danny. Of course, she had never loved Danny or anyone else, or at least she didn't remember loving Danny even momentarily.

The next week or so Cleo got excited about killing off Danny and was looking forward to being in Paris with Nicole. Seeing Nicole was important to her, but not as much as killing Danny. With Danny gone, she would be freed to focus on Vilemann and Alexander. She could move on with less baggage.

Cleo knew that she was not only getting rid of Danny, but she was also closing off the possibility of a life with someone she really loved. But what was love, anyway? Wasn't it just a

Preparing for Paris 211

form of domination? She knew that once she had killed Danny, there was no turning back. She'd made her choice. She had to reject the softer approach to life that Danny exemplified and opt for Vilemann's war of all against all. Cleo kept thinking about how her mother had been dominated by her father and how she had never fought for domination over him. Vilemann was right: There are winners and losers, and she was going to be a winner. Danny would have to lose.

These weeks were further complicated by Alexander, whose demands became more frequent. He was also trying to get Cleo to do sexual things with him, starting with sucking him off. This was not the time for this type of pressure. She couldn't imagine turning him down and putting up with the possible impact on her career just as she had to deal with Danny, so she relented. She feared that other women were doing this with him, and he would not take kindly to a refusal by Cleo. She did what he wanted. She took his penis in her hands and led it into her mouth. He put his hands on her head and rocked her back and forth to stimulate himself. She didn't like being handled, but OK, she had to go along with what he wanted. She was used to doing this with Vilemann but was surprised that it was less disgusting to do this with Alexander than she had imagined. He seemed thrilled that they had gone beyond the missionary position to oral sex and wondered what else he could get her to do sexually with him. He was enjoying himself and wanted to get as much pleasure and fun as possible. He thought that Cleo would go along with almost anything he asked. After a few minutes, Alexander pushed her back onto the couch and came into her. He wanted everything he could get. He considered her to be his.

Her more frequent visits with Alexander had been noticed by both Prudence and especially by Oliver, who had never gotten over how Cleo had dumped him. He had been really hurt, and as Cleo's early evening visits to the sixth floor became more frequent, Oliver's anger and humiliation fueled his burning need to know exactly what was going on. Prudence, too, understood what was probably happening. Now that she knew that Cleo was cheating on Danny, she was much more willing to believe the worst.

Chapter 27
Cleo and Nicole

On the flight over, Vilemann kept pressing Cleo to be tough, to be brutal. Finally, she had had enough. "Just shut up about Danny, will you! I'll handle it. Just go to Cannes and have a good time, and I'll see you down there. I don't want to hear anything more from you about Danny."

Then Vilemann pressed Cleo about Tallington. Did he know that Cleo was going to rat him out? Had they agreed never to let Danny know about them? Cleo again told Vilemann to "Just shove it."

In fact, she and Tallington had never discussed how to handle Danny. She didn't want him to know what she would do, and he was too scared of the answer to ask. Tallington panicked when Cleo told him that she was going to Paris to see a friend, Nicole. Tallington wanted to ask Cleo if she was going to see Danny but was too frightened to ask. He really didn't want to know the answer. Was she going to tell Danny about Vilemann or just about him or neither of them? Was it true that they were in the process of breaking up? Was Danny OK with that? Was it true that Danny had a girl in Paris, or was that just a lie Cleo had used to manipulate him in some way? Did Cleo really like him, or was she just using him?

He started to realize that his dream that she might fall in love with him was a dirty, shallow mirage. The ugly reality of his utter cowardice and abject social stupidity reflected right back into his eyes. Of course, he had never looked the truth right in the face.

Tallington did not understand that friendship meant watching a friend's back, or maybe he did but didn't have the guts to do the right thing. Now, he was trapped since he had not said anything to Danny about Vilemann and Cleo on either of Danny's visits to Boston. Plus, he was sleeping with Danny's girlfriend; he was betraying his best friend. He was trapped by his own failures, and he knew it. He was not going to have any influence over events; he'd just have to accept whatever happened. One thing he was sure of—other people were more responsible than he was. He'd say, "She deceived me." He knew that this flimsy, pathetic excuse was just a fig leaf, but it was all he had. Of course, he was happy to deceive himself with the facile lies he told himself.

When Cleo came into her office to ask for 10 days off to go to Paris, Prudence felt a moment of panic and despair. She feared the worst but granted Cleo the time off. In her usually straightforward way, Prudence asked, "Cleo, does Danny suspect anything? Does he know anything? Have you been honest with him?" Of course, Prudence did not know anything about Tallington. She thought Cleo's cheating had been limited to Vilemann and maybe Remington. She did not know that Vilemann was a close colleague of Danny's in the graduate program.

Prudence said bluntly that Cleo had to do everything possible to avoid hurting Danny and that she should express regret, no, remorse, for what had happened and ask for his forgiveness. Cleo had no intention of doing any of that. She felt no regret, no remorse, and absolutely no shame. Why should she? This was her story, not Danny's. She was the sole author of her story, and Danny was just another minor character. Of course, she could not reveal to Prudence what she really felt—which was nothing for Danny. She wanted to wad him up and throw him into her trash can just like the others. There would be many other guys, many other plot twists, and many other rewrites. Why was this one any different? And anyway, Prudence had no right to tell her what to do or how to live. Society's rules of morality and decency did not apply to her.

To deflect from Prudence's assertion that she should be kind to Danny and forthcoming with him, Cleo said that they were in

Cleo and Nicole 215

the process of breaking up, and she thought everything would be all right. "He'll be fine. In fact, I think he has a girl in Paris."

Prudence did not believe a word she said. Prudence was starting to recognize Cleo for the cynical, immoral liar she was. Prudence has a sense of foreboding. Ugly, destructive, sordid things were about to happen. People were going to be hurt, really hurt.

Cleo packed carefully to go to Paris. She took Danny's camisole and bikini panties, Danny's perfume, the fancy dress she had bought in SF, a formfitting, one-piece swimsuit for Cannes, standard clothes to wear when she saw Danny and Vilemann, and one set of travel clothes. As she looked around her apartment to see if she had forgotten anything, she noticed the two crystal flutes in the very back of a kitchen cabinet that Danny had given her with "Cleo and Danny" engraved on the side. She had not used them since Danny's visit because of that engraving.

"These are nice crystal flutes, but with that stupid engraving, I have to get rid of them. Another of Danny's stupid, romantic things. What a waste." She threw them into her metal trash can, where they exploded into tiny shrapnel. Crystal doesn't break; it explodes into tiny shards with edges that slice and sharp points that can puncture skin easily.

She thought, *I need to be careful when I take out this trash; I don't want those things to cut me. A cut from Danny's crystal would really hurt.*

To protect herself, she threw all of Danny's letters into the trash on top of those crystal shards. Danny was two steps closer to being killed.

As her plane droned on and on over the Atlantic, she kept rehearsing her lines and thinking about how she would stonewall him, not respond to him at all, not give him anything. She feared she would hear something about "us" and about "love." She was ready to refuse to discuss their relationship or even recognize that they had ever had one. To rid herself of him, she had to believe, no, she had to act as if he had never meant anything to her. He had to be dead to her as if he had never lived.

There could be no discussion of a breakup. Nothing she said could imply a breakup. She wanted to refuse to believe or acknowledge that they had ever had a relationship. No

216 The BeAst and the Brightest

relationship meant that a breakup was not necessary. Actually, a breakup discussion would be inappropriate if they had never really had a relationship. She would just reveal who she was sleeping with and tell him to come to terms with it. She told herself that she also could only use the names of her bedmates, Vilemann and Tallington. She could never mention that she knew that they were Danny's friends. There could be no admission that Danny's girlfriend and his friends had betrayed him. She also had to avoid any mention of who initiated contact with his two friends or any mention of any feelings between them and Cleo. All Danny would know is that they were sleeping together.

She believed she could tell Prudence that he, too, had "moved on" and that their encounter in Paris was amiable. No one was going to get crumpled up; no one was going to get hurt. No matter how many times she told herself this lie, she could not convince herself even to pretend to believe it. Vilemann made things worse when he kept insisting that she be tough, brutal, and cruel. She told him, "Just shut up!"

Once Cleo told Vilemann to shut up on the way to Paris, they turned away from each other and read something. As the plane landed, Vilemann said, "Well, that was a smooth flight. Let's get our luggage, and I'll be off to Cannes."

Vilemann had never been good at small talk except about himself, and Cleo was happy to get rid of him and focus on Nicole and what she had to do to Danny. The luggage appeared quickly, and they both rushed to get into the taxi line. Cleo got the first cab, saying, "OK, I'll see you in four days in Cannes. Enjoy yourself." She had forgotten the see-you-soon kiss, and Vilemann hadn't asked for one. He was too eager to get to Cannes.

When she arrived, Nicole was at the front door of her apartment with a big smile and an expression that showed that she was genuinely thrilled to see her childhood friend. The two girls hugged, smiled happily at each other, giggled, and went into Nicole's apartment. Nicole lived in a huge apartment by any standards, particularly in a very expensive city like Paris. Not only was the apartment very big, but it was also beautifully furnished. The entrance room led to a huge salon with multiple soft leather couches facing a large bay window. The ceiling was at

Cleo and Nicole

least 12 feet high. On one side of the room was a huge, floor-to-ceiling window. No one could miss the view: The Eiffel Tower seemed to be right across the street. Cleo knew that Nicole's mother was really rich and that she had married an even richer Italian. Cleo realized that Nicole was living in splendor.

Nicole showed Cleo the way to a large bedroom with the biggest bed Cleo had ever seen, "I had it made custom. Isn't it great? We can both sleep here; there is so much room."

On the wall behind the bed hung four large black-and-white acrylic panels, each showing a man and a woman intertwined in different positions. "Do you like the graphics? That's me and one of my friends; the guy I posed with also did the graphics; he's very talented." They weren't pornographic, but they were fairly explicit, although in black-and-white. We had such fun doing them."

Cleo thought, *I bet you did.*

The bedroom led to a large bathroom, all in marble. On one side, a Jacuzzi large enough for four to six people was hot and ready to go. Nicole said she kept the Jacuzzi on all the time to be able to jump in whenever she wanted. Next to it was a large dry sauna. Nicole said she didn't like wet saunas; they smell. Then they went to another bedroom with its own beautiful bathroom, all in marble. There was a large stand-up shower compartment, and Nicole said, "Do you remember our sweet showers in Hawaii? Cleo nodded. Nicole said that Cleo could have stayed in that bedroom if she had come with somebody, but "Wouldn't it be more fun to sleep together just like when we were so young?"

Between a large, professionally equipped kitchen and an elegant dining room, Nicole showed Cleo a little space with a spiral staircase that led to a large greenhouse on the roof. Cleo realized that Nicole had the penthouse, not just an apartment. The greenhouse was filled with beautiful tropical plants. Nicole said, "Don't these plants remind you of Hawaii? We can have breakfast here among all these plants, just like in Kaua'i."

Cleo was tired and jet-lagged after the overnight flight, so Nicole helped her unpack. Then, Cleo got under the covers for a nap. She slept for almost two hours. As Cleo woke up, Nicole said, "Hey, I bet you're hungry; let's go get something to eat."

218   The BeAst and the Brightest

Cleo got dressed and the two friends walked over to an area near the Rodin Museum just a couple of blocks away. Arriving at a restaurant on the corner, the manager, a very handsome, muscular Italian in his mid-30s, came out and hugged Nicole, gave her three bises on the cheeks, and, looking at Cleo asked, "Who is the beautiful friend?" Nicole introduced Cleo, who was led to her seat by this very accommodating, attractive manager.

They ordered salade Lyonnaise, something new to Cleo, which she loved. The salad consisted of a mix of salade frisée and lardons. The salad was topped with a soft-boiled egg and seasoned with a wonderful vinaigrette. They ate the salad with traditional French baguette bread, then some delicious cheese and a glass of red wine. To finish, they had little espresso coffees.

Nicole put her arm around Cleo's shoulders and said, "You can't imagine what seeing you here means to me; you are still my best friend in the whole world." Cleo just smiled at her. As they left the restaurant, the manager ran over and gave Nicole a big hug and kisses on the cheeks. These were real kisses, not just air bises. Then he looked at Cleo and asked, "*Permesso*. Is it all right?"

Cleo said, "Yes," so she, too, got a big hug and real kisses on the cheeks. The manager thanked them for coming, and Nicole said she'd be back. The manager said, "Please, please. Don't forget to bring this beautiful friend."

Cleo thought, *Wow, I'm really in Paris. This is nothing like Boston.*

She also wondered if Nicole had a relationship with this manager that went beyond eating in this restaurant. Cleo was still too tired and distracted by all these new things to notice that Nicole had not paid. The check would be added to a tab that her stepfather would handle.

Nicole grabbed a taxi to take Cleo to a fancy part of Paris, not far away, on the other side of the Seine, to visit several art galleries whose owners she knew and where Nicole and Cleo looked at some terrific art pieces.

No kitsch here, Cleo thought.

Nicole said she wanted to have a nice dinner with her, just the two of them, and she knew that, even with her nap, she'd get

Cleo and Nicole   219

tired early—jet lag and an overnight flight. They had a couple of hours to kill at Nicole's apartment before going to dinner, so Nicole suggested a relaxing Jacuzzi and sauna. Cleo thought that sounded great.

Both girls quickly undressed in that huge bedroom and jumped totally nude into the Jacuzzi, which was hot but not boiling. Cleo could feel every part of her body relaxing. Nicole laid back and talked about Paris and the next day's activities. Every few minutes, she'd splash Cleo with water by kicking her legs up and down. Cleo noticed that Nicole's groin was shaved, no pubic hair.

"My boyfriend, Bepe, says he likes the look, and it's better for oral sex. I had it done with a laser. Unfortunately, Bepe is in Rome for a few days, but if you are able to come back after Cannes, you can meet him. I would love for you to meet him."

Cleo had never wanted to let a guy go down there and certainly never imagined getting shaved or having her pubic hair taken off by laser, so she was a little shocked, but she was in Paris, after all.

Cleo thought, *European hedonism*, and wondered if Nicole had let that Italian guy from the restaurant do anything down there with her.

Cleo tried to put these thoughts out of her mind and just relax in that delicious hot bubbling water. Overall, Cleo was thoroughly enjoying being with her friend and relaxing. After the Jacuzzi, they spent 20 minutes in the sauna, which further relaxed Cleo. All the stress of the flight was disappearing. Nicole was giving her best friend the best possible welcome to Paris.

That evening, Nicole had them picked up at her apartment by a driver in a big Mercedes, "My stepdad's chauffeur—he left for Rome this afternoon, so the car is ours."

The chauffeur dropped them off at what seemed to be a little neighborhood bistro. In fact, it was a bistro run by one of Paris' three-star chefs whose super-fancy restaurant was just down the street. "I thought this would be perfect for your first night in Paris." It was.

They toasted each other with two flutes of champagne. Cleo had roast duck breast, which was the most succulent meat she

220   The BeAst and the Brightest

had ever tasted. It was roasted with green olives and served with wild rice and an outstanding red Burgundy. The girls then finished the meal with a pear poached in wine for dessert. They talked for a while over coffee until Cleo started to feel the jet lag, so Nicole said, "Let's go."

This time, Cleo noticed that they hadn't paid; they never got the check. "Oh, there is a tab my stepdad handles each month."

Cleo thought, *How convenient.*

Nicole showed up for bed completely nude, and Cleo noticed that she had filled out in all the right places. Nicole was a very good-looking woman. Beautiful? No, but very, very attractive. Cleo thought it might be fun to sleep with her friend in the nude, but no funny business; she was beyond that.

Nicole laughed, "Of course not; we're grown women now. We like guys, right?"

As Cleo pulled off Danny's camisole and bikini panties to get nude, too, Nicole said, "Wow, I bet you can inflame guys with those. Who gave you such beautiful and sexy lingerie? I bet it was somebody you are in love with, right?" Cleo didn't answer.

Once in bed, Nicole cuddled up with Cleo, saying, "Isn't it wonderful to have a friend for so long, someone you love and totally trust?" Then Nicole asked, "Do you remember being together in Hawaii in that wonderful hammock at the beach in Kaua'i?" Cleo thought for a moment about the task she had assigned herself in just two days. She reminded Nicole that she was going to break up with Danny and then go to Cannes.

The next day, Cleo and Nicole woke up about the same time, rested and ready for a day in Paris together. Nicole said they could have breakfast in the greenhouse. There was a little table with rattan chairs like at Parisian cafés. Nicole said, "Eating among all those tropical plants will remind you of those breakfasts we had in Hawaii, except for the wonderful pineapple."

They enjoyed a quick Parisian breakfast of a tartine—a baguette smeared with *beurre échiré,* France's most delicious butter, and the best orange marmalade Cleo had ever tasted— plus coffee and some slices of wonderful tropical fruit. Then they got dressed and were ready for the first full day together in many years. The Mercedes and driver were at their disposal, so they jumped in the back seat and headed to the Musée d'Orsay.

Cleo and Nicole

This museum is housed in a Beaux-Arts railway station built between 1898 and 1900. The entire building was completely reconfigured as a museum to display items from the 19th century, including many of the most famous Impressionist paintings. Cleo loved seeing these masterpieces but also the amazing sculptures, period furniture, and other works of art.

After a light lunch at a café, the girls headed to the Quai Branly, a museum of art made by "primary" people in Africa, Asia, and the Pacific islands. Again, Cleo could hardly grasp all the masterpieces she saw and the amazing modern design of the museum itself. Cleo thought that there was no way to top off a day like she had just experienced, but changed her mind when she heard where they were going next.

They headed in the Mercedes to an organ concert at the Saint-Chappelle, a magnificent royal chapel in the Gothic style constructed between 1238 and 1248. The shimmering-stained glass was so extensive that it covered the walls all the way up to the stone ceiling. Cleo was stunned by the beauty of the chapel as well as the wonderful organ recital. She wondered why she had never heard of all these treasures and fascinating places in Paris. This city offered a lot more than the Eiffel Tower.

The Mercedes took them back to Nicole's apartment to rest before heading out to dinner. Both girls laid down on the bed for a 20-minute nap. Before going to sleep, Nicole told Cleo, "I really love you. Friendships that last are the most wonderful." Cleo just smiled at her.

Cleo put on the black dress she had bought in SF, and Nicole said, "You look great, very Parisienne." Dinner was at a restaurant, La Crémaillère, first opened in 1900, that had conserved the original Belle Epoque décor. The restaurant offered classic French food and a performance, including a French cancan on the dance floor right next to the tables. The four cancan girls got several of the male guests to put cancan skirts over their pants and dance with them. The guys were incredibly awkward, which made everyone laugh. Nicole had arranged for Cleo to be chosen for the last triumphant cancan dance. The dancers gave her a cancan skirt to slip on over her dress, and they all kicked and kicked to the famous cancan music by Offenbach. Cleo was no professional cancan girl, but she did a lot better than the guys.

222   The BeAst and the Brightest

Everyone laughed and clapped as Cleo, and the cancan girls danced—kick, kick, kick.

Cleo thought about how much she loved Paris and wished she'd gone there many times before but didn't make the connection with Danny's many requests for a visit. Cleo had a great time. She would not think about "that guy" until the next day.

The next day, during breakfast, Nicole asked, "How long do you think you'll stay with him?"

"No longer than 30 to 45 minutes. There isn't much to say."

Nicole said that she was going to have a table for them in a private room at the Brasserie Lipp just a few blocks down the Boulevard Saint-Germain from Danny's apartment, very close to Mabillon, and had the room for the whole evening. She had invited two guys Cleo might be interested in knowing. Cleo should come to meet her when she left Danny's apartment. Nicole said, "You should stay with him as long as necessary. Don't rush for us. Past midnight, we'll be back at my apartment. Come if you leave him late, past midnight."

She knew she would not spend much time delivering her first knife. Cleo was glad to have Nicole close by, but did not intend to discuss the encounter with Nicole. Having two guys with them could make it a fun social evening in Paris, not a tearful, emotional recounting among two friends of a breakup.

The girls did some shopping during the morning and had a quick lunch at a café facing La Madeleine. Seeing Paris through Nicole's eyes made her think about the type of life Danny might have had that year in Paris. What difference would it have made if she had visited him a couple of times as he had wanted? What if she hadn't sought out other lovers? But that was water under the bridge, as they say. She had to do what she had to do.

After lunch, they headed a block away, turning onto the rue Tronchet to a little shop, Eres, that sold swimsuits, including bikinis. These were designer bikinis, each almost one of a kind or part of a small series. Nicole wanted to buy one and offered one to Cleo. "Remember those bikinis we got for Hawaii?"

The girls tried on several before selecting one. These bikinis were very cute and definitely tinier than those bought for Hawaii. Then they headed back toward Nicole's apartment, which was very close to the Rodin Museum.

Nicole wanted to keep Cleo busy so that she wouldn't get nervous about the encounter with Danny. They spent about an hour at the Rodin Museum, which Cleo enjoyed very much. After a short nap at Nicole's apartment, she and Nicole got into the Mercedes to go to Danny's apartment. The driver took them down the Boulevard Saint-Germain to show Cleo the Brasserie Lipp, where Nicole would be waiting. Then they drove a couple of blocks down the Boulevard and turned down a small street, stopping right in front of the building with Danny's apartment.

As Cleo got out and the car drove off, she wondered what Nicole was thinking about this breakup. In fact, Nicole understood that Danny was deeply in love with Cleo, and Nicole believed that he was going to be completely shocked by this sudden and totally unexpected breakup.

Nicole expected Cleo to spend a lot of time with Danny. Would she end up having second thoughts and spending the night with him? Nicole prepared a note to leave at the restaurant in case Cleo arrived after midnight, saying once again that she should come directly to Nicole's apartment; she'd be waiting for Cleo to give her the support she'd need. Nicole had written her address on the note to give to a taxi since Cleo might have forgotten it. Nicole expected Cleo to be upset about what she had just done. Breaking up with someone who loves you, especially if the rupture is unexpected, can be traumatic to both people.

Chapter 28

Cleo Murders Siegfried

Danny received a sweet, but treacherous letter from Cleo just a week prior to her arrival in Paris. She didn't mention anything about coming to Paris. She was setting him up for the kill. He wrote her back but hadn't heard from her until right before she was planning to show up at his apartment. He got a note, "Danny, I'm coming to Paris on a family vacation and will come by to see you at 6:30 p.m. on Friday, August 5."

Danny got the note on Wednesday, August 3, just two days before her arrival. Danny was completely perplexed, no, shocked, by this note. She had a very distant and complicated relationship with her family, so a family vacation seemed highly unlikely. He also could not figure out why she hadn't mentioned a vacation trip to Paris before. Family vacations usually aren't planned on the fly. And what did she mean by, "I will come by to see you." How did she suddenly get more vacation days? He was dying to be with her, why the very casual comment? Surely, she was going to stay with him. Was she coming to break up with him? He could not believe that since there had never been any indication that her feelings had changed. He had just gotten a sweet, loving letter. What was going on?

For two days, Danny worried and wondered what was going on. His faith in Cleo had been unshakable, but he was worried, very worried. He loved her and trusted her implicitly, but the note was weird and frightening. She had never given him any reason to believe that she was anything but the good-looking, intelligent, decent woman he had met at The Coffee Spot. Nobody had ever said anything negative about her. Prudence clearly admired her. Danny knew that she sometimes used an elliptical way of expressing herself, so he thought that maybe the message was just written quickly, and it didn't mean anything. In any case, she would be with him shortly, and he was eager to see her.

That Friday at 6:30, Cleo knocked on the door of his apartment, and there she was. He tried to embrace her, but she pushed him away saying, "Let's sit down." Danny's studio apartment was small. It consisted of one room with a kitchenette on one corner, an alcove for the bed, a little space off the main room just big enough for a desk and chair, a bathroom, and a set of French doors that led to a small balcony overlooking the street. Danny sat on the bed while Cleo sat in front of him in a large easy chair Danny used for reading.

Danny suddenly felt terrified. Nothing seemed real. He could almost feel the floor give way beneath him. Why no hug? Why no kiss? Why no hello? What was about to happen? Cleo's face hardened into stone, and she seemed to clench her jaw. Danny could not believe that the attractive face he loved so much, and which was normally so brightened by her smile, could look so hard, cold, and immobile. What had happened to her? What was about to happen?

She looked straight at Danny and without any introduction said, "You need to know that I am sleeping with Jim Vilemann." Then she just looked at him.

"What?" he shouted. "What did you say?"

"You need to know that I am sleeping with Jim Vilemann."

Danny felt like she had just thrust a sharp, cold knife into his chest, right through his heart. He just sat there for what seemed to be a long time but was probably just a minute. Intense pain and shock flashed through his entire body. He could feel some of his body functions dying; he felt like he was being murdered.

In an instant, that part of his personality that trusted people, that liked people, that believed his friends were really his friends, all of his assumptions about the people he knew, including the woman he loved, proved to be wrong. Danny was romantic,

Cleo Murders Siegfried

tender, and sensitive; these characteristics made him easy to kill. Cleo had just murdered Siegfried.

"Cleo, why is this happening? What's going on? I thought we were in love. You know that I really love you. I thought you loved me."

She just looked at him and said, "You just need to come to terms with the fact that I am sleeping with Vilemann?"

Danny had no idea what to ask, but finally managed to say, "When did this start? Is it very recent?" Cleo looked at him with the hardest possible expression and said, "I'm not going to get into all that; you don't need to know that."

Danny asked whether it started before or after his last visit to Boston. Again, she gave him nothing. Her facial expression did not change. She made no attempt to answer; she just repeated that she was not going to say anything else. "You never said anything in your letters. I don't understand anything. What happened?"

Cleo just repeated, "You just need to come to terms with it."

Danny felt that with every question, he was hitting a stone wall. Cleo was leaning back in the chair passively, just looking at him. "Cleo?" He was almost begging for some sign of softness, some tenderness, some recognition that they had been together in Danny's mind at least for almost a year and a half. Didn't she know that he really loved her? Hadn't she loved him? She just stared at him. "Cleo, don't you know that he is a very tough, very mean guy?" As soon as he said this, he regretted it, but it was the truth. Danny knew that Vilemann was very domineering and could be brutal; Danny could not imagine a decent woman, much less a feminist like Cleo, having anything to do with him.

Cleo didn't flinch. She was giving him nothing, nothing at all, not a single word of love or affection or regret. No reference was made to the time they had been lovers; there was no expressions of regret that their relationship was over or that they had even had a relationship; she gave no reason why she was sleeping with Vilemann. She never said anything about her feelings for Vilemann or why Vilemann. She never said whether she had approached him or he had gone after her. Nothing. In fact, she never said that she was breaking up with Danny. She didn't say anything like, "I don't like you anymore," or "I think you are boring," or "The separation has been too hard on me." Nothing. She also didn't say anything like, "I don't want ever to see you again," or "Let's be friends," or "If you try to contact me, I'll call the police." Nothing. None of the type of statements people might say during a breakup.

Danny did not perceive what was happening as a breakup; it felt more like he was being annihilated, as if the pages in her diary that mentioned him had been torn out, wadded up, and thrown in the trash can, only to be replaced with fresh pages on which she could write another version of her plot. Not only would he not have a role in her life from that time on; he had never existed. Her diary would be wiped clean of Danny.

Danny felt a rush of terrifying emotions swell up in him. He reached out his hand, hoping she would take it, but no. She just leaned back in that chair. Again, Danny felt that she was there to murder him. He could not breathe or see anything. The walls of his studio apartment seemed to turn black and cave in on him. He slowly got up and said he needed some air.

He stumbled toward the French doors and walked out onto the balcony. He slowly held out his hands to grip the railing. His whole body was shaking uncontrollably. Those black walls came closer and started to crush against him, and for a moment he thought that those black walls would push him over the railing. He could almost see himself falling four stories to the street below. He imagined Cleo and Vilemann pushing him over that railing. She had been giving him slippery glances, but when he turned around to look at her, she was just staring straight ahead. He understood in that instant that she didn't care whether he lived or died. He was right; she didn't. If he had gone over that railing, his death would have meant nothing to her. She would never have assumed any responsibility for what happened to him. She'd just invent some fable that did not include her to explain his death.

The shock of being murdered, even if psychologically and socially, not physically, spread through Danny's brain from the most advanced frontal lobe to the most primitive base of the brain: the limbic region, the brain stem, and the amygdala. These parts of the brain are responsible for breathing, blinking, and the beating of the heart. The shock he had received was

Cleo Murders Siegfried

changing his brain, altering his synapses as they tried to come to terms with the unthinkable, with this trauma. He tried to think, but evil and doom spread throughout his brain like poison. His brain was infused with horror. He was looking out at the city, at the beautiful, romantic city of Paris, but was seeing nothing; he was blind with despair and humiliation. An ugly, horrifying feeling of being murdered overcame his mind and brain. His love for Cleo was being transformed into shock, into trauma, as he saw the woman he loved actually killing him. Breathing became difficult and his heart raced, then slowed to a crawl. He heard Cleo walking but couldn't turn around. He sensed her walking near him, and a rush of emotion ran through his body as he imagined her pushing him over that railing. He imagined her actually murdering him. Again, she was with Vilemann, and they were pushing him over that railing. Danny was paralyzed. Cleo walked over to the refrigerator to see if he had an opened bottle of wine; she wanted a drink. All she saw was an unopened bottle of champagne. She swiveled around and headed back to the chair where she had been sitting. As she looked around the apartment, she saw a bouquet of anemones, her favorite flower.

Poor bastard. He just lost. I'll get a drink when I see Nicole. She sat back down in Danny's easy chair.

Danny slowly came back in and sat down on his bed. Cleo was not moving; she was just looking at him. Danny felt like a building that was being demolished. When the structural walls and columns are blown apart, everything comes crumbling down. He suddenly felt all those restraints that control our emotions let loose, and he began weeping. His mind could no longer control his brain or his emotions. The trauma of being murdered was devastating him. He was not crying; he was weeping for the first time in his adult life. All of his emotions, all of his feelings, all of his love seemed to be exploding out of him with each jolting sob.

Cleo just sat there looking at him. He tried to get control of himself, but was struggling to hold back the sobs, to breathe regularly. He finally managed to say, "My God, Cleo what happened? I need to know what I did, what has happened to us?"

She hesitated a minute then said, "Just come to terms with the fact that I am sleeping with Vilemann."

Cleo had accomplished her mission; she had just killed Siegfried. She had not flinched or said anything to make him feel OK about what she had said or help him understand what had happened. She was halfway to totally eliminating that weakness in her that had allowed her to imagine, even for a moment, that she loved him.

She knew that by killing him in cold blood, she was getting close to being able to resist loving anybody, to being controlled or dominated by anybody. In a week, she just had to deliver the next knife. If you can kill somebody, particularly somebody who loves you, in cold blood, you can never again love anybody. That was her goal, to be free from domination by love. She aspired to be Hegelian. War suited her more than love.

Again, she told him, "Just come to terms with it." With that she stood up and said, "I'll be back in Paris next Friday, a week from now, and I'll come by again a little bit earlier about 5:30 p.m."

Danny barely registered what she had just said. He could not imagine what might happen in a week, but he was encouraged a bit that she was coming back. Then in a second, she opened the door and disappeared down the stairs. She did not turn to look back at him. Danny fell on the floor, holding his hands clasped in front of him in two fists so he would not explode from shock or anger or die from despair.

After about 15 minutes, he crawled onto the bed and just wept uncontrollably. He felt like he was going crazy as his mind could no longer control his brain or emotions. His whole body shook violently. He did not sleep all night. By the morning, he felt dead.

Chapter 29
Nicole's Present

Danny's apartment was just three blocks from the Brasserie Lipp. Cleo walked over to the Boulevard Saint-Germain, turned left to go to the Brasserie, and noticed how animated and full of life the boulevard seemed to be.

She thought, *No wonder people like living here. Paris is a terrific city. So full of life.*

Arriving at the Brasserie, she was impressed by the original Belle Epoque décor and by the number of patrons already there. In Paris, diners usually arrive between 8:30 and 9 p.m. or even somewhat later, but the restaurant was already buzzing with animated conversation. Cleo was impressed by the elegance of some of the women and their clothes.

So, this is Paris, she thought.

Cleo checked her watch—6:55 p.m. That had taken just about 20 minutes, plus five minutes to walk to the Brasserie, although it seemed faster to Cleo. The maître'd showed Cleo up to the private room where Nicole sat with two very good-looking, very fit guys. Cleo thought that Nicole had two very attractive boyfriends. She wondered if Bepe knew about them.

Nicole had prepped the guys for different scenarios and told them to be ready to just be good listeners or to be as "engaged without restraint" with Cleo as possible, to do whatever it took to help her get over this breakup. They should just see where things went with Cleo. Whatever happened, they would get their

232 The BeAst and the Brightest

envelopes. Nicole had found two professionals who were ready for anything; disappearing quickly if Cleo didn't seem to want them to be with her and Nicole, sympathetically listening, offering their perspectives on breakups, or giving her whatever she wanted, a kiss, a hug or something more.

Nicole was shocked to see Cleo so early. She had thought that the confrontation might have lasted for hours, but no, there she was. Nicole jumped up, gave her a big hug and whispered, "How did it go?"

"Fine," Cleo said with a big smile. "No problem. Everything's fine."

She looked relaxed and happy and gave the two guys big smiles. Nicole introduced them as "guys you'll enjoy being with—Jean-Carlo and Frédérick."

The guys gave Cleo the usual three *bises*, and everyone smiled. Nicole thought that having the two guys with them would be good for Cleo. She might need some support beyond what Nicole could offer.

Cleo thought, *Killing Danny was faster and easier than I thought; now I have a night in Paris to have some fun.*

Cleo wondered, *Does Nicole have three really good-looking boyfriends, these two plus Bepe?*

Nicole said, "Great, let's all sit down and have a flute of champagne."

As the waiter went to get the four flutes, Cleo exclaimed, "What a lovely restaurant! It's great when beautiful things are preserved!"

The guys were very charming. Jean-Carlo and Frédérick both spoke English well, enhanced with a distinctive French accent. They knew how to appear interested in her and what she said without fawning. Nicole told stories about Cleo and her when they were young. She even mentioned exploring each other, touching each other down there when they were in Hawaii. Cleo was surprised that she shared this story with these guys, but they thought it was charming.

Frédérick said, "What could be more natural? We're all sexual, right? We all have to learn about sex."

Cleo spoke up, "Yeah, who doesn't like sex. We all do, right?" Then she raised her flute and cried out, "Here's to sex, here's to

Nicole's Present   233

wild sex." The guys thought they had just gotten their marching orders and were pleased that Cleo was good-looking. The evening would be much easier, maybe even enjoyable.

After dinner, Nicole let the check go to her dad's tab, and then they left the restaurant to find the Mercedes waiting for them. Jean-Carl and Frédérick were in the back seat. Cleo was in the middle between them. Nicole was in the front beside the chauffeur. Jean-Carlo asked Cleo for a kiss, and got one, a long passionate kiss that let Cleo release some of the tension she had felt all day. She had rarely kissed a guy so voluptuously. She was ready for fun, and he was really good-looking. She kissed him and Frédérick several more times heading to Nicole's apartment and put her hands on their legs; up high on their legs. As they got out of the car, Nicole whispered to Jean-Carlo, "I think you guys know what she wants."

In no time, they were all back at Nicole's apartment where Nicole put on some music and opened another bottle of champagne. They all danced and drank champagne. As they danced, Cleo kissed both guys several times, and let them hold her and touch her, even on her buttocks and breasts. Cleo ran her hands over the guy's pecs and down to their pants. After a short while, Frédérick said, "How about the Jacuzzi?"

Jean-Carlo shouted, "OK. Let's go—à poil."

Cleo didn't know what à poil meant, but the guys started stripping so it was obvious. Cleo took a deep breath and stripped. She was ready to completely let go and she did. She felt like getting wild. She got to Danny's bikini panties and then remembered her line. "Frédérick, I don't like to take off my panties by myself when I'm with a guy … will you help me?" She had worn Danny's present of his camisole and bikini panties to his murder as a way of signifying to herself that he meant nothing to her, not even some infantile nostalgia or soggy, romantic sentiment. She prided herself on being as tough as Vilemann. She looked around to see Nicole heading to the kitchen, still dressed.

Not only did he help her slip off Danny's panties, but once in the Jacuzzi, he came right into her. In two seconds, Frédérick started penetrating her with his very hard thing. Cleo just laid back to enjoy it. As his hard penis came into her, she felt a rush of joy and fun. She was in Paris, and she needed to let go totally.

234   The BeAst and the Brightest

As Frédérick continued to pump in and out of her, Jean-Carlo was caressing and kissing her breasts. Nicole had disappeared, but Cleo was so entangled with these two studs that she didn't really care. Jean-Carlo and Frédérick were really good-looking, real studs.

Cleo thought, *These are the kind of guys to suck off,* but before she could push Frédérick out of her and go down there on him, the guys switched again. In two seconds, Jean-Carlo was in front of her, pointing a very hard penis right at her.

She took him in her mouth and thought. *This is good, so exciting. I feel so alive!*

He let her play with his hard tool for a minute or two, and then he penetrated right into her. She was having a wonderful, wild time. The guys switched again and came in her in different ways. She was fulfilling a long-standing sexual fantasy, and it felt good. Cleo felt ravaged but happily ravaged. All of her tension had evaporated. She felt the joy of intense sexual release and pleasure.

After about 20 minutes, Jean-Carlo said, "The sauna." And they all went into the very warm, but not hot sauna to fondle each other and kiss. Both men went down on Cleo; it was the first time Cleo had let a guy explore her and play with her like that. She loved it. She understood why Nicole had shaved all of her pubic area.

Cleo thought that these guys knew just how to make a woman feel good—no great. Cleo could not believe her reaction. She was enjoying sex for the first time since Danny left her in Boston. No, she didn't want to see it that way. No. She was just enjoying sex, unrestrained, wild sex. She was letting herself go completely. She was letting all of her tension explode out of her. While Danny was weeping at the mercy of his emotions, Cleo was using wild sex to release hers.

Next, the boys led Cleo to the bedroom. Frédérick laid down right in front of Cleo, who was lying on her side so that his penis was right in front of her. She started sucking him as she felt Jean-Carlo enter her from behind. Never had she imagined letting guys do things like this with her, but somehow, it felt great. Two guys were penetrating her, and she liked it. Being penetrated by two guys made her feel alive and vibrant.

Nicole's Present

By 1:30 a.m. Cleo felt totally ravaged, happy, and satisfied. Cleo looked up to see those four acrylic panels showing Nicole and her friend interlaced and thought, *Wow, I'm enjoying it; I bet Nicole did, too.*

The guys got dressed, kissed Cleo on the cheeks and the mouth, and left the apartment, picking up a little envelope on the way out. Nicole had assured herself that Cleo would have a great experience with these very experienced professionals. They had not let her down. Cleo just laid there in that huge bed, nude, savoring this moment of total ecstasy and satisfaction.

Nicole came into the bedroom, saying, "Did you enjoy my present?" Cleo didn't noticed the word, "present." Then, Nicole undressed, gave Cleo a kiss on the cheek, and said, "I hope those guys helped you get over what happened with Danny."

Cleo didn't need any help getting over Danny, but she had enjoyed the two guys. Cleo thought, *What could be better than zipless fucking with a good-looking French guy. How about two guys at the same time*, but she said nothing.

Nicole laid down nude next to Cleo, who put her head on Nicole's shoulder. Cleo felt totally relaxed and happy as she fell asleep. Nicole lay there for a few minutes and wondered how it had actually gone with Danny; she didn't believe what Cleo had told her. Nicole was certain that Danny was totally shocked and probably in distress.

The next morning, Cleo woke up just after Nicole. They were lying in bed, looking at each other. Cleo didn't know what to say. Nicole said, "It was OK with those boys, right?"

Cleo said, "Yes, better than OK, it was really great," and they both laughed.

As they ate breakfast, Nicole asked Cleo again if, in fact, her discussion with Danny went fine, and Cleo said, "Right, he understood. No problem."

Nicole didn't believe her but didn't know what else to say, so she helped by saying, "The best way to forget a guy is to enjoy another one, or two, right?" Cleo nodded. Nicole was distressed that Cleo was probably lying about Danny. They were such good friends that she expected Cleo to tell her what had actually occurred; she expected Cleo to be honest with her.

To change the subject, Nicole started talking about how easy it was to pick up guys in Greece. She explained that they would spend the entire winter trimming down and muscling up to be as attractive as possible to women during the summer holidays, and they would not hassle women like in Italy; they'd give women whatever the ladies wanted for a day, a couple of hours, a few days, or longer. They were there to serve. The girls could be in control. Nicole ended by saying, "Maybe we should go to Greece together; what do you say? I used to go every summer until I met Bepe, that is."

Cleo wondered how this Bepe fit into Nicole's life in Paris, especially given her relationship with Jean-Carlo and Frédérick. This was another time when Cleo was totally clueless. Nicole said, "Don't forget that new cute bikini from Eres when you go to Greece; the guys will love seeing you in that."

Chapter 30

Cleo Rapes Danny

As Cleo packed her bag and got ready to leave for Cannes, she told Nicole that she appreciated everything she had done for her. She wasn't sure if she would come back that next week to stay with her; it depended on the guy in Cannes, but she'd call to let her know.

Nicole asked Cleo about the guy in Cannes. What was he like, and was she serious about him? Had she fallen in love? Was her friend, Cleo, crazy in love? Nicole thought that she must have fallen crazy in love to be willing to trash Danny.

Cleo brushed her questions away, saying, "He's just a guy I do things with."

Hugs and kisses were quickly exchanged, and Cleo got in the Mercedes to go to the Montparnasse train station for the trip to Cannes. She knew she wouldn't see Nicole again, at least not on this trip. Nicole was upset and concerned.

Cleo had reserved a first-class train ticket, so her seat was comfortable, and since she was still tired, she slept most of the way. She took a hired car from the train station to Cannes, so she was at the Hotel Vilemann had been so enthusiastic about fairly quickly.

She went to Vilemann's room, but he wasn't there. He was at the pool wearing a little men's bikini; she was shocked seeing his unattractive body in that little thing. He smiled and said, "This is what they wear down here. I got it at a cool shop in town recommended by the pool guy over there."

238   The BeAst and the Brightest

Cleo did not think he looked good in it at all. Jean-Carlo or Frédérick could have worn it with some style; she actually thought she'd like to see them in a little men's bikini. But Vilemann looked ridiculous. She told him to "put something on to cover up because I want to eat." She really didn't want to see him in that stupid bikini, although she did notice some really good-looking guys around the pool wearing the same type of thing. They looked good; Vilemann didn't. Cleo thought that she'd wear the swimsuit she brought with her if she went swimming, not the tiny bikini Nicole had purchased for her. Or maybe she'd just wouldn't swim.

They ordered salads by the pool, and Vilemann urged Cleo to tell him all about what happened with Danny. Cleo had no intention of telling him anything. She just said it went fine. Vilemann pressed her. "Come on, how did he react?"

Cleo said that he wasn't happy; he would need to get used to the idea, and then she looked Vilemann right in the eyes and said, "That's all I want to say." She did say that she had enjoyed seeing Nicole but skipped any description of her activities with Jean-Carlo and Frédérick. "So, what have you been doing?" Cleo asked.

Vilemann talked about going to the pool, an afternoon at the beach, a little shopping—to get that men's bikini—and some restaurants. He forgot to say he had been thinking about her. She noted that he had not bought anything for her. He talked about Cannes with the usual frenzy that had initially enthralled Cleo. They just hung out at the pool that afternoon and then went to town for dinner. Back in their room, Cleo said she was tired, and Vilemann agreed. Neither seemed interested in sex.

The next four days went by without any arguments, but also without any passion or sex. Wednesday night Vilemann became terribly upset,even aggressive and angry when he couldn't perform. He couldn't get it up. OK, at times, he was rather limp, but he had never been totally impotent with Cleo. This was the first time that had happened with her. He excused himself saying that he must be tired. As they rolled over, their eyes met—filled with weariness and deception, empty of any feelings, of any desire. Given what had happened in Paris, Cleo was happy just to be in bed and go to sleep. Vilemann seemed to have other things on his mind. Finally, Cleo asked if everything was OK.

"Sure," he said using the same type of response that Cleo had perfected that meant everything and nothing.

Cleo wondered if he had been with another woman. Thursday afternoon, Cleo took the train back to Paris. She called Nicole to say that she had loved being with her, but she would not be able to see her because of the guy in Cannes. Nicole begged her to come another time. "I loved seeing you and want you to get to know Bepe. Maybe you can come with the guy you are seeing in Cannes."

Actually, the more she thought about that night with Nicole's two boyfriends, the angrier she became at Nicole for organizing that wild sex romp. Cleo felt that she had exposed herself too much; that she had lost control to these two guys she didn't even know. She felt no hesitation in using a guy but did not want a guy to ever feel he had used her.

She started to realize why Nicole had a huge custom bed but didn't really want to imagine what happened in that huge space; she had seen enough, too much, actually. She imagined Nicole having sex with both Frédérick and Jean-Carlo in that huge bed, guys who had been in her, all over her. Cleo's anger toward Nicole flamed up again. She was not sure she ever wanted to see Nicole again. How could Nicole share a boyfriend with her? Both her boyfriends? Letting her boyfriends have sex with another woman seemed immoral, totally immoral. Cleo felt disgusted. She asked herself if Nicole had any sense of sexual morality, of right and wrong. Actually, Cleo had misunderstood everything.

Cleo had booked a room in the Hotel Rochechouart in Montmartre near Pigalle, so getting to Charles de Gaulle Airport at Roissy the next morning would be easy. She idled around that morning; ate some seafood at a sidewalk café and did a lot of people-watching. She had a light lunch at the café, where a couple about her age came in, sat down, ordered two glasses of white wine, and started kissing each other with tenderness and passion. Cleo just looked at them.

Parisian lovers, she thought without any reflection on Danny.

She walked around Montmartre and visited the cathedral Sacre Coeur for a couple of hours that afternoon, and then went to her hotel to take a nap and tidy up. She grabbed a cab and gave the driver Danny's address.

240   The BeAst and the Brightest

She kept thinking, *After today, it's over; that's good.*

Yes, it would be over with Danny, but it was also going to be over for Cleo; she would never again feel the radiance that Danny had illuminated within her. Other men could have given her sweet, tender, faithful love. Blondie wanted to give her his tender love, but she intended to annihilate that part of her that could respond to those feelings, to that type of relationship with another person.

People often say that once you kill someone, you are never the same, and they are right. Murderers cannot become normal people again. When they kill, they kill part of themselves. This is what Cleo hoped would happen: Her spot of vulnerability would be eliminated. She'd be stronger, more of a winner, more like Vilemann. Cleo had ended it with a lot of guys but had never killed them with the ferocity and brutality of betrayal she had inflicted on Danny, and none of those guys had loved her nearly as much as Danny. She felt proud that she had been able to watch as Siegfried bled to death. She felt like a winner. She only had one more knife to deliver to have won everything! She'd be the powerful, independent woman she aspired to be. She'd be a female Vilemann, a true Hegelian, triumphant.

As she did the previous week, she arrived right on time. Danny opened the door and tried to smile, but he looked dead. His eyes shouted, "I hurt!, Hurt!, Hurt!" He seemed to have aged 30 or 40 years. His complexion was washed out as if by a constant stream of tears. His hands were trembling. He reached out to touch her, but again, she pushed him away. "Let's sit," she said. Danny tried to say something, but Cleo cut him off. "Let me go first." Danny was shaking. His eyes were cloudy, and his lips were trembling. Cleo again looked immobile; her face was stone. Danny had thought about a dozen scenarios to anticipate how this second encounter might go, but he had not imagined what was about to happen. He could never have imagined what was about to happen. Cleo sat down again in Danny's reading chair and said straight out, "You need to know that I am sleeping with John Tallington."

Again, Danny fell back as if Cleo had struck him with another knife right through the heart. He couldn't believe what he had just heard. Cleo just stared at him.

Cleo Rapes Danny

"I thought you said you were sleeping with Vilemann?"

"I am," Cleo said coldly. "I'm also sleeping with Tallington."

Danny thought his brain was going to explode. He could feel his blood pressure drop; he thought he might just pass out or die. "Are you really sleeping with both Vilemann and Tallington?"

He could not believe what he was asking. "Are you doing it with them at the same time? Is this group sex? Are you having sex parties? Are other people involved?" Tallington was his best friend; how could he betray Danny like this? "That bastard," Danny shouted. What was going on? Danny was completely lost.

"Yes, I'm sleeping with both of them, Vilemann and Tallington. You don't need to know anything else. I am not going to tell you anything else about all that." Danny asked, "Do Vilemann and Tallington know you're sleeping with both of them?"

"Of course they do," she offered.

"Are they OK with you having sex with both of them?" Danny could not believe what he was asking.

"Sure, it's just sex, and that's no big deal. What's it to you anyway."

Again Danny asked, "Are you doing it with both at the same time?"

"I told you that you don't need to know anything about that. I have nothing else to say about that."

Cleo just sat there and looked at him. Danny's head was spinning, and he was in shock. He tried to get control of his emotions but couldn't. He looked in the direction of Cleo, who was just sitting in that chair, looking at him, expressionless. Finally, he got up and again went toward those French doors and stepped out on the balcony. He looked in the direction of the city, but he could not see anything. He was blind with anger, humiliation, and sorrow. He was angry not only at Cleo but at his two former "friends." They had all betrayed him. Had they all three participated in sex parties? Had they all laughed at him? Had he become an object of ridicule to his former friends and lover? Danny suddenly realized that male friendship evaporates at the drop of a pair of panties.

He felt stripped naked and violated as a person. An overwhelming force of evil, a suspension of humanity and

242   The BeAst and the Brightest

civilization—just raw brutality and vandalism—invaded every aspect of his person. He now understood the trauma, the profound sense of evil that women feel when they are raped, except for the physical penetration, which must be horrible, but he did feel two knives in his heart. He understood that Cleo, Vilemann, and Tallington had absolutely no respect or consideration for him. He felt that Cleo had just raped him. He felt completely violated as a human being. Would they be happy if he just fell from that balcony?

He again felt a tremor; then he started shaking as if an earthquake was ravaging him. He imagined Cleo, Vilemann, and now Tallington behind him, pushing him over that railing. He then imagined them going back into his apartment, stripping and fucking, each guy taking a turn with Cleo. He looked back at Cleo, who was not even looking at him; she was looking straight ahead. He realized that she did not care whether he fell over that railing or not. Cleo had become a murderer and a rapist. Vilemann and Tallington had become accomplices to murder and rape.

He slowly walked back into the room and asked those same questions: "Why? When? How did this happen? Don't you understand that I truly love you?" He came up against the same stonewall.

"You don't need to know any of that. You just need to come to terms with the fact that I am sleeping with Vilemann and Tallington."

"Who else knows about this?"

Cleo shrugged her shoulders and said, "Everybody, I guess."

"Does Prudence know what has been going on?"

"Yes."

Danny asked himself why somebody hadn't warned him. Why had everybody let Cleo lay a deadly trap for him? Then he looked back at Cleo. Again, not a word came from her that might be included in a traditional breakup—nothing about him or them. "Us" had died, or maybe Danny thought that to Cleo, "us" had never existed. To Cleo, "we" were a fiction, just a word Danny used, just another of Danny's romantic illusions.She said nothing about their relationship or how, why, or when her feelings had changed.

Cleo Rapes Danny

Danny became tremendously angry and humiliated. Many men would have struck out against Cleo; brutal revenge and violence would have inflamed many men to strike her, but Danny took the blow all into himself. If one of them was going to be damaged, to be hurt, it was going to be Danny. He felt like he was stepping in front of an avalanche of pain and horror, and it hit him hard, very, very hard. He took the entire blow. Danny was incapable of hurting a woman, any woman, even one as deceitful and immoral as Cleo.

Again, he started weeping; he wasn't crying; this was weeping, sobbing as his whole spirit rushed out of him, as he took the entire blow, and as the trauma of being raped was again ravaging every corner of his brain, damaging his mind. Cleo's words transformed every nerve in his brain from love and happiness to fear and dread, from joy to despair, and from goodness to evil.

Cleo just sat there and looked at him for a few minutes, then stood up and walked out, closing the door behind her. She did not look back at him or say goodbye. Cleo had raped him by showing absolutely no respect for him as a human being. She had violated him totally. She had not assaulted him physically as men do to women who they raped, but she had assaulted, murdered, and raped him psychologically and socially. She had achieved her objective of destroying him totally.

By showing absolutely no respect, no decency, no consideration at all for Danny, she had made herself into a rapist. A rapist should never expect to be treated with any respect, to be treated like a decent human being, but Cleo was happy about what she had just done. She was proud of her rape. She had enjoyed it and was proud of her performance. He was stripped of any dignity; he wasn't even a person to her, just flesh to destroy, to defile, male meat to trample. She felt free, free to be herself and do whatever she wanted regardless of the consequences to anyone else. She had no concern for Danny. She felt like a free woman. She felt like celebrating her triumph.

She quickly found a taxi and headed to her hotel. Lively music was playing, and a lot of people seemed to be having fun in the bar. Behind the bar was a lovely restaurant in the traditional bistro style. This restaurant was right in her hotel, so she thought it looked like a fun and convenient place for dinner.

244   The BeAst and the Brightest

Since she heard music and laughter coming from the bar area, she headed right in.

The bar area was packed with happy people who seemed to be having a spontaneous neighborhood party. A guy with an accordion was playing traditional French popular songs. Another person was playing piano. Many people were singing along. The atmosphere was happy and friendly. The whole neighborhood seemed to be there.

The dining room behind the bar was packed with people happily enjoying delicious food with their friends and family. Many of the patrons seemed to know one another. The scene seemed to be right out of a movie filled with clichés about Parisian bistros, but the atmosphere was delightful and authentic. She was in a real, lively Parisian neighborhood hotel restaurant.

Cleo went in and ordered a glass of white wine at the bar. Before being served, she switched to a flute of champagne to celebrate the way she had "raped" Danny. She was sure he would never bother her again. Her plan had worked perfectly; he was completely destroyed. She was proud of herself for the plan and how well she had executed it.

Cleo tried to join in the singing since she recognized many of the tunes, including many of Piaf's, but she didn't know the words to any of the songs, so she just hummed along. She got swept up in the festive atmosphere of this friendly neighborhood café restaurant.

She thought, *Paris is terrific, so lively and fun. I need to come back.*

She stayed in the bar area, enjoying herself with the crowd for almost two hours. She permitted herself a second flute of champagne. "Here's to fun in Paris," she shouted! All sorts of people showed up: business types, gays, artists, and even the fish merchant who had just closed up his stand outside the restaurant. She loved it. Finally, she realized that she needed to eat something and go to her room since she had a long flight the next day.

She asked for a table, but the restaurant was full. She had not noticed the little sign, *Complet,* no more room. A nice-looking guy who had spotted her in the bar asked her if she wanted to have dinner together. He had a reservation, and she was hungry, so she accepted. Her nickname for him was French Stud #3.

Cleo Rapes Danny   245

She was so hungry that she ordered steak frites, a steak with french fries, and a salad. Then she had a pear tart for dessert. He offered a bottle of Bordeaux. She couldn't resist a glass of good Bordeaux with her steak since she was both celebrating and trying to enjoy her last evening in Paris to the maximum. French Stud #3 and Cleo both had a second glass of that Bordeaux and then a bit more to finish the bottle.

As she finished her meal, she thought, *"Wow, what a nice, fun, friendly evening in Paris."*

The guy she shared her table with was very good-looking, actually handsome. Although he spoke very little English, they understood each other's smiles. He offered to pay for the meal, a gesture Cleo appreciated. She planned to reward him.

"I'm staying in the hotel; my room is right upstairs, number 325," she said with an inviting smile. Why not enjoy another French guy while she had the chance?

They enjoyed a zipperless moment as their clothes seemed to fly off. He was very good in bed, really good. They did it twice, including some positions and techniques new to Cleo, then turned over and went to sleep. As she went to sleep, she thought that she had just enjoyed another lovely anonymous, zipperless fuck. She thought Jong was so right; nothing like an anonymous, zipperless fuck, especially with a handsome French guy.

He didn't know her first name, and she didn't know his. She didn't want to. French Stud #3 was fine, just fine.

Cleo didn't need another guy to get over what had happened with Danny; he was completely dead to her. She was just enjoying the joy and fun of sex. All that evening, she didn't give a thought to what had just happened. It was over, totally over.

Cleo woke up early since she had to take off to go to the airport. French Stud #3 stayed in bed while she was in the bathroom, cleaning up and getting dressed. As she prepared to leave, she came over and gave him a couple of delicious kisses on the lips, then pulled down the sheets to his knees. When she saw that he was somewhat erect, she gave a quick suck and a couple of kisses on his penis. Then, with a big smile, she opened the door, turned toward French Stud #3, and blew him a final kiss. In the elevator, she thought that being in Paris had opened her

246 The BeAst and the Brightest

up to the idea of enjoying a little hedonism of her own. Paris had liberated her.

She also thought, "These French guys really know how to handle a woman in bed. Perhaps there is something to the Latin lover thing. If I kill off Vilemann, perhaps I'll go to Greece to see if Nicole was right that the Greek guys are good-looking and let you have control. But I'll never go with Nicole, no Nicole."

All in all, it had been another good day in Paris, and what a nice way to finish a trip to this fabulous city, singing along with a fun group of people, a good meal, good sex, and sleeping in the arms of a handsome French guy. What more could a girl ask for?

Wow, I've now had three French studs in just a few days, she thought with a big smile.

As she was opening up sexually, she was closing the door on the ability to have any tender, kind, or loving feelings or the possibility of having any connection, any relationship with anyone. For the next 25 years or so, everyone in her life would be de passage, just passing through … zipless.

After the second encounter with Cleo, Danny could hardly move. He ate some bread and cheese from his little fridge and drank some water, but that was all. He could not go out of his little apartment for three days. Then he had no more bread, so he headed to the boulangerie at the corner. The Buci open-air market just behind Mabillon provided a roast chicken and some prepared salads. He took them back to his apartment.

For five days, he stayed in his apartment, trying to put his thoughts together. Could he ever return to Boston or Harvard? What would he encounter back in the Econ Department? Certainly, he would encounter Vilemann and Tallington. That would be ugly and traumatic. Who else knew about what was happening while he was away? Danny reflected on the betrayal of his two "friends." He wondered how people could survive without friends. Could he ever trust another guy to be a friend? He thought not. How can someone who has been betrayed terribly by a male friend, by two male friends, ever believe in friendship, particularly with other guys?

Danny also wondered what he should do with his life. Could he teach economics at an English-language school in France?

Cleo Rapes Danny
247

He now knew more people in France than in Italy, so maybe he should commit to living there. Could he finish his doctorate in Paris? Staying in Paris was tempting, very tempting.

On the other hand, his family was all in the U.S. His father had heart problems, and Danny felt he needed to be in the States to help him. His mother and sister were also close to him, even if they lived out west, far from Boston. Maybe he should just abandon his doctorate and try to pass the exam to be in the State Department like his friend from Stanford? Being stationed abroad and traveling around the world might be fun. He felt that his whole life had been shattered; not broken but shattered. If a pottery coffee cup or plate falls on the floor, it can chip or break into several pieces, which might be glued back together. But when crystal flutes from Baccarat, like the ones he had given Cleo, fall on the floor, they shatter into hundreds of sharp, cutting shards. Danny felt that Cleo had shattered those crystal flutes inside him, those flutes he and Cleo had used to toast each other in moments of celebration of their love. He felt lacerated from the inside. This thought made Danny feel like he was choking on his own blood. Should he try to put things back together or start a new life? How would he survive this ordeal?

Two unexpected developments helped him decide the direction to take. His advisor came to Paris later that week and told Danny that he really liked his work and could give him a research project that would support him the next year while he wrote his dissertation. He did say that Danny did not look well at all and asked if everything was OK. Danny said he hadn't been sleeping well. He wondered briefly if he could do the work from Paris but realized that this was not possible. He needed access to Harvard's library and other resources. His advisor also said that Princeton was likely to have a tenure-track position available that next year, and he thought that Danny should go for it. A job at Princeton was a very attractive possibility, but every new Ph.D. in economics would probably compete for it.

The second development was a letter from another economics student, Bill Anderson, who had just married a wealthy woman. She had just finished her art history Ph.D., and they had bought a house in a suburb very close to downtown Boston. Unexpectedly, she had gotten a teaching job for one year at

248   The BeAst and the Brightest

Duke, so they were going to move down there. They wanted to
keep the house at least for a year. Bill had seen the notice Danny
had posted in the Econ Department about needing a place for
two people when he returned from Europe. The deal Bill offered
was to let Danny live in the house rent-free, utilities included if
he would take care of the house and a puppy that they had just
bought from Ireland. They were going to get an apartment at
Duke, which would not be appropriate for this puppy, a pure-
bred Irish Wolfhound.

These developments helped Danny decide to go back to
Harvard. He had spent four years already on his doctorate and
knew that throwing it all away was dumb. Plus, he did not want
to be intimidated by "those three," as he came to call them. So,
he tried to pull himself together enough to finish his research
and plan to go back to Boston.

During the next few days, he was reasonably productive, but
at night, he could not sleep and was haunted by a recurring
nightmare. In that nightmare, he was with Cleo, Vilemann, and
Tallington in his apartment in Paris. They were all dancing. Then,
suddenly, the three of them push Danny out onto the balcony
and shove him over the railing. He'd hit the pavement four stories below, and they go back into the apartment, strip, and start
fucking, each guy taking his turn with Cleo on Danny's bed.
Danny would wake up in a cold sweat, shaking with anger and
humiliation.

He kept thinking that Cleo was free to associate with anybody she wanted, but in this society, complete sexual freedom is
not the norm or acceptable. Sleeping with a parent or a sibling is
incest, and sleeping with the husband or wife of a friend or rel-
ative can be devastating. Yes, sometimes people fall in love, but
Cleo had just said they were sleeping together. It was just sex.
Doing something like that was just sexually immoral and totally
irresponsible. And why did she wait to tell him anything until he
was scheduled to come back to Boston? Why the sudden, brutal
ambush? Why didn't she send him a breakup letter or come to
Paris and tell him the truth months earlier? And why was she
with two of Danny's friends, including his best friend? Boston
and Cambridge were full of young men looking for a woman.
Had she been with one or both of them when he visited her in

Boston? How could she have been so dishonest? Who could be that evil? Was Cleo evil? Along with everyone else in the department, Danny knew that Vilemann was a bastard. He wondered if Tallington was just as evil as Cleo.

For someone who imagined herself to be a writer, who took pride in her ability to create fables, and who could always find the right phrase, truthful or not, Cleo had revealed almost nothing to Danny during their two encounters in his apartment and had used just the most brutal declarative sentences. Cleo had announced her cheating as if sleeping with these two guys was completely amoral, without any immoral or negative consequences; she acted as if her two visits were just because Danny might want to know who her current sex partners were, who shared her bed and her body. Her statements did not reflect any pride in her conquests or shame in her behavior. She had acted as if her actions were entirely amoral, neutral from a moral perspective, or simply removed from moral considerations.

Danny decided to write to Prudence, whom he considered a friend and who spent five days a week with Cleo. He told her what had happened, about his depression and severe distress, and wondered if she could give him any insight into what had happened or why. Danny wondered if Prudence had known that Cleo was cheating with two of Danny's student friends when he and Cleo had dinner with her in January or June. He told her he was fighting terrifying dreams at night and horrible daydreams as well and that sometimes the walls of his apartment seemed to turn black and push him toward that balcony. These were not suicidal thoughts; they were emotions driven by the experience of being murdered and raped. Danny told her that he was struggling to get through each day. "If you hear that I committed suicide, don't believe it. I was murdered and raped."

Prudence wrote him back immediately, saying that she had been advising Cleo for some time to be truthful with him, but she had not followed this advice. Prudence thought that it was Cleo's responsibility to let Danny know what was happening; her responsibility was to encourage Cleo to do the right thing. She wanted to believe that Cleo had regrets about what had happened but had not been able to express them or act on them. She asserted that he and Cleo had a chance to reach some reconciliation once he was back in Boston but that he needed to focus on the future. Prudence finished by saying, "You have so much going for you that you should just realize that you'll get over this ordeal and find someone who really loves you." She finished the letter by saying that as soon as he got back to Boston, she'd like to have dinner with him. She'd be an open ear. "You probably need to talk," she wrote. What neither of them at the time realized was how hard it is to describe being murdered or to recount the terror of rape.

Danny was experiencing many of the psychological reactions of rape victims: fear, isolation, anger, numbness, confusion, shock, disbelief, and denial. These are the reactions of anyone who is traumatized, whether because of war, incest, or sexual assault. Cleo had described her relationship with Vilemann and Tallington purely in sexual terms, as guys she was sleeping with. She never said she cared about them or had fallen for them or loved one or both of them. No, she was just fucking with them. She was just getting her sexual satisfaction from them, two of Danny's former friends. How low would she go? Could a woman go any lower? Had she thrown away a guy who truly loved her just to fuck his friends? Everything essential was left unsaid, except the most devastating.

Cleo's two visits had exiled Danny from the sunny side of the street into a dark, dirty alley. He'd have to walk down that ugly alley for some considerable time. He wondered if he'd ever find the sunny side of the street, the street where Siegfried had lived, or whether he'd be trapped in that alley or on the dark, shady side of the street forever. His heart was in agony; his spirit was in mourning.

Chapter 31

Wonderful Women

Danny had hardly left his apartment for a week when he got a call from Sandrine. She asked why he hadn't been at one of the cafés and wondered if everything was OK. She had thought that maybe he was traveling in France for his research, but he had never been out of touch for more than a week. She and Christelle did not know that Cleo was coming to Paris and had expected to see him at one of the cafés. Sandrine didn't want to presume anything, so she just asked when she could see him. After listening to her message, Danny called her back. He asked her if she would meet him the next day at Café Mabillon at 3:30 p.m., their usual hour. Sandrine knew from the sound of his voice that something was seriously wrong, so she called Christelle to decide what to do.

When Danny arrived at 3:30 p.m. sharp, Sandrine and Christelle were both seated at the café. Danny didn't know how to react or what to say to them. He thought that telling them what had happened would be too painful. When the waiter showed up, the girls both ordered a coffee. Danny declined a drink, but Christelle saw how upset he was and told the waiter to bring him a beer, a big one. They asked him directly if everything was OK. He hesitated, then managed to say that it was over, totally over with Cleo. She had been there, and it was over. He tried to act brave but just couldn't. He put his head in his hands and started shaking. Both women put their arms around him.

252   The BeAst and the Brightest

Christelle asked, "What happened?" Danny blurted out that she was sleeping with two of his friends, including his best friend.

"That beast!" Sandrine exclaimed.

Christelle called her a bitch in French, a *garce* and a *salope*. Christelle asked, "Was one of them really your best friend?"

"Yes," was all that Danny could mutter.

"*Quel misérable connard*! What a miserable bastard!" Christelle shouted. "What a miserable bastard!"

Danny could hardly breathe. They talked for a while. Both girls gave him the usual advice: Forget her, this is not your fault, you have so much to live for, you just have to go on. Danny kept asking himself if this was true. Had he failed Cleo in some way? Had he hurt her? Perhaps he should have been more forthcoming in his letters. He knew that when he left, she was conflicted and angry about his departure, but he believed that, once back in Boston, their love would be reconfirmed. Why hadn't he been more insistent that she come to Paris? None of these questions answered the fundamental issue. Why hadn't she said anything to him earlier? Why hadn't she been honest with him? How long had he been deceiving him? Given all the guys in Boston and Cambridge, why his two friends? Was this all a plot to destroy him? Was she deceiving him during his two visits? Of course, the answer was that she had been deceiving him for most of the year, but he did not want to believe that about her.

After an hour or so, Christelle and Sandrine whispered something to each other and Christelle left, giving Danny the usual three bises, plus she held his face in her hands and gave him several tender, lingering kisses on the lips. Her affection meant so much to him. He saw these women's reactions to his distress as further proof of how wonderful women can be. Both Sandrine and Christelle were strong, intelligent, and independent but also soft, compassionate, empathetic, and loving. They were also real friends, not fake ones.

Seeing these two women's sympathetic reactions, Danny wondered how any woman could be as tough, as unrelentingly cruel, ruthless, and brutal as Cleo had been in those two encounters. He could not believe a woman could be that cruel and brutal to anyone, particularly to someone who had loved her, even if she had never loved him. She was not only lacking

Wonderful Women

in common decency, but she was devoid of any empathy or tenderness. Danny had never imagined that a woman could be so much like Vilemann.

Sandrine asked him if she could go back with him to his apartment.

"Sure, I'd love that, but don't you have to work?"

"Christelle is going to tell them that something much more important came up."

Both Christelle and Sandrine had understood how damaged he was and were fearful of what might happen. He looked horrible. Sandrine knew that as a real friend, she had to help Danny, not just say she was sorry about what had happened to him. She had to act. He needed some care, a lot of care. Sandrine hung out at his apartment the rest of the afternoon, letting him talk. She held both of his hands because if she didn't, they would shake violently. Around 7:45 p.m., Sandrine insisted on taking him to dinner. He looked thin. They went to a little neighborhood restaurant where Danny ate the standard steak with fries, which is both nourishing and filling. That dish, plus two glasses of red wine, helped him a lot. This was his first real meal in more than a week.

Sandrine said, "This is my treat. You are our *copain*, you know." Danny got ready to say good night and thank you, but Sandrine insisted that she was going back to his apartment with him. On the way was an American-style, self-service pharmacy. Sandrine said she needed to get something. She bought a toothbrush. She was not going to leave Danny all alone.

They continued talking until late. As 11:30 p.m. approached, Danny asked her if he could walk with her to her apartment. "I'm not leaving you here alone. You need some female company. I'm sleeping with you, but no sex; that would complicate things. You are absolutely not ready for that. Just hugs and kisses. No sex."

Sandrine knew that sex needs to be a product of happiness, not a response to despair or nothing more than an exercise in cynical physical pleasure, as it was with Cleo, Vilemann and Tallington. Sandrine told Danny to brush his teeth first and asked him for a big T-shirt. She took the T-shirt and went into the bathroom. When she came out of the bathroom, she saw Danny sitting on the edge of the bed, wearing his shorts and a T-shirt.

254 The BeAst and the Brightest

Sandrine sat on the edge of the bed then said, "You don't need a T-shirt. You're a guy, and you need affection."

So, Danny took off the T-shirt, and Sandrine slipped into bed next to him. She kissed him and caressed him all over, except where she had said she would not go.

They talked a lot until Danny fell asleep. He was totally exhausted. Twice during the night, he had that terrible nightmare about being pushed over the railing of his terrace and then seeing Vilemann and Tallington fucking Cleo in his apartment. The experience of being murdered and raped had been imprinted in his mind and brain. The trauma inflicted by Cleo had been made part of him. Disappointment fades away with time, but trauma becomes part of your psyche, part of each nerve synapse. After each nightmare like this, he woke up trembling and sweating. Sandrine knew he needed someone with him. So she hugged and held him as tightly as she could and caressed him until he went back to sleep. She wanted to cry seeing Danny so profoundly hurt but knew she shouldn't. He needed all of her strength as well as her affection.

The next morning, she noticed the untouched bottle of champagne in the refrigerator. Danny begged her to get rid of it. He could not imagine drinking one drop of that champagne meant to be shared with Cleo. Sandrine put it in a colorful bag and gave it to a young woman at the agency who had just announced her engagement. She thanked Sandrine and gave her a big hug, saying that she and her guy would celebrate with it. Sandrine disposed of the dead anemones by putting them in the collective garbage bin shared by all of the apartments in his building.

Danny had just three more weeks in Paris before going back to Boston. After that first night with Sandrine, she continued having dinner, sleeping with him, and hugging and caressing him as tightly and sweetly as she could. Every night, he'd wake up two or three times, shaking with anger and humiliation. Sometimes, he'd cry out in his sleep because of that nightmare about being pushed over the balcony railing, or he'd have other similar, frightening nightmares. Sandrine realized how terribly broken and traumatized Danny was, and she was determined to take care of him as much as possible. Sandrine loved Danny but had respected his commitment to Cleo.

Wonderful Women

He had always been attracted to Sandrine, but because of Cleo, he had never imagined making a move. His emotions and commitment were focused solely on Cleo. He started wanting to make love with Sandrine but respected her no-sex limitation. He wasn't ready; that was true.

Sandrine told Christelle and Loïc about Danny's nightmares and how he would wake up suddenly very agitated and shaking. They understood that he wasn't just hurt or disappointed; he had been traumatized by what happened with Cleo. Trauma is much more serious than disappointment. Ask any woman who has been raped or a Vietnam or Iraq war veteran suffering from PTSD.

Christelle, Loïc, and Sandrine ate dinner with him at local restaurants the next Friday and Saturday night. Danny was very happy to be with them. The next week, Sandrine kept coming to his apartment each evening after work, taking him to dinner and then sleeping with him. She gave him hugs and kisses and all of her tender affection. Two evenings, Aurélie came to have dinner with them, and she hugged and kissed Danny. The first night, before she kissed him, she looked at Sandrine since she knew how Sandrine felt about him, but Sandrine just nodded as if to say, "He needs all the love and affection he can get." Aurélie kissed him again several times with a delicious, sweet tenderness and then gave him a big smile as she put her arms around him in a tender embrace. Aurélie was a wonderful woman: smart, independent, faithful to her boyfriend Andrian, and loving. She knew what friendship means—protecting and taking care of someone and being there when that person needs help.

The second Sunday afternoon, Christelle and Loïc came over to his apartment to see Danny and Sandrine. After lunch with his three friends, Christelle told Danny that she was going to take Sandrine's place for a couple of days since Sandrine absolutely had to go to Bordeaux for two days for work. Sandrine told Danny that she had a train to catch that afternoon, but she'd be back on Wednesday and would be with him again. Christelle said, "So, I'm staying with you." Then she added, "Same rules; no sex."

Danny said it wasn't necessary, but Christelle insisted. Loïc told Danny, "Christelle and I want to be sure you are OK." Loïc then stood up and gave Danny three bises. These were not air bises but real kisses on the cheeks. Danny did not recoil from these male kisses since he realized that Loïc was confirming their deep French friendship. Danny understood that he and Loïc had become true friends and that Loïc fully supported Christelle's decision to stay with him. Then he and Sandrine left. Danny was so happy that Christelle would be with him. Being alone seemed impossible.

Sunday, Monday, and Tuesday night, Danny and Christelle slept together. The only difference was that Christelle didn't wear a T-shirt. Danny remembered her comment about nudity and how all girls have girl bodies, so what's the big deal about nudity? She did keep her panties on since the rule was no sex. She cuddled up against Danny's shoulder and let her breasts lay on him. He almost burst out crying since she was such a beautiful person, such a lovely woman, and so naturally tender and kind. Even though neither was wearing a T-shirt, there was nothing sexual about her touch, just reassurance by her presence and a lovely sensuality that seemed to help him find some peace, some acceptance, some belief that he could move on. He squeezed her and said, "You and Sandrine are the best *copaines* any guy could have." Christelle answered, "You're our friend."

Then Danny asked, "Are you sure Loïc is OK with your staying with me?"

"Sure. It's just friendship; you need someone with you, no sex. What could be wrong with friendship? Loïc trusts me completely, and he is worried about you; we all are." Again, the simple, compelling logic of this statement seemed irrefutable.

Danny saw that, in practice, trust among people enables many good things to happen that are impossible without it. Trust requires truth and fidelity. Respect for the truth makes life better. It is like oil in your car or food for your body. Truth makes things work, whether friendship, love, or a society. Truth is much simpler than many people imagine, but it does require courage, integrity, and empathy, which many people lack. Recognizing the truth and knowing intellectually that truth is important are not the greatest challenges; having the character to tell the truth is what matters. Character implies courage, integrity, and empathy. Christelle had a lot of all three, so did Sandrine, Aurélie, and

Loïc. Cleo had none of these positive characteristics. Neither did Vilemann or Tallington. Deceit is poison. Danny feared that the truth would never come from Cleo since she had been a stonewall in the two confrontations with her, and he doubted that Vilemann would help him understand what happened. Danny's only hope seemed to be Tallington, and maybe, just maybe Cleo.

Christelle thought that the simple truth gave her the freedom always to do the right thing and to be herself without artifice. Cleo saw the truth as flexible and as an enemy, constraining her behavior and limiting her options, impinging on her freedom and independence. Danny thought that these women—Sandrine, Christelle, Aurélie, and the others—were not only sensitive and wonderful but were true feminists living life on their own terms, treating men as equals and demanding the same from them. They lived without artifice or pretense. They were transparent about who they were. Danny asked himself why Cleo couldn't have behaved like these wonderful women. Why had she been immoral by sleeping with his friends and why the deceit? Why the deceit? Why did Cleo not understand the importance of basic decency, the capacity to feel even a minimum of respect for other people, and why did she lack any capacity for empathy?

If Cleo had broken up with him either when he left or during the year, he would have been hurt and terribly disappointed but not traumatized. The trauma Danny felt was caused by her sexual immorality and deceit, by her lack of decency and empathy, not a breakup. OK, a breakup would have been tough, very tough, but he would have gotten over it. A breakup would have been a huge disappointment for Danny but not traumatic, particularly if Cleo had expressed any regret, said she remembered all their happy times together, or revealed that she loved someone else in a way she could not deny. Had Cleo broken up with him, Sandrine would have helped him accept the disappointment, including without a T-shirt or panties.

Danny also knew that most cheaters get caught; they don't announce that they are doing something immoral. Cleo had come to Paris to announce that she was sleeping with two guys, neither of whom she said she loved or who loved her. She announced that she was sleeping with these two guys, both

258 The BeAst and the Brightest

Danny's friends and colleagues, almost as an affirmation of her total lack of constraint; society's rules did not apply to her. If she dared to come to Paris to make her two announcements, why hadn't she had the courage and integrity months earlier to do what Prudence told her to do: "be honest with Danny"?

If Tallington believed that Cleo had broken up with Danny and that he was OK with the breakup, why didn't Tallington come to Paris with Cleo to have a good time in that lovely romantic city? What kind of a guy would pass up a chance to spend time in Paris with his lover? If he suspected that Cleo had lied to him, why didn't he come to face Danny man to man? Why let Cleo come alone? What if Danny had gotten violent and hurt or even killed Cleo? Did Tallington know that Cleo was going to Paris with Vilemann? How did he feel about his sex partner, Cleo, going to Paris with another guy, the guy she had been sleeping with for a long time?

Sandrine came back from Bordeaux Wednesday night and started staying with him again. She would stay with him until he returned to the States. Danny got a call from Nicole the next day on Thursday. She wanted to see him.

"Really, are you sure? Do you know what happened between Cleo and me?"

She said that she wanted to know more; she wanted to know where they could meet to talk. They agreed on lunch at Café Madeleine, ironically the same café where Nicole and Cleo had eaten lunch the day she murdered Siegfried. Danny told Nicole the essence of what had happened.

During the first encounter, she told him that she was sleeping with a close professional friend of his, a colleague. Then, during the second encounter, she revealed that she was also sleeping with his best friend in the economics department and that she had not offered any explanation of when the affairs started, why she cheated with two of Danny's friends, or how she felt about sleeping with both of them at the same time. Had she slept with them on different nights or was she having sex parties? She had simply said she was sleeping with them, both of them. She had nothing to say about any feelings toward them; her relationship with them was described as nothing but sex; she was just

Wonderful Women   259

sleeping with them. Danny had nothing. He understood nothing. But he knew it was over. Nicole just listened.

Nicole had enjoyed a varied and full sex life during those first years in Paris, especially during her trips to Greece, but she was very careful never to deceive anyone or hurt anyone. Since those first years, she had been with Bepe, and she had been totally faithful to him; she really loved him. She had thought that Cleo had fallen for some other guy but could not have imagined that her bed partners were Danny's friends and colleagues or that one of them had been Danny's best friend.

She was also surprised to hear that Cleo never said she had fallen in love with either of her bedmates or her sex partners. Danny told Nicole the truth, which was that Cleo had only said she was "sleeping with them." Nicole thought about the present she had given Cleo: two professional studs to take her mind off Danny. When she heard what had actually happened, she regretted her present. Nicole realized that Cleo had only told her part of the truth. No, Cleo had lied to her about something important, about a human being, a guy who loved her. Cleo had hidden things from Nicole, her best friend, and she had hidden things that seemed totally immoral and deceitful to Nicole. Nicole felt used and abused.

On the way back to the United States, Cleo thought about that night with Nicole after she told Danny about Vilemann. Her impression was that Nicole had succumbed to a hedonistic lifestyle centered on sex with men and luxurious materialism. Sex was OK; sex was necessary for women just like for men, but she thought that Nicole was not enough of a feminist to understand how to keep men in their place. A little hedonism might be OK; Cleo had enjoyed some new sensations, some new experiences in Paris and had really liked them. But Nicole seemed to be going too far. She had done that shaving thing, which Cleo found disgusting. She thought that Nicole had given herself over to some sort of dirty, exaggerated European hedonism that stroked men's egos. Cleo thought that feminists should never live to please men. Cleo was forgetting that she had become a sex toy for both Remington and Vilemann, but self-reflection was never her forte.

As the hours passed on the plane, Vilemann kept insisting that Cleo tell him everything about what happened with Danny. He wanted to know the blow-by-blow about how Danny had reacted. He wanted to savor his victory over his colleague. Had Danny suffered? Was he really surprised? Was he upset? Had he focused more on Tallington than on him? Finally, Cleo could not take it any longer and told him to shut up about Danny.

She wasn't defending Danny as much as telling Vilemann to back off. Vilemann started to laugh at Danny and started mimicking Danny's shocked and hurt reaction to Cleo's betrayal. Vilemann wanted to savor his victory. He wanted confirmation that he was the winner and Danny the loser. Cleo was both offended and upset. She could dump Danny, she could betray him, she could be cruel to him, but she wanted to make it clear that those were her choices. She did not want to be Vilemann's tool to hurt Danny. He could not take any credit for what she had just done. Killing Danny was her idea, her choice. She wanted Vilemann to understand that she, Cleo, had killed Danny, not Vilemann. She told Vilemann that he should just shut up. When he didn't, they got into a big fight. Of course, Vilemann considered her nothing but a tool to hurt Danny.

As they approached Boston, she announced that she needed time to catch up with work so that once in Boston, she would need a week alone. Vilemann said he understood. After all, he had the victory he wanted, and he was not yet ready for "female meat." At the baggage carousel at Logan Airport, they said goodbye without even a polite, pretend kiss.

Chapter 32

Cleo Moves On

After putting her suitcase in her apartment, Cleo went to the little grocery store near her house for some essentials, the *Sunday New York Times* and the *Boston Globe*. Then she got Thai takeout from her usual Tuk Tuk Thai restaurant. The flight was long and full of tension because of Vilemann, and she was tired, but she tried to stay up. All she could think about was that hedonistic romp with Jean-Carlo and Frédérick. She regretted letting them have so much freedom with her body and again felt a bit upset that she had actually enjoyed it, but she had. Actually, it had been great. She started looking through her mail and noticed Danny's last letter to her. She threw it out unopened; then she tore out the pages of her diary that mentioned him. He was now officially dead. She put new pages where Danny had been but couldn't write anything.

Monday morning, she showed up early for work, only to see that Prudence was already at her desk. Prudence noticed that Cleo seemed rested and relaxed. She asked, "So, Cleo, tell me about the trip. What happened? How did it go?"

Cleo missed the authentically questioning intonation in her voice and the use of her name, not "my dear," so she just gave the stock answer, "It was a great trip; Paris is great." The second she said that she understood from the disapproving look that Prudence gave her that she wanted to hear about her discussion with Danny.

262   The BeAst and the Brightest

Cleo did one of her linguistic acrobatic moves, a verbal back flip, and with a very serious look, said, "The discussion with Danny was tough, but he understood. We had a good long discussion, and I think we ended up in a good place. A year apart has been hard on both of us and although he might have tried to maintain our relationship, he obviously has had several girlfriends in Paris; the current one might be named Brigitte."

Prudence just looked at Cleo. She knew that Cleo was lying. Prudence had just received Danny's letter telling her what happened. She had thought that Cleo's only lover was Vilemann. Learning about Tallington, Danny's best friend, shocked Prudence more than anything she had experienced in her life. Her belief in Cleo was shattered. The word "agast" assaulted her mind; she felt terrified. As she read the letter her hands shook violently, and she asked herself how she was going to liberate herself from this woman. Given Cleo's two betrayals of Danny, Prudence now believed that the rumors about a sexual relationship between Cleo and Remington were true. Prudence stopped seeing her as a successor.

Cleo sensed that Prudence had not believed her lie. She was upset and a little angry about it. Prudence had no right to judge her. Prudence's opinions about Danny and what she should do or not do with him were irrelevant to Cleo. She didn't care what Prudence thought.

By Wednesday, Cleo wanted to see somebody, so she called Tallington, whom she knew would come running at her slightest invitation. She didn't really want to see Tallington since he had served her purpose; she just wanted a convenient penis. He had been anguished about what might have happened in Paris. Tallington and Cleo had a quick dinner at her place and had sex together. He didn't have the guts to ask her anything about the trip. Before the trip, she had lied constantly about how she and Danny were breaking up because he had girlfriends in Paris. Tallington liked hearing these lies since, if true, he would be less guilty of betraying a friend. But he really didn't believe what Cleo was saying. Once she was back in Boston, it just stopped. It was over. She never mentioned Danny again, and Tallington just accepted whatever she had done to his best friend. He did not have the courage to ask Cleo about Danny. He was too afraid to

Cleo Moves On

ask Cleo if she had told Danny about them and, if so, how he had reacted or what he had said. In any case, Tallington hoped that he'd be able to hide behind Cleo's betrayal of Danny with Vilemann. He hoped to avoid being held responsible for his own betrayal, his own immoral behavior.

He knew that Danny was coming back soon, and that worried him. Was it true that Danny had girlfriends in Paris? Had Cleo lied about everything? Did Cleo hurt Danny? If so, would Danny come back and get a gun? He didn't think Danny would kill him or any of the others, but that happens frequently in similar circumstances. Was Danny angry and jealous enough to kill him, or Cleo or Vilemann? He hoped that Danny was a better person than a jealous, angry assassin. Paradoxically, he and the others had bet their lives on Danny's good character while doing horrible, immoral things that too often lead to violence, even murder. Why did they believe so fervently in Danny's good character? As he lay there in her bed, Tallington realized that he might be savoring the last moments of sexual pleasure with Cleo, so he might as well enjoy them as much as he could. He could not go any lower; he had hit rock bottom as a guy.

Finally, the week before Danny was to come back, Cleo told Tallington that in anticipation of Danny's return, they should never be together again. Tallington did not really know why this was happening. Was Cleo going to jettison both him and Vilemann and get back with Danny? Had she told Danny about him but not Vilemann? Had she told Danny about Vilemann? What was going on? Tallington felt sick to his stomach. Then Cleo said that she had told Danny about both of them but had not told him when these affairs started, whether they were continuing or anything else, and that Tallington should do the same.

"Don't tell Danny a damn thing!" she insisted. "He should never know anything!"

Tallington decided this meant anything about Vilemann as well. Tallington just said, "OK." He would never abandon the conspiracy of silence. This was his ultimate betrayal; he could never face the truth or partially redeem himself by telling Danny what had actually happened, when, and why. When Danny returned, he would not even tell Danny whether they were still

264 The BeAst and the Brightest

sleeping together, and if not, why they had broken up or if there had been a confrontation between them about her deceit.

Even though he felt that Cleo had used him and that he had done something profoundly wrong, he was never able or willing to tell Danny anything, even when he saw how broken his former friend was when he got back from Paris or even decades later. His arrogance prevented him from ever acting with the most basic decency. He never told Danny anything he hadn't already known in Paris, even when, many years later, his former friend had another crisis related to this sordid mess.

Many years after these events, Danny wrote to Tallington, asking for some basic information in writing about what had happened and when. Danny said that he needed to know what had happened to help him deal with the pain and suffering he had experienced for so many years. Danny promised that if he got the information he sought, he would never share it with anyone and never contact Tallington again.

Tallington was too arrogant or frightened to tell him anything. The truth was too challenging for him. Maybe he had enjoyed screwing Danny's girlfriend too much to betray her? Did he feel a compelling complicity with his former bed partner? His character had never changed. He hadn't had second thoughts about respecting his pledge of silence to Cleo. Plus, by never telling Danny what he did, he could try to avoid facing the reality that he, too, was an accomplice to murder and rape. He, too, had participated in Siegfried's murder and Danny's rape. He could continue to lie to himself about his good character. So much for a person growing. He'd just aged. He told Danny that he knew he had made mistakes but was totally unwilling to describe them or make up for them. He could not make amends, not ever, not at all, not even by telling Danny the truth in writing about what had happened.

He would not even tell Danny what Cleo had done or said to deceive him. Was her deception that she and Danny had broken up or was it that she was falling in love with him? Or did Cleo admit to having had an affaire with Vilemann, and then tell Talliington that it was over with Vilemann? Did Cleo lie about having broken up with Vilemann? Tallington used the excuse that Cleo deceived him, but he would never tell Danny what she said or did that was deceptive.

Cleo Moves On

When someone is terribly hurt because of a crime or moral sin, telling them that you are sorry is not enough. Actions, and the truth, not pathetic excuses, are required. Do we let murderers and rapists get off with just saying that they are sorry? Justice requires that the person who was wronged hear the truth from witnesses or a confession from the perpetrator. Neither Vilemann nor Cleo ever accepted that they did anything wrong. On the contrary, they were proud and happy about what had happened. Telling the truth was too challenging for Tallington, or perhaps he was too proud and arrogant or happy that he had been able to have sex with Cleo. His lack of moral fortitude and integrity did not allow him to tell the truth about what happened, certainly not the truth, the whole truth and nothing but the truth. His supposed friendship with Danny meant nothing to him. He was a totally false friend.

Judith Herman, the celebrated Harvard scholar of trauma, has shown that people who are traumatized need acknowledgment, apology, and amends. Danny only got a pathetic, hollow excuse from Tallington, which, in the absence of the truth and amends, meant nothing to him. Tallington's refusal to face up to the truth and share it with Danny was just another offense. Justice would have required an honest dialogue of restorative interaction that liberates the truth.

George Washington said, "True friendship is a plant of slow growth and must undergo and withstand the shocks of adversity before it is entitled to the appellation." At the first bump in the road, Tallington's true character was revealed. Friendship is built with bricks of action, not straw of words.

Sandrine insisted that Danny stay with her at her apartment his last few nights in Paris since he had to give up his place. Those last three nights, she took off her T-shirt as she came to bed just wearing her panties, but still said, "You're not ready for sex, but just know you're a great guy, and we love you." She wanted to say, "I love you," but knew that this was not the time to say that. Danny was so damaged he almost started crying again, but Sandrine kissed his eyes as if to dry them. They talked a lot and finally fell asleep holding each other. Sandrine was doing all she could to keep control of her own emotions, which was hard for her since she really loved and wanted Danny, and she was sure that Danny felt the same. Those days and nights with Sandrine had transferred all of Danny's love from Cleo to Sandrine, the woman who deserved his love.

Chapter 33

Danny Returns

Danny arrived at Logan Airport and went directly to Bill's house to settle in. Bill was a gregarious guy, and his wife was very friendly. Danny had not been great friends with them, but they knew and liked one another.

Right after Danny returned to Boston, he went to see Prudence. She was extremely welcoming and said how happy she was to see him. She had read and reread his letter, so she was prepared for the worse. She could see instantly that he was completely destroyed. He was in despair and clinically depressed. She understood that he was battling terrifying emotions despite the care and love he had received in Paris.

Prudence told Cleo that Danny was back in Boston, but she did not contact him; he was dead to her. Prudence told Danny that Cleo probably regretted what had happened and urged him to call her. "I'm sure she is not happy about how things turned out." Danny asked for any insights she had into why these things had happened and when Cleo first started sleeping with these guys. Prudence just repeated that she had been telling Cleo for several months that she should be honest with Danny. She did share with him the few facts she knew.

Nothing prolongs pain like suffering a continuing insult, a prolonged offense. Injustice is a terrible offense; closure is impossible as long as the truth is hidden. How do you close the door on a mystery? How do you come to terms with a conspiracy of silence?

Cleo and Vilemann's compact and Tallington's compliance with the injunction to "be brutal and not tell Danny anything" was a continuing source of despair. Danny was desperate for some recognition that he and Cleo had loved each other and that Cleo at least regretted what had happened. Why hadn't she been able at least to say she was sorry she had hurt him? Of course, she wasn't sorry about anything. She was proud of her new independence, proud to be like Vilemann, to be victorious in war, in life.

Danny called Cleo but got her answering machine. He told her that he was back in Boston and that he wanted to see her so that they could both understand what had happened and reach some reconciliation. He thought this would be best for both of them. "We shouldn't part angry at each other; we shared too much love, at least I thought we did."

She didn't return his call or mention it to Prudence the next day. Danny left the same message for Cleo every day after he had seen Prudence. Often, Cleo was in her apartment and heard Danny leaving his message on her machine, but she was never tempted to pick up and talk with him. Cleo didn't return any of his calls. Sometimes Vilemann heard Danny leaving his plaintive message and was thrilled to hear the trauma, the terrible distress in his voice. He loved each taste of his perverse victory but had learned not to say anything to Cleo. She erased all of his messages every day.

Danny stayed at the house, not going anywhere for a few days after Bill and his wife left. He was dreading going to Harvard. He knew that confrontations with Tallington and Vilemann were inevitable. Danny continued to spend most nights having dinner with Prudence, who continued to say he was more than welcome. She said she understood that he needed to talk and that time would be required for him to accept this ugly new reality. As they talked, she became increasingly frightened that he might do something awful; he might hurt himself or others. He was obviously depressed and perhaps suicidal. So, after two weeks, she asked Cleo to come to her office and share her perceptions with her. "Cleo, you can't let Danny do anything awful. All you need to do is to have an honest conversation with him so that he can move on. Imagine if he were to … you know, put an end to it all. You have to be honest with him."

Danny Returns

Cleo was mortified. He was dead to her. She had no idea what being honest with him meant. He knew what was going on; he knew who she was sleeping with. What else was there to say?

Danny went to the Econ Department at Harvard to see his advisor and get the keys to his car from Tallington. He was not in his office, so Danny left a note saying, "Leave my car keys on my office desk. The door is open." The next day, he had to go back to get his keys, which he found on his desk. Tallington came into his office. Danny just looked at him. Tallington delivered his pathetic line, "I know I did something wrong, but she deceived me. I am terribly sorry," But then said repeatedly, "You're the one she loves; you're the one she loves. Not me. You'll get back together."

Tallington's hope that Cleo would fall in love with him vanished when she told him that it was over since Danny was coming back to Boston. Tallington stupidly assumed that Cleo still loved Danny and that his pathetic desire to win her love had failed. Tallington believed that he had lost in a contest between males for a female, Cleo. But nothing like that had happened; Tallington misunderstood everything. There was no contest for her love. She didn't want to love anyone, just use them, and Tallington was nothing to her but Useful Idiot #2. Hearing that statement, "You're the one she loves," repeated over and over, further hurt Danny since he had loved her profoundly. Tallington was no friend, and Danny saw him for what he was: a sniveling coward who was totally immoral but also cynically arrogant.

Tallington tried to justify himself by writing the following note to Danny:

"It has always been my belief that Cleo deceived those close to her. I don't assume she was truthful to any of us. I am not confident in my understanding of why. It has always been my belief that it had something—perhaps a lot—to do with her craft, which invaded her personality, distorting her sense of what experiences in life were all about—recording them to write about them at a distance, one where factual accuracy is selectively crafted for other

270 The BeAst and the Brightest

goals—or simply live life in the best way she could. I made mistakes in this period, and I am sorry for them. I am not confident it is the same for Cleo."

Tallington hid behind these trembling, weak words. He had betrayed Danny by not telling him about Vilemann and by sleeping with his best friend's girlfriend without knowing how his friend would react to his taking Danny's place in her bed. Christelle was right to call him a miserable bastard.

The confrontation with Vilemann was shorter. Vilemann threatened Danny to stay away from him and Cleo. Danny and Vilemann had almost nothing to say to each other. Vilemann saw Danny as the loser in this fight, and Danny saw Vilemann as an evil bastard, nothing more. Again, just seeing Vilemann raised the question of how a woman like Cleo could ever associate with a bastard, an ugly brute like Vilemann.

Danny had not yet fully accepted the fact that Cleo did not have a conscience or any consideration for anyone. He had not realized that Cleo was just Vilemann in a woman's body. She had absolutely no respect for the truth or sexual morality. Danny's Cleo was not the real one. The Cleo Danny loved was a figment of his imagination. In his imagination, she was a very attractive, intelligent, perhaps talented young woman with a strong commitment to feminism. In fact, she was all that, but she was immoral, untruthful, and deceitful. Danny had not seen those other parts of her character. Love is blind, and she was skillfully deceitful. Of course, deceiving someone in Paris was easy since Danny's friends failed the test of friendship.

After these confrontations, another event convinced Danny to spend as little time as possible at Harvard. One afternoon, he spent an hour getting things together in his office, and some guys in the department came by to see him. They welcomed him back, asked about Paris, and then one of them said, "You know, that girl you used to take out, she has been sleeping with Tallington and Vilemann."

Another guy said, "Yeah, maybe we all have a chance with her; she's so easy to bed." Despite everything that had occurred, Danny hated to hear guys talk about Cleo as if she were a

Danny Returns 271

common whore, the department's whore. Danny knew that these guys had no idea how much he had loved her or how much he was suffering; they probably assumed that he and Cleo had broken up when he left. These comments hurt him.

As Prudence had suggested, Danny continued calling Cleo but only got her answering machine. She had no interest in any sort of reconciliation and could not even imagine what reconciliation might look like. She did not return his calls, even to say to stop calling her.

Prudence kept insisting that Cleo talk with Danny, so she finally called him back to avoid alienating Prudence. Cleo was happy to get his message machine. Her message said that she'd meet him at a coffee shop on Boylston Street the next afternoon at 5:30 p.m. He left her a message thanking her and saying that he thought this would help them both.

Cleo thought, *Poor Danny, he just doesn't get it. He lost, that's all. I won; he lost.*

When Cleo showed up, Danny was already at a table in the back of the coffee shop where they could talk without a lot of people around them. Danny tried to reach out to give her even the smallest hug, but she recoiled and did not even let him touch her. As she sat down, she immediately started explaining that, as a feminist, she was free to have sex with anybody she wanted, that she would never allow herself to be dominated by a man, that he did not own her or have any claim on her, and that she was a sexual being and could enjoy herself with any willing guy whenever she wanted.

Danny just listened, crestfallen. She was obviously not interested in a dialogue. They shared no moral beliefs or personal values; their ideas about feminism were profoundly different. Cleo had no interest in what Danny thought.

Every time he tried to say something, she cut him off and just continued. Finally, he was able to ask her what had happened between them.

"You left," she said.

If somebody was "to blame," it was Danny because he had left her. Danny tried to ask her why she had continued to write to him even though their relationship was over and why she had welcomed him into her apartment, into her arms, and her body when he came back to Boston.

She just said, "Come on, Danny, you know."

But of course, he didn't understand anything. Then she got up, turned around to leave, then looked back and said, "What the big deal? You're not the only person to experience a sudden and totally unexpected breakup." Then she left without saying goodbye or anything else. The hoped-for dialogue was hijacked by Cleo to sound off about her claim to total sexual freedom and to avoid any mention of her deceit or immoral behavior. The encounter had been a fiasco.

The next day, Danny returned to see Prudence. Danny's despair had gotten deeper and his anxiety greater. Prudence said that Cleo needed more time and that he should not give up on her. Later that week, Cleo made a point of telling Prudence that she and a guy were going to a play and, "We're excited to see it together."

Prudence understood that this was Cleo's way of saying that she was moving on with another guy. Prudence didn't know if it was Vilemann, Tallington, or some new guy.

Two weeks went by, and Prudence and Danny had seen each other a few times. Danny had tried to reach Cleo again, saying that he still hoped that they could "continue their dialogue," but Cleo had not returned his calls. Finally, Prudence again called Cleo into her office and was more straightforward.

"Cleo, Danny is still very upset. In fact, I think he is in trouble, and I value him just as I do you. Please reach out to him and see if you two can clear the air a bit. I think both of you would benefit. Please make an effort to find a way to reach some reconciliation, some understanding."

Cleo knew she was cornered. She'd have to see Danny once again, for the last time, she hoped.

Prudence helped organize a dinner at The Harvard Hotel. Prudence thought a dinner at a nice restaurant would force them to spend more time together, and she hoped Cleo had heard her request to be more forthcoming. She wasn't asking Cleo to get back with Danny; she knew that becoming a couple again was impossible, but some reconciliation should be attempted one more time. Cleo knew she had to agree to go to the dinner.

Danny Returns

She and Danny arrived at the same time, so they were seated as if they were a couple. Cleo took the menu and held it in front of her face. Cleo ordered halibut and rice. Danny said that would be fine for him as well. Danny ordered a bottle of white wine. The waiter asked Cleo if she wanted a starter, but she said, "No, the fish will be fine."

Danny took this to mean that the conversation might be short. Even before the food arrived, Cleo said that she hoped Danny had come to terms with the fact that she was sleeping with other people. Danny told her that Tallington had said several times that he, Danny, was the one she loved. He also told Cleo that Tallington had refused to tell Danny if they were still sleeping together. Cleo just stared at him. She was not going to tell him anything. "Cleo, I loved you very sincerely, and I trusted you totally. What did I do to alienate you so much?"

Cleo said that their relationship, as he called it, had never amounted to much to her. Then she added, "Maybe you had a significant relationship with me in your imagination? OK, we slept together a little bit, but that was all, and sex is no big deal. Haven't you heard about women's right to 'anonymous, zipperless fucking?'"

Cleo then went on to talk about and praise Erica Jong, whom Danny had never heard of. Danny asked, "What was anonymous about sleeping with my friends? They are not anonymous to me. You knew I considered them my friends."

Cleo answered that she didn't care who he knew; she was free and would not accept any sexual restrictions from Danny or any other guy. "I'll sleep with whomever I want. I can fuck anybody I want."

Danny said that he had never "slept with" Cleo or certainly had never fucked her but had tried to express his love for her with his body with their sexual intimacy. Maybe she had not gotten the message that he truly loved her or didn't want to hear it from him.

All she could say was, "Whatever."

They then turned to their fish and rice, pushed it around on their plates for about 10 minutes, which seemed like an hour to Danny, and then looked at each other. Cleo got up and started to walk away, then she turned toward him briefly and said, "I think that maybe I may be in love with Vilemann a little bit." Then she left.

Danny paid the bill and went back to the house. Her life, defined by lies, deceit, and cynical sex, had been emptied of any empathy. Serial, zipless encounters with men had hollowed her out of human-to-human communion and had erased any empathy or sympathy from her character if she ever had any. Cleo could not reconcile with Danny since Hegel cannot understand Kant and character is destiny.

The next day, Danny bought Erica Jong's book at the Coop. A quick reading just increased his despair. The next evening, Danny told Prudence what had happened, thanked her for all her help, and said, "It's over. There is nothing more to do; nothing good is ever going to happen between me and Cleo. It's over."

Prudence just repeated what many other people would say to him, "You have so much going for you; you just have to move on." And he did move on. He promised to keep in touch, and Prudence said that she'd like that very much.

In the opening scene of Shakespeare's comedy *All's Well That Ends Well*, a mother shares this guidance with her son: "Love all, trust a few, hurt no one." Cleo's philosophy of independence and domination was to love no one, deceive all, and hurt everyone. Danny's innocence and naïveté led him to love all, trust all, and hurt no one. The philosophical and moral chasm between them made reconciliation impossible.

Chapter 34

Danny Moves On

Danny worked as hard on his dissertation as possible. The opportunity did turn out to be real at Princeton, and Danny and a bunch of other academics were invited to present their dissertation topics and their findings to a group of Princeton professors. Danny had been surprised to receive the Harvard grant to France based on just one weekend of hard work, and the same thing happened with Princeton. He did the best presentation he could, but he kept his expectations low since the competition was intense, and this was probably the best starting job at a name university available that year in the country.

Much to his surprise, Danny's advisor called him two weeks after his presentation, saying that Princeton was going to offer him the job, a three-year, tenure-track position. His advisor was ecstatic. Danny told his advisor how much he appreciated all the support he had been given and that he'd be in touch with Princeton. Of course, Danny was happy. Any aspiring young Ph.D. would be happy to get a job at a great university like Princeton. But Danny was mostly happy just to have a way to leave Harvard and Cambridge. He started making plans to "get out of town" as fast as possible. He coordinated with Bill to turn the house over to another graduate student, found an apartment in Princeton, and started packing.

By chance, one day at Princeton, Danny saw one of his lovely girlfriends from his years at Stanford. She grew up in Palo Alto and was two years behind Danny in school. Kathleen was the quintessential lovely California blonde. Everyone called her Kitten. Even given the competition at Stanford, she was acknowledged to be very, very bright as well as beautiful, friendly, loving, and sweet. She was athletic, affectionate, and laughed easily. Even with her cute name, no one underestimated or lacked any appreciation for her. Danny was so happy to spend those two wonderful years with her. When he graduated and left for Italy, they had to acknowledge the end of what had been a wonderful, loving relationship. Just as she was graduating, she married a nice guy she had met at Stanford, and they were now both graduate students at Princeton. Danny and Kitten were both amazed and delighted to see each other again. They saw each other a couple of times; Kitten wanted him to meet her husband, and they went out for dinner several times.

Kitten asked Danny if he had a girlfriend, and Danny told her his tragic story. She took him in her arms and kissed him on both cheeks. "You are too nice a guy to hurt, you know that don't you?" Danny could only mutter, "Cleo didn't see it that way."

Kitten decided to help Danny in any way she could. She started organizing dinners with her friends. At each dinner, Kitten invited one of her attractive, intelligent girlfriends. Danny really enjoyed meeting all of these lovely, smart women. Kitten was taking care of Danny. Kitten's emotional maturity and the loving end to their relationship enabled her to transition from a warm, friendly lover to a warm, loving friend. Kitten had had a number of lovers. She had always understood them as people and treated them with respect, even during a breakup. She had never hurt anyone. Some of her lovers had been disappointed by the breakup, but she took care never to injure any of these guys. One time, Kitten said that she couldn't emotionally or intellectually understand deceit or betrayal. She asked Danny, "What kind of a woman is this Cleo? How does she live with herself?"

Several months after arriving in Princeton, Danny went back to Cambridge for his dissertation defense. He drove there very early on the morning of his defense, all the way from Princeton to Cambridge. The meeting with the review committee was

Danny Moves On

scheduled for 1:30 p.m. and took less than an hour. Then, he was asked to step out of the meeting room. About 15 minutes later, his advisor came out and said, "Congratulations, doctor." He was free to go.

"I suppose you're going to have a party with your friends," his advisor said. Actually, he walked to the parking lot, got into his car, and drove nonstop to Princeton. That was the last time he was ever at Harvard. He could never bring himself to go back.

Kitten organized a surprise party for him when he returned from Cambridge with his doctorate in hand. Danny again said to himself that women can be wonderful and that friendship is essential to resilience and happiness. Danny knew he had been changed by what happened to him, but as Maya Angelo has written, he had strived not to be reduced by it, but the innocent, sweet person that was Siegfried was dead, and Danny had to carry his corpse within him all his life. Living with a corpse within him was a constant reminder of what had happened in Paris. He was trying to move on with greater wisdom and insight, but also happiness, but Siegfried's corpse would stay in him all his life. Reconnecting with Kitten and seeing her married and happy reconfirmed to Danny the value of friendship with good people. Kitten had been a wonderful lover; she then became a good, supportive friend. Women can be wonderful.

Danny wrote a letter to Sandrine telling her that he had received his degree and that he was generally doing fine. He wanted her to tell all of his friends in Paris how much they meant to him. Sandrine wrote back her congratulations and assured him that everyone was very happy for him. Then, Sandrine wrote that Alfred had proposed, but she could not find it in her heart to accept.

She wrote that she understood that during those last few weeks in Paris she and Danny felt love for each other but that he had to go back. She ended by saying that she had decided that love should guide her life and that she hoped someday to find the kind of love that she had felt for Danny, and that she hoped he'd find a new love in America. Losing any hope that he and Sandrine would ever be united in their love meant that Danny might never love anyone again. But how do you live when you can't believe in love?

278   The BeAst and the Brightest

Despite the chance renewal of a friendship with Kitten, her husband, and some of their friends, falling asleep was still very hard for Danny. He was still having those nightmares. Instead of joy or a great sense of accomplishment at getting a Harvard doctorate, he was just relieved to have left all that behind him. He asked the university to mail his diploma; he would not be returning for the graduation ceremony. He wasn't even thinking about the future or his plans for his first year as a professor. All he could think about was the disaster his personal life at Harvard had been. Kitten and her friends were shining a light, leading him forward, but the shadow from those three in Boston was dark and persistent. Often, people at Harvard and similar universities are called the best and the brightest, but Danny had learned that these three were beasts, human beasts. Hegel did capture part of life, but Danny refused to renounce Kant. He chose to live in a world where love, truth, and fidelity are honored. He would have to live in that world, however, with a deep, painful scar.

Danny knew that we live in a "world of sin and woe," as Churchill said. He understood that the trauma he had suffered was insignificant compared with the trauma and suffering of millions of other people. Danny did not consider himself a victim, but he could not forget his trauma. As he moved on, the wound Cleo and his false friends had inflicted closed but did not heal. That ugly, painful scar was the reflection of those three ugly, destructive people. Many years later, Danny would learn from the great work on trauma by Judith Herman of Harvard that moving on, while necessary, is not sufficient to heal trauma. Trauma is healed by redemptive justice. Those who inflict trauma have to reveal what they did and be held accountable.

Many years after these events, Danny was inspired by all of those women, the creators of the #MeToo Movement who were raped or abused but were able to find their voices, even after years or decades of holding their tongues and hiding their pain and humiliation, to denounce their rapists and abusers. By telling their personal truth, it became public truth, which served as a palliative and a release for those brave women. A few were able to get some form of justice in a court or the court of public opinion. They were able to surmount their anger and humiliation

Danny Moves On 279

to denounce their rapists and abusers. These women's truth also inspired other women and some men to help pass laws and improve practices and procedures that might protect women in the future and enable them to get justice when they are hurt. Danny could only applaud these women. Danny felt just as raped, just as abused, just as violated as a human being as many of these women; but what happened to him was just immoral and evil, not criminal, so he had no recourse in the courts.

Since working every day with Cleo had become a source of distress for Prudence, she spoke with Johnny Littman about a position for Cleo in his much larger division, but Littman expressed his reluctance, saying, "Hiring someone like Cleo might have reputational consequences." Littman knew that Cleo slept around and was well informed about Cleo and Alexander's sexual relationship. Comments about Cleo in the little world of Schendler resembled village gossip. By letting everyone "touch" her, she had become untouchable.

Prudence had never openly criticized Cleo to Danny, hoping that they would reconcile, but she became so distressed because of what happened that she wrote the following letter to Danny. She believed that he would benefit from knowing what she really thought; Prudence's insights would help him overcome his anguish.

Cleo's passion is literature and writing. Her life is fiction, where she shapes and rewrites the story, she tells herself and others to fit her evolving needs. To her, these are not lies, just revisits. Scenes are rewritten, and characters evolve. Those she wants to embrace temporarily are given nothing more than fragments of the truth, glimpses of the plot, never the whole truth or the essence of her evolving storyline.

These characters are trapped in a well-phrased illusion, believing they are co-authors until they no longer serve her purpose. When they seek to understand themselves and their role in the story, she protects her independence with half-truths, evasive but clever comments, and silent smiles.

When they press her to understand more, to get to know her, she invites them to come to bed. They take that to be an invitation to come deeper into her life, but it's really just a subterfuge. She gives her body to protect her life, or the lives she is living, as she writes and rewrites chapters.

Her deceit eviscerates characters she wants to erase. She uses sex shamelessly. Morality is totally foreign to her. She never feels regret or shame for what her characters suffer because they are fiction. The truth is always malleable. It's fluid. She does not have the integrity or the strength to tell the truth about anything. She can never recognize her own culpability or accept responsibility for her destructive behavior.

Her lack of any moral compass and her dishonesty inevitably led to a catastrophe with you because you genuinely and profoundly loved her. I hoped that you and Cleo would be able to reconcile, but without the courage and honesty to recognize her frightful behavior and apologize or to feel any shame, she turned into a beast."

Chapter 35

Cleo and Vilemann Finale

Vilemann was getting excited about San Francisco and the possibility of a position out there. He, too, was finishing up at Harvard and was ready to move to the Bay Area. He seemed almost giddy with excitement. Cleo wondered if what she felt for Vilemann was love or if she was still just caught up in his frenzy. She felt something but wasn't sure what love felt like. She was eager to go to SF with him in the belief that being out there with him would reveal his intentions toward her, but also allow her to make her own decision about Vilemann.

His dark charisma had invaded every part of her body and her life. He owned her, but she would never have admitted to that. She still wanted to believe that she was that independent, free feminist she had always aspired to be and that she would determine what happened between them.

Cleo's family issues started to complicate her life further. Her father had created two trusts for his three kids. One of them had been used by her brothers to enlarge their vineyards in Chile and Australia. Since she had opted not to work in the family business, her part of this trust had been ceded to her brothers. The other trust had been used to buy some land in Australia that had never been developed successfully but was costing money to keep up, or at least that is what the brothers were going to tell Cleo. There was a lot more to the story than what the brothers would share with their sister. They would tell her that the money in that trust was running out and that they had to deal with that problem. They needed Cleo's agreement to cede her share of this trust so Mark could deal with the legal and financial issues once back in Australia. By ceding her share, she'd be off the hook for any of the expenses related to the land. They were asking her to come to San Francisco to meet with them to go over all of the figures and to deal with the accountant and lawyer. Cleo was open to the idea of meeting with her brothers to terminate this remaining family entanglement and knew that Vilemann wanted to go to SF to see the people with whom he might work. She feared that if the trust money ran out, she'd have to start contributing to the costs.

The brothers were essentially defrauding their sister. A possible protection against being accused of defrauding her was to have an in-person meeting with all three siblings, the lawyer, and the accountant. Her presence would create the impression that they had been totally open with her. They could rightfully claim that she had met with them, the lawyer, and the accountant to go over all of the figures and the agreements. Of course, she was so disengaged with her brothers and the rest of her family that Mark and Tony believed she might never realize that she had been robbed.

The vineyards had made her brothers very wealthy, and they intended to increase their wealth by leasing out the undeveloped land to builders for housing, shopping areas, and an industrial park. When those deals were finalized, their wealth would expand enormously. The rent and lease payments would roll in for years, and the sums would be substantial. They had no intention of sharing any of this wealth with Cleo.

The wealth her brothers were accumulating from their vineyards was used for all sorts of activities. Her older brother, Mark, had developed a taste for sex in the brothels in Thailand, which were a short, direct flight from his vineyards in Australia. He had the means to frequent the fancy VIP brothels in Bangkok, Phuket, and Pattaya. He had tasted the "merchandise" in the brothels in Bali and Jakarta but preferred Thailand. Tony, his younger brother, had gone several times with him to the fancy brothels in Thailand, and since his first experience there with his brother, Tony started doing the same thing in Rio de Janeiro. Sex

Cleo and Vilemann Finale

is addictive, particularly when it is easy and plentiful to access with money. They started visiting each other's vineyards every three months or so, then going for some sexual recreation either in Thailand or Brazil. These trips and experiences made them even hungrier for even bigger money, and they were eager to settle up with Cleo essentially for nothing to be able to move forward with the business deals that were going to make them extremely rich.

During his visits to Thai brothels, Mark had developed a taste for younger and younger girls. He preferred them to be 13 or even younger. Yes, pedophilia. These girls were everywhere, and the police were paid off either with money, drugs, or sessions with these little girls. He kept this preference hidden from his brother. When they were together, they just used "women" 16 or older. Tony also had a hidden desire. He liked both boys and girls. Sometimes, when he was in Rio, he paid to be with a boy; other times, he wanted a boy and a girl at the same time. Just like Mark, Tony kept this a secret. Just as in Thailand, when the brothers were together in Rio, they stuck to older women, 16 and up. Of course, Cleo knew nothing about the business deals, the trips between Australia and Chile, or the side trips to Thailand and Brazil.

After lots of back-and-forth, Cleo finally arranged to meet with her brothers in SF. Vilemann said he wanted to go with her, which pleased her immensely. Cleo thought that being out there with Vilemann, who was so excited about the possibility of a job in SF, would help clarify her thoughts about him and them. Should she consider living with Vilemann; did she actually love him? Like Elizabeth in *Les Enfants Terribles*, she wanted to be the one to decide what path her life would take; she would be the last one standing. All these considerations were setting her up for a major fall, but she never thought that she could lose. Cleo had not learned Frank's lesson that cynical sex can be a two-way street.

Vilemann had decided that to finish beautifully with Cleo meant finding a way to crush her, to show her that she had lost and lost totally. He wanted to destroy her, to vanquish her. He had valued her simply as a weapon against Danny. She had not only betrayed Danny, but she had also turned on him to hurt him

284   The BeAst and the Brightest

as much as possible. Now, Vilemann wanted to demonstrate his power one last time by totally devastating her.

He started telling her again that if she wanted to be with him, she'd have to give in to his desire for anal sex. He'd say, "Why shouldn't we give ourselves to each other totally, right?"

Cleo hated these discussions but did not want this to prevent him from going with her. She saw this trip as the deciding moment—would she go to SF with him and have a life with him in SF or kill him off? She had been moving her sex red lines for a year and decided to submit to this one last demand, although it had been totally taboo. Although terribly conflicted, she submitted to his desire. She begged him to be tender and not go deeply into her. "Please, just play a little around my thing, OK? Don't go deep into me back there?"

He turned her around and lifted her bottom so he could penetrate her, but not in her vagina. She steeled herself, waiting for his penis to go into her butt. First, he slipped the penis-shaped sex toy into her vagina and then another sex toy into her butt. Cleo thought for a second it was his penis until he started playing with it—in and out. After a minute or so, he slipped the sex toy out of her butt and then inserted his penis, pounding her with all his force. He pushed himself into her as far as he could go and came in and out with all his sexual strength. She felt totally invaded and distraught, but as he climaxed, he exclaimed, "Finally, Great! Great! This is great! Super! Super! Great!"

After his climax, he stretched out on the bed and said, "Now I've had you, everything I wanted." Cleo was impotent to refuse him anything. He owned her. "That was great," he repeated. You liked it, didn't you?"

"Sure," was her reply. She wanted to cry but couldn't.

She was mortified as she thought about what she had let him do but tried to think about other things. He had always been rough with her during sex, but she had accepted whatever he wanted to do, no matter how rough he was. Vilemann had finally achieved total domination over her. He not only owned her, he was also defiling her in preparation for the final kill. After that first night, anal sex seemed to be all Vilemann wanted from Cleo. He gave her some thong panties saying, "I like to see your ass."

Cleo and Vilemann Finale 285

She started wearing them every day and letting him see her just wearing those little thong panties. Sometimes during anal sex, she'd touch herself just to feel some sexual stimulation. Was he not interested in her as a woman? Did he not understand that, as a woman, she needed some sexual pleasure, too? Sometimes, when he was doing her in the butt, she'd tremble and want to cry, but she knew she had to submit to him to keep him.

Cleo and her brothers agreed to stay at the Westin St. Francis on Union Square. When they were in downtown SF, her parents used to go there to have a drink or to get something to eat in the bar area, and the kids had fond memories of that hotel. They had always had banana splits—beautiful, big banana splits.

The plan was to arrive on a Wednesday afternoon in San Francisco and get together with Cleo's brothers that evening for an early dinner. Since Cleo and Vilemann were flying west, they would be tired. Mark made reservations for dinner at 6 p.m. at E&O Kitchen and Bar, a restaurant offering Asian food.

On the flight to SF, Vilemann talked about the job and about living in SF but did not ask Cleo if she wanted to live with him or whether she would consider moving with him to SF. She started thinking more seriously about how to win at The Game. Danny had been dealt with; now she had to decide what role, if any, Vilemann would have in her life. Danny was dead, and she had dumped Tallington once he no longer served her purpose. His role in her life had been emotionally insignificant, actually non-existent. Now, it was all about Vilemann. He had come to dominate her so much that she couldn't imagine he would not ask her to live with him. But she was conflicted.

The four of them met at the Westin's bar for a drink. There was not much conversation except for the cliché questions about Cleo's and Vilemann's flight. Then, they headed a few blocks to the restaurant. As they walked, Mark talked a bit with Cleo about the problematic land holdings, leaving Vilemann to chat with Tony. Dinner conversation focused almost exclusively on the food that they shared. Cleo had little or nothing to discuss with her brothers except the trust issue, which she did not want to discuss in front of Vilemann. She certainly didn't want to talk about anything important to her regarding Vilemann while her

286   The BeAst and the Brightest

brothers were present. As they finished eating, Cleo mentioned being tired from the trip, and Mark handled the check. Then they all walked back to the Westin and said good night without any hugs or kisses. Cleo and Vilemann got in bed, both claiming to be tired, so nothing happened between them, not even a little good-night kiss. The only thing of substance that happened that evening was that Vilemann had a brilliant idea for how to dispose of Cleo.

Vilemann had never imagined continuing the relationship with Cleo once in SF. Having achieved his total triumph, he now wanted to find a way to trample her so that she would realize that he was the triumphant winner and she was the total loser. The plan just dropped in his lap that evening.

Mark was not only the oldest, but he also always led when business had to be discussed, so he told Cleo that they would get together first and would be joined later by Tony, the lawyer, and the accountant. Tony offered to show Vilemann around SF the next day. The next morning, Mark and Cleo spent several hours discussing the land holdings, and after a quick lunch, another session was held in his suite going over the accounts for the trusts. They were able to agree easily. At about 3:30 p.m., an accountant, a notary, and a lawyer showed up at Mark's suite to finalize their decisions.

Mark had shown Cleo figures that demonstrated that the initial money, $500,000 for each kid, had been spent to buy and maintain the vacant land. Property taxes and other expenses, plus failed vineyards on that land over the years, had used up what money was left. Mark told Cleo that their father had made a big mistake buying the land since it was essentially worthless as vineyards. Every attempt to produce wine had failed. Of course, Mark didn't mention the very lucrative deals that would make him and Tony much richer. The deals were at the point of being signed, but Mark had put off finalizing these deals to be more able to defraud his sister. He wanted to finalize the deals only after seeing Cleo. If he were ever asked, he could say that these deals were purely speculative when he and Tony saw their sister.

To distract her from the potential robbery, Mark offered to give something to his sister from their earnings in the vineyards. Even though she had not had any managerial involvement with the

Cleo and Vilemann Finale 287

vineyards or the undeveloped land, Mark said her wanted her to have something, so he offered her a check for $10,000. Cleo was happy to get something since she had expected nothing and had feared she was going to be asked to cover some expenses. To Mark and Tony, $10,000 was a pittance. The lawyer drafted the necessary papers ceding her share of the land trust, and Mark cut a check to Cleo for $10,000. Cleo had been robbed, but she did not realize it. They wrapped up at about 5 p.m.

Everyone had agreed to meet at 6 p.m. for a drink in the bar at the Westin, so Mark and Cleo had a little time to go to their rooms to freshen up for dinner. At the bar, they all ordered some wine, drank it without much conversation except between Vilemann and Tony about things they had done and seen in SF, and headed to the restaurant. The brothers had made dinner reservations at Ula Restaurant, a lovely Art Deco-style bistro that offers French cuisine. Cleo's parents had been invited, so they were six for dinner.

Since Cleo's mother had bought her apartment in SF, her parents had been functionally distant, not legally separated, but distant. Each had their own lives. They had skipped the drink at the Westin, electing to meet everybody at the restaurant. Cleo had not seen her parents for more than two years, so everybody tried to smile when they got together, but the hugs were cursory, and there was no kissing on the lips. The restaurant reminded her of Brasserie Lipp in Paris, where she had met Nicole and the two guys after the murderous encounter with Danny. She tried to get that memory out of her mind by engaging in conversation with her parents, but those conversations did not take off except for a few small exchanges with her father; the four younger people had to keep things going. Cleo thought it was revealing that Vilemann did not seem that interested in connecting with Cleo's parents, but she didn't care. He was usually a torrent of opinionated comments, self-serving stories, and "informed" observations that dominated every conversation.

To get any conversation going, Vilemann asked Mark and Tony about their names. They were not Italians, so why the names Mark and Anthony? Mark and Tony both spoke up, explaining that their parents had honeymooned in Rome and were enormously impressed by all the Roman ruins. So, the boys became Marcus and Anthony. So, why the name Cleo? What did Cleo have to do with Rome? After being in Rome, their dad had become fascinated by Mark Anthony and his love affair with the queen of Egypt, Cleopatra. Cleo's name was actually Cleopatra. Vilemann remarked that he had never known that. Cleo leaned over to Vilemann and said, "After all this time, you didn't know my real name? Did you think it was just Cleo?"

"It just never occurred to me to ask, that's all. What's the big deal?"

Mark was the oldest, followed by Cleo and Anthony. Vilemann asked Mark, "So you're the oldest, followed by Cleo? How did your parents know that they'd have a son they could call Anthony?"

Mark spoke up, saying his full name was Mark Anthony. Tony's full name was Anthony Mark. Mark added that he knew this reversal of names might seem unusual even bizarre, but it worked since he was always known as Mark, and Tony was only known by his first name.

"Since the names Mark, Anthony, and Cleopatra were used for the first two kids if Tony had been a girl, what name would a baby girl have been given?" Vilemann asked.

"Well," Mark explained, "Since Cleo was taken, it might have been Alexandra, the Americanized version of Alexandria, the city in Egypt where Cleopatra studied and that was famous for its library, the most extensive in the ancient world. But that name was already in the family. One of Cleo's first cousins is named Alexandra. We almost never see her because, on a trip to Venice, she met an Italian stud, kind of a tough guy, and they got married. Nobody in the family sees them very often. What's his name anyway—Giacomo, Gianni, Guillermo? I forget, not important. They have two sons and one daughter and now they live in Padua, not far from Venice."

Actually, Mark just made up the part about the name Alexandra. The ability to create believable but false stories ran in the family, as did the rejection of conventional sexual morality. Mark's story seemed believable to almost everyone at the table. He could invent fables as well as Cleo. But Cleo's father objected, saying that Alexandra is a Greek girl's name related

Cleo and Vilemann Finale

to the Greek goddess Hera, which means "defender of men, or mankind, or warriors, something like that."

This statement caused an incredible outburst from Cleo. She shouted, "That would have been horrible for me, the worst name for me. Defender of men? No way!" She paused, then shouted, "Even for a sister, that would have been a horrible name— defender of men. What a stupid name for a woman."

Everyone looked embarrassed and a little shocked by this outburst. Once the social discomfort passed, everyone at the table was silent until Cleo's father made an unfortunate but typically maladroit remark. "At least Alexandra has two sons and a daughter, so my brother has grandchildren." This remark was met with total silence among the three siblings, none of whom had any intention of ever having children.

Mark paid for the dinner. Cleo's parents left with just a light, rapid hug, and the three siblings and Vilemann walked back to the Westin. Back at their hotel, Vilemann seemed disinterested in sex, so he and Cleo just went to sleep. This was the second night together without doing anything.

Cleo spent Friday with her father in Napa. She actually enjoyed being back in the vineyards and seeing her childhood home. A visit to the wine cellar brought back happy memories of Nicole and her among all those barrels of wine. She and her father had an early dinner in their house, and then Cleo got a car service back to SF. Vilemann had planned to spend the day with the people he might work for. Cleo expected to see him when she arrived back at the Westin, but he arrived late, about 12:30 a.m. He said that he had eaten dinner with those people, and their discussions had run late. He also said that they wanted him to spend the next week working with them so that he wouldn't be going back to Boston the next morning with Cleo. None of this was true, except that he wasn't going back with her. She asked herself what the hell was going on. They went to sleep with just a quick, cursory kiss.

Cleo got up early the next day in a very bad mood; she was actually terribly angry at Vilemann. Nothing had gone the way Cleo had hoped, or had it? She had thought that he might try to convince her to live with him out there, to try to build a life

290 The BeAst and the Brightest

together, but he had not said a word about her coming with him. All he focused on was his job. Clearly, he was going to move to the Bay Area. She was going to be abandoned again.

Cleo's idea of what she was going to do with Vilemann was becoming clearer; she needed to find a way to win. If he was going to abandon her, breaking up with him would not be enough; she had to do something similar to what she did to Danny. Vilemann needed to be destroyed, devastated, and decimated—in short, killed. She would figure out how to do it once back in Boston.

She rushed out to SF International and got on the plane to Boston. Her mood didn't get any better as she flew east. At least she had finalized the trust issue, gotten a check for $10,000, done the courtesy visit with her parents, and had a clearer idea about Vilemann. That idea just wasn't what she wanted, or was it? He had dominated her for more than a year, so imagining life without him was hard. But could she really live with this tough tornado of a guy? How did she feel about giving up her life in Boston for a guy? Could she possibly get an interesting job in SF, something equivalent to what she had found in Boston? Why hadn't he ever asked her about her name? Had she ever really liked or loved him, or was the attraction just his dark charisma and his tough Hegelian philosophy? She was certain about one thing: She didn't want to be abandoned again. If Vilemann was going to abandon her, he'd get what he deserved: a brutal killing. Like Elizabeth in *Les Enfants Terribles*, she intended to have the last word.

She was relieved to open the door to her apartment. She had eaten at a new Legal Seafood restaurant in Logan Airport before going into the city, so dinner was taken care of. The only resemblance between the new Legal Seafood and the one where she and Danny had eaten was the name. Danny's Legal Seafood had burned down; it was no more. Just like him, the old restaurant wasn't even a memory. She didn't give a thought to the dinner she had shared with Danny at that old Legal Seafood. She had a few hours to look through her mail and pick up the previous weekend's *New York Times*. She started reading the arts section, then looked at the book section and drifted off to sleep.

All day Sunday she waited to hear from Vilemann, but he didn't call. For dinner, she went out, and when she got home she still didn't find a message from him on her machine, but with

Cleo and Vilemann Finale   291

the time difference, she thought he'd probably call later. She got
a short call at 11:30 p.m., just as she was getting ready for bed.
He said that the work was fascinating and that he was working
like crazy. Nothing more. He didn't ask about her trip home or
anything else.

On Monday morning, she went back to her job, where
Prudence asked her about her trip. Prudence knew that Cleo was
going out there with some guy and wondered what this would
mean for her. Would she be following this guy back to San
Fran? Was the guy Vilemann or someone else? Cleo just said the
trip went well; she had seen her brothers and parents and had
enjoyed an afternoon in her childhood vineyards. She said nothing about the guy she went with or even if it was Vilemann or
someone else. Prudence had learned that what she didn't share
was usually more important than what she said. Prudence had
hoped sincerely that Cleo would tell her that she was leaving to
go to SF. That would have simplified many issues at Schendler.

Monday evening, there was no message at all. She knew he
was moving to a hotel closer to the job, but he hadn't left the
number or the name of the hotel. Tuesday night, she didn't hear
from him. She could hardly control her anger. What the hell was
happening?

Cleo hated feeling that she had no control; she couldn't even
call him. Then, the next day Wednesday night, at 12:10 a.m., he
called. "I know it's late there, but we just stopped working. How
are you?"

"I'm tired and was sleeping," she almost screamed at him.

"Sorry to be calling so late; I'll try to call earlier tomorrow."
And then he hung up. Cleo was so incredibly angry that she had
to read a large part of the book section of The Times to get back
to sleep.

She started thinking that maybe he had met another woman.
When he called on Thursday, she asked him directly: "Have you
met another woman?"

"No, but you need to know something. You need to know
that I am sleeping with Tony. You have never guessed that I like
meat of every kind—women and men. You need to know that
Tony is the same." Then he stopped. Cleo could hardly believe

292   The BeAst and the Brightest

what she was hearing. He had just referred to her and Tony as "meat." She felt like a bomb had gone off in her apartment.

"What? You and Tony are having sex?"

Vilemann said, "He's really good-looking, and frankly, Cleo, he's a lot more adventurous and more fun in bed than you are."

"Oh my God!" she screamed. "No, no, no!" She couldn't believe this was happening. She could not believe that her boyfriend or whatever he was had betrayed her with a man … her brother! And Tony was totally immoral! How could he do this to his own sister? His relationship with Vilemann was totally immoral. She couldn't believe it. Those bastards!

"Are you saying Tony is gay?"

Vilemann clarified: "Tony swings both ways, just like me, but mostly toward boys, good-looking boys."

Cleo thought, *Maybe even ugly guys like Vilemann.*

Cleo begged for more, for some understanding. "When did this start? Did you go after him, or did he go after you? Who is responsible for this? You have to tell me."

Vilemann responded, "You don't need to know all that. Just get used to it; just come to terms with it."

How could Tony betray her like this? How could Vilemann betray her like this? It was disgusting, totally immoral. Her own brother was having sex with the guy she had been with for over a year. She thought about Vilemann's penis and what he and Tony were doing with it and was so disgusted that she almost threw up. She wanted to vomit. She now realized why Vilemann was so eager for anal sex with her. He had not only fucked her, but he had also found a way to deny her, to negate her as a woman. He had set her up for her killing. She was just "meat." She had been made into the same kind of disgusting meat that he was enjoying with Tony, her brother.

Yes, her brother! She started trembling, and her anger almost blinded her. "You bastard, you damnable bastard, you monster, you are nothing but a beast," she shouted. "How can you do this to me?"

Vilemann just held the telephone away from his ear for a few moments, then said, "Cleo, don't play the morality card with me. Everyone knows you're nothing but a whore. You sleep with

Cleo and Vilemann Finale

everybody. You cheat on everybody. You try to deceive everybody. You're no one to talk."

She started gasping and then said, "I thought you were really interested in me, in us."

"Who told you that? We are both players, and the game ends at some point. I am the winner, and you are the loser in this game. Too bad."

Cleo shouted, "Don't you love me?"

"Oh, come on. I never said I loved you. I just fucked you. That's all we did. And by the way, I knew you were lying about when you and Tallington started sleeping together. Every time you lied about you and Tallington, I had a big laugh. And no, I didn't care who else you were sleeping with as long as you would use it against Danny."

Cleo was actually gasping; she could hardly breathe and wanted to explode. She felt like a hand grenade had gone off in her apartment, and shrapnel was ripping through her body. She started to shake uncontrollably. Why was this happening? What had she done to deserve this?

Then Vilemann said that he and Tony appreciated her introducing them to each other. "Oh, my God, no!" she shouted. She could not believe that Vilemann could treat her so badly, that he could show so little respect for her, even as a human being, a person who might have, maybe, loved him, a little bit. How could he be so cruel, so brutal, and have sex with someone so close to her, her own brother?

She thought, *I have been loyal and loving to him; how can he turn on me and hurt me so badly? Didn't I mean anything to him?*

Cleo felt her whole life collapsing. She started realizing that her expectations and thoughts about Vilemann were like those she had with Danny. Both had left her. Danny left her physically but continued to love her and tried to keep their relationship alive, but it didn't matter to her. His love for her had never died until she came to Paris, that is. He had thought that her presence in Paris would reinforce their love, not be the occasions when she denied its existence. Cleo detested him for leaving her, and his tenderness and loving attitude seemed too romantic, too unreal to her. He was too "Kant;" she was all "Hegel." Cleo thought that

294   The BeAst and the Brightest

Danny was nothing but a silly romantic and believed in love and truth and being faithful and all that BS. Now, Vilemann was in SF with her own brother. She imagined them getting together every time Tony came to SF. Would Vilemann visit him in Chile? Plus, she kept thinking about how Vilemann had persuaded her to let him "play in the sewer." She was almost sick to her stomach. All this was too much for Cleo, too horrible to think about. Danny and Vilemann had thrown her off The Game, holding out the possibility of life with someone else, not just serial guys, not just one prick after another. She chose the evil one, the bad boy and tough guy, and was paying the price.

She put the telephone receiver in her lap to try to pull herself together. Then she heard him talking and put the receiver to her ear. "You just need to get used to this, come to terms with this. Then he delivered the second blow. "I thought you'd understand I am bisexual when you arrived at that hotel in Cannes. Didn't you notice all the good-looking guys? While you were in Paris getting rid of Danny, I was fucking that good-looking pool boy and one of the waiters. The pool boy is the one who bought me that men's bikini. We had more really wild, fun sex parties when you went back to Paris to finish off Danny. Didn't you notice my lack of interest in fucking you these last few weeks? By the way, I like your butt more than your pussy."

Cleo was devastated; she could not believe what was happening. Suddenly, Cleo realized that the night she spent with French Stud #3, Vilemann, was with the pool boy and one of the waiters. She thought, *My God, he was cheating on me!*

For the first time, he said that all he had been doing was fucking her; she was just prey. "I've been thinking about boys. I go through periods when I'm occasionally with women, and then I switch to boys. I really like good-looking young boys. Can you imagine how happy I was to learn that Tony is also bi? During that walk to the restaurant in SF, we both revealed that we are bi. I told him first that I was excited to come to SF since I am bi. I told him since I could sense it in him—the way he walked, everything.

"I only approached you initially to see if I could take you away from Danny. Danny was a rival in the department, and I needed to get him, to hurt him. Why do you think I went after

Cleo and Vilemann Finale | 295

you when there are many better-looking women in Boston and women who are more fun in bed? All you did initially was the missionary position, and I got so bored with that."

He was tearing her apart, and he was enjoying it. The more she was shocked and suffered, the happier he was. Hadn't he told her that he was always the winner? "My real game was against Danny; you were just the useful idiot who allowed me to win, nothing more. And I got to fuck you, a lot, and even in your ass. Imagine how surprised and delighted I was that you not only betrayed Danny but that you then turned on him and hurt him as much as you could. You helped me win, big time. You didn't hurt Danny; you murdered him. And now I have Tony, thanks to you. I'm going to hang up now; it's over; don't try to contact me." That was the end.

Cleo wanted to cry, but she was so mad and shocked that her tears would not flow. Every five minutes, she asked herself what had just happened.

Is this real? Can he actually have done this to me? What a bastard! Doesn't he realize that I'm a human being; I have feelings? I can be hurt. Don't I deserve some respect, some consideration, just like everybody else?

She opened her window for fresh air. It was cool outside, which made her feel better. The cool air calmed her for a few minutes, but then she started to shiver. Was she shaking because of the cool air, because of what had just happened to her, or both? She poured herself a glass of wine. She drank it in two gulps. Then she drank another glass. The wine was hardly affecting her.

For the first time, she had lost to a guy and lost totally. He was writing the plot, and he had just written her out of his story. She hated him. She hated him so much that in the future, she could not even say his name. When she wrote in her diary about what had happened to her, she could only refer to him as "v," not even "V." She came to hate "v." To her, "v" meant she had to live with pain, the pain caused by the shrapnel he had lodged in her body. She would never get over what "v" had done to her. She really hated him. She couldn't hate Danny; he was dead to her. In the end, he had meant nothing to her, absolutely nothing, so little she couldn't even hate him. Can you hate someone you have killed; someone you have raped?

Nothing like this had ever happened to her. It was monstrous. How could he be so cruel, so brutal? Why hadn't she understood what was going on? She knew that he was tough, but she didn't think he would hurt her. Why hadn't she seen what a bastard he was? Cleo couldn't sleep. These questions kept harassing her until almost 4:30 a.m., when she finally fell asleep. At 7:45 a.m., she woke up with a start. She tried to make some coffee and toast, but as soon as the coffee was ready, she sat down at her table and the tears came in great waves; she was actually weeping for the first time in her life as an adult. Her emotions took control of her, and she wept.

Of the three of them, Vilemann, Tallington, and Danny, only one had loved her, and he was the one who paid the highest price. Cleo came to detest—no hate—"v" for what he did to her, but she rejected any responsibility for what she had done to Danny. Now, Danny was dead to her, and Tallington, well, useful Idiot #2 had never counted for anything. Her ultimate deception was that she had deceived herself. She had rejected Danny's love only to embrace an evil man who would hurt her, a sad fate for a would-be feminist like Cleo, who was determined never to submit to a male. In her diary, Cleo wrote that "v" hurt both her and Danny. But Vilemann only hurt Danny because Cleo decided to cheat on Danny with a professional colleague of Danny's who was a real barbarbarian, not to break up with Danny when that happened, to deceive him for months, to then sleep with his best friend, and to be cruel and brutal both in Paris and back in Boston. Those were all Cleo's decisions. Cleo had hurt Danny. She never admitted that she had hurt Danny or accepted any responsibility for her betrayal of his love. Recognition of responsibility would have implied shame, and she never felt any shame.

Just like Elizabeth and Paul in *Les Enfants Terribles*, Cleo and Danny both lost. Danny had offered love, affection, and loyalty. Vilemann offered cruelty, brutality, and betrayal. In the end, that is what Cleo got: cruelty, brutality, and betrayal. She chose Vilemann, her devil, because she was also cruel, brutal, and capable of betrayal. Frank had tried to teach her that cynical sex is a two-way street.

Chapter 36

Cleo and Remington Finale

Two uneventful weeks went by, during which Cleo became calmer, although she constantly thought about what "v" had done to her, and she would shake all over. Sometimes, she wanted to scream. Swallowing that kind of humiliation, that kind of assault on her as a woman, as a human being, was simply too difficult. She could accept some humiliation, but not total humiliation, the annihilation of her as a woman, as a person. She could swallow some of her pride, but not all of it. She could annihilate Danny with no second thoughts or regrets but accepting that treatment was impossible for her. Sleeping with another woman, especially if it were somebody she didn't know, would have been bad enough. But a guy and her brother, someone so close to her! She just kept thinking that he was totally immoral, totally evil. Yes, he had always been evil. Danny had told her that. Cleo was able, at least, to see the evil in Vilemann, although not in herself.

One Wednesday afternoon, Alexander came by and dropped off a note saying, "Tomorrow at 6:30; my office this time. I have missed you. Can't wait." Well, at least he wanted to see her in his office. He had taken more time and done more aggressive sexual things with her in the hotel, some of which she never thought she would do, at least not with him, so she was somewhat relieved that this session might be no more than another thumping in his office. She really wasn't up for sex with anyone, but how could she turn him down?

298   The BeAst and the Brightest

She decided that the moment had come to ask him for help to move to a bigger division and for a promotion. She could feel the intense tension between her and Prudence and knew the time had come to move on and up. She had been giving Alexander the sexual pleasure he wanted for a long time. At least she, not those other women, was the winner. The time had come for her to cash in to move up.

The next day, she showed up right at 6:30 p.m. Nobody but Alexander was on the whole floor; everyone had gone home as usual. She opened his big double mahogany doors and saw him already on the couch. He had poured himself a glass of red wine. "Hi, Cleo, can I get one for you, too? We need to celebrate a bit since it's been some time since we were together."

He poured another glass and handed it to her. She had been with him so many times that having sex, particularly a quickie or a standard blowjob, with him was nothing to her except for some of his new demands. She wondered if he'd want to do some of the sexual games and bizarre positions they had done in the hotel room. They chatted a bit; Cleo mentioned having been in SF. Alexander asked if she had seen her old boss, Frank. "No, she said, there wasn't time. I had a lot to do with my family."

As he put his wine glass down on the coffee table, she kicked off her shoes. He reached over and started unbuttoning her blouse. She stood up between the coffee table and the couch, paying attention to the wine bottle and their glasses of wine to avoid knocking them over. He unzipped her skirt and let it fall to the floor. She stood there in front of him so he could remove Danny's gift. He said how much he liked seeing her in lingerie like that.

"You are always sexy, but wow in those!" He lifted the camisole over her head, and after she flicked her hair back into place, he put his hands on the sides of her bikini panties, pulling them slowly to the floor. Cleo stepped out of them so Alexander could pick them up. Dropping the camisole and her panties on the floor behind the couch, Alexander leaned in as close to Cleo as possible. She knew what to do. She helped him with his shirt, said how great he looked, and then she finished undressing him as fast as possible.

Cleo and Remington Finale

Cleo said, "You know, I really liked sucking your big dick," as a way of limiting their sexual encounter to what they had already done. Alexander just smiled broadly. Cleo sat up to give him another blowjob, but he pushed her down on the couch and said, "Let's get right at it."

Cleo leaned back, putting one leg over the back of the couch, inviting him to come into her. She was really hoping it would just be another quickie. She was glad to see him bend over to come on her since she preferred the missionary position with him on top rather than her laying down on him to do it. They were both totally naked, and as he came into her, he sighed and said, "Wow, I have missed this; this feels wonderful."

Suddenly, those mahogany doors opened, and Diane Bouquet burst in. "You bastard! I told you never to let this happen again, didn't I, you old bastard!"

Alexander tried to jump up as fast as possible by pushing off Cleo, pressing his hand hard against her left left breast. She let out a cry of pain. He managed to stand up as he grabbed his pants trying to pull them on. He almost fell backward over the coffee table. Cleo found her skirt on the floor right in front of the couch where Alexander had been sitting. She held it against her chest as she desperately looked for her other clothes. Her camisole and bikini panties were behind the couch where Alexander had inadvertently dropped them. Her shoes and blouse were under the coffee table.

Diane ran toward Alexander, leaned over the coffee table, and slapped him hard across the face. Cleo thought she might get the next blow. Cleo bent over awkwardly to avoid Diane's slap, but Alexander's elbow hit her face. She stood up to get her balance, then saw Diane's arm back as if to inflict another slap, so she ducked down again to avoid Diane's hand, but she hit Alexander instead, almost pushing him over. Cleo was trying to get out from behind the little space between the coffee table and the couch, and as she stood up, she knocked over the wine bottle and the glasses, which still had wine in them.

Diane Bouquet swiveled around to look at Cleo, who was searching frantically for her camisole and panties. Since she couldn't find them, Cleo reached under the coffee table for her skirt and shoes and saw that the spilled wine had soaked her blouse. She grabbed it as fast as she could. She had no time to get her skirt on, so she just held it in front of her. Cleo held her blouse a little bit away from her, trying to keep the wine from spreading to her skirt. She pushed Alexander out of her way to go around the coffee table and lurched toward the doors. As she ran out, Diane stared at her naked backside and shouted, "You dirty, stupid little bitch. Get out, you stupid bitch. You're through. You dirty bitch."

As she heard Alexander's big mahogany doors close behind her, she looked around for a place to hide and saw the men's bathroom in the corridor. Cleo didn't think that Diane would think to look for her in the men's room. Cleo's hands were trembling almost uncontrollably as she put on the clothes, she had been able to grab. She looked like she had been stabbed in the chest because her blouse was covered in red wine. She looked like she was dying, but it wasn't her who was dying, only her career at Schendler.

She heard loud arguing in Alexander's office. She peeked out of the men's room, and when she saw that nobody was there, she bolted for the stairs. She didn't want to have to stand there waiting for the elevator, which was probably all the way down at the first floor. She almost tumbled down the stairs from Alexander's sixth-floor office to the fourth floor, where her office was located. She ran frantically down the hall to her office, grabbed her purse with her money and apartment keys, and then ran back to the stairs. She was thrilled and relieved to have remembered her purse and keys. As she opened the door of the stairwell to go into the main lobby, she feared she'd see Alexander or Diane or somebody else. Was Diane looking for her? What would she say if anybody else saw her with her wine-stained blouse? She fled down the stairs to the first floor and turned away from the lobby and the front doors to go down a side corridor and out an emergency door into the back alley. She ran as fast as she could down that dark, ugly alley to the main street, where she saw a taxi passing by. She hailed it and went to her apartment. Once there, she screamed, "Oh God, NO! NO! NO!" She understood that her days at Schendler were finished.

Sleep was impossible all that Thursday night. Ugly, terrifying thoughts assailed her all night. She could not control her

Cleo and Remington Finale

thoughts about Vilemann and her brother and about who could have betrayed her by telling Diane about her little thing with Alexander. These questions and thoughts raced around her mind like furies from hell. She was incredibly angry. Who was the rat who told Diane about her little encounters with Alexander? Nobody had gotten hurt. It was just sex, and she was just about to ask for his help to get a better job. Was it Prudence, Oliver, or Littman? Or Fred Fried? Or had some of the authors she had slept with found out about her and Alexander and told Diane? She had not offended anybody by rejecting an invitation for a night or two of sex, except Fred Fried's group sex thing. She had accepted everyone who wanted to have sex with her, except one woman writer. Did Littman know about them? She wondered if Littman had wanted to approach her for sex but had hesitated and had decided to undermine Alexander by telling Diane about Cleo's visits. Did Littman want Alexander's job? Was Littman that low? Was this a maneuver by Littman to get the top job? Who else could have done such a terrible thing? Who could have told Diane? Who had betrayed her?

The next morning, after another horrific, nightmarish, and sleepless night, Cleo succeeded in making coffee and drinking it in small sips. Prudence called Cleo early that morning. When she heard Prudence's voice on her message machine, she grabbed the phone and blurted out, "Oh Prudence, I am so sorry, so very, very sorry." This was the first time since she was a child that she had said those words, but at least she meant them—momentarily. Prudence paused and then said calmly, "Cleo, given the unfortunate events of last evening, you probably should take some time off." Cleo said she understood and that she'd wait to hear from her. She never did.

She got a letter from HR at Schendler by courier the next Monday morning notifying her that her employment was terminated and that she would receive her last paycheck in the mail. The courier also delivered a cardboard box with the personal items she kept in her office, including the folder with her scribbled notes for her book on feminism. On top of the folder, someone had carefully laid out the camisole and panties Danny had given her. Danny's camisole and bikini panties looked like a white shroud placed there on the occasion of the death of her ambition. Was the shroud also meant to cover up her raw, naked shame, or were the camisole and bikini panties there to shame her?

Cleo thought, *They are trying to kill me, but I am the author of my story. I'll write the final chapter; I'll make the last move. I'll win this game.* She crossed her living room and opened the big window. She knew what she had to do. As she felt the rush of the frigid air, she screamed, "All bastards, all damn bastards!"

The truth was never her friend; sex was her instrument, and morality was not only ignored but it was also denied. It was over. She had built her life on deceit, denial, and irresponsible sex. Everyone saw her simply as perfidious or worse. Cleo spent her whole life wandering around in a world of wrong and deception. She deceived and hurt those closest to her. In the end, the person most deceived and most wronged was the person she might have been. The person Danny loved was this unrealized Cleo, not the real one. She wanted to shine a light on feminism but fell into darkness and betrayed love's place in the light.

Queen Elizabeth II once said, "Grief is the price we pay for love." Danny thought she might be right in certain situations and among certain people, but love doesn't have to lead to grief, not in a Kantian world.

Chapter 37

Love Guides Life

Danny loved meeting all of Kitten's charming, intelligent friends and grew very close to Kitten and her husband. They seemed like such as happy couple, much like Cristelle and Loïc. While feeling friendship with Kitten and her friends, Danny couldn't connect with any of the women he was meeting. His heart as elsewhere. All he could think about was Sandrine.

Danny could not get the image of her pretty face, her loving arms, her sweet lips or her wonderful tenderness out of his thoughts. He also knew that she was strong and intelligent and that her career at the agency meant a lot to her. Danny understood that she was profoundly integrated into her family and friends. Her friends, their lives in Paris and at the beach house meant the world to her. In fact, her work, her family and friends, and living in France was her world. Asking her to give up all that to come to America would be a betrayal of her. She could never regain all that she had in France living with him in America. She was a happy young woman in France, and she needed to stay there.

Danny also didn't imagine how he could work in France. He didn't have French residency or a job. He knew that the French academic world is tough to penetrate by someone from outside. He could not imagine how he could have a work life in France to support himself, but all he could think about was how profoundly happy he'd be to live with her, to share his love with her. She had become his world.

During that first year teaching at Princeton, he exchanged letters with Sandrine, just one every 3-5 weeks. He could not write about his feeling for her since he imagined she would easily find someone in Paris and that he'd stay in America to teach at Princeton. But every letter he received from her was like a hot air balloon lifting him up into the sky, thrilling him, and giving him a broader perspective on his life. He'd read and reread these letters sometimes kissing the paper, imagining his lips touching Sandrine's. An overwhelming sense of bliss engulfed him as he read each letter and then carefully folded and slipped it back into the envelope with the little French stamp.

Danny felt excited but anxious each time he saw a letter from France. Would Sandrine just be writing about her life and their friends. Would she just be sharing her news of the day, or would she one day tell him about finding someone new? The prospect that Sandrine would tell him that she had found a new love both terrified and reassued Danny. He knew that life goes on, and had accepted the reality that Sandrine's life would be with someone she loved in Paris. Danny wanted her to be happy, but dreaded hearing that she had moved on with someone else.

Danny was surprised one day to find an envelope with a French stamp on it in his mailbox that was not like the letters from Sandrine. The letter was from Loïc. The letter started out with some news about Cristelle and him, and about Aurelie and some of their other friends. He finished by saying that he had spoken with his father about his management consulting firm and its international clients.

Loïc wrote that, "My dad's consulting firm is expanding and is looking for educated people who know finance and are comfortable working in French and English and who know something about industry. He is going to be in New York soon. He remembers your visit to our house and was impressed by your economic research and by you. I know you have always wanted to be a professor, but would you like to talk with him?"

Of course, this was all a clever stratagem developed by Sandrine and Cristelle. They had been making little, subtle suggestions to Loïc and mentioning Danny to Loïc's father for

Love Guides Life

months, and finally Loïc caught on. His father had actually gotten interested in discussing a position with Danny without connecting it directly to Sandrine. So, Loïc's letter was just telling Danny what was true of his father; he was looking for people with Danny's background.

The meeting with Loïc's father was at the Four Seasons Hotel in Manhattan. Danny was invited to lunch. The meeting went as expected. Loïc's father greeted him warmly, asked about his teaching and life at Princeton, shared some news about Christelle, and said how happy he had been to meet Danny. Participating in this usual warm up, Danny could only think about Sandrine and living in France with her. Here was the CEO of a major international management consulting company initiating a conversation likely to lead to a job offer, but all he could think about was Sandrine. Would Sandrine be happy if he returned to Paris? Did she still love him or was he just a happy memory? Danny didn't even notice when his meal was put in front of him.

Yes, he was listening to Loïc's father and trying to respond appropriately, but his emotions almost overwhelmed him. Despite the waves of emotions sweeping over him, he did hear Loïc's father invite him to their headquarters at La Défense in Paris to "meet some people you might work with and to discuss a possible role at our consultancy." Danny said, "Yes, I'd love to come to Paris."

Had he inquired about a salary? Had he asked where he might work? Would he consider giving up his position at Princeton? All he could think about was Sandrine. Did she know about this meeting with Loïc's father? How would she react to his showing up in Paris? Did Christelle know about all this? Of course, Danny suspected that both Sandrine and Christelle were aware of this, but he hadn't caught on that they had planned and plotted this initiative. Christelle had always understood that Sandrine loved Danny and when she turned down Alfred, Christellle knew that she and Danny needed one more chance.

Danny's letter to Sandrine started by saying how delighted he was by the opportunity to work in the consulting company. He also said how happy, how very happy he would be to see her in Paris. He wrote that he and Christelle were in touch and he expected her to set up a time when they could all be together.

Then he said that meeting her had been the best thing in his life in Paris, how much she meant to him, and how she had saved him when he was in trouble. He wrote that he was more than eager to see her. In fact, he was excited about the possibility of seeing her again. He signed the letter, "Still in love, Danny." This ending to his letter just popped out of him. Was it totally inappropriate and presumptuous? Would Sandine like to hear that he loved her or be offended? Danny thought about how Christelle always relied on telling the plain truth and how simple the truth makes life. So he folded the letter and slipped it into an envelope sealed with a stamp and a kiss.

Sandrine wrote him back saying that he must stay with her, and that in the heat of the summer in Paris she slept without a T-shirt or panties and that he shouldn't bother to pack pajamas either. "Please pack lightly," she wrote. Danny understood that this was her deliciously naughty way of saying that she still loved him and that they would fully express their love and desire for each other as soon as he arrived in Paris. He wrote her back saying that he would pack very lightly, no pajamas. They both knew that they didn't need time to reconnect; they had never separated emotionally.

Christelle organized the wedding at the château. The reception was held at Loïc's house. Christelle wanted Danny and Sandrine to be united where she and Loïc had fallen in love. All their friends were there including Kitten and her husband, who couldn't imagine not being there and meeting all Danny's true friends. Sandrine wanted the honeymoon to be at her beach house to signify to Danny that he was now part of the family.

Danny finally caught on to the fact that Sandrine and Christelle had plotted this all year. Women can be so wonderful.

About the author

The author is married to a wonderful French woman and has two sons and one delightful little granddaughter. He and his wife can be found traveling all over the world. This is his first novel.

He has also written essays on current American culture and politics, For the Love of America: 75 Ideas and Observations.

Printed in the USA
CPSIA information can be obtained
at www.ICGtesting.com
LVHW060617261124
797245LV00020B/358